FIVE PATHS

SID GARDNER

FIVE PATHS

iUniverse books may be ordered through booksellers or by contacting:

iUniverse
1663 Liberty Drive
Bloomington, IN 47403
www.iuniverse.com
1-800-Authors (1-800-288-4677)

Because of the dynamic nature of the Internet, any web addresses or links contained in this book may have changed since publication and may no longer be valid. The views expressed in this work are solely those of the author and do not necessarily reflect the views of the publisher, and the publisher hereby disclaims any responsibility for them.

Any people depicted in stock imagery provided by Thinkstock are models, and such images are being used for illustrative purposes only. Certain stock imagery © Thinkstock.

ISBN: 978-1-4917-9743-3 (sc)
ISBN: 978-1-4917-9744-0 (e)

Print information available on the last page.

iUniverse rev. date: 05/23/2016

PART ONE

1999-2000 Western University: The Class

Fourteen students straggled into the seminar room, juniors and seniors at Western College in Los Angeles in the fall semester of 1999. With electives on their hands, they had all decided to sample the first session of a curiously titled course called "The Fifth Child: Global Child Protection in the 21st Century." They numbered six men, eight women, stretching both terms, as demanded by the proprieties of the approaching new century, to include 20 and 21-year-olds in the full bloom of their late adolescence.

An objective observer would have described the lot as carrying themselves with considerable self-regard, though mixed with a measure of anxiety at their first view of their professor. She stood, unsmiling at the head of a long table and gestured them to the chairs around the table.

The course schedule labeled her Ms. Gabriela Lopez, so she was not of the professoriate caste, unburdened with a doctorate. She appeared to be in her early fifties, trim with a long dark braid trailing down her back. She had a definite air of command as she sat down in a large chair in front of the only window in the room.

On an early September afternoon, the room was warm, offsetting the older charm of a narrow, second-floor classroom in one of the original buildings on the campus. The air conditioning struggled with limited success to cool the room.

The students sat in their adopted poses, ranging from advanced slouch to prim, back-on-the-chair, both feet on the ground, hands folded or arranging notebooks and pens. A class notice had advised no laptops or tablets allowed.

Lopez asked the students to introduce themselves and tell where they were from. After each had said a few words, she asked a second question. "Why are you here?"

The first student to answer was named Roberto Garcia, who had said he was from California. With a greater degree of confidence than most of the others had shown in their self-introductions, he said, "I'm in computer science. I want to see if technology has anything to offer the field we're going to be talking about."

Lopez allowed herself a small smile. "I suspect it will, but you will have plenty of time this semester to tell us what it is."

As each of them answered the question, they predictably mentioned their "interest in children," their curiosity about other cultures, and their majors in international relations, political science, psychology, or languages. There were two international students, a woman from Iraq and a man from China.

A tall blonde woman introduced herself with a frown as "Suzanne Forrester, from Chicago." She added that she was especially interested in the harm done to girls. Another woman named Felicia Fiori, who was from New York, said she looked forward to discussing how "direct action" could make a difference for children. Jeremy Boxton, a short man from Texas, told a somewhat wandering story about religious groups in Texas who had gotten him interested in services to children in other countries. And an African-American man from South Carolina named Stanley Wright said he hoped to learn how better political leadership could help children.

Lopez watched them carefully as they filed in and began trying to answer her questions. She paid the most attention to the seniors, full of themselves, getting ready to make choices, to leave the sheltered campus and go become somebody. As she always did with a new class, she tried to pick out the ones that would matter, who might come to care enough to choose rougher, steeper paths.

The men were always so hard to read. Did they think it was just an easy elective, or would they be challenged by her descriptions of the ferocity of the battles to protect children? She knew the women were sometimes carrying their own deeper reasons for seeking out her class, wounded by their own experience with bias and abuse. Which ones were there out of a well-intentioned but shallow desire to "help children," and which of them would learn how to get past their own history and go to work to prevent unspeakable harm done to real children far away from the oak-lined quadrangle?

She hoped she'd catch hold of some of them, sending them forth on the Mission. She worried about the balancing act between pressing too hard, making the Mission seem like narrow idealism and, on the other side, holding out the rewards that she knew could come—but rarely quickly, and sometimes never.

She knew she could teach the class. But she wondered if she could teach the students in it what lay ahead if they wanted to join the battle— and why it was worth their lives.

Lopez said, "Thank you. You've each raised some interesting points, and we're going to discuss all of them in this class."

She rose and turned to the whiteboard behind her, and wrote the number *400,000,000* on the board. Speaking slowly as she sat down, she said, "We are here to talk about the inexcusable abuse of four hundred million children. If that number and the facts behind it do not bother you, you probably should not be here. This class will demand a certain amount of outrage from each of you." She paused. "I hope you are capable of outrage at this stage in your education."

She looked at each of them, and went on. "Our discussions, the field trips we will take, and your readings will help you begin to understand what is happening to these children. But we will spend more time as we go on through the semester on what is really the central question: *what you should do about it.* You may decide that you will go on to a glorious career in some other field, and your answer to this question may be that you will send a few dollars to the charity of your choice when you remember."

She paused again, and then added, "That would be good—but not good enough."

She went on. "I know your generation got the idea somewhere that it isn't cool—or whatever your current word is—to express emotion that is either too positive or too negative. They call you 'the whatever generation.' My response to that is based on more than two millennia of philosophy—both Western and Eastern: *get over it and get into it.*

Get over your being too cool to feel empathy, and get into making a difference. We're going to look hard at some facts in this course, but there will also be some emotions. It turns out that it is impossible to talk sensibly about children without emotion coming into it."

She looked out the window, gesturing at the campus below them. "We're not an elite Ivy League college. We don't have to teach you how to get a six-figure job. We only have to teach you to think, and how to live, if you're interested."

Then, feeling she might be too hard on them—at least some of them—for a first session, she said more quietly, "I have reason to believe that some of you will respond magnificently to this challenge. I also have faith."

She went on to spend an hour on the numbers, broken up with questions from the students, which she welcomed. She carefully reviewed a painful litany: the number of children who attended no school after the primary grades, the number of girls married before their teens, the number of children killed by leftover land mines, the number of girls mutilated for sexual reasons, the number of children under ten who worked full-time. She went on and on, through sixteen different categories of child abuse and neglect, explaining that these were the categories developed by the United Nations Children's Fund—UNICEF.

She used slides from a Powerpoint, but spent more time explaining the data than reviewing the actual slides. The whiteboard became covered with numbers, and then with arrows that she drew, showing how early marriage and child labor and leaving school at eight were all connected.

The board became almost impossible to read, and as she drew to her conclusion, she smiled, waved at the board, and said "Looks messy, doesn't it? That's part of what we'll be looking at in this course. Why are there are so many pieces of the puzzle and whether anyone is trying to put the whole puzzle together, or just parading around with their piece?"

She wrapped up the session by assigning them to pick one of the problems she had briefly described and bring in a three-page summary of the issue and some of the proposed solutions. She ended by saying "I know this is depressing at first. But even more depressing is how little anybody is doing about it."

She briefed them on the field trips they would be taking and handed out waiver forms they needed to sign to be able to travel in the van rented by the university.

As they walked out, Stan said to Roberto, "She seems a little intense."

"A *little*? Like *The Chain Saw Massacre* is a little intense."

Felicia, overhearing them, said "I thought she was great. I wish all professors laid it out like that in the first session. She told us where she's going and basically said get out if you don't want to go along. No bullshit. I like that."

At the next session, the fourteen had winnowed down to twelve. The woman from Iraq was no longer attending and one of the men had also dropped out, a junior who had introduced himself as an international relations major.

They had all Googled Lopez and learned that she had left Cuba with her parents at five, had graduated from Florida State University, worked for the United Nations and Human Rights Watch, and had been teaching for ten years. She had published three books on children's rights and lectured at conferences in Europe and all over Latin America. She was divorced, with two adult children.

After two class sessions, they formed informal study groups of three or four. Lopez suggested they group themselves based on where they were seated, and then move around among groups until they found a group that was compatible.

By the accident of seating, the four in Group A were seniors, but only two of them knew each other well. The group consisted of Stan, Suzanne, Jeremy, and Roberto. Stan and Jeremy had taken some classes together, the others knew each other casually, as seniors usually did on a small campus of less than two thousand.

After a week, Felicia asked Roberto if she could join Group A. Roberto heard from one of the other students that she had gotten into a fierce argument with some of the members of the group she had originally joined. They had suggested that she join another group. With a qualm or two, Roberto invited her to join them at their next meeting.

He vaguely knew who she was, and had an impression that she was brash, sometimes funny, and usually with a guy—but never the same guy for long.

As she walked into the group which was meeting in Stan's apartment a few blocks off-campus, Felicia announced, "Let me be clear about this—I left those other wimps because they wanted to talk about petitions and I wanted to talk about protest. So let me know now if any of you are afraid of a little hell-raising when we finally get around to helping kids."

Roberto spoke first. "Whoa there. Slow down. Why don't you tell us where you're coming from? I've got no problems with direct action—my grandfather walked with Cesar Chavez. But tell us why you disagreed with those other guys."

Pulling a chair out from a small table in Stan's kitchen and plunking herself down in it, Felicia fired back, "They're typical of most people at this rich kids' school—they think writing letters makes a difference. Lopez is talking about some real stuff that affects real kids, and letters aren't going to cut it."

She spoke fast, eyes darting around the group, seeming to dare them to disagree or even to speak up. Dressed in what they had come to realize was her typical sweat shirt and leggings, she folded her arms and waited for a response. The others were watching Roberto, as the first respondent to Felicia's semi-attack.

He said, "You're welcome to join us, though I doubt most of us are as rich as you seem to think. We've been talking about several different ways to deal with the problems Lopez has been bringing up. And they all go beyond letter writing. So, welcome."

Felicia wasn't done. "What do you say we start out," she said, ignoring the fact that the group had already met once, "with telling our stories? Not the rehearsed pablum you gave out in class, but the real stories. Who wants to start?"

They all looked at each other, faces sharing a look that said *who the hell made her boss?* But they were amused enough by her bluntness and self-revelation that they tacitly decided to go along with her demand for the moment.

Stan said, "I'll start. Middle class black family from Columbia. South Carolina. Sports in high school, football here, but decided to stay away from an athletic career based on some advice from an uncle who was in the NFL. Older brother of three boys. I came to Western because I'm going back home to get into politics somehow and I wanted to see another part of the country before I dig back into the roots at home."

Roberto said, "Guess mine is a lot like Stan's. Middle class Latino family, grandfather came up during World War II to pick crops and stayed. Rest of us all born here. Drybacks. My folks teach school in Glendale, lived there forever. Two sisters, younger. Folks gave me a kiddie computer when I was three and I never looked back. I live for technology. I'm close to my family, which is good, because they're only fifteen minutes away."

Jeremy leaned back in his chair and said, "I grew up in the hill country, outside Austin. My parents were sort of hippies who played country music when they were sober. A girlfriend took me to church when I was a freshman in high school, and I felt like I had found my escape route. I guess you'd call me a fundamentalist Christian, but I'm still trying to figure out what that means."

Felicia clapped her hands once and said, "OK, you guys are doing good. I grew up in Queens, in a typical Italian family. My father worked in sanitation, my mother stayed home with my three brothers and me. My brothers were all older and they either teased or ignored me. My *nonna*—grandmother—told me I could go to Hollywood and be a star. The rest of them all laughed, except my father, who ignored me even more when I hit puberty. I'm here because it was the college furthest away from home that accepted me and let me escape my family. I got three things from those people. I speak pretty good Italian, I can cook Italian, and I know lots of opera. Italians' gift to the world—opera, along with pasta and Mussolini."

Suzanne went last. She spoke in a monotone, looking at a poster of the 1963 March on Washington on Stan's wall. "I was abused when I turned thirteen. It made me neurotic, and I'm still pissed about it. My mother cut me off, but sends me some money. I don't get along well with most men." Then she added, somewhat mysteriously, "At first." She added, "I'm here because I heard about this course and I wanted to do something to protect kids."

They were a striking group, both in their diversity and their individual appearances. Stan was tall, with close-cropped hair he kept at a length that would have passed inspection in most basic training units. Avid movie-goers would have called it a toss-up between his resemblance to Denzel Washington or Blair Underwood. He had an athlete's walk, taking longer strides than most people. But his most remarkable feature was his ever-ready smile. He'd smile when he was in class, when he was walking to class, and when he was eating—between bites. On the rare occasions when the smile disappeared, it was a dramatic contrast.

Stan's only known vice was a liking for short, stubby cigars, which forced him to map out the very few places on campus where he could smoke and gave him a lingering aroma that Felicia was quick to detect and note with a quiet "yuchh."

Suzanne's height was the first thing you noticed about her, until you saw the details of her lovely face. She kept her light blonde hair in a boyish cut that only emphasized her fine cheekbones and green eyes. Her voice was quite soft, rising a bit when she wanted to emphasize a point. She neither smiled when she seemed amused, which was rare, nor frowned much in class; expressionless was her usual expression. Her steady gaze at Lopez seemed to say *I'm listening hard and I'm trying to put all the pieces together.*

Jeremy was a bit below average height, slightly overweight in a way that could fit the all-purpose adjective "stocky." He had thick, sandy-colored hair. He was usually at ease with his classmates, some of whom teased him a bit, but affectionately, as they got to know him and saw his acceptance of their response to his openly religious nature. His convictions were deep, but with an unusual tolerance of irreligious remarks and attempted put-downs. His usual response was a slight smile that registered as *if you think that's funny, all right—I'm not going to debate it.*

Roberto dressed as though he wanted to destroy the image of a baggy pants, shaved head look of Latino males in Southern California. He wore his hair long and apparently untreated by any artificial means. As a joke, he occasionally put a plastic pocket protector in his shirt pocket with two or three pens, as if wearing a sign *I'm a techie nerd*. He was as tall as Stan Wright, in the neighborhood of six feet, often boosted up further when he wore boots that he described, when asked, as "my El Paso Tony Lama specials."

Felicia was short and short-tempered. Full-breasted, she tried unsuccessfully to conceal it with an array of loose sweat shirts, even in warmer months. She often wore an intimidating frown, but when something amused her, a corner of her mouth turned up in a tentative half-smile. Her dark, curly hair was worn long in an early Valerie Bertonelli look—Italian to the max. Her laugh could be a weapon, sometimes humorless, sometimes genuine. She often leaned forward in class, an in-your-face body posture that went with her overall aggressiveness. But as the members of the study group got to know her better, she relaxed more often. What was left was a slight scowl that could flow into an equally slight look of approval, perhaps signaling gratitude that her friends overlooked the chips she tended to carry on both shoulders.

In mid-October, the dozen members of the class filed out of the large van that had brought them from the college, and walked into a nondescript storefront in a strip mall in southeastern Los Angeles.

"Looks authentic to me," one of the men murmured as he and the others walked into a small conference room where Lopez awaited them. As they seated themselves around a large table dotted with coffee stains, they looked at the maps pinned up on the walls, maps of the greater Los Angeles area and maps of the world with red markers covering some of the capitals.

Small signs on the front windows identified the agency as Child Protection Associates. A dozen staff members watched the students as they walked through the agency's offices. Some seemed to the students to be about their own ages, while others appeared to be in their late 40s or early 50s.

When they were all seated, Lopez began. "Basic ground rules, people. What you see or hear in these offices and the other sites we'll visit is totally off the record. No names repeated or written down.

No photographs. The work here is sometime highly confidential and involves court cases, so we can't have names tossed around."

She added, sternly, "That doesn't mean you can't take notes for the papers you will be expected to write on each of the agencies we visit. I want you to prepare at least five pages on your impressions of the projects we visit and an additional five pages on the problems underlying their work. Questions?"

There were frowns, but no questions.

Lopez introduced the director of the agency, a Latina named Salinas, to speak to the students. As she walked up to the head of the table, emerging from the group of staff who were observing along the wall, the students realized she could not have been older than thirty. Lopez had explained that Salinas had become director three years before after working on the staff as an intern while attending Cal State Dominguez Hills nearby.

Salinas leaned on the desk in the front of the room, and began. "We work with children, mostly 12 to 18-year-olds, who are out on the streets for one of three reasons: they have been kicked out by their parents or relatives, they have left because they were being abused, or they have been trafficked for prostitution by large or small trafficking organizations. About a third of the kids we deal with are undocumented, meaning they came here with their parents when their parents entered the country illegally."

She paused and said in a different, stronger tone of voice, "We do not use the phrase 'illegal immigrants' here. These children and their parents entered the US without legal standing, just as some of your ancestors did when they came from Europe or elsewhere."

She continued to describe the children they served, using the maps behind her to explain the flow of youth from their families to foster care, in some cases, and on to living on the streets. She pointed to the countries where the youth had come from: Mexico, all Central American countries, Vietnam, Eastern Europe, and, in the case of the trafficked girls, China.

Three staff members then came forward and presented brief case studies of children they had worked with during the past few weeks. The frowns on the students' faces grew longer as each case study unrolled, with examples of sexual and physical abuse that were at times stomach-turning.

The brief, tentative questions that came from the students included *How can you do this work—isn't it painful to think about? How much do city and county agencies provide services when you refer kids to them? How good are those services?* The answers, respectively, were essentially Yes, Not much and Not very.

And at the end, Roberto asked "Do you have any idea how many of those who need your services you are able to help?"

Salinas frowned and said, "Less than 1%, based on the latest estimates of kids living on the street or in prostitution houses. We do what we can with the resources we have, but the need is enormous."

Lopez thanked Salinas and began summarizing the session. "We've been talking in our class about children who are maltreated. You know that some of those children live thousands of miles from here—and today you learned that some are in this neighborhood. We're going to look at this problem of abused children on a global scale, but I hope your visits to agencies like CPA will remind you that these are not just exotic problems of faraway cultures. They are also here and now. You want to work with other, exotic cultures? Fine. But our own culture has plenty of people who think that hurting kids is OK. For some of the worst of them, it's good business."

As they climbed back into the van, Felicia said to Suzanne, "Cold bath of reality, I guess."

Suzanne just nodded.

Over the next two months, as the fall turned to Southern California's curious form of winter, cooler with occasional, brief spells of rain, the group met faithfully after class each week except during the December holidays. The study session rotated around to different apartments or dorm rooms, meeting in restaurants or coffee shops when that was more convenient.

In November, the group gathered for the first time in Roberto's apartment, which he had warned them was "a little unusual." He lived in a two-bedroom apartment high in the hills behind the college. The apartment was half glass walls facing the view, which looked out into the valley that ran down toward the Pasadena Freeway. It was furnished with modern furniture, and had two full walls of floor-to-ceiling books. When doing some low-grade snooping the first time they visited, Stan and Jeremy spotted a room with what appeared to be five monitors and an unknown number of desktops that looked as powerful as anything they had ever seen on campus.

Stan asked the obvious question as the group settled into the couches and chairs around a fireplace in the living room. "Wow, Berto, this is a pretty nice pad. You rob a bank, or is there where your secret, rich girlfriend keeps you in style?"

Roberto was trying, with mixed success, to manage his obvious pride in his place and his not wanting to show off. "No, man. It's kind of a long story. The short version is I was in a computer science class when I was a sophomore and they asked us to write some code. So I did, and the teaching assistant noticed it and asked me if he could show it to the professor, who was an adjunct from Jet Propulsion Lab in Pasadena. The guy liked the code, he got me a patent for it, we sold it, and now it throws off a little money every month that helps me pay for this place."

"What does the code do?" Jeremy asked.

Roberto looked uncomfortable. "Uh, I designed it to sort of listen in on e-conversations. But I think the feds are using it to track other countries' space programs."

Felicia laughed. "I love it. Berto is a spy. Or a spy enabler."

Thereafter, the group kept rotating around as they met. But for obvious reasons, Roberto's apartment was their preferred gathering place.

The rough spots in the five members' interactions with each other smoothed out or were mostly ignored, as Lopez' intensity kept the group focused more on the content of the course than on each other. Most of the time, the severity of problems affecting the children Lopez talked about suppressed the natural tendency of college seniors to assume the world was preparing itself to revolve around them.

As a college and a location, Western reinforced Lopez' message, working at letting its students know that they and the world were connected. The campus was a bit of paradox, a closely linked set of buildings around an oak-bordered quadrangle, with dorms and classrooms that rose gradually up a hillside owned by the college. Some of the buildings had been modernized, while others looked just as they had decades earlier when a series of movies set in colleges had been made on campus in years when Hollywood studios sought close locations. The classic look of the buildings still provided the backdrop for an occasional made-for TV or cable series.

This academic oasis, however, was located on the eastern edge of one of the world's most diverse cities: Los Angeles. Surrounding the campus were smaller homes built in the 30's and 40s, with larger apartment buildings on the major streets. Glendale, Pasadena, and the neighborhoods of what was loosely called East Los Angeles bordered Western. Students heading west for beaches or the downtown area passed by the southern edge of the expanses of Forest Lawn Cemetery.

Some students might try to disappear onto campus for four years, but the city and the world were very close by at Western—a good thing, in the view of most of its students and faculty.

Gradually, the five seniors became individuals to each other, learning more about why each was really taking the course, recognizing the strengths and the inevitable baggage each of them brought to the class. They took the study group seriously, going over the lectures, rehashing the field trips they had taken, arguing among themselves about what Lopez meant or what it meant in political and policy terms.

Felicia remained the erratic spark plug of the group, sometimes irritating the others by her persistence and sometimes forcing them to stop throwing generalities at each other and get specific. Suzanne spoke the least, harboring what the others came to realize was her own trauma. When discussions of child abuse became specific, especially about girls, Suzanne fell silent, and the others soon learned not to press her—as Lopez had quickly seen.

Jeremy talked about the issues of harm to children in essentially religious terms, but became quiet when Lopez and others pointed out abuse within the church and abuse in other religions that was sometimes justified as doctrine. Stan's lens was politics, and he usually interpreted issues through a framework of whatever the US Congress was doing about the problem. He seemed puzzled when Lopez pointed out early in the course that the US Congress was one of only two national legislatures in the world that had not ratified the UN Convention on the Rights of Children. Stan made that non-decision the focus of his final paper in the course.

And Roberto was the technology guru, peppering Lopez with questions about why hand-held computers and smartphones weren't used more widely in child protective work, asking why traffickers weren't subject to Treasury banking prosecutions, and usually arguing that every child protection nail needed a technological hammer to fix it.

In their private meetings, the five became much more heated than in class under Lopez' watchful eye. At the same time, they began to know each other well enough to see where the red lines were—where they could kid somebody about something in their life and where it was too raw.

Early on, the members of the group became sensitive to their greetings, especially across gender lines. They were of the millennial generation that freely hugs—men and women. People of their age who know each other well usually hug if they are greeting each other after some time apart. And Felicia was a world-class hugger, her Italian heritage having won out over her family neuroses.

But Suzanne was a definite non-hugger. "Hey, Suzanne" and a hearty hand wave was what the three men quickly learned to offer—and only that.

Because of his religious background, Jeremy was often the butt of some of the kidding, and he took it better than anyone would have imagined when they first heard his story of being born again. At one point, when the teasing had gotten fairly close to the edge, Jeremy simply declared with a wave of his arm around the whole room and a huge smile, "There is nothing any of you secular sinners can say or do that would keep me from loving you all as children of God."

Felicia worked harder at understanding Jeremy than any of the others. Like him, she had also grown up in a family she felt alienated from, but she had never reached Jeremy's level of getting past it. She would tease him, and then come over and sit at his feet when he made one of his conciliatory, all-encompassing remarks. And Suzanne clearly felt a level of comfort with him that she never approached with Stan or Roberto.

Stan got along with nearly everyone, showing the athlete's ease with people, the good-looking male's disregard for appearances, and the extrovert's self-assurance of someone whose role in his family was carved out early as stable older brother and beloved son. His race was never mentioned by Stan, but when one of the group occasionally saw him with a group of black students, they glimpsed a slightly different Stan and realized how easily he moved across invisible barriers that were still present.

And Roberto also had the self-confidence of a favored child, but with an overlay of a deep drive to make money that was seemed at odds with his being in the Lopez class. He was clearly trying to work out the tensions between financial success and helping kids—and hadn't gotten there yet.

He was also trying to develop a theory of women to match his theories of finance and science. He tried to explain his theory about watching women to Jeremy one night when they were waiting for the women to arrive to a study group meeting. The two had gotten burgers and some beer after classes.

It was a sketchy theory, but Roberto could embellish a sketchy theory until an inattentive listener could imagine he had just heard an earth-shaking concept.

Roberto's theory, as he told it to Jeremy, who kept falling asleep, was that there were three stages of the aesthetics of watching girls—or women, as the case may be. Stage 1 was the inevitable, limbic-brain reaction "I'd do her." Roberto was too self-confident to add the obvious corollary "if she wanted me to."

Stage 2 was the sheer aesthetics of watching. Roberto outlined it carefully: "The color of her hair, how she wears her hair, her body, of course, the shape of her mouth, her eyes, her racial type or blend, progressing to the way she moves. Is she tentative when she moves or does she walk and move around with assurance?"

He further explained that hair-flippers who played with or endlessly smoothed their hair were automatically disqualified. Excessive body enhancement was also a disqualifier. Chins mattered—Roberto explained that he was somewhat surprised that chin enhancement was not more widely advertised, given the chin-deprived features of some otherwise lovely women. But then he realized, as he pointed out to Jeremy, that such reconstruction might in fact be widespread, though invisible.

The third and most challenging stage, he claimed, was bringing an active imagination to bear on the visible facts. Roberto explained this to an increasingly bored Jeremy as follows: "The trick is to conjure up a life from what you see—elements of virtue from the visible. For example, suppose she's smiling. Is this an act? Is she really happy? Why is she happy—she's going to see her family? Her lover? Her kids? She's gotten a new job or she's escaping a rotten job—or marriage? If she's overweight, is she happy and OK with it, is she a lover of good food, a believer in a Rubenesque ideal, lacking self-discipline, or glandularly handicapped? If she's thin, is she self-denying, anorexic, a marathoner, or just naturally thin?"

Jeremy finally spoke up. "Maybe you should be a shrink, Roberto. Then you could get them to tell you what they're thinking instead of you just making it up."

Felicia and Suzanne had just come into the apartment as Jeremy finished speaking. Felicia asked "Making what up?"

Roberto quickly said, "We were just talking about movies—whether they make it up or base it on what really happened."

Jeremy laughed, but stayed silent.

Stan never mentioned football, but the other four all read the student paper, and knew that he was a starter and sometimes a star as well. When they asked Stan during a break in class if they could attend the games, he gave them a funny look and said, "Sure, if you want to see me get pushed around, be my guest."

So the four of them developed a ritual of meeting before the games, traveling to away games in Roberto's well-aged supercrew truck.

Growing up in Chicago, Suzanne equated football with her family history, and was the least interested, but the others persuaded her to come along. She gradually found herself admiring the movement of the players and even fascinated with the occasional violence of the game. Jeremy tried to forget his parents' using football as an excuse for drunken

Saturdays and Sundays, while Roberto studiously watched the patterns of the game and tried to figure out how serious betters ever made money on football. And Felicia became a rabid fan, cheering everything Stan did and at times infecting the others with her enthusiasm.

As they got to know each other, each of them worked to understand the backgrounds of the others, and the networks they belonged to at Western when they weren't in the Lopez class or the study group. Stan had the broadest connections, as a member of the athletic fraternity who spent as much time with the student leaders and self-declared intellectuals, as well as the group of black students who formed a fairly close-knit group on campus. He could move easily from one group to another, and the other four recognized that the time he spent with them had become an important part of his senior year, even though it drew him away from his other networks.

Roberto was closest to the computer science majors and a loosely defined hacker group that understandably talked little with outsiders about their exploits. Like Stan, he dated actively and widely, tending toward a tall blonde archetype that he sometimes got teased about, but rarely varied. Jeremy, predictably, was friends with the actively Christian groups on campus, but also worked with a group of progressive students who were often involved in some form of community service in the nearby neighborhoods and the downtown area.

Felicia had joined a sorority as a freshman, encouraged by some other women from New York, but became inactive after her first year due to both her finances and her growing disdain for the cliquishness of the group. Her primary contacts, outside the Lopez group, seemed to the others to be mostly serial romantic liaisons that sparked, burned, and then flamed out in succession. She would often be seen around campus with what Roberto referred to as her "stud-of-the month."

And Suzanne was seen from time to time with a group of self-declared feminists who ranged from active LGBT partisans to women who were headed for careers in medicine and education along tracks that advocated for more women in leadership positions in professional arenas.

One night the group had shared pizza and beer at Stan's apartment, which was three blocks from the campus on a side street marked with bars, donut stores, and auto repair shops. In contrast with Roberto's magnificent place, Stan's was a one-bedroom mixture of jock's lair and a library of political tracts, with maps of South Carolina voting districts covering nearly all the wall space.

They had talked about papers they were writing for Lopez' class along with some assignments in other classes that were coming due. Television was on with sound off, showing some music videos that were below the interest level of any of the five.

Felicia, as often happened, threw a new topic onto the discussion. "OK, friends and neighbors. We've talked a little in past get-togethers about grad school and what's next in our lives. So where are you all headed, now that it's December? Jeremy, you first, because you're so predictable."

Jeremy smiled and said, "True, true. I'm off to seminary in Texas, to see if they will let me work on international children's issues somehow."

His smile disappeared. "I'm not sure how it's going to work out. They seem to have only two tracks there—regular pastoring and youth ministry—which doesn't really cover the issues in the class." Then he smiled a typical Jeremy smile and said, "So I'll wait and see what happens. But I'm headed to friendly downtown Austin and whatever the Lord has in store."

Stan scoffed and said "At least in Austin you'll get to meet both of the liberals in Texas, Jer."

Roberto spoke up and said "I've been accepted at UC Santa Barbara's computer science MA program. They have an internship arrangement with Treasury in Washington, and that's where I want to end up after the first year. I need to learn how corporations and cartels hide their money offshore."

Felicia challenged him immediately. "I don't hear much kids stuff there, Berto."

Roberto shook his head. "Wrong, happy flower girl. The traffickers combine kids, prostitution, and drugs, all in the same shipments, sometimes."

Since Felicia Fiore translated roughly to happy flower in Italian, it was a nickname that Felicia sometimes received—never enjoying it much. The first time Roberto had used it, she shot back "*Si, mi chiamano*

Felicia Fiori. That's from *La Boheme,* means they call me Happy Flower. But it ain't necessarily so."

Then Felicia pointed to Suzanne, who quietly said "I've been accepted in the international social work program at Columbia in New York. It's a two-year program with strong ties to some of the women's advocacy programs in the UN offices in New York." She smiled and said, "So come see me when you're in New York, people."

Stan rounded out the reports with his simple statement: "I'm headed home. Got early admission into law school at the *real* USC— University of South Carolina. I need that home-grown network to start climbing the political ladder. And you should all expect letters asking for tastefully small but not tiny campaign contributions as I begin to build my donors lists."

A collective groan went up from the group, but followed with smiles and responses of "Sure, Stan."

Jeremy asked, "What about you, Felicia?" Then he wished he'd been softer, because she looked so sad they could all tell she was undecided. She said, slowly, with a frown, "I have no idea. I guess I'll go back to New York and see what turns up. Save me some lunches, Suzanne."

Professor Lopez was unpredictable. Just as she seemed to be winding up for a long lecture, she would stop abruptly and ask a question. By that time in their undergraduate education they had learned that this was a professor's trick of keeping them focused, but they rarely felt they were ready for her questions. She seemed to have a way of knowing when she was going on too long, running the risk of letting them tune her out—and then the question would erupt, sometimes interrupting herself to pin down a loose reference.

"Wright"—she always used last names—"what do you think causes that?"

Woe to Wright if his only response was "Causes what, Professor?" And if his answer was a formula response, "I suppose it's the economics of that country" or "Political pressures, I guess," she would frown, shake her head, and call for a different student to answer without giving the unfortunate responder any feedback. Which was, of course, worse than bad feedback.

As the class moved to the final sessions of the semester, Lopez announced that the next sessions were, in her words, "My attempt to inoculate you against naiveté." She went on to explain that trying to protect children without understanding the barriers that were likely to be faced was a kind of naiveté that could be as dangerous to children as the original harm.

As an example, she assigned the book *Weapons of the Spirit* and then showed the hour-long DVD that had been made based on the book. The film and book told the story of a village in Vichy France that had agreed to hide hundreds of Jewish children under the leadership of a French pastor.

After the viewing of the film, Lopez asked the student to read a more recent treatment of the same incident, *Village of Secrets*. This book depicted a much more complex set of events, in which the heroes were less apparent.

The students were irritated that their first impression had been sullied by the second book, until Lopez made clear that this second-guessing was the intent of her exercise. She insisted that first impressions were not always reliable, and that when emotional responses to the needs and abuses of children were involved, she had seen over-reactions occur often enough to want them to understand how this misjudgment could occur.

"You want to make snap judgments about your own life—fine. Mistake—but fine. But be very careful making snap judgments about other people's lives. That's what this assignment is about. You never get perfect information about a decision that affects kids. But you can dig deeper, and get *better* information. Then you'll have to decide. Because not deciding is deciding to do nothing."

She was quiet for a moment, and then said, "I want to talk about trafficking as a specific kind of harm to children. You have to understand where child abuse and trafficking begin. Their roots lie in a blend of profit motives, coercive violence, gender inequity, and a demand for illicit sex and labor. They are nourished by addictions—to drugs and sex and male power over women. And they are enhanced by perversion of technology into a tool for control and oppression. So if you try to take on these forces—you'd better know how powerful they are, and what it takes to defeat them.

"Above all, it takes persistence in creating a spotlight that creates a constituency. And projects just don't do that. Projects are marginal at best—they can even be harmful, if the system insulates itself by answering criticism by saying 'look—we have a project that deals with that.' And so people decide they don't need to change the policy—they just start a project."

In the next session, Lopez began with a softer tone than she usually took. "I don't want to inquire about your religious attitudes. But I do want to connect what we've been talking about to religious ideas, and to the ideas of those who reject religion. If you are a believer of any of the Abrahamic religions, children must be central to your religion. And if you are not—if your faith is in science instead—then the remarkable discoveries of neuroscience in the last thirty years or so provide us with even more evidence that children must be nurtured so they can become fully realized adults."

She paused and looked around at them. Their discomfort was palpable, but she continued. "And if you believe in sin and live in this country, then you cannot ignore the original sins of America, its acceptance of slavery and its deliberate policies of genocide toward the first Americans. Children were the most affected of those victims, and children who are still enslaved and still the targets of genocide in dozens of countries and cultures must be a part of your calculus in deciding what to do about these sins. Once you are aware of them, to not act is to decide it doesn't matter. And that moves you into the theology of sins of omission."

She went on to lead a spirited discussion on children and religion, in which the discomfort level of the class soon shifted to an active debate between those who agreed with her that religious ideas belonged in the debate, and those who felt that religion was part of the problem rather than the solution.

Jeremy's head was spinning. For him, it was the first time in any non-religion college class that theological ideas had been presented so openly. He had made more detailed notes than he had ever done before, and as class broke up, he headed for the library at the other end of the central quadrangle, full of questions. He doubted that the answers would be in books, but that was where he was going to start looking.

Lopez said, as the group was packing up to leave class, "Long trip next time, people, I'm cancelling class next week and we're going take a full Saturday and make it a real international journey this time."

Roberto, who seemed able to get away with more in the class than the others, or not to care about whether he was confronting Lopez, said with a smile, "You're flying us all to Paris in your private jet?"

Lopez smiled and said, "No, but I'll accept your invitation when you get your first one, Berto." Then she turned to the class and said "We're taking the van down to Tijuana to visit a shelter down there and maybe do a little work building an annex."

Felicia clapped her hands and said "I love it. We're going to actually touch something real with our hands."

Lopez said "Oh, yes. It's real down there."

They left campus at 6 am and crossed the border at San Ysidro around 9 after stopping for a quick breakfast in Chula Vista. The driver, a friend Lopez knew from her work, maneuvered through the side streets of Tijuana, arriving at a two-story house in the La Joya neighborhood. The sign on the outside said *Casa de Niños*—Children's House.

As they walked into the house, they noticed a fenced side yard with children's play equipment and a swing set. They had been asked by Lopez to bring toys and clothes, and they dropped them in a donations bin at the front of the house.

Lopez introduced them to the director, whose name was Gary Jimenez. After they had sat down in the front room, Jimenez began by saying, "Look, I don't like the drive-by poverty tourism stuff much. But I've known Graciela and her programs for years, and I trust what she's teaching you about what we do here—and why we do it. I'm going to get some work out of you, and maybe some of you will end up doing work like this. And that's worth it."

He went on to explain that the thirty children and youth living in the house had been abandoned by their families or were waiting for their parents, who had crossed into California to find work. "The older ones do a pretty good job of taking care of the younger ones. A few of these kids have been caught up in the smuggling business run by the cartels, and we've had to pay off the police to keep the cartel guys from coming around to 'claim' the kids they used to pimp out. Some of the older girls were on the streets here and in San Diego for three or four years before we could persuade them to come here."

Stan asked "The local government and the federal agencies don't do anything to watch out for these kids?"

The director laughed, with an edge, and said, "Both of them are paid off regularly by the smugglers and the traffickers."

He stood up and said, "Now it's time to do some work. How many of you have ever worked in construction?"

Stan raised his hand, and Roberto said, "I've installed a lot of computers. Do these kids have any access to the internet?"

"We have one old desktop and a dial-up connection that works, sometimes."

Roberto smiled and said, "Let me have your address. I'm pretty sure I can get you some second-hand desktops and a few laptops that are going to be given away by a firm I work with."

Jimenez said "That would be fantastic." Then he added, "If you can, please arrange to have it delivered by someone you trust. The mail and regular delivery services tend to take a lot off the top when they get shipments they can sell off."

Roberto said "Will do."

And Stan said "Berto the fixer. Way to go, dude."

Jimenez led them to a small foundation that had been laid in back of the house. Lumber had been laid out beside the foundation, which Jimenez said had been donated by a local charity that worked with a network of Southern California churches. "We're going to use this for storage. The house keeps getting filled up with kids' stuff and bedding, and we need a clean, dry place to store supplies."

He showed them a plan for the supports and roof, and Stan took over supervision of the group. With help from some of the older children, they worked for nearly three hours straight, breaking for lunch, and then went back to work. By 5 pm, they had put up the walls, filled in the wallboard, and roofed the small building.

As they were packing up for their return in the van, Lopez joined them in the living room of the house with a group of five children. She said "These children wanted to thank you for your work. I asked some of them to tell you their stories. Berto, will you translate?"

Happy that he had avoided the third generation's tendency to drop using Spanish at home, Roberto slowly translated the story of two of the boys who had been living on the streets. One of them had worked as a drug handler for the cartel that dominated Baja California. He had lost a shipment of marijuana to a rival gang, and the dominant cartel had put a contract out on him. He found his way to the Casa program through a local priest.

One of the girls had worked in San Diego and was able to tell her story in halting English. She looked about fifteen, with long hair she had swept up in a ponytail. She told them, "The pimps came and got us in a home where we were waiting for our parents to cross back over. They told us they were taking us to a place where our parents would meet us, but when we got there, it was a…a house where they made us do bad things. Then they took us across into San Diego in the back of a big truck that was carrying fruit. We worked around the hotels in the bad part of downtown until we got arrested twice. Once you were arrested a second time they said we were too risky to have on the streets because we had a record. They took us back here and sold us to another house. They made us do the same things, and they beat us when we didn't have enough customers. Then another girl and I tried to run away, but they caught her. I came here because the shelter downtown told me about this place."

In the van on the way back, Felicia was quiet while the others talked about what they had seen and done. Finally she said to Lopez, "I knew what you were talking about in class was real. But that girl made it so much worse than I had believed. Thank you for bringing us down here."

Jeremy and Stan were having coffee in the student union. They were totally at ease with each other by this time, their Southern roots having helped and their natural comfort level with most people having worked its smooth magic.

"Jeremy, why are you so mellow? Fundies are supposed to be all up tight and righteous, man. Why aren't you like that?"

Jeremy laughed. "Your stereotypes are pretty lame, Stan. I guess I picked up some mellow from my parents. They were *too* mellow—they let everything wash over them and didn't care much about anything—including other people. I resented their not caring, and once I found the church, I was pretty much on my own. I got into Western through a counselor at my high school who noticed my grades and liked my writing. I guess I've always been easy-going since I found the church. Trust in the Lord and all that."

"Looks like it works for you."

"So far, so good."

"That's what the guy said as he passed the fifth floor after he fell off a ten-story building. So far, so good."

"You've been watching *The Magnificent Seven* again."

"Every few months, gotta get my fix. It's all in there, Jeremy. All of life."

Early in the semester, the two of them and Roberto had rounded off a study break at Western by seeing a revival of the classic Western, based on Kurosawa's *Seven Samurai*. Stan had been the most affected, and could recite lines from the movie to fit nearly any situation.

Roberto, however, had pointed out how much the bandit gang's leader, Calvera, resembled a modern cartel boss. And the women just laughed at them—"little boys with cowboy toys" was Felicia's dismissive phrase.

At the next session of the class, Lopez began by reviewing the responses of the US government to child protection threats. She was balanced, crediting some Republicans and church groups with genuine international leadership on HIV/AIDS issues that had saved thousands of lives. But she also reviewed the recent history of the "responsibility to protect doctrine" which was emerging from a Canadian group due to present its report in 2001. In response to the genocide in Rwanda and the Balkans in the 1990's, this doctrine maintained that states have a responsibility to protect all people within their boundaries, and when the state is unable or unwilling to do so, it becomes the responsibility of the international community.

She summed it up. "If this doctrine gets endorsed by the UN, the criteria for intervention are likely to become an important new facet of the debate about genocide. And I would predict that what some have called 'femicide'—deliberate attempts to harm women—will also become a part of that debate."

Suzanne had been listening, no longer taking notes as she tried to absorb what Lopez was saying. She asked Lopez, "So what does the doctrine say the UN should do about this? Pass resolutions that everyone ignores? Form their own army? Give guns and ammunition to the families who are being persecuted?"

Lopez shook her head. "The doctrine is silent on that, other than some language about "the international community" protecting people without specifying how that is supposed to be done. And I want to be clear—this was all debated in terms of genocide—not harm to children specifically."

Stan asked, "How has the US responded?"

"The US response to these issues on the ground was strong, eventually, in the Balkans. But in child protection, we are not a major player yet. The Europeans have done much more than the US government has done so far. We are major contributors to UNICEF, but we don't play an active role in child protection or in anti-trafficking, compared to other countries or the UN."

She paused and looked at them for a moment, underscoring what came next. "Final point. Some of you are going to run into people and politicians who are all about *freedom*. It is a core idea in this country— and in other countries as well. It's a very good idea, but it isn't an absolute idea. Isaiah Berlin, one of the wisest men of the 20th century, once said that 'if men were wholly free, the wolves would be free to eat the sheep.' When the subject matter is children, that's a good thing to remember."

Stan took careful notes, paying special attention to her remarks on the US role and what Congress had contributed to the debate. And Suzanne kept frowning, struggling to accept a doctrine that said all the right things without explaining how they were supposed to happen.

The study group had decided as a break to attend a concert that was a benefit for children's programs in Los Angeles. At the end, the choir that was performing invited the audience to sing with them, and the song they chose was *Amazing Grace*.

The five of them stood together, the guys grumbling mildly, and then the singing began. Felicia stood in the middle of the group, singing loudly, and after a few measures of the music, the other four stopped singing.

Her light soprano voice was so clear, rising above the other voices, that all they could do was to listen and stare at her as she sang. The high, crystal tones of her singing were electrifying to the four of them as they listened. Their Felicia—tough guy, chip on the shoulder, aggressive Felicia—was a singer of amazing ability.

Once they were outside, on their way to a coffee bar, Jeremy was the first to ask her, "Felicia, why aren't you singing somewhere? You have an amazing voice—we all heard it. You've never told us about it. What's the story?"

She kept walking a few steps ahead of the group, then turned and said, seeming irritated, "Look, I don't want to talk about it. My *nonna*— my grandma—wanted me to take lessons but no one else in the family saw the point. And I never thought I was that good, anyway."

They were all quiet as they walked along together, torn between honoring her request and feeling how wrong it was that her gift was being ignored. Finally Suzanne said, "Felicia, I've heard you humming a lot. Do you know you do that? Don't you think something inside you wants you to sing?"

Felicia was quiet until they arrived at the bar. Then, as they were all sitting down, trying not to look at her, upset that the issue seemed likely to just disappear, she said "Cut me some slack on this, guys. Music is unbelievably important to me. It got me through some very rough spots. But I'm not ready to do anything with it right now other than climb into my headphones and drift away when I can."

Stan gave it a final try. "Just because your family was mostly clueless doesn't mean we are, Felicia. You have a better voice than most of the people on that stage."

But she just shook her head and looked away. There was nothing for the rest of them to do but to nod and change the subject, which they did.

The group was gathering for a study session, this time back at Roberto's apartment. Jeremy was quieter than usual, and Felicia was the first to notice it. She went over and sat down next to him. "Why so quiet, Jer?"

"Crummy day. I got into it with some of the brethren at the Wednesday chapel meeting after the service."

"About what?"

He was obviously uncomfortable talking about it. "They started talking about all the people who are going to Hell. And one guy went off on gays as the worst people, who would all be damned to eternity. One of the women in the group, who's pre-med, said she had taken biology courses and learned that the biological basis for homosexuality was scientifically proven, not something people choose. And then she asked why God would make people like that if it was evil. The guy went nuts and attacked her personally."

"And you stood up for her."

"Sort of. I called him a judgmental bigot, and he told me I had to leave. I didn't, and so the whole group got up and left."

Felicia was quiet, while the rest of them watched the exchange. Then she said, "I have two questions. How did you feel after they left? And was the pre-med cute?"

After the laughter died down, Jeremy smiled and said "I actually felt pretty good. And she was nowhere near as pretty as either of you."

Roberto said "Right answer, dude. Way to go."

Lopez began her lecture. "In the work to protect children, race matters. Bigotry and racism matter. When you are out in a world where most people are what we in this country call, in a somewhat mindless euphemism, 'people of color,' race still matters—and unfortunately, color matters within race and ethnic groups. As you come to understand the different forms of abuse of children, if you choose to work in this field, you will find out how much race matters, along with religion, and sects, and ancient hatreds that are more culturally based than racial.

"But you've got to get the numbers right. And you've got to understand how race and culture work in your own country, before you start telling people how to handle it in theirs. You don't have to point fingers at anyone to recognize that 72% of births outside marriage in the African-American community in this country—and 42% overall—are numbers that matter."

She was watching them carefully, knowing that she was in sensitive territory but certain that they had to learn to deal with this piece of the sad reality of child neglect. "And then we start to see how culture plays a role. The rates of teen pregnancy and single parenting among Latinas increase with every generation that has lived in this country. First generations, there isn't a real problem. Second and third, it starts to get a lot worse. The longer they live here, the worse it gets. So—culture matters. And it's not just other cultures that are the problem. Ours has some real problems, too."

Stan was watching her carefully, as was Roberto.

Lopez continued to talk about the cultural tendency to abuse children from other racial and ethnic groups, seeing then as The Other. Then she looked at the group and said, "Maybe you should go to Manzanar."

Stan said, "What's Manzanar?"

Lopez asked the group, "Anybody know?"

Roberto answered. "It's where they interned the Japanese in World War II. Interned is a nice word for imprisoned. Swept them up, took them out of high schools and even colleges, like this one, and made them live in the desert up in the Eastern Sierra. Ten thousand people, who got tossed onto buses and moved overnight to the desert. Many of them lost their homes and their businesses, because they were Japanese. Because they were The Other."

Lopez said "That's right. It's hard to forget that scene once you've seen it. So think about going to see it."

The group got together and planned a weekend trip to Lone Pine. They left early Saturday morning in Roberto's truck, Stan and Suzanne alternated in the front seat because they were the tallest, and the others sat in the second seat with their bags in the bed of the truck.

The drive was stark and beautiful, out across the Mojave into the high desert and the soaring Sierra and White Mountains that surrounded the floor of the Owens Valley four hours north of Los Angeles. As he drove, Roberto pointed out the landmarks—where Los Angeles bought up the orchards and small creeks feeding into the Owens River and Owens Lake, which was now almost entirely dry. He told the story of the battle of the Owens Lake with the Paiute Indian tribes who were once the only inhabitants of the Valley.

"How do you know so much about it?" Jeremy asked.

"My dad used to bring us up here to go camping and fishing when we were growing up. He's a history teacher, and he made sure we knew the history of Executive Order 9066, which President Roosevelt signed in early 1942. It was backed by Earl Warren, the big progressive Republican governor of California who was Chief Justice when the Brown v Board of Education decision desegregating schools came down. After Pearl Harbor, the Japanese were the bad guys. So we panicked, and down came 9066."

They arrived at the little Asian-styled gate that marked the beginning of the Manzanar camp. They walked through the exhibits which the National Park Service maintained, and looked with amazement at the guard tower where guards with rifles had watched over the camp.

Roberto continued his briefing. "We judge other nations and cultures when they throw kids and families into shelters and refugee camps because of their religion or their ethnic identities. We should be more careful about condemning them when this happens."

He paused, thinking how to express himself. "I played basketball in high school with a guy who was born here. He was the smartest kid in his class, by far. And his country made him and his family live in this hell hole, with cold blowing through the walls of the huts they lived in during the winter, and desert heat all summer. Winds blowing all the time. When they drained the Owens Lake, when LA Water and Power came and took most of the Valley's water, the winds picked up arsenic from the lake bed and blew it all over the southern end of the Valley. *Arsenic!* But these people were the closest, living in what was then the biggest settlement in the Valley. And they had to breathe it every day."

They were walking from the Visitors Center through the reconstructed buildings where the camp's residents had lived. Suzanne said, "I see why Lopez wanted us to see this. Part of what happens to the kids she's been talking about is when they get lumped into some group that doesn't matter. The Other, like she said. These people became The Other. And their kids had to grow up here for a while, until the war was over."

Jeremy said, "Yeah. I wonder if we would ever do this again."

Stan pulled out a map, and said, "Let's go up that road. The Alabama Hills are out there, along with all these volcano cones. Let's see what's on the other side."

Roberto turned in the direction Stan had indicated, saying "You always have a map, Stan. Out here, you bring a map. You collect all those voting maps on South Carolina districts. I know you're thinking about running one day, but you're really a maps guy, aren't you?"

Stan was quiet, and then answered. "I like to know where I am. On a football field, you've got to know where you are and where the other guys are—the ones that are trying to take you down. Driving around, I never want to get lost."

He paused, then went on. "In an election, you need to know where the voters are. I just need to know where I am. Maps help, sometimes."

As they drove back to Los Angeles, alternately napping and talking, Jeremy thought about the emptiness of the desert and the many Biblical references to desert lands. In his driving back and forth from Texas, he'd seen a lot of desert, some like the California desert they were now passing through, some even more arid, some high in the New Mexico mountains. Empty lands, he thought to himself, but full of revelations, for those willing to look and listen.

He leaned forward, tapped Roberto on the shoulder, and said "Thanks for bringing us out here, Berto."

In one of the Lopez sessions, Roberto had asked some questions about how the agencies in the field of child protection used technology. Lopez gave him a brief answer and then said, "Why are you asking about this?"

Roberto looked away, suddenly evasive. "I work with computers, a little."

Stan laughed. "A little. That's like Bill Clinton works with politics, a little. He's a genius, Professor. He can get you the President's bank balance in fifteen seconds. Or yours."

Lopez said "So you're a hacker. A super-hacker, it sounds like."

Roberto, still guarded, said, "I can get around in code and on the net, yeah."

Lopez smiled and said "You're messing up the stereotype, Roberto. You're supposed to be Asian."

Roberto laughed, a bit more at ease. "I know. That's why no one suspects me. What could a barrio kid know about computers—how to carry them off the truck?"

Lopez, now serious, said, "Without wanting to encourage you to commit any felonies, I will tell you this. We've talked in this course about how some of the child trafficking goes together with drug trafficking. And some of the cartels and traffickers use internet banks to move money around the world. They have whole platoons of guys like you who keep their money hidden from the feds and from their competitors. You want to be very careful in those corridors, Roberto. But there is an enormous amount of money sloshing around the Internet, much of it gained from ruining people's lives. Someone who could disrupt that could do some good. But they would be working in a very dangerous place. And that's all I'm going to say about it."

Roberto watched her carefully, taking in every word.

And the others realized that they were briefly glimpsing a world only Roberto understood—and that it was mostly a dark and amoral landscape.

Then, in the final class session, Lopez shifted her focus from the content of the course to the students themselves. She said, "I know some of you have some good intentions to continue your interest in these issues in your careers. I think that's wonderful, and I hope you keep me posted on your progress. But I want to be sure you understand how much of yourself you'll be bringing to this work. Some people seek out helping professions from a conviction that they can make themselves whole by helping others. Sometimes that works.

"But if you haven't grown up with fairness in your own family, it will be harder to imagine and work for fairness in your life's work. If your earliest years are marked by neglect—if someone has tried to make you feel like a thing instead of a person—it will be harder to learn how to value every child as a creation of God."

Felicia interrupted, clearly distressed by Lopez' words. *"But you can change it!* You can take a different path from the one in your family."

Lopez smiled and said, "Yes, you surely can. You can only blame your parents for so much of your own treatment of children and other people in your life. Then it's up to you. I'm just trying to make sure that you know that is going to be part of the work that lies ahead of each of you."

Finally the semester came to a close. Graduation and the final, largely meaningless semester were looming, and the class was further from most of the students' minds than it had been in September. Lopez seemed to know this, and began the final session with a long story about a child whose had been kidnapped by drug smugglers as she tried to reach her parents in Texas. It was a wrenching story, in which the child was repeatedly abused, the parents had disappeared, and the outcome was uncertain as the story ended.

Lopez finished her summary of the newspaper story, and said "I am not making this up. This happened. *New York Times*, October 6. Read it. And then know that it keeps happening, over and over to thousands of children and their families." She paused, because by then faces were being wiped, and a few tears brushed away. She let the reaction subside, and then asked in a tone empty of expression, "So what are you going to do about it?"

Roberto was the first to answer. "I don't know. But I will—some of us will—do something. We'll do something. And then we'll come back and tell you."

Lopez allowed herself a small smile and said, softly, "Good. We shall see, but you've made a commitment. Good."

The five of them adjourned to a coffee shop across the street from the campus that had become one of their unofficial post-mortem headquarters.

Roberto spoke first, as the others sat drinking their coffee and tea, thinking about the class. "So what do you think? Should we take her seriously?"

Jeremy said, "I can't speak for anyone but myself. But I'm going to give it a try. I've interviewed with a church group which has an internship in Austin. I'm going to do that for the summer before I go to seminary and then see what happens." He shook his head. "I don't know how anyone can listen to her and just walk away."

Roberto nodded, and said "I've done a lot of thinking about this, ever since that first class. I'm good with computers. I'm going to see if I can make some money by taking some money."

Suzanne asked, "What do you mean? Take money from whom?"

"From the bastards who do this to kids. I've been reading a lot for the paper I'm doing for Lopez about how the Treasury Department has developed a lot of ways to stop money flowing to terrorist organizations. I'm going to go to Washington and see if I can get a job there as part of grad school. They're hiring programmers. Then I'll see if they can teach me anything."

Suzanne said, with a tone of skepticism, "Might work. I'm going to look for an agency that works with girls and women. I've read about a bunch of them that fund programs for girls that delay early marriage. Maybe that will be worth doing."

She was silent for a few moments. Then she added, "But I don't know how you stop violence with words on paper. If protection doesn't mean ending the violence—using whatever it takes—it's just words."

Felicia was the last to speak. "I don't know. It all seems so futile. I don't know if waving signs or signing petitions would make a hell of a lot of difference. She told us about all these letter-writing campaigns, and all the rest—but what really happened that made a difference?"

She looked around at the four. "But if we all wander off and do our own thing, we'll never know whether any of us took Lopez seriously." She frowned, seeming to censor herself, and then she blurted out "So what if we all met in five years and then see what we've done?"

Her challenge silenced them all for a moment, and then Jeremy said "I think that's a great idea. We're here, we're all taking this class, we got to know each other, and we can check back and see if any of us really did anything about it. I'm in."

The other three quickly agreed, with Suzanne merely murmuring "All right."

Felicia was quieter than usual as they agreed to her suggestion, and then said "Thank you. I really want to stay in touch with all of you. I still don't know what I want to do—or what I *can* do. And you guys help me think about that better than anybody I've ever known. So thank you."

To lighten the mood, Roberto said "*De nada*, happy flower."

Then Jeremy asked Stan, "If Gore is elected, won't these issues get more play? Kids' issues, I mean?"

"Maybe, but he's all about the environment and government reform. I don't hear him talking about kids, except the usual Democratic pieties. And nothing international. Only person talking about that is Hillary, when she got all up in the face of the Chinese in '95. Went to Beijing and talked about girls and women's rights as human rights."

"OK, but won't Gore appoint much better people than Bush would—people who know and care about kids?"

"Probably. Though you never know. Dems sometimes appoint real duds, and Republicans sometimes get people with a personal experience—adoption, HIV exposure, or something like that—that helps them get it."

"So we'll see what happens in November."

"I hope so."

Felicia had a question for Roberto. "Berto, what about this 2000 software thing? Isn't the whole internet going to, like crash or something, when the calendar turns over to a new century?"

"Not happening. Any firm that lets the changeover to the year 2000 mess up their software doesn't deserve to get in on the boom that's happening. The next few years are going to see people making small and large fortunes out of new software."

Felicia said, "Are you going to be one of those guys?"

"Maybe. If I do, you'll know it, and I'll figure out a way to cut you all in on it."

Stan chuckled and said, "I'm not going to bank that yet."

"I mean it. You are my pals, and I want to help you do whatever you can to help kids. Maybe I can use my stuff to help you with your stuff, somehow."

Suzanne said, "That would be nice, Berto. Thanks for keeping us in the picture."

As she packed up her files at the end of the class, having graded their final papers and given them their grades, Lopez reflected on the class. She had grown to care about all twelve of them, but she had quickly noticed that the Five, as she thought of them, had a special bond that was much stronger than the other two study groups had developed. The other groups were just that—study groups. The Five were strong personalities who had managed to become a strong group, which was not easy, in her experience watching classes over her years of teaching.

She wondered about what already seemed to her to be the different paths each of them was likely to take if they ventured out into the child protection world. Stan was the easiest to read; he was bound for politics. She hoped the ugly history of race and hardball politics in his native South Carolina would not hold him back, but she had seen his steadfastness in class, with the group, and even, once or twice, on the football field.

Jeremy was undoubtedly headed for a religious route, and she knew enough about the coverups and timidity in those arenas to be concerned about his staying power. Roberto was definitely going to move down a path driven by technology, but she did not understand that world enough to be able to predict his path. And she worried about his search for financial dominance and whether The Mission would co-exist with that drive or overwhelm it in deal-making. She knew there was also a dark side to what Roberto intended to do, and she didn't know if it was safe, even for someone of his extraordinary skills.

She worried most about the women, Suzanne's anger burned low but intensely, and she knew it would be a difficult fit to channel that anger into positive work. Lopez knew that her hatred of the violence done to her was so near the surface that she could imagine it exploding out of control some day. She could not yet see what gifts Felicia would bring to the Mission, if she chose it, but somehow she knew Felicia's blunt, direct manner would make a mark. She had seen a soft side to Felicia that she could not conceal, for all her tough guy exterior. And Lopez hoped that side would be allowed to emerge somehow.

In all, she knew she had been given a glimpse of the futures of some remarkable young people. In their closeness, which she had seen repeatedly in class and on the trips they took, they had become a sort of family, drawing on the strengths of their own families where they existed, substituting for the weaknesses of their families when that was holding them back. She hoped they would gradually grow into their own potential to help other families with terrible obstacles of their own.

She wondered if they would stay in touch, and she hoped they would.

PART TWO

2000-2005

Stan 2000-2005

S tan Wright was an excellent athlete in high school, a four-letter jock. But he was also a near straight-A student. He chose Western in LA because he knew he was going back to South Carolina after college and wanted to sample life somewhere else in the country before he did.

Stan decided early on in high school that hitting people and getting hit was not how he wanted to make a living. He liked football and the other sports, and had been approached by three SEC universities and two of the traditionally black colleges about full or near-full scholarships to play football. But he knew he could play at Western without it being central to his education, and that was what he wanted.

An uncle who had made it to the NFL took him aside one day after watching him practice and said "Stan, if you can find some other way of making it than this jock shit, pick it and don't look back. You're smart, man, you can get money or power or whatever you want. But hitting people and getting hit ain't it. You're done at thirty and then you spend the rest of your life limping around and wondering why you can't remember what day it is. Use football to get an education if that works for you. But I've watched you grow up. You're going to be something better than a halfback or a wide receiver, Stan. A lot better."

So Stan was a football player because it paid for things he needed and got him to places he wanted to go, not because he wanted to make it in the pros.

Early on, as far back as junior high, teachers had seen the leadership thing in Stan. It was a measure of his evenness that he had not gotten full of himself after teachers and others had kept telling him he was going to be something special someday. Black and white teachers had both called him in and given him what he came to think of as "the Moses talk"—advice that somehow he was going to be "a leader of his people." Stan was cocky enough to think of the people of all of South Carolina as "his people," but he didn't let on that his vision went well beyond the Moses thing.

He ran for student offices, he went to statewide events like Boys State and other leadership training, and he participated in church youth groups. But with Stan, those who knew him best sometimes saw his achievements as checking items off a long list of to dos. His choices were more deliberate, less spontaneous than most teenagers were able to make.

In his junior year in high school Stan had to choose between a speech contest and a football playoff that had gotten scheduled on the same Friday on opposite ends of the state within an hour of each other. Without hesitation, he told his coach he would not be able to play. When a counselor asked Stan why he had made that choice, Stan looked at him and said "I've played football before. But I've never won a speech contest."

He won. And the team pulled itself together and squeaked out a two-point victory without him.

Stan's father ran a home-building company that placed Stan's family well into the higher strata of middle-class families in Columbia, where he grew up. His mother was a substitute teacher at the local elementary school who then became full-time when her youngest child entered first grade. Relatives from both sides of the family lived close to Columbia, so Stan grew up surrounded by a supportive extended family, with its share of strong role models and a few cousins who made their living on the far side of the law.

He had also met a distant relative with some national fame, from the Wright side of his father's family. She was a cousin who had left South Carolina where her father was a minister and had gotten involved in the civil rights movement in the 60's and then founded a national children's advocacy movement. Stan had talked with this cousin several times, on her frequent trips back to South Carolina and at her offices in Washington.

The last time Stan visited her in Washington, she had taken him aside and told him, staring at him with her intense face close to his, "Stan, you stay in touch with me. You are going places, and we both know it. I want to help you if I can, but you stay in touch. Don't go off getting swept up with fancy California nonsense. They have a lot of money out there but not a lot of common sense. You stay in touch, hear? And you come *home*."

Early on, in a continuing project that began with a high school government class project, Stan had begun collecting election results. At first it was an assignment, then it became a hobby, and finally it morphed into a passion.

Stan continued his research at Western in every class where he could justify the political research or the sheer mathematics of the analysis he was doing. He knew that there were fourteen counties in South Carolina that voted Democratic most of the time, and he knew that he lived in one of them. He knew that only one of the six congressional districts was Democratic, and he knew that if the state were fairly districted, a new, seventh district should be Democratic, given population totals. He knew that court cases were pending because South Carolina's reapportionment was one of the most egregious examples of racial clustering, drawing districts with all black voters in one large district and the others scattered around districts with strong Republican majorities.

Stan kept all these numbers and the maps that revealed them, and updated them whenever he could, He faithfully read the South Carolina papers that were available online. He had met the staff director for the lone Democratic congressman on a trip to Washington, and kept him informed of his educational progress. And he kept his home voting address and voted absentee in every possible election.

Stan definitely appreciated girls, and girls appreciated Stan. In high school, he moved around, instinctively sampling different types of girls, to the extent that his school offered the princesses, the brainy ones, the drama queens, and the quiet, self-assured ones.

At Western, he learned early on the difference between girls seeking their own kind of trophies and those who got beyond race without pretending that it was irrelevant. He was puzzled at first by Southern California black and Latino girls, who often had a strong disdain for

Southerners. One girl who had grown up in South Central Los Angeles even attacked him during their freshman year for his "plantation ways and cotton-picking style." He laughed it off, but he could pick up the overtones of envy at Stan's growing up in a majority black community.

There were a few black girls at Western from other parts of the country, but he found the four who had come from Southern states like his own were the easiest to just hang out with, even though one of them seemed to resent all the time he spent with the other groups on campus and at times made clear that she felt he was a climber.

As his education at Western drew to a close, Stan prepared himself for his return to South Carolina. He knew law school would be more of a grind than undergraduate classes, and he was ready for it. The others in the study group teased him about going back home, but they all knew why he was doing it, and most of them admired his narrow focus on what he wanted and how he was going to get it.

From the beginning in Lopez' class, Stan had made two things clear: he cared about children's issues and he believed politics was how to make a difference for children. He never put down other approaches to helping kids, but it was clear that for him, elected office was the route he was going to try to take. None of the others had anywhere near as clear a vision of their future as Stan Wright had.

The most important event in law school, in many ways, was 9/11. Stan was in class when the bulletins began reporting the planes hitting the World Trade Center, the Pentagon, and then the field in Pennsylvania. Classes were quickly dismissed so that students could gather around the television in the student dining area. Undergraduates were rarely allowed in the law school buildings, but all these distinctions were suspended in the crisis atmosphere, and the room was soon full of students from classrooms in nearby buildings.

Like everyone else in the room, Stan was trying to sort out what the tragedies meant to him and his family. A few of the students had brothers in the military, and since South Carolina was a state with deep military traditions, there were loud exclamations from those students as the news kept coming in.

"Guess my brother will get deployed wherever these bastards came from." "My dad is probably on a plane right now headed for DC." "We're going to kick the crap out of whoever did this."

Stan couldn't yet figure out exactly what the politics of the attacks meant, but he knew the counter-attacks would mark political life in the US for many years to come. And he remembered Roberto taking them up to Manzanar, talking about what happened after Pearl Harbor. He knew two or three million Muslims wouldn't get rounded up, but he couldn't help wondering how they would be treated after 9/11.

While he was still in law school, he got a call from Jeremy Boxton, who seemed at loose ends in his studies at the seminary. As they talked, Stan saw a bit of himself reflected in contrast to Jeremy's uncertainties. Stan knew where he wanted to go, and he had a pretty good idea of how to get there, though he knew he'd have to please a lot of people on his way up the ladder. He felt sorry for Jeremy, and tried to give him straight advice.

He got his law degree, he found a firm in Columbia that was carefully balanced, both politically and racially, and he joined the firm. Three weeks after setting up, he was sent to Washington for a deposition on a case, and stopped by his Congressman's office. He had wanted to pay a courtesy call, having met the Congressman while he was on a high school visit to the Capitol.

To Stan's surprise, when he gave his name to the receptionist, he was quickly ushered into the chief of staff's office, who asked Stan to sit down and then pulled out a file and began reading it. Stan was again surprised to see his name on the file, and to hear the aide, Jeff Davidson, read from it. "Graduated Western College 2000, came back to Law School, graduated fifth in your class, working now at Perry and Robinson in Columbia."

Stan said slowly, "Yes sir. All correct. I'm surprised…"

"That we have all that information? Stan, we keep track of every young man and woman in our district who heads off to four-year colleges. It's our way of making sure we know where the talent is in our fair state." Then he stopped talking and looked at Stan, who began to feel uncomfortable.

Davidson finally said, "Stan, we may want to ask you to do some political work for us back in the district from time to time. We'll pay, of course. Think that would be acceptable to your firm?"

Stan quickly answered, "I think so, Mr. Davidson. The firm does political work—on both sides, as I'm sure you know. I'll ask, but I'm sure it will be OK."

"Good, good. We like to keep bright young lawyers like you plugged into what the Congressman is doing and also listening to what people back in the district are concerned about. Two-way flow, you see? We appreciate your help."

Then he stood up, and shook Stan's hand as he smoothly moved him toward the door.

Headed back on the train, Stan had some time to think about what had happened. He knew he had been recruited, and that had not surprised him. What was harder to get used to was the fact that he had been tracked—monitored as a speculative property, in effect. He liked the feeling that he was on the radar of people who mattered to his future, but he was still getting used to the possibility that they might be making more of the decisions about his future than he would.

Stan knew he wasn't yet in charge of anything that mattered. And he began to suspect that he was getting closer to finding out who was in charge—and that it would put boundaries around his future.

Both because his mother was pressing him and because law school had given him less time for female companionship than he enjoyed, Stan began dating in a more deliberate way than he had ever done before. He met women at the law firm, he met others through friends, and he checked back with the women in his high school circles who were still single and still childless. It turned out to be a smaller group than he had hoped. But he was able to identify a list of seven or eight women who he thought might be appropriate to get to know better. And so, somewhat methodically, he began asking them out.

He had rented a small one-bedroom apartment in Columbia that was close enough to the law firm that he could walk to work when the weather was decent. A football teammate, Bo Ross, who was two years ahead of him at the law school, had been hired by the firm, and he double-dated with Bo a few times. They developed a routine where they invited women to dinner at Stan's apartment. Bo would cook a usually decent meal and Stan would be in charge of wine.

Stan's apartment had an adequate kitchen and a separate dining area, and Bo and Stan were soon able to tell which women appreciated the effort of their cooking and which just wanted to be taken out to the most expensive restaurants in the Columbia area.

Stan had kept his eye on a paralegal in the firm named Dolly Fawcett, and she became the first woman he asked out a third time. He liked her cute face and figure, he liked her obviously extroverted ways, and he liked that her father had the largest African-American-owned chain of restaurants in the state.

After dinner, Bo and his date had left and Stan and Dolly were sitting on his couch, appropriately far enough apart without it seeming distant. She looked at him and smiled—and then shocked him.

"They say you're playing a wide field, Mr. Wright. They say you're looking for Mrs. Right. That true?"

Stan prided himself on quick reactions, but he stammered a little and then said "I guess everyone is looking for someone special. Aren't you?"

"Of course. But you seem to be a little more deliberate about it than most." She laughed, showing a dimple on her left cheek. "We started a chart of who you were most likely to date next in the office or in the other firms in Columbia. You messed it all up by asking me out again."

She moved a few inches closer to him on the couch. "So what is that all about? Did I pass some test, Mr. Wright?"

Stan decided to dial it back a bit and said, smiling, "If you weren't the prettiest girl I'd dated, it would make no sense. But you are, and it does. Satisfied?"

Dolly blinked and said, "Why, thank you." She was quiet, watching him. Then she asked, "Do you know that almost everything you talk about is about politics? You're kind of fixated on it. Are you going to try to run some day?"

Stan answered slowly. "I'm thinking about it. It seems to me that it's one of the best ways to get things done. So I'm thinking about it."

"To get what things done?" She was not going to let him get away with a formula answer, he saw, and he raised his estimation of her, which was already high.

"To help people. To help kids, mostly."

"What kids? Kids here in South Carolina?"

"Yeah. And kids in other parts of the world—kids whose lives make most of our kids' lives look pretty good by comparison. Kids who go to work when they're 6 and never go to school and get married when they're ten. Kids who are really abused." He paused, and went on. "I took a course in college that told us what was happening to all those kids, and it kind of stuck with me. I want to help kids like that, somehow. And politics seems a way to do that."

It was the first time he had laid out his credo to anyone in such stark terms.

She looked at him, just staring. Then she said, "You're going to do it, you know. You're so intense about it, and you're so smart, and you're so damned good-looking. You'll do it."

She was quiet again, and then said, "I hope you find the right person to help you along the way."

He quickly said, "I do too."

They were married a year later.

Stan accepted a job in the Congressman's office in Washington, and they rented a one-bedroom apartment in Southeast, within walking distance of the House Office Building. Dolly began classes at Howard Law School, and they bought a kayak that they took out on the Potomac in the summer. Night after night, they paddled up the river past Georgetown and then back down to the edge of the airport, paddling, stopping, drifting, talking, enjoying the river and the night and each other.

Ever after, they called that year "the kayak year," with a touch of sorrow, because they never again had the freedom to go out on the river more than a few times a year.

The best part about the job was the Congressman's committee assignments. He sat on House Foreign Affairs, and better still, on the subcommittee that handled the budget oversight for the State Department and some of the many intelligence agencies. Those agencies were in a state of near-chaotic reorganization after 9/11, and Stan was able to watch the negotiations and horse-trading as the Congressman's seniority and his role in the Black Caucus allowed him more clout than most of the members on the committee.

Stan moved quickly from handling press relations and constituent mail on committee issues to preparing background papers and sitting in on some of the oversight hearings. He began to know some of the key players in the executive branch agencies, and slowly compiled a well-annotated list of contacts in each of the agencies and on the Hill.

At first Stan was quiet in the staff meetings, watching and listening carefully to the other staff assistants as they reported to the Congressman. Gradually, as he attended more meetings and spent more time touching base with the other staff, he spoke out. At first it was only in the areas where he had assignments. But then he felt comfortable offering his opinions, carefully, tentatively. "I wonder if we've thought about..." "Maybe we should also consider..." He learned how to add to others' recommendations instead of opposing them, working them around to his point of view without a confrontation.

After one session, the senior staff assistant walked out with Stan and said quietly, "You're making a real contribution in there, Wright. You've learned how to work with the team."

"Thanks. Takes ten other guys in football, Bill. I learned that fast once I saw what happened when somebody missed a block and the cornerback was coming at me."

Dolly's law studies went well, and they enjoyed the first year of married life greatly. They had agreed to wait to have children until Stan's future was clearer. But one evening after dinner at home in their apartment, she pushed her chair back and asked Stan point-blank, "When are we going to have the running conversation, Mr. Wright?"

"You want to run? I thought you hated to get up in the morning when I jog up to the Capitol and back."

"Very funny. You know what I mean."

He did. He had been thinking about it, but at 26, he knew it was very early, and he knew the Congressman had just announced he was seeking re-election. So he said, "It's early days, sweetness. The Congressman is very solid for re-election. No one will ever beat him. And Jeff Davidson has had his eye on succeeding him for a long time. That's what everyone expects—the Chief of Staff moves into the spot."

"So what are all those files you brought from your undergrad days that you keep adding to every time there's an election?"

Stan smiled, while knowing that it would take more than his usual first-rate smile to respond to her probes. "That's my insurance research. That's what I need to know to scope out the alternatives."

"The alternatives to running in our district, you mean?"

Cautiously, Stan answered, "Yes."

She then proceeded to run through the two districts Stan had been monitoring—the two that might one day turn Democratic. She mentioned the leading state legislators in each of the district who would probably want to run, the most important employers in each region, and the people her father knew. She also mentioned the deal made by black Democrats with the Republicans in the 1990's to redistrict in ways that created black legislative districts while protecting white Republicans' seats.

When she had finished, she sat and waited for his reaction.

"Damn, woman. You know more than I do about some of those towns."

"Well, of course I do. Why do you think I married you? You're going to need all the help you can get turning one of those districts over."

He stood up and came over to her chair, gently wrapping her up in his big arms, and said, "Yes, I am. And you're going to give it to me, aren't you?"

She stood up, pulled him closer, and said, "You'd better believe I'm going to give it to you, big man."

Jeremy 2000-2005

Jeremy enrolled in a seminary outside Austin in September of 2000. His parents were living in the Houston suburbs at the time, and he was able to drive over and see them when he returned from Los Angeles. He looked up the girl who had helped him connect with the church, but she was engaged to be married. He found a part-time job in Austin that helped him get re-acquainted with the area before classes began. Then at the end of August he moved into the dorm.

The first year went by quickly, and Jeremy was patient, moving through his required courses in the rhetoric of the Old Testament, Greek, and homiletics—the art of preaching. He found time to do some work in a Baptist church in Austin, working as an assistant to the youth minister.

Jeremy found he missed the Lopez seminar and study group more than he expected. The give and take at Western had been very different from what he found in seminary classes. The professors were mostly older ministers who had been teaching for decades, and who often had a world view that was restricted to a 1950s view of missions and missionaries. And the students were rote learners, for the most part, who rarely asked questions that varied from the curriculum.

Once or twice he had attempted to discuss issues of child protection and child poverty drawn from the Lopez class. But he found the professors had little familiarity with those problems and even less interest in learning about them. Their view, as Jeremy began to understand it, was that the rest of the world needed to be converted to fundamental Christianity, and that was the beginning and end of overseas ministry. Conversion would solve all problems, donations through the church were the only resources that mattered, and government programs were anathema. Once Jeremy asked about the United Nations agencies' role in international work, and his professor responded that their church never worked with the United Nations because it was full of heathens.

As he began to select courses for his second year, Jeremy realized he would really have only one elective. He found no courses that addressed the children's issues he wanted to study, but noticed a course at the

University of Texas on development issues and the family. He submitted a petition to add the class to his schedule.

A week later, he received a short note saying his request was denied. The section that made Jeremy decide to seek a meeting with his academic advisor read "We have found that allowing our students to attend secular institutions while in the seminary undermines their dedication to Christian principles set forth in a Christian curriculum. Therefore we must decline your request to undertake external coursework."

Jeremy's advisor was Professor Bancroft, who appeared to be in his late sixties and who had a full head of very bushy white hair complementing an equally bushy beard. As Jeremy sat down in the chair Bancroft had gestured him to take, he could not help but notice Bancroft's distinct frown.

"Now Mr. Boxton, what is this business about a course out of sequence? I believe we have made clear that external courses detract from the mission of the seminary."

"Yes, sir, that was what the letter stated. But for some time I've been committed to work in international children's programs as my calling in ministry. This course would help me move toward that goal."

Bancroft's frown grew darker. "Do you not feel that your mission in your own country is rewarding enough? Why do you feel you must work outside the U.S.?"

"Sir, I have been impressed with what the church—what many churches have done to help children who are abused throughout the world. That is the work I am called to do."

Bancroft shook his head. "This whole business of churches and the abuse of children has gotten very tangled up with secular politics. I don't see the need for more seminary graduates in this field. I'm afraid I must reaffirm our rejection of your request." He stood up and held out his hand. "Good luck with your second-year program."

Jeremy had not expected flexibility, and he had not gotten it. As he looked at the list of required second year courses, he knew it would be a boring two semesters—with an entire third year looming ahead. For the first time, he asked himself if the seminary was the right path toward what he wanted to do—what he knew he was meant to do.

So he called Suzanne. She was headed into her second and final year of her MSW program at Columbia, he knew, and as they went back and forth trying to sync times for a call on both Texas and New York time, he realized how much he missed the group. Especially Suzanne.

Finally they connected. "Jeremy, I'm so glad you called. I've been thinking so much about our group—and missing it."

"Same here. That's part of why I called, to see how you're doing and if you've heard anything from the others."

"I heard from Felicia, and we've gotten together a bit. But classes started in the last week of August, and I've been so busy I haven't connected with anyone else. How are you doing?"

So he told her about the course work and the refusal to allow him to take outside courses.

She responded quickly. "You sound down, Jer. More than you usually let yourself get down—you're the happy, cheery guy, dude. Don't turn negative on us, please."

"I won't. How are you doing—are you liking the courses? What does it look like you'll be doing after this year?"

"I love the courses. There's a women's group here that works on the Millennium Villages programs in Africa, and another that's working in the Middle East with grass-roots women's groups who are setting up schools for girls. One of the schools is protected by a group of women who banded together to call for protection from the national police when they are threatened. It is so exciting. And most of the courses are just what I'd hoped they'd be. I think I'll end up with one of the teams going to Africa—they're going to be hiring in the spring, so I won't know until then."

Jeremy could hear her enthusiasm, which was as upbeat as he'd ever known Suzanne to be. He felt glad that she was doing so well, and then he couldn't help but contrast her progress with his own situation.

He said, "Glad to hear you're on track. I'm going to hang in for another year, I guess." Then he changed the subject. "Are you still up for meeting in '05? Is that still on?"

Suzanne said, "I hope so, at least if I'm in this country then. I'd really like to see you all and see how you're doing. I miss the group."

"I do too." He rang off, leaving unspoken the words that came immediately to mind: *and I really miss you.*

So Jeremy went back to his second year classes, resolved to put up with the drudgery and what he increasingly saw as the self-satisfaction and insularity of the seminary faculty. He had tried to make friends among the other students, but once they found out that he had gone to a secular college in *California*, barriers seemed to go up.

In some ways, it was easier to defend a literal view of the Bible among his mostly non-religious friends back at Western than it was here in the seminary—because the narrowness of the seminary's interpretations were impossible to reconcile with the first-rate education that he had gotten at Western.

One of his second-year classes was mission and evangelism, and he had hoped that the international issues he cared about would be a focus of the class. The class was taught by a missionary who had worked in India for twenty years before returning to the US, an older minister who spoke very quietly and seemed more interested in telling stories about his own experiences than preparing the students for theirs.

In the second session of the class, Jeremy raised his hand and asked, "Will we be talking in this class about how the church works with children in other countries—children who are orphaned or abused?"

The instructor looked at Jeremy as though he had interrupted him with an inappropriate question. "Our concern with orphans is how we can get them into our churches and, when possible, get them adopted and brought to the U.S. to live with Christian families. There has been a decline in international adoptions in recent years, and our job is to reverse that."

"But sir, aren't some churches moving to secure good families for those children in their own countries so that they remain in their own cultures?"

"Their own cultures, as you put it, are *pagan*, worshipping elephants and dozens of other gods. Those are not cultures we want any children growing up in, Mr. Boxton."

Jeremy had recently read a book on international adoption, *The Child Catchers*, which presented a very different picture of the adoption field. But he remained silent, seeing how much his question had upset the instructor. And he chalked it up as one more example of the distance between his own goals and those of the seminary.

The seminary students didn't hear about the 9/11 attacks until they broke for lunch. The seminary authorities had decided not to interrupt classes with the news. Students gathered around an ancient TV set in the student lounge, trying to follow what was happening, but at 12:55 the assistant to the seminary president came in and turned the set off. "Back to classes, please. This news program will be on after you finish your afternoon classes."

The group docilely walked off to their 1 pm classes, and Jeremy thought *another strike against involvement with the outer world.* The discussion of the attacks over the next few weeks centered mostly on the evils of Islam as a religion of violence. Jeremy listened for some recognition that Islam and Al Qaeda were not the same, and that Islam was an Abrahamic religion that honored Jesus as a prophet—but heard none of it.

Then a few days later, he saw a small ad on a bulletin board in a local coffee bar, where he hung out often because so few of the students frequented the place. The ad was for a drawing class held in the local community college. In high school Jeremy had taken two art classes and enjoyed them greatly, especially one on drawing in which he had actually won a prize for a drawing of a horse.

Jeremy took the ad off the bulletin board and smoothed it out on his table. He looked at it for a long time, and then a phrase from Timothy came into his head: "Therefore I remind you to stir up the gift of God which is in you through the laying on of my hands." *Stir up the gift of God.* He pulled out his phone and called the number on the ad.

Jeremy had more or less inherited his parents' VW bus, an often-repainted relic of their on-the-road hippie days. It ran, usually, and it had the advantage that he could find a park out in the hill country west of Austin when he wanted to read or write papers for class in a more rural setting. The van was one of the pop-top versions made in the 70s, and he sometimes slept out in the van when he felt he was in a reasonably safe area.

The van got him to and from the night drawing class he had signed up to take. He had been very tentative at the first session, which he found to be made up of an enthusiastic instructor, a curly-haired fifty-something woman, and twelve students ranging in age from fifteen to what appeared to be at least seventy. The instructor appeared to use the random inspiration method, asking each of them in the first few sessions to draw whatever they wanted just to get used to the paper and the pencils and charcoal that were handed out.

But as each session came, Jeremy found himself enjoying it more and more, settling into a routine of drawing whatever object had been set up by the instructor, and then drawing free-style for the rest of the session.

He was only a little surprised in the final session when the instructor announced "a special challenge" and opened the hall door to a young woman who walked in clad in a robe, which she promptly dropped after seating herself on a stool.

Jeremy did all that a very celibate 22-year-old could do keep from being distracted, and ended up fairly pleased with his drawing. The instructor quietly said "Well done, Jeremy," as she passed by.

The drawing course was over, but he had learned that drawing the reality in the world was an excellent way of coping with the rigidity of his course work at the seminary. As he came to the end of the second semester, he began looking at his options. A third year at the seminary was starting to seem like it could be an even bigger mistake than the first two.

Jeremy found himself again thinking of the Lopez study group. In many ways, next to Jeremy, Stan was the most religiously oriented of the Lopez group. He had been raised in a church-going family, he had relatives in the ministry in black churches, and he had made clear in a few deeper-than-usual conversations with Jeremy that he was a believer, albeit in a Supreme Being very different from Jeremy's.

So Jeremy decided to call Stan. After catching up on what Stan was doing in law school and relaying the news from his recent talk with Suzanne, Jeremy said with some hesitation, "Actually, I'm calling for some advice."

"Always available for advice, Jer, old pal. Can't guarantee that it'll do you any good, but advice I've got. What's up?"

Jeremy explained his frustration with the course work and the rigidity of the seminary. "I came here to learn how to do ministry to kids—the stuff we talked about with Lopez and with each other. I still take that seriously. But these people don't seem to think that way. They're all about finding a church and working within that framework. I hate to throw away two years of effort—and the loans I took out to pay for it. But I'm less and less sure that a third year will take me where I want to go."

He was quiet, and then added, "I may have gone to the wrong kind of seminary. I picked one that was close to home and tied to a church tradition that I knew. But it's so *narrow*, Stan. They really don't seem like they want to know about the rest of the world."

Stan said, "Sounds to me like you're ready to make a move, Jer. Losing the two years isn't a loss if it helped you figure out what you really want to do. What are your options?"

"I'm not sure. I've been thinking I should look for work with one of the church-related agencies to make sure that's what I want to do. I've looked into World Vision, Save the Children, and some of the others. I'd have to start at the bottom, but I'd know after a while if that's the right path for me."

Stan said, "Some of those outfits are based in Washington and New York. Why don't you come hang out with me for a few days? I go up to Washington to do legal research a couple of times every year. You could tag along and save yourself some hotel costs." He paused, and then added, "I'm seeing some young maidens, but we can work around that. Have you been seeing anyone?"

Jeremy laughed. "There's a librarian here I've been seeing a lot of, but she's sixty with three grandchildren, so it's not looking very hopeful."

Stan said, "Let me tell you something I remember about you, Jer. You are relentless when you have a goal in view. You wouldn't let our teasing or our nasty secular wisecracks bother you one bit when you wanted to make a point. And if this seminary is making you feel that you're losing that drive, maybe it's not the right place for you to carry out your mission."

He added, "There are a lot of churches and religious organizations out there, man. They don't have to be the ones these guys are tied into."

Jeremy agreed to think about coming to Columbia and then on to Washington. He thanked Stan profusely and hung up. He had some decisions to make.

He began researching the non-governmental organizations—called NGOs by everyone in the field—that were church-affiliated. The biggest ones—World Vision, ChildFund, Church World Service, Catholic Relief Service—worked on some of the child protection issues that the Lopez class had examined.

Jeremy's hopes rose as he saw that some were hiring. He sent off some emails, knowing he lacked the qualifications for anything other than entry-level work, but making clear that he was willing to start at the bottom to get a position with one of the agencies.

Within a week, he had heard from two of them, and one, Church Children's Services, had an opening. So he sent in a resume and called Stan.

Jeremy found traveling to Washington with Stan to be more enjoyable than any social contacts he had had in two years at the seminary. Stan was bound for politics, ands regaled Jeremy with stories about the fund-raisers, candidate's nights, and door-knocking he had been doing to establish his bona fides with local politicians and their supporters.

"It's fun if you don't take it too seriously, Jer. You're going to meet all kinds of people, and some of them are as cynical as the day is long. But others are true believers, and you have to be careful not to pop their bubble. I love working with the kids I've met. I'm in a pickup basketball group that plays in a park near the law school. Those kids are all hoping to get a basketball scholarship, because it's absolutely the only shot they're ever going to get at college. The University sponsors a few of them with scholarships, and I've been able to steer some of the money to some of the kids I shoot hoops with. They go off to the U or to the black colleges, and some of them wash out after a semester. But some of them stick with it. It's the best feeling I've had in a long time to have them come back at the holidays and hear them talk about being in a good program." He laughed. "I'm also picking up some good campaign workers."

Jeremy asked, "So when are you going to run?"

Stan said "I'm not sure. I can't seem too pushy. It's partly a question of waiting to see if the Congressman I've gotten to know is going to step down. There's at least two of his staff who would go for it, but I might be able to shake things up a bit in a primary. Or I could wait for the next district in South Carolina that might elect a black congressman. That would be a bigger risk, but it would be less of a scramble to get the nomination."

"You're not even twenty-five, yet, Stan. Isn't that a little early?"

"Yeah, it is. But you get in young and you have a chance for seniority. That's tempting. You get on the right committee, and you can start to have an impact." He looked at Jeremy, serious now. "I can't help but think about Lopez writing '400 million' on that whiteboard. Those kids are hurting *now*. I don't want to just wait around to catch a break. I think I've got to make my breaks—go after it as soon as I can."

So Jeremy went to Washington, and then on to New York, and interviewed at several of the church-related agencies. He regretted not having finished his seminary work, but he knew that the experience he could get with the NGOs would be much more helpful over the long-term than a third year at the seminary. He ended up taking the job with the Church Children's Services agency in New York, with a promise that he would be considered after a year for a field rotation. He looked forward to catching up with Suzanne and Felicia.

Before he left, as he was packing up his room at the seminary, Jeremy received a call from the Dean of Students. The Dean came right to the point. "Boxton, I see you haven't registered for any classes next year. What's going on?"

"I'm not returning, sir. I'm going to work for a church agency in New York."

"Would you please come see me? I have time this afternoon at 3:30."

As he walked into the Dean's office that afternoon, Jeremy thought about why he had been summoned. He suspected it was about more than losing the tuition.

The Dean greeted him and began by saying, "Boxton, we'd be sorry to lose you. I want to be sure you and we both understand why you may be making this decision—if that's where you are."

"I'm certain this is the right decision, sir. My calling is to work with children, and my coursework here has not offered me as much room to move in that direction as I need right now."

The Dean looked uncomfortable. "I gather there was some disagreement about a course you wanted to take at the U. Perhaps we could be more flexible about that now that you're in your third year."

Jeremy paused before he responded. He knew that the offer was too little, too late, but he also knew that the Dean might remember some of what Jeremy said if he said it clearly enough. And he felt he owed it to the other students to leave the strongest message he could about what he felt was missing at the seminary.

"I appreciate that, Dean, but it's more than a single course. Frankly, this institution just doesn't offer me what I had hoped I would get when I enrolled."

He leaned forward, emphasizing his words as if the Dean were deaf. "I want to work with children. I want to work with children around the world who are in trouble and need help. But the coursework here is almost exclusively about building churches in this country, not helping children in the countries where most of them—*the least of these*—still live.

The Dean blinked, and settled back in his chair. "You've been noticed as one of our more," he paused, looking for the right euphemism for *challenging*, "questioning students. Yet your work has been exemplary— all As. Why leave when you are so close to the degree?"

"Sir, with respect, because the degree won't give me what I need. I want to be able to work with children, to raise a ruckus when it is necessary on their behalf, to challenge institutions and organizations that are harming them or not doing enough to protect them. And sir, you teach none of that here. It's not in the curriculum, and it's not in the experience of most of the faculty."

The Dean frowned, and then sat up. "Well, you've made yourself clear, Boxton. I'm sorry we don't have what you think you need. And I wish you the best in your future endeavors."

As they stood and shook hands, the Dean added, "I'm afraid you may find the world of religious agencies is not all that welcoming to your ideas, Boxton."

With his best smile, Jeremy replied, "Then I'll have to work all the harder to change that world, sir. Isn't that what we're supposed to try to do?"

Without waiting for an answer, Jeremy walked out of the Dean's office. The confrontation had gone as well as it could have, and his own mind was crystal clear that he had made the right decision.

Once he began his work in New York, a supervisor soon noticed Jeremy's skills with spread sheets, and for a while he found himself steered away from work of the agency's programs and instead into finance and administration. He stayed with these assignments because he sensed that knowing both the programs and administrative sides of the work would be an asset that most of his co-workers would lack. An older worker had taken him aside after three months in the agency and had told him after watching him in meetings and reviewing his work, he could see that Jeremy had a real future with the agency. He told Jeremy that he should try as hard as he could to move back and forth between program and administration.

The older worker explained it bluntly: "Too many of the program people—both here and in the field—have no idea how to move money or other resources around. And the admin types view the program side as idealistic and likely to waste money if the admins don't watch them every minute. You get acquainted with both sides of the fence, young man, and you're going to have a great career." He smiled. "Switch hitters—able to bat from both sides of the plate. Always more valuable to a ball club."

So Jeremy mastered the nuances of depreciation and the logistics of moving food and equipment across the planet by the cheapest and fastest means available. He began accompanying senior officials into the field, and his passport filled up with the more exotic locations of the NGO world: Ethiopia, Colombia, Guatemala, Bangladesh, and Cambodia. He arranged food shipments to refugee camps, located space and instructors to train new youth advisors to church missions, redirected funds from ongoing missions to areas where a crisis had broken out— military actions or natural disasters that were affecting children. Once he even cancelled his flight home from Bangladesh because a monsoon had inundated all the coastal facilities where children were living. He worked for two weeks straight to arrange borrowed aid from other NGOs and from the US military bases and ships in the area. He finally returned to New York after he was given a count showing where every child who had been dislocated was now living.

At the core of his work, there was still a theological center. When trying to explain it to friends outside the NGO or religious world, Jeremy simply said "The Bible tells us to help the least of those alive, and that is what our work tries to do. We work with kids and families who live on less than a dollar a day, kids who may never go to school and may start to work twelve-hour days when they are six. We are called to help them, and so we do."

He felt mostly good about choosing the path he had chosen after leaving the seminary. He knew that the work he did, both directly and indirectly, was helping children. His travels, bringing him up close with children in orphanages and refugee camps, taught him more about basic human need than anything he had learned—at least in that seminary. And he was also learning the darker side of child protection—trafficking children and their mothers out of refugee camps, parents who actually sold their children or entered into marriage contracts for daughters who were under the age of ten.

And during this time, he was also painfully aware that the churches themselves had some very dirty laundry. The child abuse scandals, he found, were not restricted to pedophiles among the Catholic clergy. Protestant agencies had also struggled with sports and residential program leaders who used their positions to abuse children of both sexes. Some denominations were working to find and root out these abusers, while others devoted far more energy to suppressing information than to suppressing the abuse.

At an annual conference of religious NGOs held in New York in 2004, there were two workshops—out of a hundred—devoted to child abuse. Jeremy decided to attend both, and was disappointed greatly by the first in which a panel of religious leaders in international programs described their difficulties in hiring staff because of all the new screening and supervisory responsibilities the various scandals had brought.

But the second was much better. The workshop consisted of a single Catholic priest who was based in Guatemala. Painstakingly he described the process of meeting with every parish priest in every region of the country that received funding from Catholic Relief Services. CRS had instituted a review of all clergy and lay personnel who worked directly with children. Father Suarez, a Jesuit, described the painstaking process that was involved and said bluntly that some of the abusers were still hidden deep within the church.

Jeremy went up to Suarez after the session and introduced himself. He thanked Suarez for the workshop, and then asked him "What makes you hopeful about all this—what do you think is getting better?"

Suarez sat down on one of the workshop chairs with a sigh. "We are slowly becoming more honest—some of the churches, in some of the places we work. We are admitting we have a problem, which the addiction people tell us always has to be the first step toward recovery.

"One day, perhaps soon, there will be a Pope from this part of the world. And maybe he will throw off the secrecy of the Old World and shine the light of cleansing on all our efforts to let the little children come unto us. Maybe one day that will happen."

Jeremy loved Christmas, both for The Story and for some of the few happier memories of his parents usually being home and sometimes being sober. Most of the Christmases of his youth, they tried to get it together, to be a family. And his mother especially, country singer that she was, made an effort to keep music in Christmas, singing carols around the house in her twangy soprano, at times wheezing from her endless cigarettes and her drinking the night before, but at times offering up her simple Silent Nights and Little Drummer Boys with crystalline tones that touched Jeremy whenever he heard the songs in later years. Sopranos and Christmas were like peanut butter and jelly in his life—at least at that time of year.

And for Jeremy, as he came into his born-again period, the added dimensions of The Story also comforted him. He was an only child, and his parents had few lasting friends or relatives. So babies were a special attraction, and the lives of those babies, poor ones, ones with health problems, became for him a way of caring about other people without anyone judging him for the excesses of his parents. Babies and toddlers responded to love and warmth, and he learned in church in the child care room during services that he could be good with children. And so The Story of a baby born in danger and hope had special meaning for him all his life.

He drove back to Texas at all four holiday breaks while he was attending Western, sometimes with friends or arranged rides, sometimes alone for the full 1400 miles. He always took the southern route, through Phoenix and Tucson, on to El Paso, across the endless west of Texas, along the Rio Grande, through Van Horn and Fort Stockton, crossing the Pecos River, through Sonora and Fredericksburg and on into Austin. He could do it in two days when he was in a hurry, but he usually stopped off in the small towns along the way and made it in three or four easier-driving days.

Those were pre-satellite radio days, so he listened to the AM stations full of country-western music and the fiercely right-wing preaching of local stations, which kept him humming or shaking his head at the sheer weirdness of some of his fellow evangelicals. With close friends after he had left the seminary, describing his evolution from pure born-again to something nearer the center of Christianity, Jeremy would adopt a deep Texas drawl and imitate some of those preachers as a way of explaining why he had shifted his ideas about "God and Her universe"—which was how he always put it, in a deliberately iconoclastic phrase.

Years later, a woman he came to love told him that she had begun to fall in love with him the first time she heard him use that phrase. "You were so straight-laced, and so pure, and then you came out with that amazing phrase. And I began to see that you were something more than the good little fundie boy that you sometimes tried to be."

Suzanne 2000-2005

Suzanne was easily accepted to Columbia School of Social Work, and found an Upper West Side apartment in New York near the campus. She arrived in a sweltering summer, but was excited enough to be setting up for her two-year sojourn that the heat didn't bother her.

Before classes even started, she went to the student advisor's office and got a list of volunteer programs for students. She had been told that she would eventually be assigned to a formal internship in a local agency as part of her coursework, but she wanted a volunteer assignment. She assumed she would need an antidote to what she suspected, correctly, as it turned out, to be a mix of first-year classes that ranged from fascinating to deadly dull.

Suzanne had worked out an arms-length agreement with her mother that financing her graduate study would be a shared responsibility, with Suzanne taking out small loans while her mother paid for the rest through her Chicago bank. Suzanne had a small trust fund from her grandmother, and her mother made clear that Suzanne would be expected to use some of that money for college and graduate school. Her mother had conducted all the financial discussions with Suzanne, and her stepfather had stayed out of the picture, which was fine with Suzanne.

Suzanne and her mother had negotiated a strange, tentative peace after the terrible explosions that came as Suzanne turned thirteen. Her mother refused to leave her stepfather, and Suzanne refused to ever speak to him. Her mother's financial position was comfortable, and by her mid-teens, Suzanne had understood her mother's strong preference that she send Suzanne away with whatever support she needed to stay away. Since that was Suzanne's preference as well, it mostly worked.

Suzanne had known for some time, since the crises of her early adolescence, that she was going to have problems with boys—and men. In her logical way of approaching a problem with an illogical root, she assumed that at some point she would try the obvious alternative of lesbian relationships. She liked girls, and found it easier to be friends with them. When she met new women, she felt a *what about her?* tingle as part of her casual search for a trial partner. Nothing had happened yet, and she felt little need to rush it.

Suzanne's birthfather had disappeared from her life when she was three. She had only a vague memory of a man who talked to her briefly in the morning before he left for his teaching job at a Chicago university. She knew that she had some unfinished business with her father, but she had postponed it until she felt stable enough to talk with him without rancor. That stability had never come, however, and she rarely thought about it. Parents were essentially a vacuum in her life that Suzanne had learned to accept, without acting as if it were normal. She built a careful wall around the subject with friends, and they all soon learned that it was simply not discussable. The architecture of Suzanne's life had little room in it for family, and she knew that preserving that vacuum was the best way for her to get on with her own journey. Suzanne realized she had over-structured her life as a reaction to the harm done to her by her stepfather. But she also knew how close she had come to losing touch with all reality when her crisis had come, and she understood that the walls and fences around her life were there for good reasons.

"You're so logical and so prepared for everything" friends would say, and she took it as a compliment, while knowing that it was also a deeply rooted defense mechanism. Nothing was ever going to hurt her again.

The one exception to her cold-blooded structuring of her life was her passion to work with girls and women who were in danger. She knew, of course, where the passion came from. In high school and her first two years at Western, she had read everything she could find on survivor psychology. What she took from it was a conviction that she had to channel her own anger into constructive activity for others who were less able to repair themselves. As she got deeper into the literature of trauma and child sexual abuse, she found that two paths diverged in survivors' lives: anger at the perpetrators and empathy for others who had been abused.

She had had a conversation with Lopez as the class at Western was ending, and it came back to her often as she moved into the work at the agency she had chosen for her internship.

Late in the semester, she had asked Lopez for a one-on-one counseling session, and had spent half an hour, amid tears, telling Lopez what her stepfather had done to her. When she finished, Lopez took her hand and said, "You are always going to have the anger, Suzanne—at your abuser and at all abusers. But anger by itself can consume you—you can burn yourself up if you can't rebuild some positive feelings about yourself by helping other victims."

"How do I do that?"

Lopez smiled, sadly. "You watch for a chance to help somebody. You look for organizations that work in this field, and you listen carefully as people tell their stories. Some of their stories will touch you, and those are the people you should try to help. Just by listening, or by helping them find their gifts—where they're still strong. You have a lot to offer them. Suzanne. Not only your empathy because you went through it, but your brains and your skills at finding better paths for the rest of their lives—and yours."

Suzanne said, "That all makes sense. But I don't think the other— the anger at the bastards who do this—will ever go away."

"It shouldn't. It will give you energy, and it will help you understand that this is in some ways a war, in which we have to help the victims at the same time we are fighting their oppressors. Just try to keep the balance. Don't let the hate burn you up, Suzanne. You have a lot to give those women who are hurting, but the hate will cripple you if you let it."

So as she began her twice-a-week volunteer duties at a women's shelter, she tried to combine what she had learned in her classes and what Lopez had told her, looking for the strong places in the broken souls of the girls and women she was counseling. She found she had a gift of her own, the ability to listen in a way that encouraged her clients to pour out their stories. More than one of the women told Suzanne that until she met her, she had never been able to tell anyone the full story.

Suzanne also learned that it was critical that she find the right moment to ask "And what are you going to do about it?"

She loved the work and she loved finding out that she was good at it. She imagined that she could do this work for the rest of her professional life. She had occasional moments of loneliness, and welcomed Jeremy's call about his struggles at seminary. She looked forward to meeting with the Lopez group in three years, and one day she called Felicia to see how she was doing. She got hold of her at her apartment, and Felicia explained that she had just quit her third job in two years.

"I'm having a little trouble sticking somewhere, Suzanne. I keep digging out problems with the agencies where I work or the ones we're trying to improve—but nobody in the agencies wants to hear about it. At the last job, they said I was a 'classic half-empty neophyte.' I guess that means I keep uncovering rocks and telling them what's under them."

Suzanne smiled. "But that's what you do, Felicia. You lift up rocks. Somebody has to do that, or the crap never gets discovered. Where are you going to look next?"

"I'm not sure. There's an agency over in Brooklyn that works with kids—I thought maybe I'd see whether working directly with kids is better for me than trying to change what agencies do."

"Sounds like a good move. You want to have lunch?"

So they met for lunch, and Suzanne listened to Felicia's complaints about her work, and her worries about keeping a job. She tried to be helpful to Felicia, and toward the end of the conversation, she deliberately steered it away from talking about work, going over good times at Western. Suzanne told Felicia about an "exercise class" she was attending weekly, and when Felicia pressed her on it, she admitted it was actually a martial arts studio.

"Wow. You're learning to kick ass? How does that feel?"

"Better than it probably should. The instructor is a woman who was actually a boxer for a while. She combines Asian martial arts with Western boxing—great exercise and a pretty good confidence builder. You know I always…I used to get stuck in this victim thing, because of what happened to me. But this is helping me to get rid of that. I work out and spend a lot of time on upper body and leg exercises."

"Terrific. Looks good on you. Maybe I could use some of that, too." She was quiet, and then asked, "Suzanne, do you ever think about going somewhere else—working in another country?"

Suzanne said, "Funny you would ask. I'm taking a course now on international social work, and it's helped me identify some organizations that work with kids in other countries. Why do you ask?"

"I've started to wonder if I could do more good on the Lopez agenda"—she said it with some embarrassment—"if I were in another country where things are even worse than they are here."

"Why don't you come up to Columbia next week and we can have lunch again and I'll show you some of the stuff I've been looking at?"

Felicia agreed, and as she left, Suzanne realized that she had another project, which she looked forward to: helping Felicia find a job she liked.

Suzanne had always liked Felicia, seeing her aggressive stance as a different version of her own defensive posture. She knew Felicia's family life had been painful, never comparing it with her own trauma, but sensing that in some ways Felicia had been emotionally harmed as much as she had. She had seen Felicia at her best, persisting with a good point in class or in the study group when someone else would have caved in to criticism or being ignored. She admired Felicia for that toughness, and sometimes wished she had more of those qualities herself.

When they sat down to their deli sandwiches in Suzanne's dorm room a week later, Suzanne spread out the brochures and one-page fellowship announcements she had collected. She explained "I got these from a bunch of places—there's an international office at the School that is supposed to help with placements in jobs in other countries. Some of them get dropped off by recruiters. Look—" she pointed to two of the brochures. "Some of these say that they do both direct service and advocacy. They may just say that because it sounds good, but maybe it would give you a chance to do both. What countries are you interested in?"

"I have no idea. Is there anywhere they speak Italian?"

Suzanne laughed. "I doubt it. You guys gave up your empire faster than most of the others."

"Yeah—and we picked the wrong side in a couple of wars. But maybe Libya and Somalia?"

"Quiet places now—but I wonder how stable they are. Don't we have some kind of boycott against Quadaffi?"

"Let me look into it. Suzanne, are you thinking you would go on one of these fellowships or take a job in one of these places?"

"Not yet. I need to work with a women's group here and see what it is like to hold down a job. But in a year or so, maybe I could look at it. Lopez would say we need to go where the problems are worst."

"Lopez! She's still in our brains, huh?"

"I guess."

They agreed to have regular lunches, and Felicia promised to try to find a more stable job.

Suzanne went back to her job at the women's agency with a more critical perspective after she had talked with Felicia. She disapproved of what Felicia called her "bouncing," but at the same time she wondered about her own stability in the job she had while she was finishing up course work. The agency head had made clear that they would offer her an entry-level MSW position when she got her degree. But when she tried to project what she had been doing into a permanent position, she wasn't at all clear what that would bring her.

The agency worked on women's employment issues, but tended to define that task, as Suzanne saw it, as screening out women who weren't employable. They only accepted a third of the women who applied, and when Suzanne looked at the files on intake interviews, she found that what was causing the screening out was often a combination of drug and alcohol issues, domestic violence, and literacy problems.

When she asked her supervisor, a few months before graduation, what happened to the women who were screened out, she was told "We refer them to other agencies who handle those problems."

Suzanne couldn't stop herself from asking the next, obvious question: "But if we are trying to get them jobs, and that's the barrier, why don't we offer those services?"

The supervisor looked at her with surprise. "We're an employment agency, Suzanne. We don't do those other things. It would detract from our core mission."

In her course work, Suzanne had already been exposed to the silo syndrome, in which each sub-category of problems was handled by a different agency, with different training, different funding sources, and different attitudes toward the clients. She realized it had a real-life counterpart in her own agency.

A few weeks later, she had her interview with the agency director about a permanent position. The director, a woman of mid-fifties, said "We really like your work, Suzanne. You have excellent credentials from Columbia, and you've been able to establish good rapport with our women. I'm sure you will fit in well here."

Then she asked, in a way that made it seem like a formula part of the interview, "Do you have any questions for me?"

Suzanne took a deep breath and said, "Yes, I do. I've noticed that we screened out most of the women who come here because they have more serious problems than we can deal with here. Are there any plans to expand our ability to deal with those issues—substance abuse, literacy, and domestic violence?"

The director blinked twice, then frowned. "No, I can't say that we do. Were those issues that you felt you want to work on? Because there are other agencies that do that kind of work."

The tone of "that kind of work" was unmistakably *work which is beneath us*. Suzanne heard it, and the look on her face made the director realize it. She said, "I don't mean to denigrate those services. But it's just not what we do."

Suzanne decided to give it one last try. "But if those are the services those women need, what assurance do we have that our referrals get anybody connected with those services? Wouldn't it work better if we provided those services here?"

"We're not funded to do that, Suzanne." Then she looked at the clock behind Suzanne's chair and said, "I'm afraid I've run out of time. Please let HR know if you will be able to accept our position."

As she rode the subway back to her room, Suzanne knew she couldn't take the job. She had adjusted some time ago to the lack of any contact with children. But she knew that any effort she made to help women would mean that she was going to repeatedly run into the agency's narrow definition of what that help meant. She smiled to herself as she thought back on her conversation with Felicia about "job-bouncing." It looked like she was about to take a bounce herself.

When she got back to her room, she pulled out the international brochures she had shown to Felicia. She reviewed them more carefully, especially one that described work with a human rights agency based in London, which had offices in Africa and Asia. When she found a section in the brochure on rights for girls and women that referred to the UN Convention on the Rights of the Child, she opened her laptop and began her new research project.

Felicia 2000-2005

Felicia had reluctantly gone back to her family in Queens after graduation, but after a week she was ready to move on. They expressed little interest in her studies, asked her when she was going to get a job, and rudely wondered whether she was ever "going to get a boyfriend." To taunt them, her standard answer was "No, but I have a lot of girlfriends." They soon learned to stop asking her.

She needed a job, she needed a place to live, and she needed somehow to connect with the passion she and the rest of the group had all felt in Lopez' class. She wanted to work for children—not necessarily with children. She had talked with Suzanne a few days after graduation, and some of her ideas about her next steps had begun to clarify.

Spring 2000

Felicia was packing up her apartment in Eagle Rock, and Suzanne had come over to help. As they negotiated between Felicia's *throw everything in a box and tape it up* approach and Suzanne's carefully labeling things in logical order, they tackled the question Lopez had imprinted on their brains: *how can we do this work?*

Felicia said, "You can work with kids. I've seen you do it in some of the volunteer work you did in the schools. I'm no good with that, I'm too impatient. I want to take action. I want to make things change at the highest level possible."

Suzanne smiled. "So, like Stan, you want to run for President."

"No! You know what a joke that would be. I want to force the President to do the right things."

Suzanne said, calmly, "All right. How can you do that?"

"I don't know! That's what's pissing me off—I know the direction I want to go but I don't know how to get there."

Suzanne said, "There are dozens of direct action groups, from the national and international advocacy organizations to those that could get you put in jail. So pick one of the good ones that's safe and see what working for them is like. You don't have to lock down your career in the first job, Felicia. You have to try things. See what you're good at, see what feels good."

Her tone changed to pleading. "But please, try to stay out of jail. I'm pretty sure that being locked up wouldn't agree with you."

Felicia laughed, noting once again that one of Suzanne's many skills was calming her down. "I'm going to need you around as a therapist, OK? You're going to be in New York, at Columbia. So I'll stay in the city somewhere and you can talk me down from time to time. All right?"

Suzanne reached over and patted Felicia as she was lifting a box. "Of course. Since I'm so well-integrated in my own personality, I'll tell you how to run your life. Great idea."

"You know what I mean. You can help me see things clearer, keep me from going off half-cocked."

"Dr. Never Half-cocked. That's me."

Felicia laughed her wicked laugh, and said, "I never want to be half-cocked, Suzanne. I go for the full cock every time." Felicia knew Suzanne's comfort level with her lewd comments was low, but she also had seen that laughing about sex was one of the things that eased the subject for her. And Felicia could rarely pass up a chance to laugh about sex. Although at some level she knew she was engaged in one of the oldest con games in the world—the effort to convince herself she was worth something. And she knew that she was going about it the wrong way.

Suzanne had asked her about it only once, and then had dropped the subject. One time when Felicia had come home half-sober from what was obviously a disastrous encounter, she asked her "Do you ever get tired of that BS, sweetie?"

Because it was Suzanne, Felicia's immediate comeback had died on her lips. And finally she said, "I'd drop all those bastards in a second if I could connect with one decent guy."

"Like Jeremy, maybe?" Suzanne asked.

Felicia paused for so long Suzanne thought she wasn't going to answer. And then she murmured "Never happen," as she weaved off to her bedroom.

Suzanne sometimes felt that Felicia was high maintenance, but then she reminded herself that there was really no one else in her life for whom she made any maintenance efforts at all. She was as close to a sister as Suzanne was ever going to get, she supposed, and she tried to help Felicia see her own strengths.

Felicia Fall 2000

Once she decided she needed to leave her home in Queens, Felicia had found a job working with a child abuse prevention agency on the Lower East Side. She negotiated for an apartment with one of the other staff members at the agency. The apartment was in the East Village, in an older building that was still more money than Felicia had wanted to pay, even sharing the rent.

Felicia had saved some money from working in the cafeteria at college during her senior year. When she did the arithmetic, she figured that she could survive for six months on the small salary at the agency and her savings. Beyond that, her plan was very sketchy, and her college loans were always on her mind.

The agency functioned as a kind of watchdog over the city's child welfare system, funded by a national foundation that supported child welfare reform. She began working as an entry-level data collector, reviewing the information published by the agency. The problem was that the data typically lagged two years behind the actual caseload, and, as she got deeper into its records, she suspected that the data also concealed as much as it revealed. So in her own cut-to-the-chase style, she decided to call Roberto.

"Roberto, could you get into an agency's data system? We need some numbers from this agency I'm trying to oversee for my job."

"Unless it's the NSA, I probably could. How soon do you need it, and what are you looking for?"

Felicia explained that she wanted the actual reports of child investigations and what happened to them—in real time, without the two-year delay that the agency used to clean up their records.

"Sure, no problem. You trying to see what they're hiding? We did a project in grad school on county child welfare data upgrading. Turned out they would never put some of the data on some of the families in their case files or on the state system because if they did, they would then have to do something about it—try to help the parents keep their kids instead of just pulling the kids out and sticking them in foster care."

"Something like that." Felicia didn't want to go into details until she had the numbers.

"OK, send me the details—let me give you an email that I use for... uh, special projects."

Felicia knew that meant it was encrypted so that no one could see his email.

Roberto went on. "How you doing, Felicia?"

"I'm all right. This job isn't too so hot, but it pays some bills. I left home after a few days—it was either me leaving or they would have thrown me out."

"Sorry to hear that. You seeing anyone?"

"No, pretty much only work right now. Doing some writing."

"Good. You write like a whirlwind, friend. Keep it up."

After a week, Roberto sent back the data she wanted. Her hunch had been right, the numbers from the agency were changed from the raw data coming in from the front-line workers who actually visited families, to make it look like they had gotten to the cases sooner. In some cases the central office had also eliminated or downplayed the families' problems so that the agency would not be blamed for not responding. The rule Roberto had pointed to was in force: *if it isn't in the file, it didn't happen. So they just don't put it in the file.*

When Felicia took the new data to her supervisor, she was met with a very troubling response.

"Where did you get these numbers? These aren't from their website or the data they've sent us."

"I have a friend who was able to review some of the files that aren't on the website. It's all public data—the feds pay for these cases, so there's nothing confidential about it. These are just totals—there's no information here about actual cases."

Her supervisor, a man named Wilson Miles, had retired from a thirty-year career with the city's child welfare agency. Felicia had noticed his reluctance to criticize the agency when their performance was discussed in staff meetings, and now she could tell that he was very upset at her findings.

"I'm going to have to discuss this with the Director. I don't think we can use any unofficial data like this."

"But it answers the question we've been asking—how many cases have problems that never get into the record. That's what we've been looking for, because we have all these reports about people who need services who never get them."

"Maybe. But it would compromise our relationship with the agency if they find that we've been getting into their files to get data they never gave us or never posted on their website. I'll talk to the Director."

A week later, Felicia was called into a meeting with the Director and two other staff, in which Miles began by presenting his case against using the data. The Director looked at Felicia's findings, and said, "This is very serious, Felicia. This is not data they've given us, and they're going to be very upset if we present your conclusions."

Felicia heard *your conclusions* and realized she was being cut adrift. She was getting angrier, and throwing caution aside, she said, "Look, I was asked to find out about services these kids and their parents need. I did that, and now you're saying I screwed up somehow? Why are we protecting these people? They're the ones who screwed up. Isn't our job oversight—not comforting them?"

The Director, a woman who had a reputation as a well-known children's advocate, said haughtily, "I'd prefer you not telling me what our job is. My decision is that we can't use the data. Thanks for coming in."

Felicia quit the next day, after writing the agency's funders a letter describing the disagreement. She never got a response.

Her next job was with an agency that advocated for women who were at risk of having their kids removed by the child welfare agency. After a few weeks of working with these women, she went to her supervisor to discuss why they didn't track what happened to the clients and their kids after they were re-unified. "The agencies are bragging that they've reduced the foster care caseloads, but when I look at the number of cases where kids that were sent home were removed again—they're increasing. Why don't we follow them for longer than six months?

Her supervisor at first patiently explained how difficult it was to follow the clients, who moved a lot and didn't respond to attempts to contact them. The patience disappeared, however, when Felicia continued to press for more effort to follow up and offered to do some of the interviews herself. "That's not what we do," she was told.

Two jobs later, she decided to call Suzanne. They talked, and agreed to meet a week later to explore options for work. For Felicia, the continuing uncertainty about working *for* children or *with* children was bothering her more and more.

Spring 2003

When she sat down for lunch with Suzanne a few blocks away from Columbia, she began by running through her job ups and downs. "The pattern is that I ask them why they don't do a better job, they get defensive, I press harder, and they suggest that I should go work somewhere else. I'm getting tired of this bullshit, Suzanne. I just don't know if I can do it any more. I get so angry, I can't stay with anything with frustrating barriers and people."

"How do you do it?" she asked Suzanne. "How do you put up with all the bullshit? You got an even worse deal than I did growing up. How can you stand it?"

"I don't know, sweetie. I guess I just let it harden inside, and wait for a chance to use that hard edge against something. You let it out right away—I let it build up inside."

Felicia frowned. "Let me know when the explosion is coming, will you?"

Suzanne laughed, "It won't be aimed at you, happy flower." And then she asked a question Felicia wasn't ready for.

"How did your brothers treat you?"

"They never touched me. They just degraded me with every word they ever spoke to me."

"What are they doing now?

"The older two work on odd jobs in roofing—we have an uncle who runs a construction firm. The middle one did time for a hit-and-run that happened when he got drunk one night. He was in prison for two years. The younger one, Mario, wasn't as bad. But he went along with the older two when they were all together. He was only decent to me when they weren't around." She paused and said "Why do you ask me that?"

Suzanne said, "Sometimes the thing with guys and anger is about brothers. A therapist told me that once. Happily, I never had any."

"Sometimes I wish I hadn't either."

Then she changed the subject. "I've had a lot of time on my hands, so I've been doing some reading. About what happened in Italy and France and the rest of Europe, during the War. A lot of people went along with the Nazis, helped them, or did nothing to stop them. You read about that, and you keep getting nagged by this question: if we lived then, would I, would any of us, do the right thing by resisting? Or would we just go along? Would we be listed in the names of the Righteous Gentiles at Yad Vashem—the ones who acted to try to save the Jews from Hitler? Would any of us have worked to keep a Schindler's List? Or would we just have kept working, pretending not to know what was happening?"

"Pretty high bar to set, Felicia. This is not genocide."

"Maybe. But it goes back to Lopez asking us what we're willing to do to save children's lives. I don't want to get on some honor roll, that's not what I mean. But some people risked their own lives, and most didn't. Most went along."

"Yes, they did. They had jobs, and families, and debts, and they went along. And it was morally wrong, what they did to inform or what they didn't do to shelter people—to protect kids from what happened to millions of them."

She was quiet for a moment, not wanting to insult Felicia, nor to denigrate her passion. "But if we quit every job we have that's imperfect, we won't have jobs. And then who can we help?"

From anyone else, Felicia would have heard Suzanne's words as excuses for harm done to children. But Felicia knew Suzanne's passion was at least as deep as her own, and she remained silent, thinking about how quickly she had left jobs that frustrated her in the last year. She had even developed a phrase for it: *the bouncing career syndrome*. She knew that someone who held multiple jobs in a short period of time could be giving up the standing that you needed to make your case. And she admitted to herself that those who stuck it out without giving up on their goals sometimes—not always, but sometimes—strengthened their own ability to get things done.

And she kept wondering about it as she headed home to her apartment. She had at least managed to keep her apartment through all of her job-bouncing, and had even settled in to a decent relationship with her roommate. She shared Felicia's interest in opera and sat with her in the nosebleed seats at the Met every chance they could.

She looked for a week and connected through a high school friend with a child care agency close to her apartment on the Lower East Side. Expecting that it would be temporary, she found she liked it and soon developed strong ties with some of the parents. The program had a strong parent education component, and within six months, Felicia was placed in charge of it.

She arranged outings for the parents to music performances in the neighborhood, and then took a large risk by taking a group of twenty parents and their children to a children's concert at Lincoln Center.

They loved it, and Felicia realized that her love of music was part of what she could bring to children. She saw parents giving their children the attention she had never gotten as a child, parents who sometimes had two jobs but were able to juggle schedules and backup help so that they could spend time with their children. The makeup of the group was about half Chinese and half Puerto Rican, and the efforts to communicate in all three languages—Mandarin, Spanish, and English—was half the battle, she found.

When she checked in with Suzanne after her first six months was over, Suzanne could hear the enthusiasm in her voice. "I really surprised myself—I'm good at this, and the kids like it. I don't want to do this for the rest of my life, but I feel like I understand a hell of a lot more about these families than I would have gotten counting beans in some agency research shop."

Suzanne said, "Good for you, Felicia. You needed that. Time for another dinner. I'm getting a little itchy."

Felicia took a deep breath and said, "All right. I'm going to risk it. You're coming to my apartment, and I'm cooking Italian. You only have to try it once, and then never again if you don't like it."

Somehow Suzanne knew this was a much bigger deal than just having dinner, and she quickly said, "Wow—sounds great. Time and place, please."

When Suzanne arrived, Felicia had been in the kitchen for several hours. Suzanne had brought two bottles of Lambrusco from Tuscany, which Felicia quickly approved.

Suzanne said "The smells make it perfect already. Can we just sit and sniff for a while?"

"You sit, I'll finish up in here."

The size of the apartment made sitting an easy choice—there was one overstuffed chair that took up almost the entire "living room," which was indistinguishable from the kitchen. Soon it was ready, and Suzanne began to marvel at the prosciutto and a huge round of parmesan cheese from which slices had been cut, ravioli stuffed with spinach, the tenderest veal Suzanne had ever tasted, and a tiramisu dessert that by itself could have commanded deep double-digit prices in the best New York restaurants.

They had talked and drank, then drank and talked during the meal, and both were mildly buzzed by its end. "Felicia," Suzanne said, "how about you switch careers, open some restaurants, and we give all the profits to kids? This was stupendous!"

"Thank you. I haven't had the chance to cook lately—my roommate tends to live on ramen noodles and she works late. So this was a treat for me."

She brought out a bottle of limoncello, which Suzanne had never tasted before. She tasted it tentatively, waited a moment, and then her eyes lit up. "I have never drunk anything like this. This is the greatest alcoholic drink I've ever tasted. Lemony taste that goes down so smooth and warm. The perfect farewell to a wonderful meal. Thank you."

"You're welcome. Ready for business?"

"Deciding what we're going to do next?"

"I think so. Neither of us is thrilled with what we are doing now. I've learned that I'm good with kids, and that's something. But Lopez didn't tell us to go out and do little service jobs. So what's next?"

Suzanne carefully said, "I've been looking at the London office of HRWR—Human Rights/Women's Rights."

"I've heard of them. Good outfit?"

"I think so. I think we should go to London and interview."

Felicia clapped her hands and said, "Tomorrow? Next week? When?"

"Hold on. We need to be sure we want to do this. They have a headquarters office, which is in London. But their real work is going to refugee camps and trafficking intersections, where lots of trafficking goes on. They write reports, and they have standing at the UN as associate members of the Human Rights Committee, so they can present their findings to the UN. Nothing happens right away, but the spotlight gets brighter and then the UN Refugee office gets pressured. But the front lines are where they go to some fairly rough spots and see what's happening."

For once, Felicia wasn't doing her brash act. "That could be very tough work. Do they travel with any security?"

"I can't tell from the written material—that's a good question to ask. I'm glad you're cautious. I think the work sounds unbelievably important, but we should find out a lot more about how they take care of their staff."

"So let's go ask them."

They made plans, and started booking their flights. Suzanne agreed to loan Felicia the money, and Felicia agreed to pay her back once they got the jobs—if they got the jobs.

Suzanne and Felicia May 2003

Two weeks later, they found themselves in London in front of an older four-story building south of the river. They went in, were greeted by a young, energetic woman who quickly said she was a volunteer and that their appointment was with the director of human resources.

The HR head turned out to be a mid-fifties, no-nonsense British matron who seemed to Suzanne and Felicia to have stepped out of a British TV series.

"Welcome, ladies. How was your flight?"

Felicia said, "Fine, thank you."

"Now, I have your resumes here. You've been working in direct services and advocacy. Useful backgrounds. Now, I must ask, are you a package?"

Felicia said, "What?

"Are you together—are you professional associates or life partners?"

They were equally embarrassed. Suzanne recovered first. "Oh no, we…we just went to college together and have stayed in touch."

"Ah, I see. Well, that's fine, too."

Felicia wondered for a moment if they had just lost points. And Suzanne was trying not to laugh.

In answer to her question about security, the HR staffer said "You'll need to discuss that with our program staff. I believe our usual arrangement is to have our people accompanied by local contract staff. So someone would be with you at all times—we wouldn't ask you to go out into unsafe places by yourself."

Felicia wondered what "local contract staff" really meant, but stayed quiet.

The woman went on. "I must tell you that we've had a bit of trouble with Americans who come here to work. They seem to want more to be in London than to work in the field. How do you feel about that?"

Suzanne said, "We want to work in the field. We've talked about needing to be here at first to understand what you do, but we're looking forward to seeing what is happening and to gathering the facts that you use with the UN agencies,"

"Very well. We usually have staff work here for a trial six month period and then have them begin going out with our more experienced staff. As it happens, we have two vacancies right now. I'd like you to meet with our field supervisor, but I imagine she will be glad to have you on board. How soon can you begin?"

Felicia looked at Suzanne and then said "If we could have a week to get settled, we could begin right after that."

"Excellent. I'll set up the appointment with Ms. Williamson, who runs the field operations."

After the interview they had tea—they decided to try it since they were in England. They dissolved into laughter as they replayed the interview episode on their "relationship."

Felicia said "Were you as surprised as I was?"

Suzanne answered, "Probably." She was very quiet. Then she said, "I should tell you, Felicia. I've been with women. I tried it."

She saw how hard Felicia was trying to be casual, but with shock winning out on her face, Suzanne quickly went on. "After I got to Western, I decided that my own history might make me disinterested in men. So I tried women. It was OK, but it wasn't for me."

Then she smiled. "I'm telling you this because I think we should get a place together and I don't want you worrying about me jumping you."

"Wow. That's quite a story. I had no idea." Felicia shrugged. "Of course, I'm such a predator myself, taking advantage of every available stud I can find, so my radar is pretty useless."

"We probably need to discuss your predatory habits. We can't have you bringing poor British boys in all the time to have a shag."

"They call it shag?"

"I believe so."

"What a weird word." She attempted a posh British accent. "I should try that, don't you think? Just a shag or two, please." And then they couldn't go on because they were laughing so hard.

They looked around for an apartment and after a few days of depressing trudging up and down stairs and in tiny elevators, they found a decent two-bedroom place close to their work in Kings Cross. They decided to rent the minimum of furniture, and arranged for a service in New York that would send them their personal possessions from New York and sell the rest. Suzanne was still receiving a small subsidy from her mother, which helped.

They settled in, and on the weekend before they started work, they sat in their bare kitchen drinking dreadful instant coffee.

"The life of single swingers in London," said Felicia.

"Right. That's us. If only the Lopez group could see us now."

"God, I miss those guys more than I thought I would," Felicia sighed.

"I do too."

Felicia said, "I guess I think about those guys as sort of family. Roberto is like the all-accepting, generous uncle we all wish we had, always there when you need him, always ready with his amazing skills. Stan is a big brother, solid as a rock, bound for greatness and willing to share some of it with us. And Jeremy is the sunny, happy, youngest child, always smiling, wanting to help, believing in the good of people."

Then she smiled, softer than Felicia's usual hasty grins. "Guess when you don't have such a great family, you make one up."

Suzanne said, "I know what you mean, but I still have trouble getting that close to them. I like them all, but it's hard for me to open up all the way." She smiled at Felicia, "Unlike you, who have already adopted them—and then you beat them up, just like in a real family."

Felicia laughed and said "You have to try to keep guys in line."

They spent their first month rotating among the different sections of the agency, learning what each did. They found the staff to fall into two groups: those who were glad to accept the help from any source and those who were stand-offish, assuming they were, as an especially blunt one put it in her briefing, "more Americans come to show us how it's done."

They were trained as a team, and made their first trip to a resettlement center in Ukraine for women from Eastern Europe who had been lured into prostitution. When they arrived after a flight routed through Vienna, they were driven to the "shelter," which was a converted school building outside Kiev. It was winter, and very cold.

When they walked into the shelter, they saw classrooms converted to dormitory-like conditions, and then were shown an auditorium which was a "family recreation area." About thirty women, some looking as young as 12 or 13, were sitting in three conversational areas, all clustered around space heaters that were only heating very small spaces around the chairs and couches.

Suzanne and Felicia had been told that they were only to be observers, but some of the women came over to them while their trainer was working with the staff. In broken English, they asked where Suzanne and Felicia were from. When they heard the US, the women brightened up and began talking about relatives who had made it to the US. A few quickly asked if Suzanne or Felicia would sponsor them, When told they weren't allowed to do that, the shelter occupants looked so disappointed that Felicia surreptitiously gave them her card and phone number.

"You weren't supposed to do that," Suzanne whispered to Felicia as they walked back to their van.

"I know. But they looked so down when we told them we couldn't do anything about getting them to the US. Did you see those little girls? That was the worst part."

Their trainer was sitting in the front seat with the driver, talking on the phone to the central office. When she got off, she turned and asked them "What did you think?"

Felicia said, "Pretty depressing. What do we actually do besides give them a place to live? And do any of them have anything to do with prosecuting the guys who trafficked them?"

The trainer nodded and said "A lot of this work can be depressing. But you have to think about where they were before they got to that shelter. Some of them were living completely on the street. Their pimps did nothing to give them a place to stay."

She looked away at the gray landscape, and then said. "We're having a lot of trouble getting them to testify against the guys who recruited them out of their villages. They promise these girls jobs in stores and restaurants. Some of them are runaways—the younger ones are often from abusive homes, and they'll believe anything to get a chance to get away from their own families or their pimps. But even when we get them to leave that life or they find us, they're deathly afraid of these guys. They threaten the girls that they will come and slash their faces or cripple them if they go to the cops. And of course half of the cops are on the take anyway."

Over the next several months, Suzanne and Felicia took similar trips, sometimes separately, sometimes as joint backup to the lead staff. They accompanied the HRWR staff into court, assisted them in interviewing women, and logged information about each of the clients which was kept in a large data base at the central office. They learned how to compile a dossier on each client, including information about where she had been trafficked and what, if anything, had happened to their traffickers.

As they moved out of their probationary period with HRWR, they began traveling to sites where the agency operated. They had both seen poverty and children in unsafe conditions, but neither was ready for what they found in the worst sites they visited. And their sense of urgency and their anger grew with each visit.

Their initial site visits on their own were to Uganda, India, and Mexico/ They traveled with as few additional staff as possible, sensitive to charges of NGO "victim tourism." They tried to time their visits so that there was no special assembly of the children, but instead an opportunity to sit in on regular therapy sessions and staff meetings.

But even when they were as low-key and unobtrusive as possible, children would sometimes come out of their classrooms and dining halls and stand staring at the white women. Wearing every conceivable brand of T-short and short pants—incongruously labeled at times with the names of American sports teams, rock stars, or fashion icons—the children were a patchwork mixture of castoff clothing from around the world. As they compared notes on where they had been, they quickly agreed that India and Mexico were in many ways the worst—India because the scale was so immense and Mexico because the link to US-driven trafficking and drugs was so obvious and the corruption was so rampant.

Suzanne tended to react with increasing anger at the causes and the ineffectiveness of fragmented NGO efforts, while Felicia had to struggle not to get so depressed that her sorrow made it impossible for her to respond. At times, Suzanne had to goad her, saying at one point outside a shelter in Mumbai, "These kids don't want to see you cry, Felicia—they want to see you *act*."

Felicia said, "I know, I know. But it is so sad. And there are so many of them. What gets me most of all is the finger-clingers—the little ones who come up and reach up to grab a finger and then won't let go. You want to take every one of them home."

"Our job is to make *this* home safer."

In each camp, shelter, or orphanage, Suzanne had a standard set of questions that became a ritual. She would ask, "How is your security?"

And the staff site leader would usually answer, "It's adequate."

And then Suzanne would ask, "How many guards are on duty today?"

The answer, even in the largest facilities, would be two or three.

And finally Suzanne would ask, "Do any women work as part of your security team?"

And typically, there was a long pause as the leader tried to control his or her expression of shock and disbelief, and then the answer always came: "No."

After a few visits, Felicia developed her own refrain. She asked the site operators if corruption was ever a problem for them. Some, when protected by international NGOs, would venture to say that it was, explaining how they had to share some of their funding with national or local governmental officials. But others, funded by their own governments or needing permits to operate, were much more guarded in answering.

Then Felicia would say, trying to soften her implied criticism, "Corruption is everywhere. We have problems in our own government in the US. Wealthy people are able to get legislation passed because they contribute to the legislators. But when it takes from the children, it is especially wrong, and we all need to speak against it when we can." Then she would add, "It makes it hard for people in wealthy countries to raise the funds that you need when they know that some of it will be taken by corruption and will never get to the children who need it."

Each of the girls' stories seemed worse than the last one. One escaped from an abusive marriage, which was contracted by her parents when she was 8. In Mexico, several of the children had lost parents who had been caught in cross-fires among rival gangs. The center staff added that some of the parents were apparently working for one of the gangs, which meant that relatives had refused to take them in after the parents were killed, since they feared retaliation.

In India, a few of the girls were so under-nourished that 12 year-olds looked like they were no more than 7 or 8.

"They are so skinny! What do they feed them?" Felicia asked.

A staff member answered, "When they come in that under-nourished, we have to start them out on a special protein mix and then move them to regular food after a few weeks."

In a therapy session for girls who had been trafficked, with a translator quietly telling Suzanne and Felicia what they were saying, the horrendous details unfolded. Some of the older girls had been part of a trafficking ring that specialized in pre-adolescent girls, and they had been discarded when they reached puberty. Many of them had been abused so badly they needed surgery.

In India, they met with some of the leading advocates who worked on child labor problems. As the country with by far the largest number of children under 16 who worked full-time or part-time, India's over-regulated economy was tragically matched by its barely regulated child labor laws. They visited shelters where children who had been removed from labor sites were living apart from their families because when their parents lost the income produced by the children, they delivered the children to orphanages or simply turned them out into the streets.

The human rights dimension of HRWR work included documenting harm to children and meeting with advocates in each country. Where possible, they also met with government staff in ministries of women and children. They found that the many human rights agencies in India were typically small and struggling to deal with the decentralized nature of the government and the wide variations in wealth, leadership, and corruption.

One of their most difficult, but instructive visits, was to an agency in Kenya that worked with local civil society groups to prevent female genital mutilation. The women in the group explained to Suzanne and Felicia that they had worked village by village in a very deliberate, cautious approach. With the help of UNICEF and researchers in American universities, they had designed comic books that showed girls who had not had the procedure living happy and productive lives.

The leader of the group explained their methods: "We talk with the women. We show them the evidence of the harm cutting does, in ways that sometimes last a whole lifetime. We show them that their daughters will not be ostracized if they refuse the procedure, and that more and more mothers are refusing to have this done to their daughters. Then we ask them to talk with their husbands. Then we ask the husbands to talk with the elders. It is a slow process. But in more than one hundred villages now, there is no cutting."

It was bottom-up, grass-roots organizing at its most basic. Felicia was also struck by hearing that one of the methods used to build community among the women was forming a small choir of women who were part of the organizing effort. They learned to sing both African and European songs. Felicia was unable to hear the group singing, but their fund-raising arm had developed a CD which she quickly bought.

When back in London, Suzanne usually spent her free time volunteering at a local women's shelter in East London. Felicia had gotten to know a few of the workers from HRWR and hung out with some of them after work, meeting the inevitable young British males. For a while she had a "Russian phase," as she described it to Suzanne, having met one of the young plutocrats who had bought real estate in London's Kensington and Belgravia neighborhoods, favored venues for Russian winners in the kleptocracy lotteries. She stayed overnight with her brief conquests or her friends on weekends, since bringing them back to their apartment had been ruled off-limits by Suzanne early in their joint tenancy.

Explaining it to Roberto once in a catch-up phone call, she said "I'm taking advantage of them, just as you're probably doing, cutting a swath through the techie world of LA and Silicon Valley. Or is it Silicone Valley these days with all the upgrading?"

Roberto laughed and said, "I don't know, I never notice that kind of thing, Felicia."

"Right. Like you never spent class time staring at my boobs."

"I am shocked—shocked—that you would accuse me of anything other than purely aesthetic observation," he said in a mock-hurt tome.

"I heard about your aesthetic theories. Jeremy tried to explain to me once what you tried to tell him about your nutty theories on ogling chicks."

"I'm afraid poor Jeremy didn't get the deepest nuances of my innocent intellectual frameworks for appreciation of pulchritude."

Their teasing was of the friendly near-brother-sister kind, and both of them enjoyed it. He signed off with a more serious tone, saying "I'm sure looking forward to seeing you guys in New York. Time for an accounting. And by the way, I'm good for your air fare if you need it. Tell Suzanne the same thing."

"What, you've robbed a 7-11?"

"I'll explain when we get together. For now, I'm good for it if you need it."

"Thanks, pal."

Roberto 2000–2005

After getting his M.S. in computer science, Roberto quickly got into the internship program at Treasury and after a six-month period, they offered him a position. He was living in Georgetown in a walkup apartment off Wisconsin Avenue, taking the bus to work, and staying as low profile as he could while he worked twelve-hour days.

As he learned what he could from the cyberwarriors at Treasury and the consultants they brought in from time to time, he quickly absorbed the skills he wanted to get from working on the inside. He had devoured reports and articles by Juan Zarate, who had worked in the White House and at Treasury and the Justice Department under Bush. Zarate had graduated from Mater Dei High School in Santa Ana before he went to Harvard and Harvard Law, and was a real hero of Roberto's. Zarate was reportedly writing a book about his efforts in Treasury to interdict drug and terrorism finance networks.

At first, Roberto was assigned routine logging of terrorist and other websites. Gradually, his supervisors trusted him with the training he needed to know how to penetrate not only the public postings of the groups they were tracking, but also their private, deeply coded communications. He went on one-month training details to both NSA and the U.S. Cyber Command at the Pentagon. Then he decided to work beyond his brief, testing his ability to move on his own into the emails and coded instructions of the illegal groups.

Roberto got into a deep flow state when he was programming. He didn't fully understand it, but something in his brain took over his body, with his fingers flying over the keyboard, building new code, making connections across programs. A supervisor in Treasury had watched him for a few minutes one day and told him "If you could teach that as well as you do it, we'd just send you over to NSA and fire most of the instructors."

After he had been in Treasury for a year, his supervisor came in and sat down in the other chair in Roberto's cubicle. He didn't look happy.

"Roberto, we've gotten some reports over the last few days that a war has broken out between the Zetas and the Sinaloa cartel. Some kind of hacking battle that started when one of them—we can't tell which—apparently tracked some banking done by the other one and siphoned off some of it. They're really going after each other, and the traffic we pick up says they both think some kind of truce has been broken."

He looked at Roberto, almost glaring. "You've been working on cartel stuff. You know anything about this?"

"No sir, I don't."

"Look, I know you're smart enough to make it look like one of them did this to the other, and you could probably cover your tracks well enough so that neither we nor either of them could trace it back to you. But don't think you can juggle dynamite, Garcia. Sooner or later everybody slips up. And these guys don't give any second chances when they catch you. Not to mention you'd get fired in a split second if we caught you."

"I know all that. I'd never try something like that."

"Yeah." He kept looking at Roberto, who was careful not to look away. Then he said, "You're the best entry level guy we've ever had, Garcia. You've come up with some tricks that I hope you never teach to anyone else. But don't think you're invincible. In this business no one is invincible. Sooner or later, there's always another guy who has better moves."

"I know that."

"Good. Because it's one thing to get these guys pissed off at each other. It's another to take their money for yourself. That's looking at real federal prison time."

"I understand."

When he was just beginning high school, Roberto had spent time at family events with a cousin named Luisa Menendez. She was older, and attractive, and she teased him gently with the knowing wiles of a late-teenager toying with a younger one. When the families gathered, the two of them would go off and talk softly about what they had been doing lately and who they "liked." It was Roberto's first serious attempt to talk with a girl, without the high stakes of needing to impress her. Gradually, he learned the art of listening that took some men decades to master—or simulate.

And then she was dead—suddenly killed in a cross-fire of drug-driven battles between two rival gangs in Highland Park. Until then, Roberto had thought of the drug wars as far-off craziness, kept distant from his own life by his parents' middle-class lives and his own academic prowess. But losing someone close to him made it horribly real. From that moment on, his hatred of the savagery of the gangs and the cartels behind them began growing.

Roberto knew that his days at Treasury were numbered. He had carefully taken the money he had drained from Zeta accounts and placed it in accounts he knew no one could ever discover. He assumed his own accounts were all being audited regularly with the same tools that he and the rest of the team were using to probe cartel and terrorist networks. He had planned a software venture with a friend from his graduate days at Santa Barbara, which would give him a cover for new wealth. But now that he was being watched, he knew he had to move cautiously toward an exit.

He longed to tell the Lopez group what he was doing, but he knew that was also risky. So he kept to himself, dating a few women he had met at Treasury but without any serious involvement. And he waited anxiously for the 2005 gathering of the study group.

Felicia had called him when he was still in graduate school, asking for some help connected with her job with a nonprofit agency in New York. Roberto found her request easy to satisfy, and was glad to help her. He sensed some real dissatisfaction in her noncommittal replies to his questions about how she was doing, but assumed it was just Felicia being Felicia.

His graduate school friend had gone to work in a small software firm based in Venice, California. When Roberto visited the firm, he liked the highly informal atmosphere, which consisted of a loft with a view of the ocean in an older industrial building. The typical open design layout included a gaming area where the five staff members took breaks by combining their energy drinks with online live gaming, usually in beta-testing roles for friends of theirs in other, similar firms.

Fred Kawazaki was the loosely designated CEO, and he and Roberto quickly resumed a conversation they had been having since graduate school about security software. Without revealing any of the details of his skimming ventures, Roberto caught Fred up on what he had been doing in Treasury. In response, Fred briefed Roberto on some cutting-edge security innovations that their firm had been testing for a large, unnamed firm. Roberto assumed the firm was either Google or a major banking holding company.

The new software as Fred described it, was a substantial advance on encrypting funds through a hidden site that bounced signals around more "innocent" servers than any other system had yet managed to design.

Fred said, "That's worth some serious cash if it works, Roberto."

"I know. Fred, I need to make some money, and I need to park some money. I've got some cash from an inheritance that I need to locate in a secure account somewhere. What's your advice?"

Fred, intrigued and suspecting that the "inheritance" was just a cover story, reviewed offshore investments and shadow banks that would encrypt and then invest funds from people they had first put through an exhaustive screening.

"What if we traded them some of our software for an account that is totally secure?"

"They'd go for it."

"All right. Fred, what if I worked for you for a year, we agree to split profits on anything I produce or help your guys produce, and we see where we are after a year?"

"As long as you guarantee me that no feds are going to come kicking the door down because you're using stuff you 'borrowed' from when you worked for them."

"No worry." Then he asked Fred, "What do you know about trafficking?"

Within six months, Roberto had parked his Treasury "earnings" in a safe place, resisting the temptation to make any withdrawals so the account wouldn't show up anywhere if he was being monitored. He had worked feverishly on a revision of the security software that Fred's team had been designing, and they had agreed with a major bank to test it with a firm of hackers who probed financial systems to find holes. When the test resulted in a complete passing grade, with the hacker leader declaring it one of the tightest systems he had ever tried to crack, Roberto knew he had his next nest egg.

He and Fred negotiated briefly, but each knew how much Roberto's modifications had made the system effective. They agreed to a 60-40 split of proceeds of the sale of the software in Roberto's favor. Within a week after they had advertised the software, they had queries from six banks and two venture capital firms. The bank that they had run the test with came up with the winning bid, at $40 million for the software and a year's support. Roberto told Fred he couldn't help staff it, and Fred reluctantly agreed to the deal, telling Roberto he always had a job if he wanted to come back.

As the firm packed up to move to newer space in Santa Monica—with an even better view of the ocean—Roberto put his own office necessities in a few boxes, said goodbye to Fred, and went home to see his parents.

Roberto's parents were middle-class professionals, both teachers, who had lived for many years in a home in one of Glendale's older suburbs. They had never fully grasped either his computer skills or what he was able to earn from them, so when he offered to move them into a new house, his father said "What are you talking about? On what you make looking at a computer all day you can buy us a house?"

"Dad, I designed some software and then sold it for a lot of money. I'm not going to have to worry about money for quite a while. I have enough to buy you a house with no mortgage."

His mother came over and hugged him and said "You are such a good boy, Roberto. You don't have to go in debt to buy us a house. This house is fine. You and your sisters grew up here and it's just fine. We're going to retire in a few years, and we've figured that we have enough with pensions and some savings to pay the mortgage for just a few more years. And then it's paid off." She smiled triumphantly.

"Mom, you don't understand. I made a lot of money. Can I at least get you a new car? That junker out there isn't going to last much longer."

"Could you help your sister with her college bills?"

"Yes, of course, Mom. Why didn't you tell me you needed help? What does she need?"

"I don't know. You should go talk to her. But don't go in debt."

"Mom! I keep telling you, I have a lot of money now. A lot!"

"All right. I hear you." She looked at his father. "It would be nice to have a better car. Your father is always complaining about something or other going wrong with that car. But first go talk to your sister."

The negotiations took a week, but eventually Roberto got his sister to agree to take out a no-interest loan on her tuition at UCLA. His father did not complain when a new Ford Explorer showed up in the driveway a few days later. And finally his father agreed, after Roberto showed him the balance in one of his above-ground savings accounts, to take his mother on a trip to see relatives in Mexico.

Roberto enjoyed using his proceeds from the software sale for his family. But then he was faced with the challenge of deciding what he would do next. He decided to see if he could connect with Professor Lopez, who was just around the corner at Western.

Lopez met him in the Student Union after her class was over. He was a bit uneasy, knowing the student-professor distance would always be there. But she was warm, much warmer than in class, and asked him all about grad school and the work in Washington.

They sat down to their coffee, taking a table as far away from the chattering students as they could get. Lopez said, "And then you came back here, and worked in software? You were always a techie, Roberto. How is that going for you?"

"Actually, I just left the firm. We did some software that sold to a bank and I ended up with quite a bit of money."

"I knew it," she said delightedly. "You have an air of prosperity about you, Roberto. So now you're up there with Bill Gates and the rest of the dotcom moguls. The Mexican Gates."

She stopped smiling. "So when are you going to go to work on the kids agenda?"

"That's what I'm here to talk to you about. You know the five of us in our study group got pretty close at the end of the class. We agreed to meet every five years. That's two years away. I need to figure out how to get into working on the kids agenda before then. I decided I needed to make some serious money first, but now that I have, I have to decide where to go next."

He paused and watched her, gauging her reactions. "You remember the session we had when we talked about technology and how much the traffickers use it?"

"Yes, I do. You were at the center of that discussion, as I recall, Roberto. I assume you learned a lot more about all that during your time in Treasury."

"Yes, I did. I worked in the unit that was experimenting with new ways to get into bank accounts and monitor offshore financial hideouts." He was quiet, wondering how much to reveal to her.

She anticipated his thinking. "And you found how much sex trafficking and drug smuggling were connected, and that children were involved."

"Yes. We could see, looking at their books, that some of the cartels are smuggling people, and some of them are also in the sex business. They get kids that have been promised a border crossing but never get past a sex ring."

He looked at her, unsmiling. "I'm pretty sure I could take one of those outfits down. But I'd have to go underground to do it, cut off all contact with my parents. And I'd still worry about someone coming after my family. Those cartel *pendejos* play for keeps. Even if I use every cut-out I can think of, their tech guys might still find me and then come after my folks, or my sisters."

"Tough decision, Roberto. I assume what you're talking about would be semi-legal. Or all the way illegal."

"That's right."

"Well, as I said in class, I won't encourage you to commit a felony. And putting your family at risk is a very hard call to make." She was quiet, and then asked. "How well can you mask your identity?"

"It's pretty technical, Professor."

"Call me Gabriela. We're out of class now."

He smiled. "I'll try." He went on. "It's very tricky. From right after 9/11 happened, Treasury and other agencies," Lopez nodded, knowing that "other agencies" probably meant the CIA, NSA, and the Pentagon, "worked overtime developing these tools to reach into banks and other financial institutions to see where money was coming from and where it was going. So far, this has mostly been aimed at terrorists and Iran.

They found where Saddam had hidden his money, they tracked which banks in Europe were trying to get around the Iran boycotts and which were holding Al Qaeda money. While I was there, I didn't see any of it really aimed at the cartels or the groups that are selling kids."

He was quiet for a moment, and then said, "That's what I want to do."

Lopez looked at him, and then reached out and touched his hand. "That's the right target, Roberto. But it's very dangerous—you know that. It's not like Al Qaeda that has to infiltrate people through our borders. The cartels have people all over this country, already on their payroll. The worst kind of people."

"I know. And so what I have to do—and this is where our software— what we just sold—can help. What I have to do is hide so deep inside the internet, behind so many screens, that they can never find out who or where I am. I have to bet that I am better than their best guys—the guys they have hiding their money and buying legitimate businesses. I'd be going up against the best they have, and I'm not sure yet that I am the best on our side."

"Is there somewhere you can go to get more training—to get the extra skills you would need to be sure you stay safe?"

"The feds aren't too happy with me right now. I left after they sort of accused me of something I shouldn't have done. They saw the leftover effects of what I did, and they figured out that I could have done it. But they never had any proof. So they started watching me so closely I had to leave."

"What about on the corporate side? Are there any firms that would back you?"

"They all contract with the feds, so that probably wouldn't work."

Lopez was quiet, thinking about what he had said. Then she said "Don't answer me if you don't want to. Was what they thought you were doing aimed at the cartels?

Roberto looked at her, and nodded, saying nothing.

She put her hand to her mouth, saying, "*Dios mio*. Roberto, I want so much for you to nail these bastards. But I want you to stay safe, too. If you took money away from them, you're already at risk."

"I know. It's been over a year, and I took so little they might not have noticed. I tried to leave a trail that would make it look like it was an inside job, too. It was a test. So far, I passed."

He brightened up, aware that the conversation had gotten somewhat morbid. "Anyway, my plan at this point is to lie low and set up a company that can keep working on software that doesn't have much to do with internet security. I want to see if I can work out some software that will help some of the NGOs in foreign assistance to keep better track of their results. You know the State Department and USAID have contracted out most of their funding now to NGOs, and they're beginning to demand results, under pressure from Congress. Stan has been able to get me some good contacts now that he's working in Washington."

Lopez warned, "Stay away from the Middle East. I hear the foreign assistance programs in Iraq are a mess, with corruption by the locals and tremendous waste by our firms. A friend of mine just left AID after twenty years, and he said it was the worst he'd ever seen it. Try Latin America—you have the language. Some of the church groups are still doing pretty good work. Literacy, schools, stay with the education area if you can. They could use some help."

"Good advice." He paused. "What do you think is going to happen in Cuba? Any hope there?"

She waved her hand, frowning. "Not yet. Sooner or later, the demographics in Florida are going to shift, but it hasn't happened yet. The younger Cubans in Miami don't have the terrible anti-communist blindness the old ones still hang on to. But Fidel and Raul still run the show in Havana, and they are as stubborn on their side as we are on ours. It'll change—I just hope I'm still alive when it does."

He thanked her, gave her a hug, and they agreed to stay in touch. As Roberto drove away, he marveled at her energy and her continuing ability to inspire him up with her vision of what was possible. And he felt an even greater responsibility to use his earnings wisely.

Roberto was rarely without a very attractive woman—or women— in his life. But the pattern was that the smarter, more self-assured ones soon saw his obsession with technological power and found that they would always be in second place to that drive for control. While he was working in Venice, he had become involved with one of the programmers in the firm, and spent six months with her before she left him in a dispute about taking some time off for a ski vacation.

He soon recruited a new girlfriend who stayed in his apartment while she wasn't auditioning for small parts in TV shows. She had been a Miss Something in a town in Minnesota, and had decided to come to Hollywood, which turned out to be Roberto's apartment in Santa Monica. She was, as they all were, lovely, a tall blonde in the Gwyneth Paltrow genre, but with somewhat less acting ability. Quite a bit less, actually, and her search for success was not going well. Her name was Jessica Svenquist, her Swedish origins overpowering her American ambitions. Roberto enjoyed her statuesque looks and her energetic approach to things of a physical nature, but tired eventually of her complaints about casting calls.

And so he moved on, and on, seeking company but not companionship, attracting short-term connections but without anything that mattered to him as much as his hacking and his software design. Those were at the center of his life and his drive, without room for anything or anyone else.

He tried to explain it once in a phone call to Stan, who had marveled at his succession of lovelies. "It isn't that I'm obsessed, Stan. I'd just rather program than talk to someone who doesn't understand what I'm talking about."

"So go recruit your next one at Cal Tech."

Roberto made a face. "That's such a bad idea I'm going to try it out just to prove how wrong you are."

It seemed that Stan *was* wrong. Roberto accepted an offer to give a lecture at Cal Tech on cyber-security, and found himself in a classroom with twenty computer science majors, all but four of whom were male. One of the women, however, fell into his tall blonde syndrome, and he asked her to coffee after the class was over. Her name was Cassandra Gramercy, and she agreed to meet him.

They walked over to one of the newer coffee bars that had sprung up in downtown Pasadena, and five minutes into the conversation she asked him for a job. He explained that he was working solo at that point, but she quickly said, "I looked you up in the trade newsletters—looks like you sold some software a while ago for a pile of cash. Aren't you going to continue with that? And don't you need some worker bees?"

Taken back at her forwardness, Roberto said, "No, I don't think so. Actually, right now I'm exploring some software that could be used by international non-governmental organizations to keep track of their outcomes."

"Outcomes for what?" she asked.

"For programs that deal with child abuse and trafficking in children."

"Trafficking? You mean selling kids?"

"Yes. And forcing them into prostitution and pornography."

The look on her face was in the *ewww* category, and he quickly realized she was the typical techie who was comfortable only with the software side of life—not the lives it might touch. As gracefully as possible, he extricated himself from the date.

But he had learned something, which was that bright women from the tech world were likely to want to work for him and to share his profits, rather than his passion to do something about kids. And he began to wonder if he was ever going to find a female companion on his wavelength.

He set himself up in a small office building in Eagle Rock, around the corner from Western. Tired of apartment living, he bought a top-floor condominium on the Glendale-Los Angeles border, and equipped it with first-rate security devices and Mexican art he had bought from a contact who ran a gallery in San Francisco.

He flew to Washington, meeting with Stan for lunch and then arranging sessions with some of the NGOs who had expressed an interest in software that could track outcomes better than what they were using at that point. He worked on the programs for several months, delivered a prototype, and got a decent payment for his time and the rights to the product. He stayed in close touch with his family, who still expressed amazement at his apparent ability to make a living "playing with computers."

But all that time, he felt the growing itch to dig back into his real love, which he had talked to Lopez about when he had seen her. He wanted to go back at the cartels, to see which of them were involved in prostitution and human trafficking as well as drugs. He began making small forays into some of the Mexican and Caribbean banks that were known to shelter some of the cartels' revenues, learning quickly which ones had been made "an offer they couldn't refuse" and had, in effect been acquired by the cartels. He tested his ability to make small skims off the deposits in a few of the banks, and found that with the techniques he had learned at Treasury and his own software, he could route his taps through servers in any country he wanted and completely mask his presence. He kept the taps small, never taking more than $5,000, just to see what was possible.

More than the money, what he was looking for was the involvement of the cartels in trafficking women and children. He worked in Tucson for a few months, trying to see how different the operations in Arizona were from the much larger flows of money and people in California. Then he moved on to El Paso, and added to his understanding of the Texas version of the trafficking. He read avidly all the online materials and congressional testimony from Treasury and the trafficking units in Homeland Security as well as the Civil Rights unit in the Department of Justice, He also tapped carefully into the internal data of these units, finding that the protections that most federal agencies were still using were very easy to move around. By the end of his prospecting, he had a map of the trafficking operations that was as good as anything the federal agencies possessed.

Roberto was cocky, but he knew enough about cyberwar counter-measures to know he was never truly safe. He knew he could make money, both legally and in the darker shadows of international finance. The question was whether he wanted to make trouble for the worst people who had money. He asked himself if revenge and his hatred of the cartels had become the real drivers in his life and work.

Sometimes he loved living and working on the dark side. It had become his high. And sometimes it scared the hell out of him. He'd heard stories about people who had gotten caught up in the dark side, most of whom ended up prosecuted by the feds or simply disappearing because the bad guys got to them first.

PART THREE

The 2005 Gathering: New York

June 2005

The first gathering of the group since graduation was awkward. Most of them were a little surprised that their fervent promises of a half-decade ago had lasted through all the turmoil of their first jobs, their wandering romances, and their locations spread across the world. Only Felicia, with her special brand of intensity, had never wavered from her commitment to reconvene the group. The others, in varying degrees, came out of a blend of curiosity and concern that they would be the only ones who didn't show.

Felicia, of course, was the first to arrive. She had left London ahead of Suzanne, having set up her schedule to be able to spend some time with her grandmother. The group had agreed to meet at Jeremy's apartment and then go to dinner. Jeremy lived on the East Side, near his work with a religious non-governmental organization that sponsored orphanages in seventeen countries. Since the United Nations and its Children's Fund were often the targets and funders of their programs, their East Side location meant that Jeremy was initially forced to room with two other professionals from his agency.

The apartment was a typical East Side two-bedroom apartment, with small bedrooms and a smaller front room and kitchen. It was Friday, so his roommates had taken off to visit family or friends in New York and Connecticut.

Jeremy offered Felicia a glass of wine, and they sat down to wait for the rest. "So you're working for the human rights outfit in London. How do you like it?"

Felicia swallowed a sizable amount of the wine, frowned, and said, "It's all right. Suzanne and I have seen some terrible things in the travel we've been doing to gather information for the HRWR investigations. You must run into some of that."

Jeremy nodded. "Yes, we do. Sometimes I wonder if our work with the local churches we support is making a difference in the countries where we work."

Felicia and Jeremy had always been a little wary of each other, coming as they did from such different places. Felicia had always had a feeling that Jeremy was deeper than his church-boy surface, but as much as she had tried, she could never figure out what it was.

She excused herself to use the bathroom and as she walked past a half-open door into what she assumed was one of the bedrooms, she noticed a drawing on the nearest wall of the bedroom. Looking over her shoulder to make sure Jeremy couldn't see her, she opened the door widely enough to see the drawing.

It was a nude, sketched in a few strokes, but with an erotic pose that was striking. The woman's head was thrown back as if she were laughing, her hand at her throat, the other upraised as if saying, *Stop, you're making me laugh too much.* The angle of her tilted head and arms raised her full breasts to command the center of the drawing, unavoidably the focus, undeniably erotic. She noticed pictures of Jeremy and what she assumed were his family on the dresser.

As she came back from the bathroom, joining Jeremy in the kitchen, she said "I couldn't help but notice the drawing in your room. Quite remarkable. Who's the artist?"

Jeremy kept working on the salad he was tossing and then stopped, glancing at her and then looking away. "That would be me, I reckon."

Felicia was amazed. "You? But…you like that? You drew that?"

"From life." He waited for the next wave of disbelief to pass across Felicia's face, and then said "I decided a couple of years ago in a bad time at seminary that I needed a diversion. So I took an art class. I'd done some drawing in high school but someone told me it was idolatrous, so I gave it up."

"But Jeremy, I thought you were…you know, saving yourself for a vestal virgin or something like that. That is a *very* sexy drawing."

He held up his hands in a mock-surrender pose and smiled, saying, "Guilty. I guess I'm one of those fundies who figured out that sex is fundamental too. Ever read the Song of Solomon, Felicia? It's more erotic than most of the slime that's on the internet now."

He leaned back against the counter, folding his arms. "Felicia, God gave us bodies and made men and women attractive to each other. So what's with all the guilt?"

Then he laughed. "Besides, I *am* saving myself for someone else. But in the meantime I can learn to draw beauty and give thanks for it."

The doorbell rang, saving Felicia from yet another lame remark revealing how little she knew about Jeremy.

All three came in together, chattering. Roberto, Stan, and Suzanne had somehow managed to coordinate their arrivals at JFK from Los Angeles, Washington, and London, and had shared a cab to Jeremy's apartment.

When they had all gathered and gotten through the first stage of the *what have you been doing* conversations, Roberto tapped his glass and said "I have an announcement to make."

Stan said, "Oh, oh. Techie is going to tell us he's hacked all of us and we're broke."

"That's no surprise," said Felicia.

Suzanne said "Be quiet and let him talk."

"Thank you." He took a deep breath, and said. "Let me explain something. Hold your reactions until I'm done."

He went on to describe the software he had designed, staying general about its details, explaining enough so they could grasp why it was valuable. And then he told them that he had sold his interest in the company and the software.

"How much did you get?" Felicia quickly asked.

"I would expect you to ask, happy flower. It was in the low eight figures."

Felicia had always been good with math. "Ten million—you got ten million? You're a multimillionaire!"

Roberto nodded and Stan said "Totally cool, man, Nice going."

Jeremy, quicker to understand why Roberto was telling them about the money, asked "What are you going to use it for?"

Roberto smiled and said "I was hoping you all would have some ideas about that." He paused. "For openers, it has occurred to me that none of you can get serious about the Lopez agenda if you're paying off college and grad school loans for the next twenty years. So they're gone. Give me the numbers—and they're gone."

Suzanne said, eyes wide, "You can't just do that."

Roberto looked at her and said "Yes, I can. If I have to hack your bank accounts and mark the loans paid, I will do that. I'm very serious. I can help you, and I will. So let's move on."

None of the other four could yet fathom the fact that upwards of two hundred thousand dollars in debt had just vanished from their lives. No one spoke, until finally Jeremy said, "What a blessing that it's you who can do this, Roberto. Thank you."

Stan said, "Yeah. Thanks, man."

And Suzanne and Felicia, not yet trusting speech, went over and hugged Roberto, placing kisses on both his cheeks.

Felicia said, "I just have one question."

"Just one? Fire away."

"How can you be such a great person and such a lecherous pig?"

"What?!"

"I refer to your objectification of women."

Roberto, affecting an injured look, said sadly, "I can see you don't understand my theology."

Both women spun around and looked at Jeremy, who quickly said "I have nothing to do with this!"

Roberto said, "All right. I'll explain. I look at a woman and I see a person. You say I see an object. But what if I see her as a beautiful creature created by a Supreme Being who wants us to enjoy the beauty in Her world? And so I merely observe the grace and beauty of this person, without accosting her in any way. I observe, gratefully."

Stan joined in, saying, "Is there lust in your heart? Are we in New Testament lusting territory here, pal?"

"Not a bit."

"Then either your brain is disconnected from other vital parts of your body—or you are lying."

"I am not lying. I believe it is possible to construct a theology of God-given grace and beauty, and conclude that her beauty is a gift I can peacefully and gratefully observe. None of that is about objectification.

If I make an inappropriate remark, if I make her uncomfortable, if I stare at her in a rude way, then yes, that is objectification. But I do none of that. I merely observe and give thanks."

As Jeremy laughed, Felicia said to Suzanne, "Should we humor him or shred him?"

"Humor him. He means well. And he just gave us a ton of money."

Stan said, "All right, all right. What's next? How can we help Roberto out here?"

They talked for a rushed hour, nibbling on snacks Jeremy had set out and drinking his wine, tossing out ideas, debating pros and cons, arguing about priorities. They talked about what the growing wars in Iraq and Afghanistan meant, how they were affecting children in each country and whether any of the organizations they knew could make a difference. They quickly rejected giving all or part of the money to existing NGOs, given what they had already learned in their work.

Stan said, "Let's see if I can sum it up. We're taking different routes, but we're all trying to do something about the kids Lopez talked about in class. I'm trying to get into politics, some of us are working in services agencies, and Roberto is inventing new ways to watch the bad guys. I say we've been faithful to what we said at the end of Lopez' class—that we wanted to help these kids. We're not there yet, not by a damned sight. But we're sharpening our skills, hitting some bumps in the road, and figuring out what we're good at and what we can't stomach. Sound right?"

They all nodded or said yes. Then Felicia laughed and said "Some of us started out doing more bump-hitting than skill-sharpening."

Roberto said, "But now you guys are in a great niche, Felicia. Just keep telling them the truth."

Then Jeremy said, "Maybe we should form our own NGO. 'The Lopez Group.'"

Roberto said, "I thought about that. But I don't think that would work. Hear me out."

Carefully choosing his words, he went on. "Each of us has different talents—Jeremy would say differing gifts." Jeremy nodded and smiled at Roberto's use of New Testament language.

"I've spent a lot of time thinking about what we could do. I want to help each of you to use your talents. Stan's right. We've started down what amounts to five different paths. Stan's headed for politics, I'm a techie. Suzanne works with girls and women, Jeremy with church groups. And Felicia has the world's best BS detector. If you smushed all that together, I worry that we'd just end up with watered-down versions of what we do best. Besides, Stan has a master plan all set and he can't leave South Carolina to join some flaky NGO. He has to get ready to be President."

Stan laughed. "Right. It's 2005. Maybe we elect a black guy—or woman" he hastily added as two sets of perfectly shaped eyebrows rose in unison—"by 2050."

Roberto continued. "So the question is how I can help each of you head further down your own paths and get there sooner than you could if money were a barrier."

They were all quiet for a few moments, each of them thinking what his offer might mean to them. Before anyone could speak, Roberto added, "One more thing. No ingratitude to Jeremy for offering this fine pad for our gathering, but I'm willing to make our 2010 gathering a bit more comfortable, in a venue of your choice—if you can agree on some place. Your suggestions are welcomed, but if you don't make any or can't agree, I'll decide."

Falling into a playful mode, worn down by the serious talk, they began throwing out exotic destinations.

Suzanne said "Paris."

Stan said "Cancun."

Jeremy said "Rome."

And Felicia said "Two votes for Rome, if we add Florence. The UN Children's Fund research office is based there. I did some work with them last month. And I have family close to there."

Roberto laughed and said, "All right. Italy's in the lead. We'll keep thinking about it—we've got five years."

He added, "I've got one more serious thing to say, and then we can go celebrate. I've been thinking a lot about us, and about my brothers-in-law. Good guys, hard-working, good dads to their kids. But they are a million miles away from what we've been talking about. And I worry about that gap."

He went on. "You know only about a third of people our age get BA degrees. And less than a tenth get the kind of education we are getting—four years living on and near campus, part of a college lifestyle. Most people in college our age are commuters, living at home or holding down jobs, sometimes two or more jobs. Sometimes takes them five or six years, even longer, to get a BA. And most people our age aren't in college at all.

"We're a uniquely privileged group. We worked for it, and our parents worked for it. We took out loans, most of us, and without my good fortune, we'd have taken a long time to pay them off. But what we get is this unique four-year experience, and it isn't the typical experience anymore."

Stan said, "So what are you saying?"

"I'm saying that we need to understand that we aren't like most people our age. We aren't 'the typical American 21 year old.' So when we go out in the real world—here in the US or out where these kids live—we need to understand that we don't 'speak for America.' We speak for a privileged slice of it."

Stan said, "Ok, I see what's you're saying. But there's another piece of it. I see this side when I go home, with Parris Island and Fort Jackson and other bases all around the state. We're in a war now—two of them, actually, if you count whatever's going on in Afghanistan. And with a volunteer army, less than 1% of our generation has anything to do with that. It's part of why it was so easy for us to go to war in Iraq. Find an enemy who supposedly harmed us, send our planes and then a few hundred thousand guys—and women—who are career military or volunteers—and bingo, we're in a war. Don't increase taxes, don't ask people to do anything. Just support the troops."

"Cheap grace," Jeremy said.

"What?"

"It's theology—but it's also politics. Dietrich Bonhoeffer talked about people who do the basics—go to church, play by the rules, give a little to charity—and expect to get God's grace without ever having to look at what Christ said and how he lived. We get into wars by just going along with the basics. Support the troops. Yes, but how about supporting them by asking harder questions about why the troops are there in the first place?"

They were all silent for a while, and then Roberto said, "Look, I didn't mean to drop a heavy load on all of you. Just pointing out we're not very typical. Guess that means more of a burden, though."

Stan said, with his trademark smile. "Yes it does. But now let's lay that burden down for a few hours and *party!*"

The rest of the night was devoted to food and drink at a number of New York's finest restaurants. They were gradually getting used to Roberto's largesse, and they were beginning to see its pluses.

The next day, as they nursed various levels of hangover, Suzanne was the first to ask the question none of them had thought to ask Roberto. "What are *you* going to do, Noble Benefactor?"

Roberto looked away, and said "I'm still thinking about that. Something in software, I guess. I'm not sure." He briefly explained the research he had been doing on trafficking along the US border with Mexico, leaving out the details of his skimming forays and their targets.

The others knew him well enough to know when he was being evasive. But only Stan, who had recently sat in on a congressional briefing on internet security, was quick enough to say "Maybe best not to probe, friends. Berto will tell us when he's ready."

Nodding his thanks to Stan, Roberto said, "Yeah. I'm still thinking about it." And they left it at that, knowing that there was another layer to Roberto's agenda and that they were probably not going to get much of an explanation about it.

Felicia decided to change the subject. "So we're all working to help kids. Right? So why don't any of us have kids?"

It was a classic Felicia question, cutting through all the layers of politeness and convention that she didn't care about, or wasn't even aware of. Her mind simply took direct aim at a problem without worrying about any of the embroidery around its edges.

Roberto said, "Uh, because we're not married?"

Felicia dismissed his response with a wave. "40% of babies born in this country are to unmarried women."

Jeremy said, "That doesn't make it a great idea. Come on, Felicia, we're still in our 20s. Lots of time for babies."

"I know. It just seems strange that this is all second hand. Suzanne and I have learned a lot from working with women, but only about half of them have kids."

Stan said, "It'll come. And you're right, Felicia, we'd probably have a better feel for this if we were dealing with kids every day ourselves. Although our own middle class kids, when they come along, may not have much in common with the kids Lopez talked about, or the ones our agencies are trying to help."

Suzanne remained quiet, and they all noticed it and let her alone.

Then Roberto asked the group, "Do you ever wonder how Lopez got so far into our heads? Think about it. Somehow she managed to infect all of us with her obsession, and make it our own."

Stan said, "I don't know. I don't see it that way—it's not our obsession. It's a career we decided on. We all decided to take the course because it sounded interesting. And then we chose to take her seriously, because she was so clear about why it matters. That 400 million number is unforgettable."

Roberto frowned and said, "Sounds obsessive to me."

Jeremy said, "Maybe there's good obsessions and bad ones. This one looks pretty good to me, compared to gambling or booze or sex addictions."

Roberto laughed and said, "Speak for yourself, Jeremy."

Jeremy gave them all the invariable smile he offered when he was being teased and asked, "Has anyone heard from her?"

Suzanne said "I dropped her a note when I got the job at WAV. She answered right away, chatty about classes and interested in what I was doing. She's still at Western, said she teaches that class every other year."

Roberto mentioned that he had seen her after he came back from graduate school.

Felicia had been quiet, but then said, "Sometimes I hate her. I really do."

Jeremy, irritated, said "How can you say that?"

Suzanne, much quieter, asked, "What do you mean?"

Felicia didn't back down. "Roberto's right. She infected us with this—this *idea* of hers. So we all charge off trying to change the world. We're 26, for God's sake. We have no clue what our lives or our careers are going to be like."

Stan shook his head and said "You can call it infection if you want. I call it inspiration. We caught a break, having a professor who had an idea bigger than to go memorize the material and parrot it back in a term paper. You're right, Felicia—we don't know exactly where our careers are going to take us. That's what planning your life is about, instead of just letting things happen to you."

Roberto said, "Easy for you to say, pal. You're married, you've got the great job in DC set up, you're headed for election—nice clear path."

Stan smiled and said, "I'm not going to apologize for having roots or a clear idea about where I want to go. And I still think politics is the best way to make a difference for kids. You all try your ways and I'll try mine. That's the beauty of us getting together, to compare notes. Study group grows up—but we can still compare notes."

He went on, "I learn something from every one of you, every time we see each other. Even you, Felicia—from you, I learn to stay pissed off and not settle all the time."

They all laughed, even Felicia.

Roberto said, "We've already made a difference, Felicia, and we're just getting started. In five different ways, we're already pushing against the barriers that make people say we really can't help these kids. And we have. We just haven't figured out yet where to push hardest, and how to take it to scale."

Felicia scoffed. "Take it to scale. That's corporate talk. What does that mean, anyway?

Jeremy said, "It means, like Stan said, that we don't lose sight of that terrible number Lopez put up on the board in our first session: 400 million. That's scale."

Occasionally the group needed comic relief from the severity of their discussions about harm to children. Jeremy provided some of it by reporting on a visit to an NGO that had been working on land mine detection in an area where two children had been killed playing in a former war zone. The best response that any group had been able to develop involved training rats to detect the mines and set them off.

Felicia said, "Rats?! Why rats?"

Jeremy said, "They can train them to smell the explosives. They smell, it, they start digging, and boom, sometimes no rat, but no kid gets a leg blown off—or worse."

He went on. "So they caught over a hundred rats to use as 'trainees.' The problem was that before they could send them off to the program that trained them to smell the mines, they escaped. The further problem was that they escaped into the military barracks where the soldiers who had laid the mines were sleeping. These are not small rats—they are rats about the size of dogs. The soldiers finally caught all of them and quickly managed to locate the maps that showed where the mines were placed, just so they wouldn't have to deal with the super-rats again."

As their laughter died down, Felicia told a story about meeting with a civil society group that had made a presentation at a conference she had attended in Rome. "I'm not sure any of this is true, but the woman making the presentation swore it had happened. It seems that one of the groups working on female mutilation had run into a group of elders who were completely unwilling to consider any changes in practices in their region. They argued that the procedure didn't really hurt the girls and was needed to preserve their chastity. An older woman who had been working on the problem for a long time stood up in a community meeting with the elders and held up a long knife. She cried out, 'This is what they use on the girls, and now I'm going to use it on you. You say it doesn't hurt—let's see if we can preserve *your* chastity!' Before she could be stopped, she had cornered the elder and was beginning to cut off his clothes. She was finally grabbed and disarmed. As she was wrestled to the ground, she kept shouting, 'Every woman here has one of these and knows how to use it! You'll never sleep again!'"

They began getting ready for a visitor.

A few weeks before they were scheduled to get together, Stan had called Jeremy, saying he had a question for him.

Stan said, "This is very strange. I got a call from a woman you may remember from Western. She attended the first Lopez class and then dropped out. But she had heard from someone that we were meeting regularly and she wanted to talk with us." He paused. "She's Muslim. A student from Iraq."

"Wait, I remember her. Dark hair, long dark hair. Wore a hijab. Kind of pretty, in a Middle Eastern way. Can't remember her name, though."

"Yes, that's her. Her name is Ghadah Ali." He spelled it. "Turns out her father works for the Iraqi embassy and got her into Western somehow. Knew somebody on the Board or something. Anyway, she found out I was in Washington and wanted to meet with us. Said she had some things to ask us. She works with their embassy herself now."

"You know, Stan, it's funny. I've been thinking that we all sort of agree on most of the issues we work on. But we're Westerners—Americans. Non-Western cultures don't agree with some of what we work on—with a lot of the girls and women's equity stuff. And I wondered if we could ever convince anyone on the other side of that gap that they're on the wrong side of history."

Stan said, "So this is our chance to explore that some more. Maybe."

Jeremy replied, "Invite her to join us. Maybe the second or third day we get together."

"Will do."

Then Jeremy asked him, "Why did you call me about it? Why not one of the others?"

"You're our religious studies guy, Jer. She's Muslim. Figured you'd know about other religions."

"Oh. Well, we'll see."

She walked in wearing Western clothes, a skirt and blouse, with a lightly colored hijab worn around her face. Jeremy offered her tea, and she sat in a chair in the center of the room.

"Thank you very much for agreeing to meet with me. It is very fortunate you are all in New York. I had to be here to meet with our UN delegation, so this was most convenient."

Her English was very lightly accented, and she was seemed very much at ease with the group.

Felicia, as usual, asked the question everyone else wondered about. "Why did you drop out of the class?"

"I felt that Professor Lopez and I were on very different wave lengths and that it might be..." she paused, looking for a word, "disruptive if I were in the class. Please don't take offense, but there didn't seem to be much understanding of non-Western values and culture."

"And why did you want to meet with us?"

She was silent, gathering her thoughts. "I had heard, from one of the professors that I've talked with since I graduated, that the five of you had stayed in touch and were all working in children's programs, in the US and overseas. I work with our ministry of women's and children's affairs. And I thought we could exchange ideas in ways that might be useful for both of us. I know you are working on child protection—that is what Professor Davies told me. I'm sure Professor Lopez left you with a good understanding of those issues—which are very serious in our country and around the world. I don't disagree with working on those problems. Many children are affected. But the part I have had difficulty communicating with Americans and Europeans about is what you call gender equity. I usually work with older women, women from human rights and national ministries. I thought perhaps among younger people—people closer to my own age—I could share ideas more fully."

Suzanne had been listening with a skeptical look on her face. She said, "I'm sure we all appreciate your effort. But we've been working on trafficking issues and other issues in which women are harmed by some of the cultural values you are talking about. Let me ask—do you believe in human rights? Do you agree that women's rights are human rights?"

"Definitely. But where I think we may have some differences are in how we define women's rights. We believe, for example, that if a woman wants to be submissive to her husband, that is acceptable and even honorable in our culture."

"And so if a mother wants to have her daughter's genitals mutilated because it happened to her, that's acceptable and not a violation of human rights?"

Ghadah smiled thinly and said, "Somehow that is always the issue where the discussion begins. Just as I am tempted to ask if you think the pervasive displays of virtual nudity in your culture are respectful of women. You start with mutilation, and we start with pornography. That is perhaps arguing from extremes."

Suzanne wasn't buying it. "Playboy never mutilated any little girls. I'm not sure the parallel works. Look, you throw off the shackles of colonial, imperialistic powers and replace them with the shackles of patriarchy. The oppression by the West replaced by oppression by males? That's a victory?"

Jeremy spoke up, saying, "Maybe we could hear Ghadah out, Suzanne. She's come to us asking for an exchange, and I'd like to listen to her. We've all seen examples of girls and women being harmed in our work—and we've seen some terrible neglect and abuse in our own culture as well. Let's listen."

Suzanne's body language was dismissive, but she remained silent.

Ghadah continued. "I loved my time at Western. It was very difficult at times to adjust to Southern California—although the weather was sometimes very like Iraq. But some people were very open to talking about our differences, and learning about Arabic and Persian cultures.

"What has been most difficult is that when we try to make common cause on the issues we seem to agree on, the issues that we see differently often disrupt our attempts to communicate. I know that if we keep our women and girls confined to their homes and without higher education, we will never become part of the non-oil global economy. We will never be able to compete with you, the Israelis, or the Chinese. I know that. But Iraq has more college graduates per capita than three-fourths of the nations in the world.

"It is the arrogance of many Westerners, especially those in the human rights field, who look down on us, that bothers me most. We could do as you do and simply dismiss it as coming from 'those backward people.' But we are going to have to live in the same world, and your troops and aid agencies have been going through a very intensive exposure to our culture. And it just seems like a good time to see if any increased understanding and common efforts are going to be possible.

"I should make clear that I'm not here on an official mission. Some in my ministry thought an informal meeting would be a good idea, others—including my father, I must add—felt it would achieve nothing. But I wanted to try. We perhaps have more in common from our years together in Eagle Rock than most discussions like this. So I wanted to try."

They were all, even Suzanne, impressed with her demeanor. She was talking about issues that had caused great strife, and yet she was doing it in an even-handed tone that made them all want to hear more.

Jeremy said, "Thank you for making clear why you're here. I admire your willingness to sit down with us, and I hope we can somehow make it worth your while."

Stan said, "As you know, I'm part of the government and will report this conversation to the Congressman I work for. But I'll treat it as an informal discussion among friends and not an official contact. That said, I hope we can spend some time telling you what we've been working on and what we hope to do in the future."

Roberto spoke up and said, "Even though I'm a 100% American dude, I've had some experience with the cross-culture thing—more than most of these guys. Good luck in trying to make the bridge work."

Felicia asked, "Why do you cover your head?" They all laughed politely, for Felicia had once again asked the question the others were curious about, but were unwilling to ask directly.

Ghadah said, "The simple answer is that it is custom in our culture for women to cover their heads. The longer answer is that the Holy Quran says we should be modest and not display our beauty. We also believe that female beauty should not be exploited for any man to gaze upon, but should be reserved for the beloved one. Some of your Christian sects, such as the Mormons and the Amish, have similar views."

She paused, then frowned. "If you've walked through a mall or a high school corridor in this country, as I have, you know that it is culturally acceptable for males to 'check out' girls and women with lingering gazes, and sometimes with disrespectful words. We believe that is improper contact, and lowers the respect for women."

Felicia said, "I get it. A kind of protection. Not a belief that all guys are creeps, but keeping them from the temptation."

"Exactly."

Jeremy then suggested that each of them take five or ten minutes and tell Ghadah what they had been working on so that she would have a better understanding of what they were doing and how they approached some of the issues she had raised. They agreed, and except for a little tension when Suzanne referred to her work with traffickers and some mystery when Roberto discussed his work with Treasury on international banking transactions, it went well. Ghadah made copious notes.

When the roundtable finished, she asked the group "How are you covering the 16 conditions that UNICEF works on? I heard you mention work on child labor and trafficking; what about the others?"

Jeremy said, "The churches I work with have units that work on child marriage, gender equity in schools, child soldiers, sexual violence, orphans, and children's justice issues. We work with a loose coalition of NGOs in each of these areas."

They talked some more about what they had learned from other NGOs about their efforts in the Middle East. Ghadah acknowledged that girls and women in Iraq and other countries were a long way from being treated equally, but again pointed out how widespread secondary education had been in Iraq "before your troops came to help us get rid of the dictator," as she put it with a smile.

Suzanne then said, "I'd like to return to the human rights perspective. Our agency has been doing some work with the neuroscience of trauma. Kids get measurable changes in their brain chemistry when they are abused. The biochemical changes affect their emotional stability in later life. So the question becomes whether these changes are less when all children in a cultural setting are what we would call abused—when all of them are disciplined severely in school, or punished for being girls. If the changes are the same for all kids, regardless of culture—if culture doesn't mediate trauma—then it makes the case for universal human rights. And then cultures that harm children are human rights violators, regardless of what their religion or cultural traditions may practice."

"That's fascinating. A group of women psychiatrists in Baghdad have been working with children exposed to trauma from the war. They've found the same kind of biochemical changes you're talking about, involving cortisol and other biochemical reactions. But without any comparison or control group, there's no way of making a judgment on what you've suggested—which is that universal human rights are more important than culture."

She paused. "That's very important work—and a very important question."

Suzanne was impressed, clearly, that Ghadah had followed her argument and saw how it might undermine her case for non-Western values being equivalent to Western practices. She said, in a friendlier tone than before, "I guess a Western education—that's the university, not the culture—can give us the tools to have a serious discussion about this."

Ghadah said, "I agree. I am indebted to the University—and I even recognize how much the culture has helped me bridge some of the gaps. I want to thank all of you for your time and attention. We haven't solved any of the world's problems here, but I've loved the conversation. I hope we can think of a way to keep it going."

Roberto said, "I agree. I may be able to help if financing such discussions became an issue."

Ghadah said, "If invitations to work on any of these issues in Iraq would be helpful, I'm sure we could arrange this." She smiled, "I recognize that the military efforts under way may make that difficult in some parts of the country, but we could find places that are peaceful. Relatively peaceful," she added with another, sadder smile.

Stan said, "If I could ask one more question, following from what you just said. How do you see Iraq's future?"

She sighed. "We need to reclaim our past from the terrible recruitment of children as soldiers and suicide bombers. There are forces worse than Al Qaeda, worse by far than bin Laden, who are going to come out of their caves when you leave. I am Shia, but your government made many mistakes in ignoring our religious wars. Some of the worst people on both sides are still out there, ready to fight endless religious battles. That's what worries me most."

Jeremy said, sadly, "Europe fought its religious wars for hundreds of years."

She said, "Ours have been going on for over a thousand years. But we have run out of time—the pace of change in the world has finally caught up with us. We will become a country again, remembering that we believe we were the first nation, Babylon. Or we will perish, divided into a dozen little enclaves of hatred."

After she left, they spent some time talking about the conversation. Stan said, "Took a lots of guts to come here and have this session. Imagine one of us in a similar position in a Middle Eastern country."

"No thanks," Suzanne said. "But she was impressive. She was open to additional information, which is always the test with one of those people."

Roberto said, "Those people?"

Suzanne, defensive now, said, "Yeah. Those people who make excuses for marrying their daughters off at seven and refusing to let women attend college."

Roberto said, "Not relevant, Suzanne, You heard her numbers about college."

"That's for the daughters of the elite, the dictator's flunkies. You think a little girl out in the rural outback has a shot at college there?"

"About as much as kids from the Delano migrant shacks in California." Roberto shook his head. "Let's not get too righteous here. It took guts and brains for her to get in touch with us and have the conversation. I say we figure out a way to stay in contact with her. If we're going to do this work, we're going to have to do some of it in countries like hers."

"Amen," said Jeremy. Then he added, very cautiously, "Suzanne, I know you and Felicia have seen some horrendous things when you travel. Our workers deal with some of the same things. The ways girls and women are treated in some of these places is beyond belief."

He paused, and then said, "But I've talked to a lot of people about gender equity, both inside the religious community and outside. And many of them have said that there have been successful programs that can rehabilitate some abusers and others that can sensitize boys to understanding that both boys and girls can succeed, that they're not in a zero-sum game."

He went on, watching her. "So I don't know why you're working on a gender agenda that excludes men and boys completely. Why does it have to—"

Felicia interrupted him, almost shouting, "Because nobody is trying to fuck you, Jeremy. That's why!"

Suzanne, frowning, said, "I've heard about those programs too. More power to them if they work. But that's not what's going on in camps where girls and their mothers are being kidnapped at gunpoint or promised jobs when in fact they're going to be treated like slaves. That's what we're working on. That's all."

Felicia, calmer now, said, "Let me try to explain it. I never got why you guys loved that damned movie *The Magnificent Seven* so much. I bought it and watched it—three or four times. Finally, I got it. At the end, when the villagers who have been preyed on by the bandits pick up their scythes and chairs and attack the bandits—they were back in control of the village. That's what this is about, Stan. Not an army coming in to protect these women and kids. It's them finally deciding they have to protect each other. And all women deserve to have the tools they need to protect themselves and their kids. If the rule of law doesn't exist or is corrupted, they need to take the control like the villagers in the movie. That's all. That's *everything*. They took on the responsibility to protect themselves."

Suzanne said, "A final note, if I might. Some history we missed at Western. I've been doing some research. It turns out, dear colleagues, that the Amazons were historically real. They came out of Central Asia and played hell with the Greeks for a while before things back home caused them to retreat. Archeologists have found remains that documented a race of women warriors who scared the crap out of the armies they faced at their peak."

Felicia said, "Wow. And now women in those countries walk around covered. They need some kick-ass historians."

Suzanne smiled and said, "Yeah."

Later, her historical note made more sense to the group.

As they were breaking up to go to dinner, Felicia came up to Jeremy, and said "I'm sorry for yelling at you. I know how hard you work, and I shouldn't be yelling at you."

Jeremy smiled and patted her shoulder. Then he said "If you weren't yelling at someone you wouldn't be Felicia. I am the safest person you will ever yell at, happy flower."

And she looked at him and murmured, "I know."

As they were packing up to get ready to leave for their planes, Roberto asked Felicia, "What are you humming? You're always humming."

"Oh, just some song."

Jeremy said, "She's humming *Va pensiero* from Verdi's opera *Nabucco*."

"OK. I know why she knows that—she's Italian. Why do you know that?"

"It's an opera sort of about religion. It's about the Hebrew slaves in Babylon. We studied it in Religion 201, and I went with my church group to see it performed in Dallas."

"OK, now my question is why do I feel so stupid? What does *Va pens*...how did you say it? What does that mean?"

Felicia said, quietly, "'Fly, thoughts, on golden wings.' The Hebrew slaves are singing about being captives in a foreign country, and how much they miss Jerusalem."

And Roberto said, knowing this was a sensitive area, "You are amazing."

She didn't answer.

PART FOUR

2005-2010

Stan 2005-2010

S tan loved his work on the Hill, finding the Congressman, his staff, and the staff of the other Congressional committees to be far less full of themselves than he had expected. There were, to be sure, the predictable prima donnas and divas who had to be kept happy with the right sparkling water at their committee chairs. But on the whole, he found the work and most of the workers to be the stimulus he had expected as he prepared for his own run at the greasy pole of politics.

Two or three of the women in the Congressman's office had reputations as fast-movers, and each had casually let Stan know that they were available for the kind of no-commitments liaisons that were common on the Hill—and elsewhere in Washington. He skillfully resisted any response beyond light joking, while enjoying their attention. He knew that politics demanded a kind of flirtation with voters and backers that needed to suggest a sexual dimension without actually enacting it, and he imagined he could evade any problems by keeping things light.

Dolly's studies at Howard were going well enough that she had been selected for law review. She had developed a special interest in white-collar crime, which was in the headlines due to the emerging banking scandals as the economy turned down. Stan could see her as a fine prosecutor, and wondered how that would blend with his fund-raising. But he was placated by her strong relations with a group of donors to the incumbent Congressman who had been organized by her father, whose networks were widespread throughout the state.

They had moved on from their Southeast apartment to a town house on the edge of Georgetown. They entertained, alternating Stan's colleagues with Dolly's classmates, watching some enjoyable connections fusing in the ever-fluid atmosphere of 20-somethings in a city full of intelligence and ambition.

Stan's work on the committee and subcommittees was his real arena, and he quickly learned its written and unwritten rules. He studied the formation of alliances with other staff, the process of developing networks in State and the other executive agencies that handle international issues, while making sure that he was reflecting what the Congressman would fight for—or against.

He had gotten a brief tutorial from Roberto on Treasury's role and the international banking scene, and soon acquired some formal and informal contacts within Treasury, both at civil service and political levels. One of Dolly's professors had specialized in banking law, and he was a fine dinner companion who was glad to brief him on the legal intricacies of US financial policy weapons. With these legal tools and Roberto's mastery of the technological weapons now in use, Stan felt that he knew as much as anyone on Congress about these issues.

The problem, he came to see, was that no one gave a damn about how these problems affected children in other countries. The "orphan track" was occupied by Michelle Bachman and other religious-oriented members, along with Senator Mary Landrieu of Louisiana. Another group had focused on the AIDS/HIV front, continuing the initiatives of the Bush administration that had been church-inspired. Stan had Jeremy down for a briefing on those issues, but soon found that this too was an enclave within Congress that had been well defended against any newcomers who didn't agree with the positions of these congressional leaders.

But that still left a lot of the "Lopez issues"—the 16 different categories of child protection used by UNICEF that Lopez had first framed for the class. Finding allies on those issues proved very difficult, however. Stan had listed some of the key ones for a briefing by NGOs held in 2006 and again in 2007. They included child labor, child marriage, female mutilation, landmines, child soldiers, gender equity in education—and trafficking. These briefings were attended mostly by staff, not members themselves, but they were useful ways to introduce issues that had never really gotten a spotlight.

The briefings went well, but only a core group of five other staffers attended them and participated actively in question and answer sessions following the briefings. There were three Democrats and two Republicans in the group. They were also the staffers whom Stan had liked best, because they cared about the issues as well as the politics and the media attention they could eke out for their members. They agreed to keep raising the issues, and made plans for some oversight hearings over the next few years.

In late 2007, Stan's Congressman had a health scare and was hospitalized for chest pains. He had managed to keep three prior emergency room visits for atrial fibrillation out of the media, but the chest pains continued for two days and finally his wife and the senior staff insisted that he check into Walter Reed for a thorough set of tests.

When he came back, the word put out to the media and the staff was that he had passed the tests with flying colors and was on a new diet and exercise program. But the result was still a flurry of press speculation about his plans for the 2008 election. To complicate things, Obama was running nationally, emerging as a serious alternative to Hillary Clinton, and the Congressman was caught between a strong, long-time connection with the Clintons and his obvious affinity for a potential black President. The South Carolina primary would be an important test for both candidates, and the Congressman was caught in the middle.

A few articles in the South Carolina press speculated about who would run if the Congressman didn't seek re-election or was appointed to a new Obama administration post. One of them mentioned Stan as a rising star in South Carolina black politics, along with the Congressman's chief of staff and two state legislators from the district. Stan was pleased at the mention, but knew he was going to be at the bottom of any of the lists that would emerge, because of his age. The reporter who did the "possibles" story had called Stan, but he had deliberately not returned the call.

Then the Congressman announced for re-election, and the speculation dried up. Stan was relieved in a way, because he knew it was too soon for him to make a credible run. He devoted himself even more avidly to his work on the committees, and found plenty to keep him busy.

In early 2009, after Obama's inauguration, Stan had been included in a list of potential appointees the Congressman had sent to the transition team. Stan talked with Dolly about an appointment, but told her that unless it was in State Department and was at a level high enough to get involved in international child protection and trafficking issues, he saw his work in the Congressman's office as a better route to running someday. The only feeler that came back from the Obama team was about a position in public affairs, which Stan quickly dismissed.

The Congressman's health issues continued, and the staff could see that he was struggling some days to stay focused on his work. He cut back on evening meetings and turned over more of his committee work to staff. All of this increased speculation, and in mid-2009 another set of articles about successors began appearing, with Stan's name even more prominently mentioned.

Then the Congressman announced that he would be stepping down after his current term. The race was on, and Stan was going to have to decide if he was in it or not.

He talked about it with Dolly, met with her father, and went back to South Carolina on weekends and at length for longer periods during holidays to see his family and talk with them. Most of the advice he got was to wait, given the list of older, better-connected candidates.

In September 2009 Stan was called in for a meeting with the Congressman's oldest advisor, who was visiting from Columbia. As Stan came in and sat down, Willard Sampson stared at him, in a cool way that Stan knew was intended to put him on the defensive.

But Stan didn't play defense, and so he smiled and said "How are you, sir?"

"I'd be a hell of a lot better if there weren't so many upstarts around here who think the world owes them a congressional seat."

Stan kept looking straight at Sampson, realizing that he had already lost any chance of an endorsement. But he put that behind him in a few seconds and leaned forward, saying, "I'm sorry I may have come across as too demanding, sir. But with all respect to the other possible candidates, I have the best chance of holding this seat for a very long time. And that means good things for this district, which I know is what the Congressman has worked for all his life."

Sampson kept glaring at him. Finally he said, "You are really full of yourself, young man. Just because you're some ridiculously young age, you think you're entitled to this seat."

"No sir, I don't. No one is entitled to be in Congress. If I run—and I am a long way from deciding that at this point—I'll work harder, with more energy," he added, "than the other candidates. And I'll do better if I take the seat. But I'm also aware of my age, and that I may need to step back."

"You step way back, son. You may think your Wright clan is all-powerful. But you—"

And then Stan went on full offense. He stood up, pointed at Sampson, and said, "Sir, I will let you humiliate me. But I will not let you criticize my family to my face. I am ready to do all I can, everything in my power, to continue the Congressman's great work in this district. If it's not my time, so be it. But do not bring my family into this in a disparaging way. I will not listen to that."

"Sit down, sit down, I apologize. That was an inappropriate reference." He paused, studying Stan. "You do have a backbone, young man. I like that."

"Learned it out on the football field, sir, with three linebackers trying to nail me all at once."

"Yes, I heard that. Saw a few of your games myself. You could maybe have gone all the way, into the NFL."

"I thought I had some more important things to do, sir, than getting my brains bashed in for half of the year."

"All right. I understand that. Look, Stan, this isn't your year. You can be Jeff's chief of staff, you can work in the district if you want, but it isn't your turn. Jeff's fifty-five. He won't be there forever. And you're the natural for next in line."

Stan shook his head, "No disrespect sir, but waiting for twenty years is not part of my game plan. I see a second seat opening up in the state, and I may want to take a shot at that if this one is closed off."

Sampson was visibly surprised. "A second seat? Maybe, but that's a ways off. No one is going to get that many redneck, back-country votes in one of the other districts. Not yet, anyway."

Stan smiled and said "I have some ideas about how to speed that up a bit. I'll be sure to let you and the Congressman—and whoever succeeds him—know if I decide to go for it."

Sampson smiled, shaking his head. "You do have some balls, son. You surely do. I suspect you've had a Plan B all along and you know how soon you can take your shot over in the coastal area. Keep us posted, and good luck."

Stan said, knowing he had made a firm ally. "Thank you sir, I'll do that."

In fact, Stan had a Plan B and a Plan C as well. He had studied the demographic details of the 2000 census and the American Community Survey updates very carefully, and he knew to the second decimal point how many African-American professionals had moved into the two districts most likely to go to a Democrat in the next decade. He also knew how the districts had been reapportioned in 2001, and what was likely to happen in 2011 after the 2010 census. And he had two bright interns working on election and registration data in both of those districts. He met every month with the interns, and went over their findings carefully, swearing them both to secrecy. Dolly was his secret weapon, with her own and her father's networks to add to his own carefully researched lists of contact.

Stan planned. Whenever he could, he sought to out-plan his adversary. In high school and college, he spent more time than anyone else—including his coaches--watching the films of the defense he was playing against the next week. After he went to work for the Congressman, he reviewed the biographies of each of the officers of any organization he was scheduled to speak to—a month before the event.

His target date was 2010. He knew he might have to wait for redistricting, but the faster track was heading for 2010, meaning that he would have to run against an incumbent in a district that had been aligned for Republican votes. He would lose, but the trick was running a strong enough race that he would be the favorite in a primary when the new seat opened up.

In December, he and Dolly took some time off to vacation at Hilton Head after Christmas with their families. In their suite at the resort, they stayed up late each night, going over the options. The previous

Democratic candidates had never risen above 38% in the November election, which meant that Stan would need about 30,000 more votes to come closer while losing.

They went back and forth, until finally Stan said, "We've gone over every piece of this puzzle, Dolly. I don't know what else we could do to make the decision clearer. It's still a close call. There's still two questions—can we find 30,000 votes and can I run for sure in a new district in 2012 if I'm a loser in this one?"

He was quiet, as she watched him. Then he said, "I never liked losing. When we played and lost—which wasn't often, but often enough for me to know what it feels like—I walked around for days in a depressed mess. Coach would always say 'shake it off and look to the next game.' That was always hard for me."

"So?"

"So maybe I sit this one out. Take my chances on redistricting, let someone else lose this one. There's going to be some backlash against the health reform stuff—they're already calling it ObamaCare."

She smiled, and reached over to kiss him. "I never liked losing either, big man. We've got some time. You can keep working on the committee stuff that you care about." She moved off the bed.

"Where are you going?"

"I've got to get you packed. We need to get home. We've only got two years before you dive into the deep end in 2012."

One night, after Stan came home to their condo, Dolly came into his den where he was reviewing some testimony. She looked troubled, and said "I need to talk to you. It's about Lewis."

Her brother had enlisted in the Marines out of high school and had served two tours in Iraq. He had been wounded, and had ended up addicted to pain medications. Dolly's father had tried to give him a job, he had been to the VA for repeated sessions of therapy, but he had not been able to get himself out of his downward spiral. Stan had met with him after his return and had done what he could to connect him with the best VA therapists he could locate, but it hadn't worked.

Dolly said, "He's disappeared, and my folks are really worried. He's been living in an apartment in a crummy section of Columbia, and they went by there yesterday, but he wasn't there. They went in and it looked like he hadn't been there for several days. I don't think I've ever heard them so worked up about Lewis, even with all the problems he's had. He's been talking about giving up and they don't know what he'll do."

"Did they call the cops about missing persons?"

"Yes, but they haven't turned anything up."

"Do you want to take some time and go down there to be with them?"

"I've got a new case, but I don't know—I think I should be there."

"Go, Dolly. Whether he turns up or not, your folks are going to need you. The firm should understand, and if they don't, it's the wrong firm."

She left, and Stan made some calls to the state police and to her parents. But no one knew anything.

Then, after she had been home for two days, she called him. Lewis had been in a hospital, in a secure facility because he had been arrested after getting in a drunken brawl in a bar outside Parris Island. He had arrived without any identification, so they didn't know how to locate his family. He had major injuries, both from the fight and from an auto accident he had been in before he went to the bar. "We're all so grateful that he's alive, but we have no idea what to do next."

"Let me talk to the Congressman and get some time off. The least I can do is come down and be with you and your folks."

"I didn't want to ask, but I really do need you. Thanks, love."

Stan spent time with Lewis, who was barely coherent. Then he went to the nearest VA facility and asked to meet with the Medical Director. The Bryan Dorn Medical Center was outside Columbia, and Stan had met with some of the staff in connection with some constituent work he had done for the Congressman.

When he met with the Director, he explained Lewis' problems. The Director sighed and said "I've got dozens of stories like that, Mr. Wright. I looked up Lewis' file after you called. He's gotten pretty good care from our folks here—not the best—but pretty good. But we are so swamped right now, I wish I could tell you that we could do something more, but we really don't have it. We can keep trying to get him into therapy and try to cut down on the meds. But he's got to do some of the work, and his family has got to do some of it, too. I promise you I will assign our best team to work with him, but I can't give you any guarantees that we can pull him out of it."

Stan said, "Are there any vets' groups that he could be connecting with? Forgive me, but most of the people around here seem to be older, and I wonder if being with guys his own age—who went through what he did—would help."

"You're right about the age difference. We still have a lot of guys who are Vietnam era, and they take up a lot of our time. But now we're getting swamped with the post 9/11s. You know the data—22 vets kill themselves every day. That's what we're trying to catch up with. And it isn't headed in the right direction—it's getting worse, not better. Lewis is one of thousands of vets like him, along with hundreds of thousands who came through it OK."

"Has Congress done their part—from your perspective, and off the record?"

"We could always use more resources." He looked troubled. "But if we're off the record, I'd have to tell you that we're playing some games with the record-keeping –not so much here, but in a lot of the hospitals and other centers around the country. It's a lot worse than the numbers show—and the numbers are not looking good."

They talked some more about the backlogs, and Stan coaxed the Director into suggesting some questions that could be asked in committee hearings. Stan had realized early on that congressional staff who were doing their job were really surrogates for people affected by the programs Congress paid for—but who never had the chance to ask the question. The trick was getting out into the country and asking the right questions so that the people closest to the programs could suggest the next batch of questions that needed to be asked—and answered.

The Director promised to keep an eye on Lewis' case and let Stan know if he felt there was anything more he or the family could do to help Lewis.

As he drove back to Dolly's family, Stan thought about the problems he was trying to deal with in his committee work—many of which were also caused by war and its aftermath. That included refugee children, pre-teenaged children recruited into militias, children trafficked out of refugee camps. The nearly obscene phrase *collateral damage* didn't begin to communicate the horror and tragedy behind it. Lewis and a child whose leg got blown off by a leftover land mine in Sudan had little in common as individuals—but they shared a lot of what had put both of them in harm's way.

Jeremy 2005-2010

Jeremy continued his work with Church Children's Services in New York. He had thoroughly enjoyed seeing his friends, and knew that the commitments they had made—to stay in touch and to work on the Lopez agenda—were good ones. He was amused by Felicia's amazement at his drawing, while wishing that it had been Suzanne who had discovered them.

He grieved, however, at Suzanne's distance from the group—and from him. Out of a deep honesty with himself, acquired after growing up with the casual lies of his parents, he admitted to himself that Suzanne was one of the most important unresolved problems of his life. His caring about her had begun in the first moments of the Lopez class, and seeing her again had only worsened his distress that she seemed so unapproachable.

Gradually, his administrative skills had the paradoxical effect of allowing him to go nearly anywhere that CCS programs were operating. He had become able to bridge "admin" and programs better than anyone else in the agency, based on his unerring eye for making things more efficient. The CEO had called him in one day and told him that his reforms had saved them millions of dollars in his time with the agency. He said that anytime Jeremy wanted to go visit programs, the CEO knew that he would find something that would eventually pay off for the agency. "Your travels make me money, Jeremy. So keep it up."

He took advantage of the license to travel, and over the next three years, he went to almost every area where the agency had program staff or local churches that ran programs funded by CCS.

During this time, Jeremy went through a phase naïve Westerners sometimes go through when they first come to New York. Without much effort, he somehow became the object of amusement for attractive young women who had realized they could achieve a measure of control over a male. He didn't fully understand it, but once he figured out that many of them really didn't want commitment, but only wanted companionship, he let it happen. He really believed what he had told Felicia about the God-given grace of bodies together, and his eye for beauty helped him in his submission to their wills.

"Sometimes," he told Roberto in a call one day, "I think it's because I'm not some aimless young stud trying to figure out what I want to do with the rest of my life. Thanks to you guys and Lopez—and God's grace—I know what I'm called to do. And some women like that."

He laughed. "One told me I'm the most grown-up kid she knows."

He found a gym near his work and soon built up his body and slimmed down to a point where he needed new clothes. He had gotten by with two suits and a sport coat for several years, but he found that women also sought dominance over what men wear—and he submitted to that, too. It improved his overall appearance substantially.

But few of these women wanted permanence, and he came to view this phase of his life as an effort to discern what mattered in friendship, as well as in romance. He kept friendships with all but the most flighty of the women he encountered, who tended, anyway, to be eventually scared off by his seriousness. He became the friend some of them could "talk to" without it needing to end up in bed. He enjoyed that role, too. He'd seen *Harry and Sally* and he knew how it ended. But he also knew it was only a movie, and that friends could be just that.

If he had been asked how his theology was evolving, he would have easily answered that it was mostly child-centered, meaning he simply relied on a test of what was right was what was good for kids. The Lopez class had discussed what he had now seen in the faces and lives of thousands of children. And he had seen how, sometimes, with the right resources and leadership, those conditions could be made better. And so, he believed deeply, they must be.

In a conversation with a faculty member at Union Seminary whom he had met at work, the professor told him at the end of their conversation that he felt Jeremy had made an excellent choice in focusing his ministry on work with children's problems through his agency. *Ministry*, he thought to himself. *Well, yes, that's what it is, isn't it?*

Yet his dissatisfaction with the church—with organized religion in its charitable roles, more precisely—had increased. He had seen that the agency and others in the religious field easily allowed small projects to stand for real change. And he began to see how blind some churches and church leaders were to their passivity when they learned about abuses of children within the church.

He attended churches all over New York City, but refrained from membership in any of them. From the austere environs of Episcopal high churches to the vast spaces of St. Patrick's, he also moved in and out of dozens of neighborhood churches in Harlem, Queens (once attending her local parish with a very restive Felicia), and Brooklyn.

Priorities became the watchword for his work. He sought priorities in his administrative work, and when he made visits to programs, he led the program staff through a kind of Socratic dialogue that was ultimately about priorities.

On one site visit in Uganda, he asked the site team how many children in that province needed the literacy program that the agency was sponsoring for fifty children in their churches. The team looked at him as though he asked them why the streets weren't paved with gold.

Finally the program director hesitantly answered "We don't know the answer, sir. Because, sir, we only have enough resources for these children." There were about twenty staff and local church leaders in the group he was addressing, and many of them nodded.

Jeremy said, "That is true. But should we also remember Matthew 6:21? 'Where your treasure is, there your heart is also.'"

Then he asked, "Do any of the fathers in your village drink alcohol?"

The answer came back from a few of the group, "Yes, many do."

"Does your country have minerals that are being mined and taken out of the country?" "Yes," they said.

"Do parents give gifts when their daughters are married?"

A staff member said, "Yes, sometimes many cattle and other goods."

"Do your nation's leaders ride in big cars when they come to visit the villages?"

A louder yes was heard.

"And when there are holidays, does your government pay for big, expensive celebrations?"

Again, "Yes."

Jeremy was quiet for a moment, and then said, gently, "Then there *are* resources, it seems. But perhaps there aren't priorities—at least not for the children." He quickly added, "We have the same problem in my country, I am sorry to say. But sometimes priorities can be changed if the people want it and work for it."

He waited, and then concluded, "God loves these children. Perhaps we don't love them enough to make the right choices for them."

The group was quiet. Then the leader of the church members smiled and said, "Sir, I thought you were the administrative director. Are you sure you aren't the preacher also?"

Jeremy smiled all the way back to his airplane.

His conversations with Stan convinced him that the agency needed to be closer to Washington issues, and he worked with the director of advocacy to sharpen the message the agency had developed in its work as a contractor to the State Department. He helped prepare the agency's presentation at the congressional briefings Stan had convened, and it got good reviews.

Jeremy and Stan were able to learn from each other. Jeremy's CEO appreciated his relationship with a key congressional staffer, and Stan was able to bring Jeremy into his network of outside contacts. Jeremy easily fit into the group of congressional aides that Stan had assembled, and found himself enjoying the give and take when he went to Washington for briefings.

Stan and Jeremy met to go over the efforts by US-based religious groups to respond to trafficking and other child protection problems. Jeremy began the discussion by saying, "You know, Stan, our international efforts are running into a clean hands problem."

"What do you mean?"

Looking at some notes, Jeremy said, "There are several things that weaken our advocacy when we try to move other governments on these issues. First, the kids who live on reservations in this country have lousy odds of succeeding, or even being healthy. We're in countries trying to tell them not to discriminate against their minority groups—the castes in India, the Roma in Europe, and others. But we have this terrible problem among more than a million kids in this country,

"Second, we talk about child labor as a global problem. But there are kids as young as 7 working in tobacco fields in this country. Human Rights Watch has done a report on workers at tobacco farms in North Carolina, Kentucky, Tennessee, and Virginia. These kids work beside their parents—which is legal if the parents allow it. The kids get sick from the nicotine. Labor Department officials tried to prohibit anyone under 16 working in tobacco. Congress opposed it—but the administration could prohibit it on their own.

"Third, everyone knows we're one of the world's biggest markets for trafficking. And finally, as you know, we're the only nation that hasn't ratified the UN Convention on Rights of the Child." He paused. "Pretty crummy track record."

Stan frowned and said, "None of that's a surprise, I guess. But you're totally right, Jer—you add that all up and we look like crap trying to tell anyone else how to protect kids." He sighed. "We have a lot of work to do. What are the chances that the Bishops and the other groups will ever get together on these issues to push us harder?"

Jeremy smiled ruefully. "Ah, now you're pointing at *our* fragmentation. There's never been a unified statement by all the churches that have advocacy efforts on these issues. I know—I looked for that soon after I went to work at CCS. Each group issues its own statement, and then leaves it at that. There have been a few ecumenical efforts, but nothing like what you're talking about. Never a totally unified coalition, speaking with one voice." He added, "We have a bit of a clean hands problem ourselves on that score."

Stan said, "Another thing, Jer. I've taken Roberto's advice and asked a lot of questions about what Treasury and Justice are doing. I met with their top staff and pushed them on how much they target the traffickers as well as the terrorists and cartels. You know, Jeremy, I've also read some of the stuff you sent me about your agency. You're right—it *is* about priorities as much as it is about resources. Maybe more. Our agencies just don't pay the same kind of attention to the traffickers when they look for laundered money. And they don't know as much as they should about traffickers who are also in the drug business. It's not a priority to them.

"So that's why we've made some the changes in the new legislation on the Millennium Development Goals. The US is going to insist that trafficking get a higher priority in the MDG revisions in 2015. We're asking that child protection gets listed as one of the goals, separate from the others. We've made clear in the legislation that without those changes, the US contribution won't increase. It will piss off a lot of the UN bureaucrats, and some of the people in Treasury aren't that enthusiastic about scaling up what they've been doing on those issues. But it's the right thing to do—setting the right priorities."

Jeremy had scheduled a trip to Thailand, and one of his staff who had been in the region for several years suggested he meet with a Foreign Service Officer named Steve Jefferson. When he arrived in Bangkok, he called the Embassy and made an appointment to have dinner with Jefferson, who was quick to respond and suggested a place to meet.

When Jeremy arrived, he found himself at a thoroughly Thai restaurant, with a tall Eurasian man in Western clothes waiting for him in the small lobby area.

"Steve?" he said, and Jefferson answered, "Yes. Glad to meet you."

They sat down, Jefferson suggested what to order, and they began talking. In response to Jeremy's questions about his background, Jefferson explained that he had been in Bangkok for four years, which was his first assignment. He had begun his tour working on agricultural aid, but found that he was continually running into issues about who worked in the fields, and was able to shift his focus to child labor and schooling for younger children.

Jeremy asked, "How did you get into this work?"

Jefferson smiled, and said, "A lot of ancient history, I guess. My mother is Vietnamese. My father was a US soldier who then went into the State Department himself. You may know of him—Will Putnam? He's just wrapped up an assignment as Ambassador-at Large in Baghdad."

Jeremy said, "Oh yes, I've heard good things about him."

Jefferson said, "He's a good man. My adoptive father, Bill Jefferson, married my mother after his own service in Vietnam. Will never knew that I existed until I graduated from college and went to meet him. He's been very helpful to me since then."

Jeremy asked, "How much contact do you have with the religious agencies out here?"

Jefferson said, "Quite a bit. I have the assignment as liaison to the private aid groups, so I see most of them regularly." He paused, frowning. "Some of them are great, the best people I've met out here. They work to get the language, they eat the food, the whole bit. But some of them are really weird. They don't seem to want to adjust at all to how people live out here—always trying to Americanize them and make them into good little Christians. They stick to themselves a lot, live in their own compound with lots of servants, and they don't go out into the city much. You can tell they really don't like the culture at all. They use their own converts as translators, so none of them learn the language or even try to."

Jeremy said, "That's how I've seen it, too. We tend to lump all the religious agencies together, but as you've seen, they range all over the place. Some try to understand the local culture, and some are just determined to ignore it or change it—or remove kids from it altogether and send them to the US."

Jefferson grimaced. "Tell me about it. We've had some problems with local adoption agencies and orphanages that aren't really for orphans, but a way to make money off US adoptions. When we tried to set up some standards, working with some of the church groups, we got furious traffic from Congress about how we were blocking adoptions. As you know, adoptions are at a pretty low rate right now because of all the scandals, but a group in Congress pushes hard to get the numbers up, backed up by American adoptive families. They call the unscrupulous agencies 'a few bad apples.'"

They talked more, and Jeremy was again reminded that for all the idle talk about ugly Americans and diplomats who didn't understand the rest of the world, there were some within the legions of foreign assistance who knew what they were doing and cared about the countries where they represented their own.

And he worried more about the uneven methods of the religious agencies Jefferson mentioned than he did the sometimes inconsistent policies of his own government.

Jeremy had scheduled a trip to work with one of the church sites in Nigeria. The site had worked out an unusual joint venture with a Catholic hospital that cooperated with an elementary school that was run by a Methodist mission, and Jeremy wanted to see how the cooperation was working. He hoped it would be strong enough to serve as a model for other ecumenical efforts, but he had received mixed reports from the Methodist central office in Washington, and wanted to see the programs for himself.

He arrived in Lagos and arranged for transportation that took him two hundred kilometers north to the hospital which was west of Okuta, near the border with Benin. His local contact was a cheerful young minister from the church in Okuta which had built the school in the more rural area to the east.

As they drove, Jeremy asked the young minister whose name was Ari Apogu, how the school was doing.

"Very good, sir. We have more than two hundred children enrolled, from grades 1 to 8. We've been open for three years, and we have nearly as many girls as boys now."

Jeremy asked, "How do you work with the hospital?"

Apogu said, "At first it was difficult, sir. They have their ways, and we have ours. They are mostly women, too, and that was hard for some of the elders in our church to get used to. But they were very strong, they came several times to ask us if any of the children had illnesses that they could treat. And gradually the families felt comfortable sending their children, some of the younger ones who aren't old enough for school now, who had diseases that the local doctors weren't able to treat. Those nuns are very good doctors and nurses, sir. They treated one of the elder's daughters who had a very bad case of pneumonia, and she completely recovered. After that we found we could work more closely with them. It has been very good for the children."

Jeremy smiled as the Land Rover drove slowly through the near-tropical countryside. "We all pray to the same God, right, Ari?"

"Yes sir, we do."

When they arrived at the school, Jeremy was glad to see that there was no welcoming ceremony, and that the children were all in classes. He did, however, realize that each class had prepared a song that the children class sang as he walked in and out of the ten classrooms. The building was a mixture of wood and adobe, and reminded him of schools he had visited in rural New Mexico the year before.

Then they drove over to the hospital, which was a kilometer away from the school. It was a large modular structure, which he assumed had been trucked in with the sections assembled on the site. He was taken into the lobby, where the senior nun, Sister Maria Tanko, greeted him, along with a remarkable mixture of twenty white, African, and what appeared to be Asian and Latin American nuns lined up behind her.

Sister Maria was a short Nigerian nun who wore hospital working clothes with a white nun's cap and a cross hanging from her neck. She greeted Jeremy and Apogu with a wide smile.

"Welcome, Mr. Boxton. Thank you for coming to visit us. You are our first visitor from the United States, and we are very happy to have you come to see our work. Bless you for coming, sir."

They had lunch, and then Jeremy sat with Sister Maria and two of her nurses in what appeared to be the front office.

Jeremy began the conversation by thanking the group for their hospitality, and then he asked, "We are very interested in the cooperation you have established between the school and your hospital. We are hoping that more work like this will be possible, in Africa and around the world. Tell me how it is going."

Sister Maria smiled, and said, "I think it is going well. We and the Methodists have had to get used to each other, but we are out here in a rural area where the usual structures of discipline and religious boundaries mean less than the need to help the children and their families. And we have gradually learned to work together to serve both the minds and the bodies of the children from the villages nearby."

She described some of the recent history of the area. They had been attacked the year before by a radical Muslim band of terrorists, and the central government's army had proven almost completely ineffective in defending the school-hospital combination. Most of the attacks on churches had come in the north and west of the country, but this group had infiltrated from Benin and had rampaged through several villages before a helicopter crew from the African Union troops had driven them across the border.

"Do you feel safe now?" Jeremy asked.

She frowned and said "Yes, most of the time. There have been reports of a rebel group over in Benin again, but we have not seen any signs of them." She smiled again, and said, "We have tried to prepare for what may be necessary to keep the children safe."

Jeremy asked what those preparations involved, but she just smiled and changed the subject. He had made arrangements to sleep overnight in a guest house, and after a pleasant dinner and some more conversation with the school staff and the nurses, he went to bed around 10 pm.

Three hours later, all hell broke loose. He was awakened by shooting and explosions, and as he cautiously stuck his head out the front of the guest house, he saw five or six vehicles filled with men shooting wildly into the air. They were about a hundred yards away from the hospital, but they were drawing closer.

As he watched, he saw off to the side what appeared to be several of the sisters and some older children running crouched over, with gasoline cans in their hands. Then they stopped and he lost sight of them.

A voice came from the rebel trucks, and as he heard its shouting, he saw Apogu carefully edging up to the guest house. He whispered to Apogu as he drew nearer, "What did he say?"

"He demanded that we send out the girls between the ages of eight and fourteen. He said they will leave if we send out the girls."

"Like hell we will," said Jeremy, and he then asked Apogu, "Do you know where we can get weapons?" But Apogu shook his head.

The firing continued, and then suddenly a long sheet of fire erupted. Jeremy could see in the blazing new light that a trench filled with gasoline had been ignited. He could hear screams of anger and pain coming from the rebels. One of the trucks which was too near the trench caught on fire, and then exploded. In the bright light. Jeremy could see that the nuns and the kids with gasoline had poured it into a protective trench that ran around the hospital, and had then lit it.

Jeremy heard a new sound, in the confusion of cross-fires, explosions, and screams, which he quickly made out to be rapid firing from the hospital grounds and the bushes beyond the hospital. The shots were well-placed, and several of the rebels fell, as others picked up their comrades and tossed them in the back of the trucks. He heard the trucks revving up, and within a few minutes, they had all driven away.

Slowly, the defenders moved out from the buildings where they had been sheltered. Jeremy saw that they were nearly all nuns clad in camouflage gear, together with a few teenagers who were carrying AK-47s.

He spotted Sister Maria standing on the front steps of the hospital, caring for a young man who had been shot. The wounded man was quickly taken inside and made comfortable on a table that Jeremy could see through the front doors of the hospital.

Sister Maria had moved back to the top of the steps leading up to the hospital doors. She stood with a rifle over her shoulder, her smile in place. "I am so sorry your visit was disturbed by this violence. I did not expect this—but we were ready, as you could see."

"You sure were. I am very surprised that your group was able to defend itself so well," Jeremy said.

"My father was a general in the old Nigerian army, sir, and he taught my brothers and sisters and me how to use firearms and how to set up defenses. We do not like to do it, but when children are in danger, we are certain that God would want us to protect them from harm. And so we do just that. I think we have surprised the rebels, who may have thought we were just a harmless group of nurses."

She laughed and added, "Usually, we are."

She went on. "We have a study group that meets every week, to try to stay current on world affairs, out here so far from our homes and from any newspapers. We have been reading about the new doctrine at the United Nations—the 'responsibility to protect.' We are not sure what that means at the UN. But we are very clear what it means out here, Mr. Boxton."

She gestured to where the rebel trucks had been. "Those evil men prey on the weak. So we have to show them we are not weak, and that we will protect our children."

As they drove back to Lagos, Jeremy made some notes, and his thoughts turned to Suzanne and Felicia, as they often did on a site visit. He knew they had seen villages very like the one he had just visited, and wondered about their safety. And he thought about how fiercely the nuns had protected the children in their care.

He called Roberto, as he had tried to do at least monthly, to check in and let him know what he was doing with CCS. He told him about the raid, and how the nuns had responded.

"I need to figure out how to help them, Berto. I don't want to do the Save the Children kind of adoption; I want the nuns and the others caring for these kids to have the money to pay for their school or college or medical treatment or just give their parents enough to get their kids off the streets."

"But it would take billions to help them all, Jer. I'll help, but the need must be enormous."

"I know. But if I could leave something behind in each of the places we work, that would help. Enough to challenge the grass-roots church people we work with to think about the longer term—about what it would take to free some of these kids from the worst that may happen to them.

He went on. "As I was leaving the site in Nigeria, after the night when the nuns set up the fire defense, I watched the kids. They had been badly scared, obviously. They still huddled around the camp workers and the sisters, clinging to their hands and holding onto their skirts. I heard them asking over and over if the bad men were coming back. The girls knew that the attackers had asked for them to be sent out to get loaded into the trucks, and some of them were still whimpering. And the sisters were talking to them softly, patting their heads, rubbing their backs."

He was quiet, and then added, "We can't just visit these places and move on, Berto. We have to leave something behind."

Roberto said "I'd be glad to help, Jer. Let me know where to send the money."

Suzanne 2005-2010

Suzanne and Felicia returned from the New York gathering and plunged back into their work. Suzanne had begun to specialize in working in refugee camps, where the trafficking was worsening as refugee numbers increased due to climate change and civil wars in Africa, as well as the continuing strife in the Middle East. Suzanne was asked by the central office in London to present testimony to the annual human rights reviews in Geneva, and Felicia accompanied her. Suzanne had become a powerful speaker, using her height and her commanding presence to lay out the facts the agency had gathered, interspersed with anecdotes and, where the facilities permitted, pictures she had taken in the camps.

In mid-2007, Suzanne and Felicia were sent to New Mexico and then to Texas to interview staff and inmates at two of the refugee camps that had been opened to house women and children who had been detained after they crossed the US border. They arrived in Artesia, New Mexico, and were met by a short, vivacious woman named Maria Ochoa who worked for a volunteer legal firm representing the women who had been detained.

Ochoa explained to Suzanne and Felicia what had been happening. Beginning in 2007, the refugee problems along the US border had become as severe as some of the other sites in Africa and Asia where Suzanne and Felicia had done research. Gang wars in Central America, mostly in El Salvador, Guatemala, and Honduras, and the vicious operations of the cartels in Central American and Mexico have forced thousands of families to try to get out of their villages and make it all the way across Mexico to the US border.

Ochoa said, "When they get here—and only half of them make it –they get shoved in these camps. And then it takes months for them to get a hearing. Some of these judges send nine out of ten of their cases back to Central America. They ignore federal court cases that mandate how the women and kids should be treated, they don't open the schools that are supposed to be operating—it's just a chaotic mess."

Felicia asked "Who's to blame for all this?"

Maria Ochoa laughed, but angrily, and said "Everyone is. Congress, ICE, the administration, the judges, the President—*everybody*. None of them have wanted to admit how big the problem is, or what happens when these women and kids are sent back to their homes. The stupid fight between the President and Congress over immigration has frozen everything, and in the meantime, thousands of women and kids have been caught up in the cross-fires."

Suzanne asked, "What happens to the women and children when they are sent back?"

Ochoa said, "We've tried to find out, but it's hard getting definite word back. There's a loose network of priests which has tried to track them, but they've been intimidated by the gangs, who've told the priests they will burn their churches down if they help the women once they've tried to escape."

She shook her head, a sad look on her face. "Most of these women have either lost their husbands or have been targeted by the gangs and raped because their husbands tried to resist. When they get back, what we have been able to find out is that many of them have disappeared, captured and taken back into the rural areas where the gangs have their hideouts. We never hear from most of them again."

Suzanne asked, "What have the US churches been able to do?"

Ochoa smiled, and said, "Look, I'm a Catholic. I've fought against the church's positions on abortion and birth control, and their terrible homophobia while so many priests have been involved in abusing children. But I've never been prouder of my church than when I see what the US Catholic Bishops Conference has done on its anti-trafficking activities, and what they have tried to do in these camps. They have been magnificent. They work with International Justice Commission and the Polaris organization, they work across ecumenical lines with Protestant charitable organizations—they've been great. But they haven't been successful in their lobbying efforts to get these camps to do what they were supposed to do to care for these women and children. Nothing has budged this administration, and nothing has been able to move Congress to get off its ass and do something to push the administration."

Suzanne and Felicia looked at each, both thinking *We've got to talk to Stan.*

Ochoa took them to meet with four of the women who had come from El Salvador, and it was all they could do to keep from crying. Two of the women had their children with them, and they could see that the children, looking about 2 or 3, were listless and possibly ill. When they asked when the women would get a hearing, they were told it would take at least two months before any of them was going to get a chance to explain why they would be endangered if they returned to El Salvador.

Suanne and Felicia went back to their motel and wrote up their notes. Then they called Stan, who was able to get back to them later that night. They explained what they had seen, and Stan told them he had a staff member who had been meeting that week with the Immigration and Customs officials and the Justice Department lawyers to try to get answers—with little success.

Stan said, "We've been trying to schedule a hearing, but most of the Republicans on the committee don't want to even talk about those families, because it makes clear that our real policy is send most of them back, after keeping them in those rotten camps. We need a battalion of pit-bull lawyers to come after us, because we are violating the provisions of a court decision that says we are supposed to be taking much better care of them and processing these claims much faster than we are right now. It's a mess. The last numbers I saw indicated that more than 60,000 families and more than 50,000 unaccompanied minors crossed the border last year."

After they got off the phone, they talked for another hour, getting more and more depressed. Suzanne said, "This isn't on the other side of the world—this is here in the US! And nothing is happening to turn it around. Nothing!"

March 2008

Suzanne and Felicia continued their work investigating human rights violations that were tied to trafficking women and children. After visiting three refugee camps in Lebanon, all overcrowded with refugees from Palestine and the beginnings of the civil war in Syria, Suzanne went to Sicily. She had made arrangements to work with a Sicily-based organization that focused on trafficking from North Africa to Italy and Spain, including women from Nigeria, Benin, and in lesser numbers, from Middle Eastern countries.

Women trying to make the trip had increasingly reported traffickers kidnapping girls and younger women, as well as luring them with promises that they could work in restaurants to pay off the debts they had incurred. It was a familiar pattern, reminding Suzanne of what she and Felicia had seen over and over in Texas and northern Mexico. The Sicily group had investigated the groups that were involved with the camps, and through them, had identified some of the traffickers. They had reported their findings to the UN refugee offices in Geneva, but had received little feedback thus far on what would happen as a result of their reports.

Suzanne's mission was to talk to some of the refugees and document human rights abuses. She had spent her first morning, after being picked up at her hotel in Siracusa, in the closest camp.

The camp was a depressing mixture of tents and old brick buildings left over from World War II military facilities. Over a thousand people were jammed into the camp, which was originally laid out, she was told, for about three hundred.

It was a hot day, the camp's rudimentary sanitation facilities had been overwhelmed, and the smells were the worst Suzanne had ever experienced. Her tactic of smearing Vaseline under her nose failed almost completely to reduce the stench.

The staff explained to her how the traffickers operated. Gangs of smugglers roamed around the camp, picking younger women and older girls and offering them passage to Italy and jobs in restaurants. With the help of a translator, she had interviewed some of the women in the camp. They told the same story. They had contracted a sizable debt—usually at least five thousand euros, which they owed to the shadowy organizations that had brought them from Central Africa to North Africa and then, in leaky, ancient boats, across to Sicily. Most of the camp dwellers had long ago given up their cash and jewelry to the groups that had brought them from deeper in Africa. So the traffickers' offer to let the women work off their debt for passage to Italy seemed to some to offer an escape from the unbearable conditions in the camp.

The first three or four waves of women had quickly signed up, but the traffickers were meeting more resistance as a few women escaped and made their way back to the camp. They warned the other women that there were no "restaurants"—instead there were brothels scattered throughout southern Europe where the women and girls were forced to live and provide sex with customers.

The camp operators from the Sicilian agency had tried to keep the trafficking gangs out of the camp, they told Suzanne, but their security force was untrained and unarmed, and they were simply pushed aside when the gangs entered the camp, usually arriving at night in their trucks and vans.

When she heard these details, Suzanne asked why the security was so lax and how women were leaving the camps to go to the boats that took them to Italy. The supervisor of the camp shrugged and lifted her hands, saying "What can we do? We are feeding more than three times more people than we are funded to do. We have almost no medical supplies. There is nothing left for more security." She added, looking away at the blue-tarp covered tents, "These women will do almost anything to get out of the camps—even believe the lies they are being told."

"Where are their husbands?" Suzanne asked.

"Most of them have already gotten to Italy, Greece, or Spain. These women are trying to join them."

Suzanne asked about the well-known Mafia organizations that existed throughout Sicily. She was told that some of them were actively involved in the trafficking, while the others ignored it and concentrated on their own operations.

Again, Suzanne flashed back to her work with Felicia in Mexico, remembering the role of the drug cartels. The pattern was depressingly similar: families trying to reunite, looking for work and safety, preyed upon by men who exploited the weak. The women here were trying to get to Europe instead of Texas and the slaughterhouses of the Midwest, but otherwise, it was the same.

She got in the beat-up van that was taking her back to her hotel where she planned to write up her notes and try to find a decent internet connection to send them to London. As she approached the downtown area, she motioned to the driver to let her out a few blocks from the hotel. She wanted to walk and hoped to spot a restaurant that might offer more than the pathetic meal she had gotten at the hotel the night before.

As she walked, she replayed the interviews at the camp. She noticed that the driver had let her out on the back side of the hotel, instead of the main street it faced. There were few cars passing by, and only a few stores open.

That's when she realized she was being followed.

A tall, lean man dressed in Western clothes and with his hands in his pockets was about twenty yards behind her. When she stopped to look into a storefront, she saw him stop out of the corner of her eye. She turned and kept walking, quickening her pace.

The hotel was only two blocks away, so she assumed her pursuer was going to make a move before she got there. She carried a small bag under her arm, and reached into it to pull out a lipstick-shaped container. Then she heard hurried footsteps behind her.

She heard his broken English before she turned around. "Lady— American lady! Why are you in the camps asking questions?"

He had rapidly moved around in front of her and was blocking her path. He was dark-skinned, but a European, she thought. He was standing so close that she could smell him—a pungent mix of body odor and alcohol.

"I don't understand you," she said. "Please stand out of my way. I'm going back to my hotel to join my friends."

"You understand me, lady. Stay out of the camps. It is business that does not concern you." Then he reached out to grab her arm.

When he touched her arm, Suzanne felt a surge of rage and instinctively raised the pepper spray and sprayed him straight in the face from a few inches away.

He screamed and fell back, off to the side of the street. Her route to the hotel was open, and she knew she could out-run him.

Instead, she moved toward him, and as he clawed at his eyes, she grabbed his greasy hair and kneed him in the groin with all of her weight behind it. He fell to the ground moaning. The rage was still racing through her. She went blind for a moment, and then all she saw was this disgusting man on the ground who had tried to hurt her.

She bent over, grabbed his head on both sides, and with her full upper body strength behind it, gave it a rapid twist. Then she heard a loud crack.

He gurgled once and fell back, lying motionless on the ground. She knew she had broken his neck, and that he was dead.

She looked around, and saw only a few people walking a block away from her, past the hotel. She consciously slowed her walk as she entered the hotel, went up to her room, and arranged for a taxi to the airport.

On the way, she called London and said she had contracted a severe digestive problem and was going to try to fly to Rome.

At the airport, waiting for her flight, she replayed the attack and her response. The traffickers had thought they could send a low-level street guy to frighten her away. She knew she had left DNA all over the man, but assumed forensic police work was far from advanced in Sicily. But then she realized that the traffickers or the police would find him, track her visit to the camp, and find that she had checked out of the hotel immediately after. She might as well have left a business card on the thug.

She knew that the traffickers could probably buy off any police or prosecution. So then the question became whether the heads of the trafficking organization would write it off, because she had left the area, or decide to go after her as a lesson to others who might try to investigate their profitable business.

She checked her pulse and her breathing. Both were nearly normal. When she thought about it later, that's what bothered her the most.

She got to Rome, checked into a small hotel in Trastevere, and wrapped herself deep into the blankets of her bed. And there, she finally admitted to herself that in the final moments of her deadly rage, her attacker was no longer a cheap street thug. He had become her stepfather.

She tried to sleep, but she couldn't. The memories were too intense, and she couldn't shake them.

After she turned 13, her stepfather had begun coming to her bedroom when her mother was on one of her frequent business trips. At first he just stroked her hair, which was long then. But it went from there to his touching her, and then raping her.

When she told him to stop, he threatened to tell her mother that she had come to him and asked him to help her understand sex, and that he had refused and sent her away. She knew her mother would believe him to save the marriage. She always thought that her mother knew, based on her growing coolness toward Suzanne.

It went on until she was 15. One night she hid a kitchen knife in her bed, and when he entered her and began moving, she reached under her pillow, pulled out the knife, and dug a long slice into his back. He screamed, hit her, and drove himself to the emergency room, telling them he had fallen on garden tools.

He never came to her room again.

Her mother never mentioned her father's injury. A few weeks later, they sent her away to boarding school. She quickly plunged into academics and athletics, excelling in both.

After realizing she wasn't going to be able to sleep, she called Felicia, who arrived from London the next day. She rented a car and they drove up to Florence. Felicia found a villa outside the city and they rented it for a week. She had taken leave from the agency, telling her supervisor that she needed some time off.

When Suzanne asked her where she had gotten the money, Felicia said, "I called Roberto. He wired me enough. Don't worry about it."

"I hate asking him for money."

"I don't. He has it, he always wants to help us, and we need it right now. Case closed, Suzanne.

"All right." She gave Felicia a weak smile. "One less thing to worry about, I guess."

When Felicia asked her what had happened in Sicily, at first Suzanne just shook her head. After a few days, she said "Maybe it would help if I talk about it."

She started slowly, telling her about the visit to the camp, the drive back to the hotel, and the attack. Felicia listened, saying nothing.

"He warned me to stay away from the camp, and then he touched me. I went crazy, I guess. I sprayed him with that pepper spray you got me, and then I jerked his head around as far as I could." She looked at Felicia, then looked away. "I killed him, Felicia. I broke his neck, and I killed him."

"Good!" She reached over and patted Suzanne's arm, awkwardly. Then she asked, "How likely are they to track you?"

"I don't know. I haven't wanted to check with anyone in London, and you've covered our traces well enough, getting rid of the car in Florence."

"We may need to leave here in a few days, then. Do you feel like you can travel?"

"Yes. I'd rather go right away, now that I think about it. If they can track us to Florence, they might be able to find us if we stay around here."

They took a train from Florence to Milan, and rented a condominium apartment, using a false identification that Felicia had gotten from the agency when she was on an inspection tour. The agency had already been hacked by a group of websites used by another group of traffickers, and false IDs were part of its defense.

After the first talk with Felicia, Suzanne said nothing about the attack. Felicia called London and said that Suzanne was not recovering well from the digestive problems she had experienced in Sicily, and they asked for a six months leave. Reluctantly, their supervisors granted it.

Gradually, they began talking about the attack and what it meant to their work. Felicia carefully explained what she thought their options were.

"We can go back to London and keep working for HRWR. Or we can find another agency through our NGO contacts and get into work that doesn't involve trafficking." She paused and watched Suzanne for a moment, then went on. "Or, we could work with Roberto and other guys he knows to go back at some of the traffickers with as much firepower as we can assemble."

Suzanne showed no expression that Felicia could detect. Slowly she said, "Let's talk about number three some more."

So they began a surreal, sometimes deadly, two-hour review of what the two of them could do to combat trafficking. Felicia got on her laptop and they carefully drew up a list of the agencies around the world that were combatting trafficking, with a special emphasis on those that were concerned with children.

"Some of these agencies haven't posted anything for five years. There are dozens of them."

"We're going to have to make a list of who's who and what they're doing, unless we can find someone else who's already done it."

"Surely somebody has. These agencies can't just be going off on their own and doing their own thing. We were lucky to get connected with HRWR, but there may be hundreds of agencies that work on trafficking kids—or say they do."

So they set about doing the work in a systematic way. They went through the archives at UNICEF, making day trips down to the UNICEF research office in Florence. They got library and internet privileges at the University of Milan, and logged in for at least eight hours a day for a solid month.

Suzanne expected that she would have post-traumatic stress, and kept watching for it. But gradually she realized that she wasn't replaying the attack or the death. When she thought about it—which the work with Felicia had kept away most of the time—the only emotion she felt was satisfaction that she had defended herself and that the attack had failed, this time. She wondered if her calm exterior had somehow turned into cold-bloodedness. And she devoted most of her energy to trying to find a way to get back at those behind the street thug—those who had sent him and who employed thousands like him all over the world.

At the end of the month, they had produced a 50-page matrix of all the anti-trafficking organizations that seemed active and a description of what each organization had accomplished. There were more than 200 organizations with websites on trafficking, and most of them claimed to work to prevent child trafficking as a specific activity. One directory listed over a thousand organizations that had anti-trafficking components.

But when they dug into the details of what these organizations actually did, they found a different picture. Most of the organizations provided some kind of support for victims of trafficking. A few lobbied governments to increase the resources devoted to anti-trafficking efforts. But they could find none that claimed to act directly against the trafficking organizations.

"Toolkits for helping victims are great. But it doesn't catch anyone who is trafficking, and it doesn't prosecute anybody. The UN itself says only one out of a hundred victims is ever rescued. These groups all leave the real fighting to governments—and then they admit that governments don't treat this as a priority," Felicia said. "The US spends about $18 million a year on anti-trafficking programs—not even 1/10 of 1 percent of the estimated revenues of $32 billion a year from trafficking."

Suzanne said, "Yes, but if any of the NGOs were going after the bad guys directly, they probably wouldn't admit to it on their website. We've gone as far as we can on the internet. Now we need to talk to the best of these NGOs and see who may be serious about shutting down the slimeballs. We know enough now to ask some good questions."

She paused and said, "The other good news is that we haven't heard anything about the problem in Sicily." She looked at Felicia and said, deliberately, "I think I can forget about it now."

"Good." But saying it, Felicia wondered what it would cost Suzanne to have to forget about killing someone. And then she wondered why Suzanne thought it would be easy.

They were pacing themselves. Their determination to attack the traffickers was driving them, but they were also taking some time to see the area around Milan, to go out into the countryside, and to have some great meals together. They had met some American students at the University and had dinner with them a few times, describing their work as "research for a British NGO."

After a hard day of adding new information to their inventory of organizations, they sat at their favorite trattoria and glumly reviewed their progress. Felicia spoke first.

""We're not making any progress finding NGOs or anyone else who is taking them on directly. We need some way to get into the traffickers' communications—some way to find out what they're doing before they do it."

Then they looked at each other, and at the same time, they said "*Roberto.*"

They called him, but got his cellphone message. Suzanne left a message asking him to call her.

While they were waiting to connect with Roberto, they decided to meet with staff of one of the NGOs based in Geneva that worked on trafficking issues. They took a train into Switzerland, and found themselves in the lobby of a distinguished-looking five-story building facing the lake. When they were shown into the office of the director of the Trafficking Group, they found that the director was a young woman named Marilyn O'Hara who was about their age, with fiery red hair and a stylish suit. She offered coffee and tea, and then began speaking in a decidedly Irish accent.

"You said you were working on a research project."

"Yes, we formerly worked for HRWR in London, but we're now doing research on our own for a book we're thinking of publishing.

We'd appreciate your helping us out with some of the questions that have been difficult to research on the internet."

"I'd be glad to try."

Felicia dove in, knowing that Suzanne would take longer to get to the point and unsure of how much time they would get. "We've read as much as we can about the NGOs and the UN and national efforts to deal with trafficking. We read what was available about the financial interdiction efforts, to block money laundering from trafficking. But what we couldn't tell was how many of the traffickers are being shut down or locked up. Is every one that is arrested replaced with another, or is any real progress being made?"

O'Hara smiled, and said, "You've cut to the heart of the matter, as Americans tend to do." Then she looked away, glancing at a map of Europe on the wall opposite her window to the lake. "The honest answer, which I cannot say on the record, is that it is getting worse. The technology the traffickers are using is no better than the technology we're trying to use against them—but there's so bloody damned more of them. We're scraping along with a few million in anti-trafficking resources, and they're working with billions. The last estimate made, which you've probably come across, was that trafficking is a 32 billion dollar industry worldwide. And when we do launch a major effort to shut down the money laundering, terrorism and drugs always take precedence over the human trafficking issues. The UN Office on Drugs and Crime estimates that 2.4 million people are trafficked every year, and that 80 per cent of them are sexual slaves. Twenty percent of them are children—and that's increasing. UNODC, which is based in Vienna, says that only one out of 100 of them is ever rescued. Only one out of four traffickers arrested is convicted, and the vast majority of traffickers never get arrested. The ILO, which includes labor trafficking—people moved across borders as exploited workers—estimates 21 million, more than half of them women."

She smiled, more sadly this time. "Long answer. Sorry."

Suzanne, choosing her words very carefully, said. "No, we appreciate your candor, and of course we won't quote you in any direct way." She paused. "Some of those we've talked with have come to the same conclusion you have, and have then tried to force the logic to the next step. Which for some of them leads to more direct action against the traffickers. Are you aware of any efforts of that kind?"

O'Hara's eyebrows had risen as high as possible with the final words of Suzanne's question. "Vigilante efforts you mean? Hackers going after the traffickers' websites and trying to crash them? A few selective assassinations?"

She paused, her face angry now. "No, we haven't seen any of that. Is that where you're coming out with your research—calling for more violence to cure the violence?"

Felicia knew she was probably a better liar than Suzanne, and quickly answered, "No, it's not. But we've read and talked with some people who seem headed in that direction." She changed the subject. "Most of these organizations work with victims, rather than trying to affect the traffickers. Doesn't that seem disproportionate?"

O'Hara shook her head. "Not at all. What may not be evident is how much helping the victims is about stopping the practice. If victims won't testify against the perpetrators, they go free. When the victims' reluctance to testify is added to the disgusting ignorance and malfeasance of the police and the courts—the perps win. You've seen the data—hundreds of thousands of abductions and only hundreds of convictions worldwide. That's partly about victims never wanting to face their attackers again. So we don't look down on any organizations that work with victims, as long as they are trying to get them to testify."

Felicia said "Thanks—we hadn't seen that connection yet."

Suzanne asked, as they stood up, "May I ask, how did you come to this job? You've been very helpful, and I'm interested in the career path you've taken to get into this position—if there is one."

O'Hara laughed and said, "I'm afraid my career path is unique. My father is quite wealthy, and he provided our organization with the money it needed to get started. I was raped when I was in school in Ireland, and he thought setting this organization up was the best revenge he could have."

She looked away. "He also managed to have the rapist disappear." She seemed embarrassed now, and Suzanne realized it was about her earlier reaction to the possibility of violence. "I confess I've never looked into that too closely."

It was an extraordinary response to Suzanne's question, and both of them were thrown for a loss. O'Hara mentioned the money, the rape, and the "disposal" of the rapist in a smooth narrative that presented all three events with a tone of *I know this seems amazing, but think nothing of it.*

Suzanne recovered first. "Not your typical NGO start-up, I guess."

"No. But I've found that a lot of us in this work have similar beginnings—if not the resources we've been fortunate to have." She smiled at Suzanne, and at that moment Suzanne felt completely transparent, as if O'Hara knew her life story. And she smiled back and said, "Yes, we've found that, too."

Outside, on their way to the nearest coffee stop, Felicia exclaimed, "Wow! A lot of information we needed, and some we'd never expect."

Suzanne frowned and said, "Yes. But a bit dissonant. She's opposed to violence except when it's about her own revenge, and then she's hands off because Daddy is taking care of it."

Felicia said, "Yeah. But isn't that where we're headed? Isn't that why you asked her about how she got started?"

In her typical fashion, Felicia had called the question. They had never explicitly said they were moving toward a violent response. But O'Hara's frankness had forced the issue to the surface, and as they began sipping their coffee, they quietly laid out the options.

Felicia ticked off the possibilities, making arrows on a napkin. "Aren't we looking at three, maybe four options? One: we work with the government agencies that are going after finances and prosecutions. Something like the agency Roberto interned with in DC. Two, we hire someone—maybe Roberto would fund it—or do it himself—to hack the traffickers and try to divert their funds Attack them at their financial checkpoints. Three: we approach one of the trafficking organizations and try to..." she paused, looking for a euphemism, and then giving it up, "terminate their top people."

She was quiet for a moment, and then added, "And maybe four: we set up a contract group like the US military has done and they provide protection for women and kids who are at risk of being trafficked. And if that fails, then they go after the traffickers." She sat back, glad that she had named the stark options, but also aware that she had just suggested placing their own lives in considerable danger. Not to mention becoming assassins—or hiring some.

Suzanne's response was slow in coming. Finally she said, "Have you ever read any of Diana Russell's work? She writes about *femicide*—the argument that when attacks and killing of women are institutionalized in a culture, it has the same moral content as genocide. Her work has had a much bigger impact in Latin America than it has in the U.S. She's written about the killings of dozens of women in Juarez and elsewhere in Latin America. I came across her work when I was at Columbia, but none of my professors wanted to go down that road. Too radical, they thought."

"What's her solution?"

Suzanne noticed that one of the coffee house patrons was trying to listen to them, and stood up, saying "Let's walk."

They headed toward the lake, passing under trees in full mid-summer bloom. Suzanne returned to Felicia's question. "Her solution? Well, it's not homicide. It's changing the UN conventions on genocide to include femicide, so that the same sanctions that apply to genocide could be applied to those who persecute women."

Felicia threw up her hands. "But what good would that do, when the convictions and prosecutions are so low? You heard O'Hara's numbers. The laws already on the books aren't doing any good—why spend energy trying to amend them if no one enforces them now?"

Suzanne frowned. "That's the right question. I don't know the answer yet."

Just then her phone rang. Suzanne glanced at the number, and said, delighted, "It's Roberto. Hey, friend. Great to hear from you. Thanks for getting back to us—I'm with Felicia and I'm going to put you on speaker. And thanks for sending us the help we needed to get out of… of where we were."

Roberto's voice came out of the tiny speaker. "Hey, you two. What's up? Glad to help out when I can—you know I always will."

Felicia said, "You're the best, pal. We need to talk to you. Don't you want to meet us somewhere cool?"

"Sure. Where are you?"

They told him they were in Geneva but made plans to meet him in London.

Two days later, they were all in the apartment Felicia and Suzanne had taken in London. They exchanged *who have you seen lately* stories quickly, and then Roberto said, "So tell me what we need to talk about."

Suzanne began, looking at Felicia to invite her to chime in when needed. "We've had some problems with traffickers." She explained what had happened in Sicily, leaving out the final outcome and describing the encounter as something that frightened her but that she had gotten away from successfully.

She went on. "The whole thing made us wonder if what we have been doing through the agency we work for here is the best way to get things done for kids—and their mothers. So we met with an NGO staff person in Geneva, who pretty much admitted what they were doing through the UN and other agencies wasn't very effective. Then we wondered if we could find out more about the traffickers by using some of your...uh, *unique methods.*"

Roberto laughed. "Could be." He explained that he saw his past efforts as a more effective form of what the government lamely called its "asset forfeiture" policy. "Supposedly when traffickers are caught, their assets could be confiscated and sold to pay for services to victims or additional enforcement efforts. But no data has ever been released on what the level of these assets has been, other than a recent UN report than estimated it at less than six million—worldwide. Which is a joke."

He smiled. "So they forfeit their assets to me, only they don't know when the assets are going away, and they don't know who took them."

"Isn't that risky—can't they trace you the same way you trace them?"

He smiled and shook his head. "No, they can't. Not if I'm careful. And I'm always careful. See, the final rule in this arena is that the hacker always wins the first round. The hackee can put up walls and put out tracers and do all that stuff—but only after they've discovered that someone got in and got out with something they care about."

Then he asked them a question. "How much do you see the drug traffickers and the sex traffickers overlapping?"

Felicia said. "We've got a lot of info that the drug smugglers and the gangs that smuggle people for labor and sex are converging—they're in each other's business and sometimes they're the same outfits. First they kidnap for ransom, then they kidnap for prostitution. So maybe your lines of business and ours aren't that far apart."

"Maybe not. I can verify some of that through the back channels I've set up. But let's assume you're right. Are you asking me if I can get into these traffickers' accounts and trace what they're doing? And then rip them off?"

Suzanne said, "That's one possibility we've considered, without knowing any of the details." She stopped, choosing her next words carefully. "We've also been wondering if any of those assets could them be used to improve protection of these women and kids."

Roberto said, "Protection—like armed guards or something like that?"

Felicia said "Yes. Something like that."

Roberto frowned "You're not thinking of taking these guys on directly, are you? Because some of them are better armed than the police or even the armies in these countries. They play for keeps."

Suzanne was silent, and then she said, "We want to protect these kids and their moms, Roberto. If better protection works, that's fine with us. But I don't like being attacked on the street because I was trying to help kids. If you can help us by nipping at these guys on the internet, that would be great. Then we'll see what happens next." She spoke in a level voice, looking straight at him so he would see they were serious.

And he did. He shook his head. "I'll see what I can find out. But I'm not going to do anything that would put you guys in harm's way."

"We're past that, Roberto." Then she decided to lighten up the conversation. "And now are you ready for some serious curry? There's a great place around the corner—if it's not too hot for you."

"Too hot? For the jalapeño kid? Bring it on!"

They talked some more at dinner, but in a general way. Roberto had promised to see if he could find out which trafficking organization was involved with the camp Suzanne had visited, and that was what they had hoped for.

Roberto flew back to LA after two days in London, and within a week they heard from him. He had found two separate organizations that had been identified by NGOs as working in the Sicily-North

Africa area. He had then, in his words, "tickled" each of their banking accounts. "They're baby-simple to get in and out of. What do you want me to do next?" he asked on the speaker phone in their apartment.

Felicia, looking at Suzanne, said, "See if you can move some of their..."she paused trying to think of a code word, realizing that neither phone was safe, to the best of her knowledge. "Their, uh, equipment." Suzanne nodded and silently mouthed *Yes*. "And be *careful*."

"Always, happy flower girl." He paused and said, "Does either of you have an account left in a bank here in LA?"

Felicia laughed and said, "Yes, I kept my savings account open. I'll email you the numbers."

"Don't do that!" Roberto quickly said. "I'll send you instructions on how to get that to me. Don't *ever* leave a trace of any account numbers on the internet."

A day later, they received a package with a code that Roberto promised was tied to an edition of *The Tale of Two Cities*. Roberto had always made a big deal out of having the same birthday as Charles Dickens—February 7. So that was the base for his code. All they had to do was turn to the right page and match the letters.

Two days later, Felicia opened the account and found that it had $50,000 in it.

Over dinner, they were quiet, both trying to handle the knowledge that they were now co-conspirators in international money laundering. They were only partly comforted by the fact that the funds had originated from the worst imaginable source, with the best possible intent.

Suzanne summed up where they were. "This is going to take a lot of time to get ready. We can't do it alone, or we'll risk screwing it up. We're going to need partners, including some of the stronger women's organizations. I'm going to ask Roberto for more startup money, but I think we can get hundreds of donors eventually if we show them a good plan."

Attempting to distract themselves from the pressure, they talked about the election that was then heating up in the US. All four of the group had gleefully emailed Stan a few months earlier when Barack Obama had gotten the nomination, teasing him about his prediction that a black president might not be elected until 2050.

Felicia said, "I've got a great idea. We need a break before we dive again into the deep end of this pool. What do you say we try to connect with the three guys if Obama wins and go to the inauguration? It's history, Suzanne."

Suzanne smiled and said, "A break sounds good. It's been pretty intense lately. Let's send them an invitation right away. Roberto would love to pay for it, I'm sure. I'm getting used to spending Roberto's money. And we can do a quick checkin before our gathering in two years."

In mid-November, three months later, they booked their flight to Washington. They had returned uneventfully to work at HRWR, where both were assigned to processing reports from the field. They talked off and on about their next steps in dealing with the traffickers, but they had both decided to step back from the intensity—and the risks—of what they had been discussing with Roberto, at least for the next few weeks.

They had found that after visiting several sites, they had to take time off to decompress from the secondary trauma they were feeling. Then they figured out, after several trips to different sites, that they could vary their investigations from the sites where things were worst to those where progress was being made. It helped, sometimes, to meet with a group of women and staff who had assembled the ingredients for a good program: staff who knew how to both comfort and challenge women who had been victims, and a location where resources could be pulled together to get jobs for the women and education and therapy for those that had children. The women were not all trafficked; some had been refugees for more than ten years, buffeted by civil wars, climate change that destroyed their crops, or natural disaster that made it impossible for them to return to their homes.

The common lesson, however, was that the good projects were always small, often isolated from each other, and nearly always plagued by a lack of security. When trafficking was their target, which it was for well over half of the sites they visited, they could expect that even the best sites would eventually be threatened and sometimes attacked openly by the local gangs hired by the trafficking syndicates.

And so they tried to disengage, looking forward to the celebration in Washington, wondering what it might mean to the work that lay ahead of them.

January 2009

In Washington, after a lengthy catch-up dinner with Stan and Dolly, the group huddled together in grandstand seats on a bitterly cold January morning on Pennsylvania Avenue. Stan had tried to get tickets closer to the inaugural stands, but he was only able to get two seats, and he and Dolly chose to be with the Lopez group.

The day began before sunrise, and by the time the inauguration itself had been broadcast over loudspeakers at noon, they were fighting near-frostbite conditions.

But the overwhelming, historic waves of celebration of the extraordinary day overcame the cold. Even the incessant repetition of the Chaka Khan version of *Tell Me Somethin' Good*, which seemed to come blaring out of the loudspeakers every fifteen minutes or so, could not dampen their enthusiasm. The bands marched by, the military units followed, and then, when the new President and his wife came walking behind their limousine, there were few dry eyes among the Western alums, as they tried to grasp how profoundly their country had, for at least the next four years, chosen a new course.

Each of them had lost a layer or more of their naiveté, and they were learning how cruel the world can be. But for a shining moment that January in 2009, they felt the inspiration earlier generations had felt in the early 1960's. And they were glad they had felt it together.

Felicia 2005–2010

March 2009

Two months after their return from Washington, Suzanne came back to the apartment and found Felicia sitting on the floor with tears running down her face. She dropped her briefcase and sat down beside her.

"What is it? Why are you crying?"

"It's my *nonna*—my grandma. She's dying, and she wants to go to Italy to die there in her village. They tried to talk her out of it, but she thinks she can fly and wants to be there at the end." She looked over at Suzanne, sobbing. "I have to go be with her. I don't know how long it will take, but I have to be with her. She..." and then she couldn't go on, and broke down. Finally she got out the words "She always let me sing to her, and maybe I can make her comfortable. I *have* to go. She's the only one in our whole damned family that cared about me."

"Of course you'll go. Let's book it now."

After a week, Suzanne called Felicia, asking when she answered the phone if it was a good time.

"Yes, she's sleeping. I'm so glad you called. I've started to give you a call several times, but it has been a little crazy getting nursing care for her during the day and talking to her doctors—my Italian is all coming back, Suzanne. It's what I used when I'd talk with her, and somehow it's all just flowing into me when I'm with her."

"How is she doing?"

"It's going to be only a few weeks, I think. She had advanced cancer, all over now. She takes painkillers for it but it has been rough." She sobbed a little. "I've had to take care of her, Suzanne, just like she took care of me—diapering her and making her comfortable, tucking her in at night. It feels so good. But it is so sad."

She went on, "I downloaded a lot of the music she loved, operas and Vivaldi. She gave me all of that, Suzanne. I wouldn't know an opera from an onion without her. She gave me such a gift." She sniffled. "She asks me to sing to her every night, and I just love it. I haven't sung so much since I left home."

"It's good for you, sweetie. You know we all told you that it's good for you. And it must be so soothing for her to hear you again."

"I have to tell you, there is this perfect song—not opera, but a popular Italian song that Andrea Bocelli sings. *Con te partiro.* The translation is…" and then she couldn't talk over her sobbing. Finally she said "It's called *Time to Say Goodbye.* She loves when I sing it."

She was quiet for a moment and then added, "I've been talking to Jeremy. He has been so great about writing and calling when he can. He is so comforting—none of the 'happy in heaven' stuff, but just letting me talk about her life and what she has meant to me. She's the only family I have now—except for you guys."

Suzanne said, "Is there anything I can do? Do you need anything?"

"I'm OK for now. I'll let you know if I need help. Roberto heard from Jeremy and, as usual, he sent me some money without my asking for it. So I'm OK for now."

Suzanne said, as gently as she could, "You'll always have family, sweetie. You know that. Keep us posted."

Two weeks later, Felicia's grandmother died peacefully in her sleep, with Felicia at her bedside. Suzanne flew over for the funeral, which was a quiet ceremony in the Catholic church where Grandma Fiori had been baptized eighty years before. Suzanne stayed with Felicia as she disposed of her grandmother's possessions, giving most of them to her church.

Over a meal of risotto and wine, the two of them talked about Felicia's grandmother.

Felicia said, "You know what her last words were to me? She whispered '*Cantare, carissima.*' Sing, dear one. She told me to sing. I'm still trying to figure out what that means. But you know what? I'm going to stay here in the village for a while. People who knew her have been so great. And it turns out I have some cousins here. And somehow they aren't the jerks my own family turned out to be. So I'm going to hang around for a while. Take some bereavement leave and just hang out here. Her other kids—the ones who stayed here—have plenty of room and they've asked me to stay with them."

"Good idea. You need some rest. It's been a tough few weeks, I guess."

"Yes, but it was wonderful, too. We told all the old stories, the good stories. I tried to explain to her what we are trying to do with the work—what the Lopez class and all of you guys mean to me. I think she understood some of it."

She laughed, and said, "At one point she said, translating loosely— 'give it to those bastards.' She knew what we were fighting for, and she approved of it."

She continued, watching Suzanne. "I really feel different here. I feel some of my roots—she made me feel it, watching her with the people from the village who knew her and her family gathering around. I want to just bask in that for a while. And then, I don't know."

She paused, and Suzanne could tell she was concerned about her reaction. "You know there's an anti-trafficking group that I think works here in Italy—La Strada? It means the street. They're based in Amsterdam, but they work all over Europe, and have annual conferences on trafficking. I may see if they have some openings."

"I'm going to miss you, happy flower. But this is a good place, for now. You take it easy, and see if you can make some connections while you're here."

Felicia said, "Suzanne, there are thousands of people, mostly women but many men as well, who work in anti-trafficking organizations. When we say their efforts are ineffective, we're putting down all their work for many years. We need to be careful not to sound as if two women from the US have appointed themselves to lead the charge. It helps that we're working in Europe now, but we've got to be more broadly based. If we're going to organize on an international basis, we need to get some women involved from some of these other organizations—in Europe, Asia, and Latin America as well as North America. So maybe I can help with that part over here."

Suzanne didn't answer her, thinking how to approach a sensitive subject. Then she said, "Felicia, honey, I know you don't want to talk about this, but listen. The one thing you love is the one thing you're resisting most. Why don't you do something connected with the music? You're so good and you really could go someplace with that voice."

Felicia was quiet. Slowly, she said, "Maybe you're right, I don't know. But…the thing about the music…"she started to sniffle a little, "is that it's always seemed to me that it's supposed to be shared. The music is for someone else to listen to, *with* me, or to listen *to* me. And I just never had anyone special who cared about it, or who I even wanted to share it with. Only my *nonna*."

Suzanne smiled. "Then you just have to find the right person to share it with."

Felicia laughed. "Sure, why didn't I think about that? Simon Rattle and Esa-Pekka Salonen are out there and I should just call them up and ask them to come listen to music with me."

"Seriously, Felicia. You should think about how the Lopez agenda and your music stuff could fit together."

And as they turned to dinner and other conversation, Felicia began to tuck away the idea of making the music part of her mission. She had no idea how to do that, but it seemed to make some sense to try.

Felicia had worked hard at her assignments at HRWR, and she enjoyed traveling with Suzanne and then with some of the rest of the staff. But she had often felt that something was missing. The attack on Suzanne had clearly given Suzanne a new sense of mission, and even though she had worked hard to lay out the options with Suzanne, she knew that she was not going to be able to go all the way down that path. And she also knew that getting adjusted to a new location was going to be difficult. She decided to call Jeremy to check in.

Jeremy was glad to hear from her. They talked for a long time, trading stories about work, talking about the differences between living in New York and London. She brought him up to date on her grandmother's death and her re-location to Italy, and Jeremy marveled at her courage in making the move. She probed a little about his private life, which he parried by saying "I had a date a year ago, but it was with a nun."

Encouraged by her laugh, he said "Now don't yell at me, OK. But I thought of you when I heard this. I was talking to some of the therapy people in one of our churches here in New York. They work a lot with street people and former prisoners. And they've been trying a new kind of therapy—music therapy, they called it. They have choirs, and some people play instruments. Seems like there's a whole national organization that works on this kind of therapy, and you can get degrees in it and everything. So I thought of you."

She was quiet. Jeremy, nervously, said, "You getting ready to explode? I know you never liked to talk about your music."

"No." More quietly than he had ever heard Felicia talk, she said. "No, I wasn't going to yell at you. I was just thinking about what you said. Suzanne said something just like it. Thanks, Jer, thanks a lot. I'm going to look into that. Thanks!" And she hung up.

After Suzanne returned to London, Felicia talked with the coordinators of La Strada who were in Amsterdam. When they heard her background, they invited her to meet with them. She traveled by train to Amsterdam, and had two days of meeting with the La Strada staff. They had no offices in Italy, but were anxious to involve Felicia in their work and were fine with her remaining in Italy, because the migration issues from Africa were worsening in Italy. She agreed to an initially part-time role, and returned to Florence to set up an office with an attached apartment, using some of Roberto's money and a small grant from La Strada.

She ended up working with a survivors' shelter in Calabria, among women who had been trafficked from Africa and others who had been rescued from brothels throughout Italy. About half of the women had children with them. The group spoke six or seven different languages, but most of them knew some English, and others had picked up enough Italian that Felicia could communicate with them by going back and forth between the two languages.

The La Strada group was trying to get these women to testify against their traffickers and pimps. They had found some judges who seemed likely to rule for convictions, and they had lined up attorneys to prosecute the cases. But the women were mostly reluctant, exhausted by their months of travel and sex work, frightened of the threats that had been made against them and their families. Day after day Felicia and the other women operating the shelter tried to coax the women to testify, but it was slow going.

One day Felicia decided to conclude a therapy session with a viewing of the movie *The Shawshank Redemption*. When she got to the scene where an inmate plays a Mozart aria over the prison loudspeaker, some of the women asked her to stop the video and run that scene again.

The group was visibly moved by the scene, and Felicia went back to her quarters at the shelter wondering what their reaction meant.

The next day she asked the women if they would like to learn to sing some songs. Only a dozen or so of the group of thirty agreed, so she began working with that group, playing a beat-up electric organ and choosing a few songs she could pick out herself by sound. The first song they tried was "Climb Every Mountain" from *Sound of Music*. She found a version of the song that she could download from the internet, and played it for them several times.

She typed up the words in English, and practiced with the group, working apart from the other women. After a week, she asked the full group if they wanted to hear the results. There were enough nods that she told the singers they had a performance scheduled for the next day. Some of them protested, saying they weren't ready, but Felicia offered them the bribe of an extra dessert, plus the chance to skip a therapy session, and that kept the group intact.

What happened was beyond her imagination. As the group began singing, the listeners fell totally silent. The group was mostly on-key, helped considerably by a former prostitute from Albania who had a perfect soprano voice. When they concluded, the hush in the room lasted several seconds, and then the women began clapping and shouting in each of their languages.

Felicia had her choir.

She called Suzanne, talking so fast about what had happened that Suzanne had to slow her down and tell her to start over again. "Suzanne, they were amazing! Some of them have never sung in a group before— never. And the others listening to them were quieter than I've ever heard them. Usually there's someone chattering away in group in their own languages, because they can't really follow what I'm saying. But they were completely still."

"See—you were given this gift and now you're sharing it. Good for you, Felicia."

"Suzanne, I had this awakening when I went back to my room after it was over. All the time I've been here, we've been working trying to get these women to testify—to hold their traffickers accountable. But Suzanne, they don't trust us, and they don't trust the court system here at all. If I can win their trust—the accountability stuff follows! I never got that before. They were great at the song, and they *knew* they were great. For some of them, it's the first time someone counted on them to come through—and they did."

Suzanne said, "I wonder if there are any other shelters that are trying that approach. Let me see if I can do a survey among the groups we work with. Maybe there are others who are trying it."

"That would be great. I'll ask the La Strada people in Amsterdam. I feel so great about this, Suzanne. It's like my *nonna* left me this gift, and now it's part of my work."

A few weeks later, Felicia decided that songs about slavery might be able to draw out even more feeling from the group, since many of them had been virtual slaves themselves.

And so she carefully explained to her choir the chorus from *Nabucco*, the *Va pensiero* scene, and why the Hebrew slaves were singing it in their exile in Babylon. She showed them a moving video of the chorus singing it in the opera as performed in New York. She added the song "Going Home," Dvorak's great melody from his New World Symphony, and the spiritual "Nobody Knows the Trouble I've Seen."

She briefed the camp director on what she was doing, and asked if she could make a video of the women singing these songs and others. She promised that she would blur any of the faces of women who did not want to appear in the video. But she said she thought it could be a very effective fund-raising tool, publicizing the slavery inherent in trafficking and showing women who had recovered from its worst harm.

And as she conducted them, Felicia loved watching their faces as they sang. Some were still expressionless, trapped within their trauma, not yet daring to let the emotion of the soaring music lift them out of their pain. But for others, Felicia watched the joy win out, bringing first a flicker of a smile as they sang, then freeing them up to full smiles, as they heard the passion of the composer, echoing their own slow-growing comfort in the safety they felt, surrounded by their friends and fellow-sufferers. They were all women who had borne a common grief and were now finally able to also share their pride in lifting up their voices as a communal offering.

They made the video, with some funding support from Roberto and captions translating the lyrics in multiple languages. They offered it free to all NGOs that worked on anti-trafficking efforts. It turned out to be the most effective fund-raising tool ever produced by any NGO in that field. All the talk about trafficking defined as modern slavery was given far greater power by the faces and voices of the former victims singing songs by and about slaves, but singing triumphantly and with pride.

Roberto 2005-2010

After returning from his session in New York with the rest of the group, Roberto took stock of what his next moves might be. He had loved being able to help his friends, which had given him the same satisfaction he'd gotten from helping his own family. He wondered if he would make a good philanthropist in the mode of Bill Gates and other emperors of the software world who had begun funding charitable programs after assembling their fortunes. His suspicion, however, was that he would miss the online predatory activities that gave him such a charge—and that he might be able to do as much good in that arena as he could as a funder.

He knew there was at least one missing piece in his life on the romance front. He continued his aesthetic interest in women, but the tech world he moved in was not proving to be a good venue for meeting permanent or even semi-permanent women. His social life tended to be among tech types in his former firm and people that he met through his occasional consulting. He knew he had not yet found the balance he sought between a woman who understood his passion for his work and the Lopez agenda—and who had the other kind of passion as well, ideally in abundance. But he kept looking, and hoping.

He maintained his Eagle Rock office as a base of operations, but moved around from that headquarters. Checking in on his friends from the Lopez group by phone from time to time, he resisted the temptation to reach into their online lives.

In one of their phone calls, Stan asked him point-blank, "So are you watching us through your long cyber-tentacles much these days, Roberto?"

He answered truthfully, "No, I draw the line short of finding out what kind of books you guys buy and what's in your bank balance. Just seems like a good idea to respect my friends' privacy."

"Good for you. I have a strong sense that you could crawl pretty far into our affairs if you wanted, and I appreciate your restraint. I'm sure the rest of them do, too."

As he carefully considered his options in supporting anti-trafficking efforts, he stayed in loose contact with a few of his former associates in

Treasury, keeping current as much as he could from outside with their growing ability to monitor and intercept financial transactions. Felicia and Suzanne had updated him on their use of the funds he'd transferred to them after Suzanne's attack. They explained that they had given some of the money to the agencies they were working with, paying for some their travel to hot spots in trafficking which their agencies were unable to support. At one point he sent them both messages asking them to let him know if they needed additional funding to ensure that they had adequate security for these trips.

But for the time being, he stayed away from any further taps on the cartels' funds, focusing instead on the groups known to be primarily involved in human trafficking. He monitored court proceedings any time traffickers were arrested, scanning the reports for indications of which of the groups were involved in trafficking children. He continued his probes of the southern border trafficking groups. He made a few small trial taps on their funds, continuing to leave marks that suggested another trafficking group had done it, in an attempt to cover his own tracks and to pump up their rivalries with each other.

He experimented with GPS software, some drones he had bought from a federal contractor who worked with the Defense Advanced Research Projects Agency, and facial recognition tools as a way of tracking specific couriers who appeared to be the money contacts for the traffickers. He was able to follow some of them in and out of Caracas and Switzerland where he suspected they were making money drops. As a test, he sent an anonymous tip to TSA when he thought he had detected a courier who was using false-bottom suitcases, and actually saw the courier getting arrested on an airport security videocam he had accessed. He talked with Suzanne about the broad outlines of what he was doing, telling her that in a $32 billion business—which is what trafficking and smuggling had become—there were bound to be some cracks in the system.

His chartings of the financial dealings of these groups continued to grow, and he wondered often if there were a way he could share the data with the federal agencies without their becoming aware of his own role.

So during his visit to Washington for the inauguration, he spent one-on-one time with Stan, explaining carefully that he was trying to help Suzanne and Felicia with their anti-trafficking work. He also said that he had been able to pick up "some traces of the traffickers' financial transactions" based on his experience at Treasury.

"Stan, international crime needs international banking. They've got to move money from where they make it to where they can keep it safe and buy what they need to grow and protect themselves. So from the 1990s on, through the Patriot Act in 2001 and the big changes in Treasury in the next decade after the Act, the government has been trying to keep up with the different schemes to move money around. Bitcoin, Liberty Reserve, the Silk Road, banks in Cyprus, Costa Rica, Hong Kong—this arms race keeps going on between the bad guys and the agencies that are trying to track their money. Dirty money can buy very sophisticated ways of moving money and keeping it secret, and penetrating those methods has gotten harder, even as the US and others have thrown more and more resources into the war. That's the war I'm watching from the edges."

Stan asked, "How does that work? And how dangerous is it for you?"

Roberto, with his usual air of confidence said, "Not very. They have thousands of people working for them, these gangs. Guys in the jungle, guys in the cities, guys along the smuggling routes. They have guys flying planes and driving trucks. And all I need is one lazy guy who sends money to the wrong place at the wrong time, and I get a ping."

"And you think you can beat them."

"I don't have to beat them. I just have to find a crack in the walls around the gangs and their agents. You use other servers, other IP addresses. There are software fixes where you are basically going into a place on the internet where things are so scrambled no one knows who anyone else is—totally anonymous. It's the dark side of the Internet, which some people say is ten times larger than the Internet we use. But what I saw in Treasury was how those hideouts can be broken down, piece by piece, until you can find who's behind it. The Pentagon was able to trace totally anonymous hackers to a specific building in Beijing, so they knew exactly who the hackers were."

"What keeps them from finding out who came in through the crack?"

"There's no total guarantee, Stan. But I'm pretty good at covering my tracks. It shouldn't be a problem. So who do you think I can talk to about what I'm mapping out?"

Stan suggested a few contacts at Justice that he had met, and told Roberto to be careful. He said he would.

But for the first time, Stan could hear a note of something other than total confidence in Roberto's voice, and he filed it away for future discussion.

Roberto was careful not to tell his beneficiaries whether the money he was sending them was from the licit or illicit side of his ledgers. After the original hit on the traffickers following the attack on Suzanne, he never specified the source of the funds he donated—and they never asked. Suzanne, however, took some comfort in knowing that her efforts came at least in part from the taps on the traffickers. But she never revealed that to any of her other backers, for fear it might endanger Roberto.

There was one exception to Roberto's rule of non-disclosure. Early on, he had told Stan that his support for Stan's campaigns would always come from his software earnings, which were in separate accounts. His support for Stan came through his donations to a political action committee. Both of them knew that Stan's career would be over if he were accused of receiving funds from illegal activities conducted by a college classmate, even though the funds originated with criminal activities. "Payback hacking" had received some attention from Congress after several incidents of foreign nations' penetration of public and private US-based networks, notably by China and North Korea. The US—or its contractors—had counter-attacked without admitting it. But that kind of aggressive counter-strike was not yet public policy, as Stan and Roberto both knew.

Roberto had decided to diversify, venturing into non-financial probes, trying to piece together what US and international agencies were and weren't doing about the Lopez agenda. He began with some tentative probes into federal agencies' data bases. He knew he was moving into Snowden-Manning territory, which meant that many of the easier access points to government documents were more tightly closed off than they had once been. But he took it as another challenge, cautiously contacting others on the fringe of the hacker community who had targeted US agencies. He also went after the UN agencies, where he knew that many initiatives proposed by staff had been blocked by national governments that feared prosecution or publicity.

But as he read more and more about the different forms of child abuse, he realized that private multinational firms were often behind the issues of child labor that affected hundreds of millions of children. And when he got into those files, he was amazed at how much information existed inside global corporations' personnel files that proved that those companies knew far more about their foreign contractors' use of child labor than they ever admitted in public. He found corporate legal staff memos explaining carefully how to deny knowledge of contractor practices in hiring children in order to avoid liability and unfavorable publicity. Several of the largest retailers in the US were implicated, most of which had signed and posted on their websites fair labor standards which the internal memos revealed to be complete fiction.

He began cautiously extracting information on contractors' use of children in their manufacturing plants, especially in textiles and agriculture. Through a false front he provided the information to an advocacy group which was able to verify the data from their own sources, once they knew where it was hidden in corporate information bases. A year later, he was pleased to read about International Labor Organization and US Department of Labor investigations of the firms he had targeted.

Back home in California, Roberto spent time with his family, watching his parents' aging with concern. His sisters now had growing families of their own, and as much as he could with his own travel schedule, he played the role of doting uncle for his three nieces and his nephew. He tried not to show up his sisters' husbands, but could not resist buying the children gifts for their birthdays and Christmas and getting them annual passes for Disneyland and Universal Studios. He set up trust funds for each of the children, telling his sisters only that he had begun some college savings accounts to reduce the pressure he knew they felt.

His family still did not understand what he really did for a living, other than working with computers, but they welcomed his generosity.

They knew that whatever he did, he was very good at it. And all of them, with varying amounts of subtlety—least of all with his mother and sisters—urged him to find a girl and settle down. In the abstract, he agreed with them.

He'd met a few women who were programmers in his work with other firms, and some who worked on the marketing side. Trying to avoid stereotypes, he still found the first group to be hopelessly tech-oriented and the second to be invariably chatty Kathy types who wanted to take about "awesome software" more than gruesome harm done to kids. When he ventured outside the boundaries of the software/hardware environs, he quickly found how incomprehensible his work was to most tall blondes. He even varied his ideal type, but the short redheads and brunettes were no better. He gave up his quest for months on end, and then found his yearning for female company was distracting him. So he launched new searches, but always with frustrating results.

Sinaloa 2008

The bookkeeper, Domingo Ruiz, sat in a nondescript office facing an oversized monitor connected to a late-model desktop. He peered at a spreadsheet, sitting motionless with a quizzical look on his face. Then he turned to the door and called out, "Carlos—come in here."

The younger professional came in and sat down in the chair next to the desk.

"Look at this." He pointed to a row of figures that had been highlighted in yellow. "We made a deposit in the Arizona bank, moved it through the three ghost cutouts, and here it is over in the bank in the Caymans. But look—there's $10,000 missing."

Carlos followed the row of figures, and then said, "Yes. Something happened."

"No shit, something happened." He sat back, still looking at the spreadsheet. "The Zetas used to use that same bank. I wonder if the Zetas are trying to skim the cream off our coffee."

"Sir, you said last week they didn't have the brains to pick their nose."

"True. But maybe they have the brains to hire someone who can pick our pocket." He turned to face Carlos. "I want you to trace every step of these transactions. See if you can find any tracks left in our accounts. Before I pass this up to El Jefe, I want to be able to tell him what we think may have happened."

"Yes, sir. I'll get right to it."

As Carlos left the room, the bookkeeper, whose name was Domingo Ruiz, murmured to himself. "Pinche Zetas. Was it you? Or someone pretending to be you?"

PART FIVE

The 2010 Gathering: Florence

Although they had all seen each other in Washington at the inauguration in January 2009, the Lopez group were all looking forward to their meeting in Italy. With Felicia based there, the original plan to meet in Italy made even more sense. The other four had never been to Italy, and they planned a combination of tourism and time in a villa that Roberto rented outside Florence. After some negotiations, they agreed to Roberto's insistence that they rent a private jet that would pick up Stan and Jeremy in Washington, stop off to collect Suzanne in London, and fly to Florence.

They arrived in May, just as the tourist hordes were building up. Felicia had arranged a leisurely tourist schedule for them, and they saw all the main attractions: the Ponte Vecchio—the old bridge that was the most famous bridge in Italy, the Pitti Palace, the Medici Palace, Santa Croce Cathedral, the Uffizi Museum, and the Cathedral of Santa Maria del Fiori with its amazing Duomo, the classic landmark of Florence. Felicia showed them where Savonarola had held the "bonfire of the vanities" in 1497, and also where the arch-conservative friar had himself been burned at the stake when the Medici and the papacy returned to power in Florence.

Jeremy had done some reading in Florence guidebooks, and he insisted that they walk out on the Ponte Vecchio to see something. He looked around on the wall at roughly the mid-point of the bridge, and then he pointed out to a plaque and said "There—there it is. That plaque tells how the German general in charge of blowing up all the bridges when the Nazis were retreating decided to save this one because it was so historical. Martin Wolf—that was his name. See—even the Germans sometimes knew how to do the right thing."

And Felicia had cried only once, when she walked into Santa Croce and heard the organ playing softly. She sat in a chair in the back of the section reserved for worshippers, while the others quietly walked through the cathedral, marveling at the tombs and memorials to Michelangelo, Machiavelli, Dante, Galileo, and, over in a corner of the courtyard, a plaque honoring Florence Nightingale, who was born in Florence and who is credited with founding the nursing profession based on her work in the Crimean War.

At the end of two days they gathered for dinner at an outdoor restaurant on the Piazza della Signoria. The sunlight was fading on the Duomo, the church bells had just rung 6 o'clock, and they settled their weary bodies into their chairs, with predictable, but colorful accordion and violin music playing behind them on the piazza.

Stan said, "What a day! Felicia, you are a great guide. And again, Roberto, our thanks for your gracious support for our travels. When I start out on 'congdels,' as my bosses call congressional delegations, I doubt I'll ever have as enjoyable a day or such fine companions."

He added, "I am prepared to forgive Italy everything—the inefficiencies, the occasional ripoffs in souvenir stores, the rudeness of some of the waiters. I forgive all of it, for the sake of the art, the architecture, the music, and the landscape. What a beautiful country."

"My pleasure," said Roberto. Turning to Jeremy, he asked, "Jer, have you seen enough churches these past two days?"

"And how," said Jeremy. "I can't help but notice the beggars outside each of these gold-encrusted cathedrals, however."

Felicia said, "Some of them are real, and some of them are very well-off, especially in the summer months when they make out so well with the crowds."

Suzanne was quiet, as usual, and then she said, "This has been such a good time seeing you all. I hadn't realized how much I missed you, even though we saw each other in Washington last year at the inauguration. Thank God the weather here is nicer. London can be so dreary sometimes."

Roberto asked, carefully, "How are you feeling, Suzanne? You had a rough time there for a while, and we didn't have much chance to talk about it in Washington."

She replied, "I'm fine. Your help, as always, was perfectly timed. And my nurse here," looking at Felicia, "was very skilled." Then she changed the subject, asking "How are we going to do our updates? We've been out of Western for ten years now, and we've all been busy."

Felicia jumped back into the conversation and said, "Why don't we wait until we're back at the villa where we can take our time? I'm not sure I want to compete with those accordions. And I have a million questions for all of you."

Roberto said, "I'm sure you do, as always, happy flower."

So they enjoyed the dinner, the wine, the music, and each other. And Suzanne noted that Felicia had delayed the lively exchange they were likely to have.

They took Roberto's rented car back to the villa, with Jeremy serving as the designated driver. Jeremy tended to be more careful than the others when around alcohol, which was based, he said, on his parents' history. He didn't say that he worried about the others driving—but he did.

The next day, the group sorted itself out into the early risers—Stan and Jeremy, the mid-range crowd—Felicia and Suzanne, and the late-comer—Roberto. By 10 they had moved through their breakfast of Italian espresso, prosciutto, croissants, and parmesan cheese, with juice from blood oranges. They casually arranged themselves in the easy chairs and on the couch in the large living room that faced large windows looking out onto a vineyard that stretched for several acres in front of the villa.

Stan said, "Felicia, you're usually our mistress of ceremonies. Take over."

"Yes, Senator. I propose we each take turns telling what we've been doing and then open it up for the usual free-for-all."

They agreed, and spent the next two hours telling each other the high and low points of their work. Jeremy talked about his travels and the minutia of administrative work, which turned out to be the difference between kids getting fed and local workers getting trained so they could replace contractors from developed nations. His low points included beginning to run into church bureaucrats who were resisting his inquiries about screening child care workers for abuse charges.

Roberto was somewhat veiled, as usual, but explained that he had been working with NGOs that had not been measuring the results of their work as often as they counted those "served." He also reported how his investments were doing and the real estate he had been able to purchase in California—some of which included group homes for formerly trafficked children from the foster care systems in the Western states. He also mentioned what he called "cyberinvestigations" into the banking practices of drug traffickers. No one asked him to explain it further.

Stan talked about his work on the Foreign Affairs committee staff, and went on to say, "You work your butt off and you run into these incompetents and the egomaniacs. And you start to give up on it. And then you run into someone who is so clear in their head and so pure of heart and is doing such good work—it just stops you in your tracks. And then you ask yourself who am I to go around judging these people? Some of them, at least, are making a difference. Maybe they haven't yet 'scaled up,' in the jargon. But they're making a difference.

"There's this great quote I read somewhere from a guy who was a senator from New Jersey—Bill Bradley, a pretty good senator and a great basketball player for Princeton and then the Knicks in his day. Bradley says to someone that he loves being a senator and being able to pass laws and see something happen. But he only got it half right—you pass laws, but that's only the first chapter. Then you have to make sure it gets enforced by the agencies and doesn't get wiped out in the courts and doesn't get chipped away over the years by the lobbyists. I never forgot that. And so I always look for the landmines that are out there after you pass a law."

Felicia began hesitantly, unlike her usual rush to tell her story. "You all know that I lost my grandma this year, but it meant I was able to come back home, in a way. And you'll all be glad to know—I think— that part of my new job involves singing."

There was surprised applause from everyone, and Roberto said "Excellent, happy flower. We love you, and so will everyone who hears you."

She went on to describe her work with La Strada, touching briefly on "pending plans" that she and Suzanne were making to "branch out" into some new areas next year.

Suzanne had been quiet, listening to the others. When it came her turn, she said "You all know that I had some rough spots two years ago when I was doing some work in refugee camps in Sicily. I don't want to go into it—I was attacked, but it worked out OK in the end, and as I said earlier, Roberto and Felicia came through for me."

She paused, and then said, more deliberately, "As Felicia mentioned, we have some planning under way and when we get further along, we'll want to talk to each of you."

Stan said, "That sounds a bit mysterious. And not much of an update. You want to give us some idea of what you're talking about?"

"Not yet," she answered. "It may involve a big change in our direction, and we need to be sure that we have other organizations that want to work with us."

Roberto said, "All right. Keep us posted, so that we can help if you want it."

Then Suzanne said, "I'd like to go back to what Stan was talking about with the legislation he sees." She turned to Stan. "Does your committee get involved in trafficking issues? Are you able to affect that?"

Stan said, "We're Foreign Affairs, so we have a license to get into pretty much anything a member cares about. And sometimes, even with Congress split along party lines as much as it is, we can get both sides to agree on stronger language. The HIV-AIDS legislation is a good example of what they can do when they get together. Bush pushed it because of the churches," nodding at Jeremy, "and then Obama kept at it. It's really made a difference."

Then he frowned and said, "But with the child protection and trafficking stuff that you all have been working on, we don't do anywhere near as much as we could. The total allocations for child protection aren't even added up—it's just lumped under a catch-all category of social services. So we don't even know what we're spending right now. But it isn't much."

Suzanne nodded and said, "We may want to come and talk with you once we get our new direction fleshed out."

Stan said, "Look forward to it. But I've got to tell you, it's uphill work. If I didn't work on veterans issues—and I don't do it because it's a political cover, I do it because I found out from a family member that the VA isn't doing its job—I'd be in even more trouble. Last year I got a call from one of our biggest contributors. Guy who has worked for us for a long time, who runs a software firm that grew out of some research at the University. He has done very well and has a lot of money. Very generous in his charitable contributions, as well as to our campaigns. And you know what he told me? He had read some of the speeches I've been giving on children's issues and an op ed I wrote for the Congressman. He said 'Stan, you've got to stop talking so much about foreign aid. People are starting to say you care more about kids in Africa and Asia than you do our own kids here in South Carolina.'"

He shook his head, frowning. "There's this gut-level opposition to anything that looks like foreign aid when there are so many needs at home. The state has a high poverty rate, it's 50% in some of the towns in my district. So they say keep the money in this country. They talk about corruption—who are you going to trust to spend our tax money on the right things in those countries? They have no idea that foreign aid is less than 1% of the federal budget—and that counts all the military assistance as well as the people programs."

They were all quiet for a few moments, digesting the wide array of reports and events, while still wondering what Suzanne's new direction meant. Then Jeremy asked, "So how does all this add up? What would Lopez have to say about what we've been doing?"

Roberto said, "Tough question, Jer. My guess would be that she'd be happy that we've all enlisted in the battle for kids who are abused. But she might be wondering what the total effect will be."

Felicia said, "I don't know. I don't want to be Ms. Gloom and Doom, but as much as I love what I'm doing now, I'm not sure things aren't getting worse faster than they're getting better. Suzanne and I talked with an NGO staffer in Geneva last year, and she was pretty pessimistic about the overall results."

Suzanne said, "Why don't we invite Lopez to the next one of these? Get her perspective on the problems, and on how we're doing? Five years is going to go by faster than we think."

Stan said, "Actually, we may be getting together sooner than that. If things fall in place, I may invite all of you to come help me with a little campaign that I'm considering in 2012."

Felicia said "Wow! Is that an announcement?"

"I'm still 'exploring,' as they say, but if all goes well I'm going to go after the second congressional seat in South Carolina that may open up after reapportionment. We get a new seat because of population growth, and that shakes things up a lot. If I go for it, I could use some help."

Roberto said, "Count me and my checkbook in, pal."

"I was hoping for that," Stan said.

The others all pledged their support, and they began talking about the logistics of getting together in 2012 and when Stan's campaign could best use their help.

Felicia asked Jeremy if he wanted to go for a walk with her.

Surprised, he said "Sure."

They started off on a cypress-lined lane winding down the hill where the villa sat. Neither one spoke for a whole, just enjoying the Tuscany countryside.

Then she said, with less assurance than Jeremy had ever heard from Felicia, "I needed to talk with you."

"With me? What about?"

"About Suzanne."

He was quiet. She went on. "I know you have always had deep feelings for her. She knows it too. But she has been wounded, more than once. And I don't think she can be there for you, not in the way you want. That is the first thing I need to tell you."

He was quiet, trying to understand what she was saying. Then he asked "What's the second thing?"

"The second thing is that we are in Italy…"

He interrupted, trying to lighten the moment. "I figured that out, Felicia. But I appreciate the geographic pinpointing."

She giggled, a most un-Felicia-like sound, and went on. "And since we are in Italy, we are near Assisi. And I know enough about you to know that you would love to take a trip to Assisi and be in communion or whatever you do with St. Francis."

"You're right. How did you know that? Oh, you figured it out from my fundie Protestant background."

"Jeremy, you may not know this. But you are the most Catholic Protestant I have ever met. And you should not leave Italy without going to Assisi."

"I agree." He waited for the punch line.

"And so I am offering to take you. You and me. In my family's sturdy little Fiat."

And then a mental haze lifted, and he remembered her sitting at his feet a decade earlier, listening in some of the study group sessions, talking with him in his apartment about his drawing, and a dozen other times when she had shown more interest in him—in him as a person she cared about—than anyone else in his life. And he was speechless.

She misunderstood. "Maybe some other time?"

"No. Now. *Now*." He looked at her, in some ways for the first time, and saw this gorgeous, fully Italian woman who came up to his chin, who was smiling up at him with hope. And he left behind his dream of a life with Suzanne as a distant illusion, and began hoping that he was not just a passing fancy of this woman standing in front of him, whom he had known for so long, but who had just come into his life.

The other three were sitting in the front room of the villa, when the door opened, and Felicia came in and picked up some car keys from a bowl on the front table. They could see Jeremy standing outside the door.

"We're going to Assisi. *Ciao*." And she left.

Stan and Roberto stared after them. Stan said, "What just happened?"

Suzanne smiled and said, "A very good thing. If you feel like it, pray for them."

And two more men were struck speechless that day.

At the end of their day in Assisi, Jeremy and Felicia agreed that the centuries-old hill town had lived up to their expectations. Felicia had been there before, but going with Jeremy was totally different. They saw and felt Assisi together, buoyed up by her having declared herself to him, combined with the aura of St. Francis, who seven centuries before had endowed this hilltop in central Italy with grace and compassion known in few other places in the world.

They went to the basilica, they climbed up the steep streets of the hill town, they saw Sister Clare's burial place, and they saw the hedgework on the lawn of the great cathedral that spelled out PAX in big, green letters. They dealt with the waves of tourists and kitschy shops and streets so narrow that those walking had to duck into storefronts when mini-buses drove by.

And then, on the wall overlooking the lawn of the cathedral, they held hands and looked at each other, and whispered words that bound them together. And each was amazed that it taken so long to connect, but at the same time each knew that they had the rest of their lives to work out their blended futures. And they felt blessed, and in that place, they were.

And as they walked back to their hotel, down a steep street from the cathedral, Felicia looked up at Jeremy and said, "Do you suppose any of those stores sell art supplies?"

Jeremy looked puzzled, and asked "Art supplies? Maybe. But why?"

"So you can draw me, dummy."

And then—and only then—he noticed that the stylish, undeniably Italian sweater she wore was profoundly different from her usual baggy sweat shirt. And he silently gave thanks, remembering all the museums he had walked through in Florence, for the generous curves God had bestowed upon Italian women throughout the ages.

When they got back to the villa, the silent speculation of the other three was instantly confirmed, as they saw the hand-holding couple walk into the house.

Felicia lived up to type, however, by saying "One smart crack out of any of you, and I'll beat you to a pulp."

The only response was from Roberto. "Stay calm and be happy, happy flower."

As they were beginning to move toward leaving, Stan decided to make one more effort to get Suzanne to reveal what she was doing. He suspected at some point that his association with the group and his work on children's issues in Congress might become a problem, and he wanted to have as few surprises as possible.

So he asked Suzanne, as she put her suitcase down by the door, "Suzanne, can't you tell us anything about what you're doing? I'd really like to know if it might affect our work."

Suzanne looked at Stan for a few moments, and then looked over at Jeremy.

"All right. Let me tell you about some of it. Jeremy, do you remember when you talked to Felicia and me at our first gathering about programs for boys and men? You asked us why we were focused only on women. And Felicia and you had a…" she laughed, "a brief, heated exchange."

Felicia groaned. "Why are you reminding me how mean I was to him?"

They laughed, and then Suzanne continued. "I haven't forgotten that. I know some of us—me included—have some long-standing issues with men. But I've been thinking about it. Giving up on 3 or 4 billion people all at once is kind of stupid. And I've had the good fortune," she waved at the group, "to hang out with a few exceptions to the rule, you might say."

Stan said, "Yes, you might."

"So a while ago, Berto," who was smiling quietly throughout her explanation, "led me to some software and hardware people connected with Google who are doing some pretty amazing things with 360-degree headphones. Those headsets that cover your eyes and ears and put you in a virtual reality? We've got some people writing programs for rehabilitating men who have been imprisoned for abusing women. It's all voluntary, but they get time off and a little money if they participate."

"How does it work?" Jeremy asked.

"They're in a total environment inside the headphones. In other testing, people have gotten physically sick if the scene moves too fast, because it's so realistic it can induce dizziness. The program starts out with them being harassed by unseen men, who yell insults at them. Then the harassers come into the scene, and they're big guys, guys at the scale of most men to most women. They come closer, and start pushing the guy wearing the headset. The screen jumps as if they've been shoved. All the time this stream of violent language is coming at them, calling them all kind of names—using their own names. Finally the screen jerks and the guy is grabbed from behind, and virtually raped. Not with any kind of penetration, but with screen movements and sounds in his ear, right behind him, that leave nothing to the imagination."

Felicia gasped and said, "Wow."

Stan said "How well does it work? What are your results?"

Suzanne said, "Too soon to tell. But some guys rip off the headphones and refuse to go on, even with the reduced sentences and the fees. They can't take it."

She paused. "We hope it works. If it doesn't, if there is no successful treatment for male abuse, then we have to accept violence as the answer. We're trying to find an alternative."

Jeremy said, "Obviously we'd all support that, Suzanne. But is there a chance that it might make them more violent, by forcing them back into the emotions in their own life that makes some of them abusive?"

"Some of the psychologists we have working on it—this is all going on in prisons in Europe—are worried about that. We've got an alternative program that doesn't end with rape but with other men—and sometimes women—rescuing the guys who are being attacked. We're going to see which is more effective."

She paused, and then said. "I won't deny it. This power thing is not just a gender thing. I know that. I've felt it. When you can punish someone who has attacked you," she glanced at Felicia and then quickly looked away, "you sort of lose control."

Frowning, she said, "I don't like losing control. But some of our group say that shooting up a bunch of traffickers may be the only answer when they come into camps to harm women and kids. Maybe there's another answer to the problem behind that. Maybe not."

Then her voice got cold, and she looked away from the group. "Otherwise, the logical next step is to start killing or permanently harming men who use the women and children who are enslaved. And that leads to gender wars, which none of us want. Even though we've had a kind of gender war going on for millennia."

She paused again. "We've already had women volunteer to wear suicide vests and take bioweapons into brothels, designed to kill only the patrons. There are bioweapons now that can make men sterile—or worse. We're not there—but some of the women are."

Stan folded his arms said, "Well, that pretty well defines the outer edge of rehab, doesn't it?"

She said, "Yes, it does. So we hope the other stuff works."

Then she asked Stan, "How do *you* interpret responsibility to protect, Stan? Just a bunch of words that we pretended to agree to take seriously?"

"I'm doing all that I can to get those words taken seriously."

"It isn't working, Stan. Your well-meaning centrist ideas never work because they are half-measures. They never put real resources—Pentagon-level resources—behind the rhetoric."

"Let me ask you a question. What would convince you that the government was serious?"

"Like I said, Pentagon-level resources. We're talking about 400 million kids, and right now we are spending about two cents a year to help each of them. Just get it up to a dollar or two, Stan. That would start getting serious."

"You're right. I don't disagree. But there is no way we could get that kind of money without convincing people that it has something to do with terrorism or an epidemic that might come here."

"But Stan—don't you see—some of those 400 million kids are going to blame part of what happened to them on the biggest target they can see—the richest society in history. And they're going to come looking for us. Some people would say we already have an epidemic of angry young men who hate the US. Suicide bombers, drones, and nuclear weapons—put that all together and we are headed for a tragedy."

"There is no way that 400 or even 800 million a year would prevent that from happening."

"No, it wouldn't. But the Marshall plan that revived Europe was 150 billion in today's dollars. Once upon a time we had the guts to fight evil with something besides weapons. It's the old saying, Stan—put your money where your mouth is."

Roberto decided it had gone far enough. "Hey, you two. Enough. You disagree. We get that. You're coming at this from polar opposites, even though you agree on the end results. So let it rest for now."

Suzanne frowned and said, "I'm not sure we do any more." She turned to Stan, and said, in a softer tone. "But I'm sorry I was so strident. I know you're working inside different boundaries than we are. And it remains to be seen whose way works better. We'll need to talk some more to see how that works out. I want to stay in touch with you, Stan."

Then she smiled. "It helps me clarify my thinking."

"Ditto. And thanks for saying that. If we had just one member of the committee who was as clear-headed as you, my life would be a lot easier."

The group drove off to their flights, and Jeremy and Felicia went back to her Florence apartment. It was the summer of 2010.

PART SIX

2010-2015

Stan 2010-2015

After the Italy gathering, Stan came home with renewed enthusiasm for his campaign. The redistricting to create a seventh district was still in difficult negotiations, and looked like it might end up in the courts, but the spotlight on Republican voter suppression efforts was helping his voter registration efforts considerably.

He had made his intention to run clear to his own Congressman, and the media speculation was widespread that he was the leading Democratic candidate if a new district were to be created. He had returned to South Carolina at least twice a month for events in the towns most legislators thought would be in the new district, and his reception was good among all the usual Democratic groups, and better than expected on the Rotary-town hall circuit which was dominated by Republicans.

Stan had developed a riff on fiscal conservatism which aimed at the exact enter of polarized politics about government spending. He gave the set speech to every group he could, condensing it to a 10-minute, Rotary-refined version that Dolly had helped him craft. She listened to him give it in an after-church version at a mostly white Baptist church in January.

After a lukewarm introduction, Stan began by saying, "I want to talk to you about government spending. I know religion and politics are not supposed to mix (inevitably laughter bubbled up on this one) but I do remember the scripture that says '*he who gathers money little by little makes it grow.*' That's from Proverbs, and that makes sense to me.

"Now you know I'm a Democrat, and Democrats sometimes— *sometimes*—support government spending to help others who need a helping hand. Scripture is also pretty clear about that: Jesus said *give to the poor and you will have treasure in heaven.* But I don't read that scripture to mean we need to pay for programs that don't work. And I have to tell you that there are programs that come out of Washington, and even some that come out of state capitols, that just don't work. You probably figured that out for yourself.

"So that leads me to go on a search. You remember the story about Diogenes, the Greek scholar who walked all over Greece looking for an honest man? I am on a similar search. I am looking for a true fiscal conservative.

"Now when I say a fiscal conservative, I don't mean somebody who opposes all government spending. We need police, and a strong military, and health services for our parents and grandparents when they get old. So when I search for a fiscal conservative, I am looking for someone who hates *dumb* government spending. Someone who can tell the difference between dumb spending and smart spending.

"When bridges start to fall down—and about one-third of the bridges in our state don't pass inspection anymore—you fix them. When schools aren't producing kids who can go to college and make enough money to help take care of their parents when they need it—you fix it, with better teachers and better connections to the internet, which is where they keep the libraries now.

"But when programs that are supposed to help kids or grow the economy don't show any results—you stop funding them.

"We introduced a bill last year that will make sense to any of you that have run a business. We said that after a program has run for three years or more, if it can't show results—you stop funding it. Then we said that the lowest-performing ten percent of all programs should be cut each year—with those funds going to the best-performing programs. No new money. Not a dime. Use the money from the worst programs to fund the best ones. It's that simple.

"Now if you're a car dealer, or you run a clothing store, and some lines don't sell year after year—you don't order them anymore, right? That's all we're saying. *Stop funding things that don't work.*

"You'd think a fiscal conservative would love that idea, right? Well, I thought so too. But we couldn't find any of those card-carrying self-declared conservatives who would back that bill. Maybe they were afraid that some of the programs they were quietly in favor of wouldn't be able to pass that test. I don't know. Maybe they were worried that subsidies that go to wealthy agribusinesses in Iowa or oil drillers in Texas wouldn't pass the test of results. I don't know. Some of those conservatives have given speeches—really good speeches—about what they call, in their words, not mine, *corporate welfare*. But we gave them a chance to go after some of that welfare, and they just didn't want to do it. I don't know why, but they didn't.

"But what I do know is that I am still looking for a true fiscal conservative. And maybe you folks could join me in that search.

"Thank you very much."

The speech went over very well. Stan's "searching speech" received some press attention, gaining him useful visibility as a centrist Democrat.

March 2012

The new seat had finally been carved out of a deal between the dominant Republicans and the Democrats. Stan waited until spring of 2012 to send out the call for help to the Lopez group. His primary was looking good, and he knew that the really uphill run was going to be against the Republican who came out of their primary for the new seat. So he asked the group to convene in June in Charleston at the Planters' Inn, enjoying the irony of the location. He was pleased that everyone immediately accepted. As he had expected, Roberto quickly sent him a check to pay for the accommodations and travel.

When the group gathered, they renewed their acquaintance with Dolly, whom they had all met at the inauguration. She was at ease, welcoming their teasing of Stan as a useful corrective to the fawning admiration he usually received. Roberto had brought Stan a large, framed copy of the famous Picasso drawing of Don Quixote with his lance upraised, which Dolly thought was hilarious. The drawing was immediately placed on an easel in the hotel conference room where they were meeting.

"Nice hotel, Stan, but where are the planters?" said Roberto.

"The Yankees ran them off years ago, dude."

The sessions lasted for two days, and the only outsiders who joined them were Stan's chief of staff, his old roommate Bo Ross and his campaign manager, Sue Wellington, a South Carolina native who had been assigned by the Obama campaign to help Stan while running the South Carolina voter registration drive.

Once they had settled in, Roberto began by saying "I need to get a few things clear on the finance side. Forgive me for stepping in, but I've already talked to Sue. She says your budget for the campaign is a little over $2 million. We're doubling that" –cheers and clapping broke out—"and there's more as needed. Thanks to the Koch brothers and Karl Rove, we now have the chance to put in quite a bit of money through national support funding. So I've arranged for some California and Hollywood-based friends to be helpful. There will also be a separate line item to beef up your data processing and analytics team—which look terrific," he added with a nod to Sue, "but could always use some extra help."

Stan had spoken to Bo and Sue, warning them that Roberto would have a few ideas of his own about the analytics, along with the funding to pay for it. Fortunately, neither were turf-minded and welcomed both the cash and the advice.

Roberto had rented an extended RV that had been used by Willie Nelson and his band for a road tour the month before. Its only drawback was that they still found pot stashed all over the RV. Jeremy and Felicia had the master suite, and Roberto and Suzanne each had their own bedrooms. Roberto had equipped the RV with a full set of communications uploads and downloads, along with the predictable cloud-based maps and voting information from throughout the district.

They hired a driver who knew the district well, and tagged along behind Stan to some of his events, but spent most of their time visiting voter registration and turnout sites. Stan had assigned contacts from each of the major towns, and getting to know them and see Stan's campaign through their eyes was a whole new experience for all four of them.

Roberto had met with the national Democratic Party voter analysis gurus and had then gone to work with a team he hired who had all worked in South Carolina elections. They mapped out a turnout campaign that one visiting political operative from Washington called "the most sophisticated turnout plan I've ever seen."

Gradually, as the Lopez group began to understand all the intricate details of the campaign, they caught the excitement of it. Jeremy was the first to put it into words. They were sitting at dinner, the inevitable pizza and beer. They had started their assignments at seven that morning, and had worked all day.

Jeremy said, "This is fascinating work. What we do, in our jobs most of the time, has no finish line. We help one child, twenty children, a thousand children. But there are thousands more. The finish line is invisible, receding from us all the time.

"But this" he gestured at the headquarters office, with maps of the district's cities and towns covering the walls and twenty desktops lit up with data and calendars, "all this ends on November 6. It's over. Stan wins—or he doesn't. It has a finality that's different from anything else we do."

Felicia said, "That's what's so frightening—and so important. We could lose. They could be stupid enough not to see how much better Stan is than that idiot he's running against."

Stan's opponent was a state legislator who had subscribed 100% to the Tea Party agenda. He had called Stan a "left-wing apologist for terrorists," because he had supported Obama's withdrawal from Iraq and Afghanistan.

"It's a war with only one battle," Suzanne said. "Then it's over."

Dolly had joined them. She frowned and said, "Well, over until November 2014, and November 2016, and every two years after that. This one ends and then we have to start getting ready for the next one the day after." Then she smiled. "It's exciting, though. There's no doubt about that."

Roberto asked her, "How do you think he's holding up?"

She said, "Oh, he loves it. It's what he was born to do. Traveling across the district, making speeches, asking for money—he can do it all. He feeds off the admiring masses." Her tone was flat, with a touch of bitterness.

Felicia said, "How about you? How do you like it?"

Dolly said, "I'm glad he's in it. But it can be draining. I go with him to some of the events, and do the adoring wifey thing. I've gotten pretty good at it. But I'll be glad when this one is over."

Roberto said, "You know the last poll we did found that he was behind by 4%. But he's come up from much lower than that, and the trend is headed in the right direction. If we make the turnout targets, he'll take it."

Dolly looked at him and was quiet for a moment. Then she said, "He's going to win. The turnout is going to blow people away. My parents told me the other night that they had never seen college students and high school kids so active in any election in this state. He'll win."

She went on. "You have no idea what it means to him to have you all here. He told me that you all made him feel like he was doing what he was supposed to do—what you all expected him to do from the first. You're very important to him."

She paused, and added, "And you remind me how long he has been thinking about this—how much this is a part of his mission. So thanks. I sometimes need that perspective, in the midst of all the grabbing at me and the idolizing he gets. This is exactly what he is supposed to be doing."

Election Night came, and all four of the group decided to stay in South Carolina and wait for the returns. They had gathered at the campaign headquarters, and watched nervously as city and town results, then county results were posted. Stan's opponent took an early lead, but as the larger cities and towns began to come in, the gap narrowed, and at about 10:30, Stan pulled into the lead amid great cheering by the crowd of nearly 500 supporters. The lead held, and at about 1 am his opponent conceded.

Stan's victory speech thanked everyone imaginable, including his "stalwart friends from Western University in California" and his wife Dolly. As they headed for their planes back to their own work, the four vowed to each other to come back together in 2014 and do it again. They had enjoyed the work, they had enjoyed being together again, and they had loved winning, having learned one of the most important lessons of political campaigns: winning is much, much better than losing.

Before they left, Stan met with all of them for a farewell dinner before he returned to Washington. He thanked them all, and then said, "Dolly told me you all were talking about how an election is an all-at-once thing, and you're right. But what the rest of you are doing is like a campaign without an election. You all have to watch the bottom line, too—not votes, but safe kids. You have to have a clear message—if it gets too complicated, you'll lose supporters. You have to figure out which campaign spending seems to be working and what is wasted or just symbolic—stuff you have to do, but nobody expects it to make a real difference. And in both kinds of campaigns, kids—young people—can make an enormous difference, with their energy, their low tolerance for bullshit when they can figure out what it is, and their enthusiasm. If you can get them on board, they are an antidote to the cynicism that washes across so much of our politics and our foreign aid as well. So keep it up! And thanks again, my friends."

2013-2015

During his first year in Congress, Stan learned a great deal more about Congress than when he worked on its staff. Mostly, he learned what didn't work. And mostly, to his surprise, the problems didn't come on his end of Pennsylvania Avenue but at the other end, among the executive branch agencies.

The well-known polarization of Congress between Democrats and Republicans was a fact. But after a few years of ascendant right-wing Republicans, the rest of Congress had adapted in many ways to the standoff—and to quiet ways of moving around it. In his staff position, Stan had seen that it served both parties' interests to complain about polarization. But with his own instincts towards centrist policies, he found more Republicans than he expected with similar leanings. The difference was that the incentives for visibly staking out centrist ground had lessened. It didn't make occupying that territory any less important—it just made it look worse to the loudest segments of the voting public, the media, and the big funders.

But it was the executive branch agencies that frustrated Stan most. And his resolve to work on global children's problems made the agencies' inertia all the more important—because those issues were easily eclipsed by larger spending and more visible problems.

Stan had read the remarks of a former Clinton aide at a symposium held at the Clinton Library that "the default position of the federal agencies was to do nothing." The charge rang true to Stan, after his years in a staff position and his first year in office.

Stan had assumed, naively, he admitted to himself, that executive agencies would try to be helpful to members of Congress who shared their goals. But his mistake, he realized, was his assumption that executive agencies had goals other than self-preservation. Early in his tenure in Congress he heard references to the civil service attitude that they were the "B team—those who would *be* here after the others moved on." And as a staff person he had realized that making a request on behalf of a congressman was not the earthshaking demand that he had supposed it to be—it was just another request that goes in the in-box.

He also over-estimated the helpfulness of political appointees. With tenure less than the typical member of Congress, with academic posts to return to or the prospects of well-paying jobs in the private or nonprofit sector, those appointees had neither the incentives nor the understanding, in most cases, to provide real leadership. Taking risks was to risk their future positions for ones they held for an average of only two or three years. And so they, too, defaulted to doing little or nothing.

An older Member took Stan aside in his first year and explained what he called the "rule of three years."

He said "You have to ask them three times before they take you seriously. You ask them the first year, they make a note. You ask them, preferably in an appropriations subcommittee hearing the second year, and then they ask somebody else to get the information. And when you ask the third time, they get on it, because they see you are *tenacious*."

He smiled. "We don't have much of that around here—that tenacity—except for trying to get on the TV. And most of these guys," he gestured at the nearly-empty House chamber, "don't have the follow-up smarts to go at it for three years in a row."

The best proof of these tenets came in Stan's efforts to gather information on what the agencies were funding and how well it was working. Stan had studied under a political science professor at Western whose slogans included "the budget is the policy" and "decisions to do nothing are more important than decisions to do something," which was sometimes reframed as "what's not happening matters more than what is." Working from those premises, among others, Stan sought to document total federal spending on child protection.

What came back in response to his repeated queries in advance of the oversight hearings were excuses about how each federal agency was responsible for its own spending and its way of categorizing the purposes of spending. When he shifted his target to the Office of Management and Budget, which was responsible for the entire federal budget, he received a response that they were "working on it," which they refused to put in writing or to give him any estimate of when it would be completed.

In 2013, Stan's subcommittee in Foreign Affairs conducted hearings on the newly created Center for Excellence, at his urging and his Republican colleague, a woman from California who was deeply involved in the international adoption field.

He grilled the senior staff of the Center on their proposal for a "3-6-5" approach—the designation of six countries to implement three priorities for the next five years. The staff were well-qualified, led by a former academic who had excellent credentials in global health—which was where child protection issues were housed in the State Department.

But the Center had such a small budget—and even smaller powers to leverage other agencies' budgets—that its staff spent most of their time in meetings with external agencies pleading for enough funding to make a visible impact beyond their occasional press releases. Off the record, foundation staff told Stan that they were reluctant to put serious, non-token levels of funding into joint ventures with federal agencies. They worried that either domestic politics or international conflicts could call attention to the foundations' roles in sometimes embarrassing ways.

At the same time, anti-trafficking efforts and gender equity, as "priorities" that had at least gotten White House and Secretary-level attention, competed with dozens of other diplomatic and military line items with far more power and resources behind them. When the video *Girl Rising* came out in 2013, a product of CNN, Intel, and

Microsoft founder Paul Allen's Vulcan Productions, Stan arranged for every member of Congress to get a copy, in hopes that at least the gender equity segment of the child protection agenda would benefit from the increased visibility.

The other part of his job, for which Stan was mentally prepared from his staff days—but not fully—was fund-raising. His district was not safe enough to protect him from being targeted by the Republicans, and within six months his seat was already appearing on targeting lists for the 2014 election. Dolly and his finance committee from the 2012 election were resources he could count on, and he met with them monthly, receiving weekly reports from Dolly.

He went back to the district every weekend, adjusting to a Thursday night-Monday morning schedule in South Carolina that fortunately could be done on a direct flight. He had his staff, which had been assembled by Dolly and himself from some of his original Congressman's team, research the ethical boundaries for his accepting flights on private planes from the many South Carolina firms that went in and out of Washington. He even explored military flights which flew in and out of Fort Jackson, Shaw and Charleston Air Force Bases, and Parris Island. By combining these options, he ended up having to pay for only one flight a month on the average.

When he ran for re-election in 2014, Stan won by 5% of the vote in what was otherwise a national Republican sweep.

Once he got to Congress, Stan visited Parris Island at least once a year, finding the visits to be a kind of essential base-touching, reminding himself that a critical part of his constituency was doing things that mattered much more than mall-crawling and debating over which TV reality show to watch.

On his visits, Stan always looked up a drill instructor who had graduated from his high school the year Stan became a freshman. Ernie Jackson was the fastest football player Stan had ever seen in high school. He had served two tours in Iraq, won some medals for a series of lethal battles in Anbar province, and had landed the DI position soon after returning to the States. Stan had talked with him several times as part of his work on the veterans committee, trying to understand what supports were needed for the veterans in his district.

Stan was standing with Jackson watching the fresh recruits running through an obstacle course. He said to Jackson, "I wonder if I could do that today."

Jackson looked at him and said, "Maybe, if you're in shape. But you couldn't do it in my platoon. I'd run your skinny ass off."

"Probably not." He was silent. "I don't regret not serving, I guess. But I sometimes wish I'd had the experience."

Jackson looked at him and smiled. "So you never served? Man, you serve up there in that crazy house. I call that service. You got vets some things they never would have gotten if you hadn't pushed for it. I'm glad you're where you are, Wright."

"Thanks, Ernie. Good reminder."

They watched the recruits some more. Then Stan asked, "How is the race thing playing out these days. Is it as smooth as Defense says?"

"It's never all smooth, Stan, you know that. But it's pretty good. The Latino-black-white stuff is pretty much under control now. There's always somebody who needs somebody else to look down on, though, and we have to break up fights and name-calling from time to time. But it's a hell of a lot more peaceful in here than it is out there," motioning to the gates of the base.

Jackson went on. "People handle it differently. I remember when the Mexicans first came to town, working crops. Sometimes they would come around to the back door when the crops were done, and ask for a handout. Mom always said feed 'em and Dad always said shoo 'em away."

He paused. "Kind of like the whole country, y'know? Different folks had different ideas about those people, I guess."

Stan said, "Yes. Still trying to sort all that out."

Stan had built a strong network while serving on the Congressman's staff, and once elected, he redoubled his efforts. He had stayed in contact with Jeremy, and Stan had hired two former staffers from Jeremy's network who were helpful in working with the more religiously oriented members of Congress.

Within his own office, Stan had a total of five staff who worked on the Lopez agenda. Two of them were funded from his House staffing allowance, and Jeremy had steered him to a family foundation in Seattle that had agreed to support his efforts on trafficking and veterans. The staff included a veteran—a woman who had served as a medic in Afghanistan—and two other women who had worked with UNICEF on internships and met Jeremy while they were in graduate school during those assignments. The two men on his staff were both African-American, from his home district, both possessing strong computer skills which included building a large library of sources for Stan's committee work. They had flown to California for tutoring sessions with Roberto, and Stan suspected that both were learning more about hacking than he wanted to know about, telling them to be sure never to use congressional networks for any "Roberto-type exploring."

Stan met with this team regularly and enjoyed his role as the senior member of the group, teasing the younger staff about their taste in music. He insisted that all five of them watch *The Magnificent Seven*, with the predictable gender split in response, although the veteran said she liked the action scenes, but not the endless talking. They teased him back, at times using another classic line from the movie when they were getting ready to meet with him: *Let us go and ask the Old Man. He will know what to do.*

Roberto and Stan talked at least once a month—on a secure line that Stan had borrowed from the House Intelligence Committee once he explained to them that he had a source who was giving him information on trafficking that needed to be totally confidential. Without revealing his exact targets or methods, Roberto had given Stan valuable information about the movement of cartel and traffickers' profits into banks all over the world. He had also coached Stan in the arcane details of intrusion detection devices, spyware that could watch keystrokes on any computer in the world, and other methods of tracking money and people throughout the Internet. Roberto's help and Stan's staff quickly made him one of the most knowledgeable member s of Congress on cyberterrorism and cybersecurity, which soon became obvious in hearings and informal conversations with agency staff.

Stan was conducting an informational session with State Department staff. Reading from the summary in front of him, Stan said, "A 2011 UN report estimates that the total amount of money in illegal money laundering was $1.6 trillion in 2009. The report admitted that only 1%

of this illegal money flow was detected and prosecuted. It also estimated that illegal drugs represented about a fifth of the total, or over $300 billion."

He looked up. "So the $32 billion estimate for trafficking that has been floating around seems very, very low."

"Congressman, we respect the efforts of the UN agencies to develop these estimates. But they are unreliable in our view."

"All right. What are your estimates?"

Looking only slightly embarrassed, the Assistant Secretary said "We are still compiling them, Congressman."

"Are they likely to be higher or lower than the UN estimates?"

"I can't release that information until our research is complete, sir."

Stan raised his hand over his head and said. "Higher?" He lowered it to the dais he sat behind. "Or lower?"

"Probably lower, sir."

"And why is that?"

"We use different methods than the UN Office."

Stan sat back and then said, "I feel as though I'm extracting a tapeworm here, Mr. Secretary. Very long, very slow, and very messy. Could you be a bit more responsive?"

Stan had been in enough hearings to be able to read the expression on the Assistant Secretary's face. It said, essentially, *We can go through this as long as you want, but I have instructions to give you nothing that can embarrass our agency, and I am going to follow those instructions. So you can embarrass me, but I will not embarrass our agency.*

After three hearings, Stan realized that witnesses, however powerful their second-hand testimony, were no substitute for deeper exposure to the problems of child abuse. So he arranged for a series of videos to be shown to members of the subcommittee and their staff. He had gathered coverage of trafficking, child labor, and child soldier recruitment from the international advocacy groups that worked in each of these areas. He picked a Friday afternoon when he knew most members would be back in their districts, which he knew would guarantee a better-than-average attendance by the staff.

Congressional staff tended to be young, eager beavers in their mid- to late-20s. Some of the outsiders who worked with congressional staff referred to them as "the 12-year-olds," and some of them definitely seemed even younger than they were. But among them were bright, ambitious young professionals who wanted political careers of their own and were always looking for issues that could give their bosses a good spotlight.

The videos were sometimes horrific to watch, and he warned the staffers who showed up that the images and language could be traumatic. He made brief introductory remarks.

"What you're going to see has been compiled from many hours of videotape, collected sometimes at great hazard to those who did the work. Some of the teams doing this work have been attacked by traffickers and brothel owners. But you are going to see and hear a powerful answer to the question 'Why do we do this work?'"

The first video he showed was from the International Justice Mission. It showed a tape of a raid on a brothel in Guatemala City that succeeded in removing eight girls ranging from nine to fifteen years old. The girls looked terrified as the police and IJM staff moved into the front room of the brothel and confronted the owners, who protested as they were being handcuffed that all of the girls were over 18 and said they were only giving massages.

The next part of the video showed three of the girls in a room at the IJM shelter, telling their stories through a translator. With tears and hands sometimes covering their faces, the girls talked about being promised jobs in shops and restaurants in Guatemala City. One girl said, as she sobbed, "My father said I would be able to work in a nice store and send them money. But I think he knew what was going to happen. And he sent me away anyway!"

The IJM staff then came on camera and explained how long they had worked before the raid to make sure that the local police and the judge who would hear the case would follow through on the prosecution and sentencing.

The next videos were of child labor in India, tracking children as young as six as they left the hovels they lived in to go to work in brick-making factories. He could hear gasps from the congressional staffers as the video showed tiny boys lifting the huge bricks and carrying them over to trucks. The narrator said that the estimates of the numbers of children who worked and never attended school in India were as high as 10% of all children 5 to 14 years old.

The final video was focused on child soldiers in Africa. It consisted of excerpts from two recent documentaries that had been collected from underground websites that recruited children, and then followed the young ex-soldiers after they had been rescued and returned to their families—some of whom refused to take them back.

Stan watched with both anguish and gratification as the staffers made rapid notes on the narration. He marveled at the power of pictures to tell the painful stories of children in harm's way. And he gave thanks for the brave videographers, some of whom had risked their own lives to get the pictures of these children.

Stan was back home in South Carolina, relaxing with Dolly and briefing her on his last two weeks. She watched him carefully, trying to decide whether her timing was right. Then she went ahead.

"You have only one problem, big man. You're too perfect—or you seem too perfect to most people."

"You know better, huh?"

She laughed. "Oh, yes. But they don't. Most people are more comfortable with a guy who screws up once in a while. A guy who's human."

"So I'm not human now?" Stan was smiling, but he could hear that she was trying to tell him something, and he didn't want to laugh it off. He'd learned that Dolly's judgment on people—including himself—was extraordinary. After they would come home from a party or some other social gathering, she could sit and point out things that people did and said that he had missed. She had social antennae that were much more acute than his, and it had saved him from several major mistakes in dealing with people in the office. She'd pointed out who was insecure, who was overconfident and who, in her view, was "on the prowl." The latter was a strong signal that she was aware of congressional office sex scandals that had derailed both staff and elected members. And Stan listened.

"Maybe I need a tragic flaw? We studied that in English classes at Western."

"You already have many flaws, big man. And I love all of them, but some are not as lovable to other people." She was silent. And then she said, "Maybe if you limped—an old football injury. Maybe I could shoot you, just a flesh wound, but you could limp."

He looked at her, watching her try not to laugh. "Well, this is a great conversation. From me being too perfect to you needing to shoot me." He yawned, half-acting and half-tired. "I'm going to bed. The guns are all unloaded, anyway."

"One last thought. Serious now, baby. Another thing I'm sure you learned at that fancy California school was the idea of a quest. If you take on a quest—something out of reach that you can't find—maybe that makes you more human. Maybe there's a way to make people understand that those things about kids that you work on are out of reach—and that you'll keep trying, and sometimes failing. Going for things that are out of reach can sometimes look heroic, and sometimes like you're obsessed. But you won't always get what you're going after. And for some people watching you, that's sort of a flaw. Think about it."

"I will. And now I'm going to bed."

"Me too."

Sinaloa 2011

Domingo Ruiz placed a phone call he hated to make, but knew he had to. The call was to Vera Cruz, to a former classmate whom he knew was working for the Zeta cartel, Tomás Gutierrez.

Gutierrez answered and said, "It's not every day I get a call from a fellow financial wizard. To what do I owe this pleasure?"

"Tomás, when we were in accounting school together, we both agreed that if we had to, we would take jobs with whoever could pay the most. You did that, and so did I. I am calling you because one of two things is happening. Either someone with your skills is tampering with our banking channels, or someone with better skills than either of us is jerking us around. So I am asking you, what do you know about this?"

There was a long silence. Then Gutierrez spoke. "Domingo, I have been trying to find the courage to make this same call to you. Someone has been doing the same thing to us, and I wondered if it was you or one of your team."

Ruiz quickly said, "It's not us." He paused, thinking. "So someone is diddling us both. It could be the thieves from the PRI deciding they want a bigger, quieter slice of our profits, the feds in the US Treasury Department, or some free-lancer."

Gutierrez said, "I think we can rule out the first. The PRI is much better at taking bribes than at hiring people who can track money that pays bribes."

"I agree. So that leaves the Treasury trackers or someone who's working on their own. Whoever it is, he's very good. We've tried everything we know how to do, and we can see the money leaving our accounts, but we have no idea how it happens or where it goes."

"Same here." He paused. "I'm glad it's not you, Domingo. Our chief has sworn to kill whoever is doing this."

"Ours also. The amounts are now in the millions. It happens for a few weeks, then it stops for as long as a year or so, then starts up again."

"If I am able to, I will let you know if we discover anything more than what we know now."

"I will do the same. Thank you, Tomás."

Jeremy and Felicia 2010-2015

After Assisi, Jeremy and Felicia took some time by themselves to try to plan their next moves. As much as they now wanted to be together, each cared enough about the other to know how important their work was to each of them. The music now at the heart of Felicia's work had softened and deepened her approach to children and families. And Felicia saw how good Jeremy was at his work with church-related agencies.

By the end of their week together, Jeremy thought he might have a partial solution. He had increasingly worked as liaison between his agency and Catholic Relief Services and other Catholic services agencies. His administrative abilities had gained wide recognition throughout the religious agencies that worked on children's issues, and he had already received invitations to meet with Catholic agencies in Rome and elsewhere in Europe. He called his CEO in New York and arranged a year's posting to the CCS office in Rome.

The election of Pope Francis in 2013 had begun a significant shakeup in the Vatican, which had begun to ripple out to the services agencies as well. The administrative arrangements in some of these agencies were decades old, with few efforts to collect data on the results of programs. Jeremy's standing to address these issues was at first tenuous, but improved considerably after a conference convened by the Vatican at which he was invited to speak on administrative reforms. He was able to take the dry, sometimes bewildering details of managing charitable organizations and infuse them with theology of stewardship and appropriate Scripture in a way few management consultants could do. He could also see that the agency bureaucrats had gotten the message from the top of the Vatican that reform was not negotiable.

At one point Jeremy was told a story about the Pope. During his private meetings, the Pope enjoyed referring to his earlier career, before going into the priesthood, as a bouncer in a bar. A Vatican higher-up said to Jeremy with a cryptic smile, "He keeps talking about how easy it was for him to throw people out of the bar when their time had come."

Jeremy was fascinated by the several paradoxes that came up when he worked with the Vatican agencies. In the US, there was no agency as strong in protection of immigrants' rights as the Catholic bishops. Yet the Church had opposed some segments of the expansion of health care, which affected hundreds of thousands of children. And worst of all, the Vatican had joined with representatives of Islamic countries in opposing UN policy statements on children's rights for fear of diminishing the authority of the family.

As he became more and more familiar with the Catholic constellations of agencies in the US and around the world, Jeremy repeatedly flashed back to his first time at the Wednesday audience of the Pope in St. Peter's Square. Thousands of visitors gathered in the square, and the Pope sat up on the dais—surrounded entirely by men, talking about the work of the Church in service to the world. But away from that dais, around the world, that work was carried out primarily by the women of the church, while men presided. As he began to learn of the work of religious women in anti-trafficking, shelters for victims of domestic violence, and prison work uniting women with their children, Jeremy knew he was beginning to understand who did the real ministry in the church. And he also saw how much work the Pope still had to do—if he wanted to.

They had found a small apartment in Rome near Vatican City, and Felicia had arranged to work in Florence half time and in a Rome-based agency half time. Inspired by the fresco over the door to the UNICEF offices in Florence, Jeremy had begun collecting art with the theme of Jesus and children. He had a copy of Rembrandt's *Receiving Little Children*, and a half dozen other copies of more recent paintings and stained glass windows, which warmed their apartment and made them feel more at home.

They had some difficulty adjusting to the size and pace of Rome. Jeremy could not at first understand the difference between Rome and New York City—both huge, both busy, both plagued by visible and invisible corruption, both containing extremes of poverty and wealth. But Rome had a much deeper sense of itself, given millennia of history rather than a few hundred years. Rome was full of small cars and huge ruins, too many tourists and not enough public restrooms. And restaurants that insisted that the evening meal did not begin until 730 or 8, which were anathema to Jeremy, who was still on early to bed, early to rise time.

While they were in Rome, Felicia insisted that they attend the opera. Jeremy protested that they didn't do opera in Texas, but Felicia said that was all the more reason for him to get exposed to it while they lived in Italy. And she reminded him that he had begun to steal her heart when she found out that he knew the Slave Song from *Nabucco*. He said that was the only opera he had ever been to, and that was only because the church made him go.

She said firmly, "Now *I* am making you go."

She broke him in gently, taking him first to *La Boheme*, telling him they needed to get box seats so she could whisper translations to him. She refused to tell him the plot, telling him that she would take an extra handkerchief. He laughed, and said she should save it for herself.

But when Colline sang *Vecchia Zimarra*, the Coat Song, lamenting the selling of his coat to get money for Mimi's medicine, Jeremy's face was covered with tears, which she shared. And when Mimi died, he was a wreck.

As they walked out, he turned to her, his face still wet, and said, "Why didn't you tell me she dies? How could the music be so *sad*?"

"That's opera, my beloved. Wait until you see the rest of it."

Felicia interpreted for Jeremy in many more than linguistic ways, arranging for his mid-afternoon snacks so that he was not ravenous by dinner, explaining how buses and taxis operated, showing him routes to avoid the wandering hordes of tourists around the Vatican. She tutored him in Italian, which he was sometimes brave enough to attempt in restaurants, to her frequent enjoyment and the befuddlement of waiters.

And their time together was bliss interrupted by work, relieved by more time together. Jeremy accompanied Felicia to Florence once or twice a month and spent the day immersing himself in the city where the Renaissance began. He found two agencies that worked with the poor in Florence and volunteered to work for each of them. He soon found that the staff welcomed his administrative advice as much as his hands-on work with the children.

He also met with the UNICEF staff in Florence and learned what they had been doing to improve the management and oversight of the many UNICEF programs around the world. They were the research arm of the agency, separated from the headquarters staff in New York. But there were a storehouse of research on children's issues, with an international staff that welcomed the chance to interact with a US-based colleague.

In one of their meetings, they were discussing the US response to trafficking and child protection. The UNICEF researcher, a woman named Jessica Burns, asked if they had spent any time reviewing what Congress had done recently on these issues.

Jeremy said, "Yes, we have. Actually a friend of ours is on the congressional staff to one of the committees that works on these issues. He's running for Congress in 2012 and has a good chance to be elected."

"My goodness. I had no idea you had that kind of connection. And you say he understands your work?"

"Yes, he was part of a group we belonged to in our undergraduate days that took a class together on child protection."

"Who was your instructor?"

"Gabriela Lopez."

"From Cuba? Originally from Cuba?"

"Yes."

"I've met her. She lectures in Europe from time to time at our meetings. She's an extraordinary woman. You're very fortunate to have connected with her so early in your careers."

Felicia said, "We know. She influenced all of us. Including Stan Wright, the friend who's running for Congress."

"Well, good luck to him. That would be wonderful to have an advocate at that level. Congress and UNICEF have had some disagreements on adoption policy recently, and it would be marvelous if we had someone to talk with about those issues who could be more...objective."

She explained that international adoptions had decreased substantially in the US after revelations of baby-selling and adoption "mills" that had led to the international agreement embodied in the Hague Convention on Adoption. Some members of Congress had opposed the changes because of their effect on international adoptions in the US.

Jeremy was familiar with these conflicts because some church groups were part of the congressional coalition that favored increased international adoptions. He was also aware that some of the more progressive churches had moved to a position that favored adoption of children in their own countries through church groups who worked with children who could not live with their parents or whose parents were dead.

And Roberto continued to send both of them what he enjoyed calling "travel stipends" that eased their decisions about where to live and how to travel. They had learned that it made Roberto happy when he could help them, and their mild guilt at accepting his money lessened as they realized how much it helped. And they continued not to press him on the exact sources of his support.

Jeremy had made contact with an organization that worked with adolescents in countries where gay and lesbian youth were persecuted, and at their request began discussions with religious organizations that operated youth programs. It turned out to be one of the most disappointing projects he had ever worked with. With the exception of a few of the so-called mainstream denominations—most of which were losing members as the church-going mainstream population began "aging out" of active involvement—he could find no US-based denomination that was willing to sponsor work with these youth.

He came back from one of the meetings and fell on the couch. "Why are religious people so irreligious about homosexuality?"

Felicia smiled and said, "As I recall, your phase for people like that at Western was "judgmental bigots."

"Yes. Today I would probably use more pungent language. These kids are persecuted and beaten unmercifully. But they are invisible to most churches, here and in most of the rest of Europe, too. We finally let them into our armed forces. Maybe Suzanne is right—maybe these kids all need to be in some kind of gay ROTC units."

"Now that's a concept that would get you some real publicity. Why don't you try that idea out on your next fund-raising trip to Texas?"

Felicia stayed in touch with Suzanne, following up on a long conversation they had in London after she returned from Assisi. Felicia said that Jeremy was going to try to stay in Italy and that she was going to spend as much time with him as possible.

"I will work for you from here, but I can't get involved with the security effort."

"Because of Jeremy?" Suzanne asked.

"Not really. We've talked about the Dietrich Bonhoeffer thing—he's sort of an icon for Jeremy. He's talked more than once about Bonhoeffer agreeing to join the conspiracy to kill Hitler, and what you have to do when you know that an evil is so deep you have to commit evil to end it. Although he does still want to talk to you about boys. No, my real reason is that I don't think you need me as much anymore, and I just need to spend time with the music. I can't..." she struggled for words. "I can't make the music work if I'm thinking about hurting people—even if they're the worst people in the world. I just can't balance it out."

"I think I understand," Suzanne said. "And there's a lot you can do from here to stay in touch with the other European groups, and to work on the therapy side of what we're going to be doing."

Suzanne looked at Felicia, and then hugged her tightly. "You need to stay with the music, and with Jeremy. What drives me affects you differently—and that's OK. What is that phrase Jeremy uses—differing gifts? I may be cold and angry a lot of the time, but you are *family*. And I know what's good for you."

She smiled. "And I'll be glad to tell you, as needed."

Jeremy found himself becoming involved in the 2015 revisions of the Millennium Development Goals created by the UN. The goals, originally set in 2000, had set targets for reducing poverty and improving health. A global process involving hundreds of agencies and thousands of participants had developed recommendations for the new MDGs, which had been re-labeled Sustainable Development Goals. Jeremy had also discussed the changes with the UNICEF staff in Florence, who had briefed him on the dozens of proposals for new goals, including formal mention of child protection goals for the first time.

In Washington, Jeremy and Stan met to review the likely recommendations from the US agencies involved in the SDG revisions. In 2012, President Obama had addressed the UN General Assembly and had talked about trafficking as slavery. Legislation focusing primarily on domestic trafficking issues had passed the US Congress in 2014, but no major allocation of resources had yet been made. US allocations for other child protection goals were not significant, although the creation of a new Office of Children in Adversity in 2013 brightened the spotlight on some child protection issues.

When he flew back to New York for a check-in with his agency CEO, Jeremy again raised the possibility of a joint statement with the other denominations on children's issues as a priority for all international religious agencies. Pope Francis had mentioned children in danger in his Christmas message in 2014, and that brief attention, combined with discussions he had held with CRS and Vatican officials, seemed to Jeremy to suggest that an opening existed on the Catholic side of the discussion.

He told his CEO "I think we have an opportunity to go beyond our own general advocacy, sir, to make a unified statement that the UN would have to take seriously. I've had some great conversations with the Vatican charitable staff, and I think they'd respond well to our initiative."

The CEO had a long career in Protestant ministry, and had been close to several major donors in the Southeast who continued to send money to CCS. He frowned and said, "Jeremy, I appreciate what you've done over there with those people. It can't be easy working across the lines like that. But they don't always see things like we do, and I'm leery of getting too close to them in our advocacy efforts. They've had some big disagreements with the President lately on health stuff, and I sure don't want to get in the middle of all that."

"But sir, on trafficking and child protection, they're in total agreement with the President—and with our positions on those issues. Why couldn't we issue a joint statement with them that would aim at the SDG revisions?"

"Son, those are United Nations goals, and we have a lot of donors who still think the UN is run by commies and heathens. You and I know better, but that doesn't make it a great idea to get too far out in front of our donors. I'm afraid you're asking for us to go a bit beyond our comfort area, and I really can't see us doing that."

Leaving New York to return to Rome, Jeremy was seething and as angry as he ever got. *Beyond our comfort area*, he thought. *It's not about our comfort—it's about millions of kids who will never have a moment of comfort in their whole lives.*

When he got back to their apartment, he began talking with Felicia about what it would take to leave CCS and set up his own organization. He tried to explain it to her, saying "I can keep between the lines they've drawn, but they still want to work as a single organization. I think I've grown past that. I want to try to work across the lines and break out of the silo they're stuck in."

He laughed. "Maybe some of your impatience has infected me, love. But I don't want to spend the next ten years inside the box. Time to make our own box." He watched her, carefully. "I know you love it here, and I promise we'll come back every year, whenever you want. But New York is where we need to be now, I think."

She agreed on one condition—that he would ask Jeremy for a start-up grant to make the fund-raising part of the job easier. He quickly agreed to the condition, and they began packing.

Setting up a new agency with a religious identity proved to be fully as difficult as Jeremy had imagined—and then some. He had decided to call the agency "Matthew 19:14," the scripture about Jesus asking his followers to let the children come to him. The obstacle was not just that the field was crowded. He got a recurring response from people he approached for funding and contacts he could use to staff the agency. Funders consistently asked him, in the words of one potential grantmaker, "Why do we need one more religious program office? Why not just merge with one of the existing ones?"

Jeremy didn't want to start out by criticizing the existing agencies, but he tried to explain that the fragmentation of existing agencies was the problem that few of the others were addressing. He proposed an inventory of the largest programs as a way of showing what was and wasn't happening in funding, and how small the current funding was compared with the needs. After several meetings, he was surprised at how low a priority most funders gave to such an inventory. But he finally got some startup money he could combine with Jeremy's initial grant, and he began to set up an office in New York. He expected to be able to hire at least five staff to start with, and began interviewing some of the candidates who had been referred or who had heard about the new agency and expressed interest.

Two months later he was ready to begin operations. He had hired staff from UNICEF and Catholic Charities, including an intern from Western who had heard about his work from Gabriela Lopez and was originally from New York. He and Felicia had moved to Brooklyn—she'd refused to live in Manhattan or Queens—and they had begun to get used to another big city. Happily, it was one they had both lived in during earlier lives.

In another two months they had an inventory of funding for children's protection programs run by religious agencies. The total spending was as small as he had expected. He approached four of the largest agencies, including Catholic Charities, and proposed a small conference to review the results of the inventory. Three of the four agreed—CCS, unsurprisingly, refused.

The meeting was a good beginning, which was all that Jeremy had hoped for at that point. The group agreed that an inventory was valuable, they agreed with the conclusion that the total was too small, and they agreed that they should stay in touch.

Jeremy continued to travel to Rome, as the efforts of the Catholic Church to purge itself of its own abusers grew more intense and caused some backlash among the Catholic press and the bishops appointed by prior popes. Pope Francis remained vigilant on those issues, aided by increasingly vocal nuns and other women in the Church who had formed an auxiliary organization in support of the anti-trafficking efforts of the Church and the its therapeutic components. This, too, brought backlash—along with millions of new and returning members of the Church.

Matthew 19:14 received grant funding from several foundations who made grants to religious organizations, and within a year the staff had expanded to twenty, five of whom were located in Rome. A major project of their second year was an accounting—drawing upon Jeremy's administrative experience—of the proportions of religious donations in the US that went to maintenance of church buildings and staff compared with the funding for programs for children. Jeremy began negotiations with several of the mega-churches, some in Southern California, aiming at creating their own pooled fund for child protection.

In a presentation at a World Council of Churches meeting in London in late 2015, Jeremy gave a speech that reviewed the status of funding for child protection and the work yet undone by ecumenical organizations.

As he was gathering his materials after his speech, he noticed a priest in the audience who was waiting to speak to him. He recognized Father Suarez, whom he had met long ago at a similar meeting, who had predicted a pope from Latin America.

Embracing Suarez, Jeremy said, "And here is the best predictor of papal succession in all the Americas. Congratulations." He invited Suarez to visit him in New York, and he and Felicia had many happy hours with him, finally inviting him to work as an unpaid consultant to the staff of Matthew 19:14. Suarez agreed, and became a key part of the agency's outreach to Catholics.

During their meetings in Rome, Suarez had described his work to try to get the Vatican bureaucracy to move more aggressively in pursuing priests and bishops who had been shielded from any serious responses by the Church to predatory behavior. He had become very discouraged about the initial hopes that the new Pope would take strong action on those issues.

One evening while he was still in Rome after the conference, Jeremy received a call from the Vatican—at least he thought it was the Vatican. A soft voice announced itself as Monsignor Savro, and after telling Jeremy he had heard many wonderful things about his work with CRS and other agencies, he invited Jeremy to have lunch the next day.

"May I ask what this is about?" On half-alert because of the recent meetings with Suarez, he wondered if this was an initial reaction to his being seen with Suarez.

"I'd like to talk to you about some further joint ventures that may be possible for children's relief efforts."

Jeremy agreed to meet him, still wondering what the call was really about.

The next day was raining. Savro had suggested a small trattoria two blocks from the Vatican walls. Putting his umbrella down, Jeremy saw a thin man smiling at him and giving a slight wave toward his table, set as far back in the room as possible.

Jeremy was used to lengthy Italian preludes to food and prepared himself for a mostly circular approach to whatever Savro wanted to talk about. But to his surprise, after they had ordered, Savro touched his arm lightly and said, "I'd like to talk about your meeting with Father Suarez."

Not totally surprised Jeremy cautiously said, "He is an old friend that I met several years ago. We talked about my work and his—and some of the recent problems that he has been trying to deal with. I admire him greatly."

Savro nodded, and said, "As we do. His work with children has been a great blessing." Then he shook his head slightly and said "But sometimes he allows his passion to overcome his discretion. You see, we like to solve these things within our own circle, where all of us understand the stakes and how to fulfill the ultimate mission of the Church. As well-meaning as outsiders can be, they sometimes miss the nuances of what we prefer to handle ourselves."

I'll bet you do, thought Jeremy.

Savro frowned slightly, and his tone changed from calm assurances to something else. "Mr. Boxton, I would advise you to leave these things alone. For an outsider, you have built remarkable credibility with our agencies, for an American who is not even a Catholic. To join Suarez and others who would harm the Church would risk all that you have developed with your hard work and your patience since coming to Rome. There is much that can be done in continuing to build the bridges from your agency to the Church. But that future would all be at risk if you choose to join with those who are belaboring the past."

Then Savro looked at him and all suggestions of softness disappeared. In a voice that Jeremy heard as pure menace, he said, "Leave it alone."

Back in his hotel room, he tried to explain it to Felicia, who was visiting from New York. He found he did not understand enough of it to tell her the full story. Savro's soft-hard-soft shifts were too difficult for him to follow. After an approach that had been nearly opaque, too faintly suggestive of the real subject, he had abruptly changed to a near-threat that Jeremy's work with the Church would be halted.

Was this official Vatican policy—to oppose Suarez and all his allies who were calling for more openness? Or was Savro running a rogue operation to try to pick off Suarez' possible allies one by one?

He wished that he had the full Lopez group around him. Stan would have understood the politics and the intrigue, Roberto would have seen the layers of information that needed to penetrated, and Suzanne would have cut to the heart of the harm that had already been done and would have sensed what was likely in the future.

He lay his head back on the large overstuffed chair that was his favorite place for reading and napping. He closed his eyes, and sighed. Felicia came over behind the chair and began rubbing his temples, humming softly. At first, he did not recognize the tune, but as she kept on humming, he realized it was John Rutter's short song, "Deep Peace," based on a Gaelic prayer. She had found a Youtube version of it with the perfect images to go with the words, and they sometimes played it as a post-dinner form of saying grace.

He murmured "Thank you, love" and his eyes closed. But he could not sleep.

Back in New York, Felicia continued her own balancing act, as she blended her music therapy with support for some of the shelters set up by Suzanne. She and Jeremy took full advantage of the many opportunities to experience religious music in the New York metropolitan region. Their home in Brooklyn became a haven for various music therapy professionals as they passed through New York.

Felicia had developed a special interest in organ music, and announced to Jeremy one day that her new quest would be to visit all of the world's ten largest pipe organs. Fortunately, seven were in the US, five on the East Coast, two in Southern California, and the other three in Milan, Italy, Passau, Germany, and Mexico City. Jeremy organized some of his travel in the next three years around those sites, and Felicia was able to complete her quest over the following decade.

Suzanne-Stan 2011-2014

In early 2011, Suzanne had called Stan from London. She got right to the point. "Stan, I know you're getting ready to run. I want to come over when you think we can be helpful and do whatever you need from us. I'll do door-to-door, I'll call for money—whatever you need. We may not always agree on tactics, but having you in Congress would be a good thing, and I want to help."

Stan said. "Thanks. Why do I think there's a 'but' coming?"

She laughed. "There is. But I'd like to come talk to you now, while you're still in your staff role. I want to bounce some ideas off of you and see if you can help us."

Cautiously, Stan said, "You know I'm just a staff guy. I can't make any decisions without the Chairman and the committee members agreeing to it. And we're in the minority now. So I'll hear you out, but I can't make any guarantees."

"That's all I want—for you to listen. And then we can talk about what's next."

They agreed to meet in Washington in three weeks. Then she asked, "What do you think your chances are?"

Stan said "I'd make it 50-50 right now. Obama is looking good for re-election, and that could help. Can you believe it, Suzanne? We're about to re-elect a black President."

Suzanne said, "And it's not even 2050 yet."

Stan laughed. "I'm never going to live that prediction down with you guys. Hope my political foresight has improved since then."

When she arrived for her meeting, Suzanne began by saying to Stan, "I want to get your reactions to what a group of us have been developing. It's sort of a manifesto—what we think is happening to kids and women and what we think the options are for responding effectively."

"All right. Fire away."

"There are five parts to our manifesto. Let me finish them all before you give me feedback." She took a deep breath and continued. "First, we are resting our case on the ineffectiveness of current anti-trafficking and child protection programs. The US government, the NGOs, the UN agencies, other countries—they're all in the act, but they're not turning it around. Trafficking is getting worse, and more women and children are being harmed. The huge migrations out of the Middle East have made it worse—much worse. The data is terrible, but there is no data that shows things getting better—and what there is shows it is getting worse. The allocation of funding to most of these problems is tiny compared to other problems. And nearly all of the agencies still work inside their own silos."

She continued. "Second, this is a human rights issue, and all the arguments against slavery apply to it. Third, the UN adoption of the responsibility to protect doctrine must be extended to protecting these women and children. Most forms of trafficking are femicide, which is a form of genocide. Fourth, we are invoking what we have called the Bonhoeffer doctrine. Dietrich Bonhoeffer, one of the best-known theologians of the twentieth century, decided in the end that the Holocaust justified an attempt to kill Hitler, in which he participated."

She paused, watching Stan's frown grow deeper. "Finally, if the measures we are calling for are not adopted and are not effective, we intend to proceed to forming armed security forces as a way of carrying out the responsibility to protect. That resistance will be carried out by women, for women and their children."

Stan was silent. Then he said "You know I can't endorse the last part of that."

"Yes, I do. Let me explain what the actual steps in our program are going to be. And please don't ask how we're funding them. It would be dangerous for you to know that part."

She went on to outline a deliberately staged, escalating set of measures, moving from armed guards in refugee camps and other trafficking locations to creating shelters for women and children. That would be followed, she said, by tracing trafficking organizations with the help of women who would be kept safe in shelters. The shelters would be run by and protected by civil society organizations, led and staffed by women and funded in part by widespread, social media-based fund-raising among women's organizations. She said they had seven international groups already signed up to do that part of the fund-raising. Once traffickers were identified, what she called "intensive interrogations" would be conducted by contract agencies. There would be separate locations for security around shelters and sites where interrogations would be conducted.

Stan was getting angry. "You're talking about contractors to carry some of this out? Hiring your own hit men—or women? How can you possibly control them?"

In a deliberate tone, Suzanne answered, "The same way the US military has controlled its contractors in the Middle East and in embassy protection for the past ten years, Stan. You know that. Congress has signed off on a $100 million contract for embassy security with a private firm and a $250 million contract with Academi—which is Blackwater's new name—for CIA contractor services. That's in the public budget, Stan. God only knows what's in the secret budget. Not to mention a trillion dollars for the wars in the Middle East since 9/11. That's compared with less than $20 million in the anti-trafficking budget, according to the State Department."

In a tone that was almost pleading, she went on. "Stan, there is a real enemy here. It's not the Russians nor the Muslims nor the Chinese, but anyone who hurts children deliberately or even inadvertently, without thinking of what they are doing to the future of those children. And you can't defeat that enemy without serious resources."

She continued, "Countries who refuse to prosecute those whom we identify should be dropped to Tier 3 in the State Department's annual report on trafficking, with sanctions following. We have signed up lawyers and forensic accountants who will assist us in prosecuting the traffickers and the banking fronts they are using to hide their resources. We're ready to testify at the UN hearings on the special rapporteurs' findings when each country's turn to be assessed comes up.

"Next, we'll ask the NGOs who work in this field to join us. We know that some of them will refuse, both to protect their own funding and because they disagree with our methods and our criticisms of their ineffectiveness. But some of them have already agreed to work with us on some parts of the agenda. We'll see who signs on as we roll out the first parts of it."

She leaned forward and held her hands together in fists. "Stan, we already have more than a thousand women who have volunteered from armies and private security firms all over the world. They've heard about this through their own networks. You should read the Defense Department report on the female engagement teams they have formed in the Middle East. There are some very well-qualified people who want very much to do this work."

She stopped, waiting for his response. He finished making some notes, and then said, "So what do you want us to do?"

She smiled and said, "We've thought about that a lot. To start with, we'd like a full day of oversight hearings on trafficking and child protection. We're going to follow that up with a week of media briefings in Washington that will create the brightest spotlight these issues have ever had in the US. CNN is doing a special, and we even have Fox interested because this is—in their view—another foreign policy failure of the administration."

Stan muttered, "Great. So now I'm a tool of Fox news if we do hearings."

"No, you're about to become a hero to women's organizations all over your district-to-be."

"Maybe. All right, I'll talk to the Republicans and see if they will go along. I can always do it as an information briefing if they turn me down, but I think they'll sign on. The chance to beat up the administration will be tempting to them."

He shook his head. "But that part about private armed forces is going nowhere. You want my reaction? My reaction is that it will sound like an empty threat, and Fox and others will call you femi-Nazis. Your tactics will become the story, not the trafficking and the abused kids."

"Maybe. But success breeds success. And we are going to be running a demonstration of this tactic soon, and we will see whether it succeeds."

"Suzanne, if you come into a briefing with blood on your hands, all bets are off."

She shook her head, irritated. "There's already blood on all our hands, Stan. We've done nothing while women and kids are still being sold into slavery. Sins of omission, Jeremy would call them. And he'd be right."

"Let's agree to disagree on the tactics. Maybe you could tell the briefing that these tactics are what you are considering, not what you've done. Can you separate yourself from this…this trial run you're talking about?"

For the first time Suzanne seemed uncertain. "Maybe. I'll have to talk to our group about that. But Stan—we are not going to fight fire with disposable lighters. So it will depend on whether women and children are safe. That's our bottom line."

She went on. "Stan, remember our freshman history course at Western. The wars in Europe were fought by private armies until the 18th century. The British sent mercenaries from Germany over here during our revolution. Privateers—pirates—were sometimes given formal endorsement by kings and queens. When national and international armies can't do the job—or don't even exist—private security forces have been there."

Then she smiled, wanting to lighten things up. "Tell your Republican pals it's just letting private market forces work their wonders."

Stan said he would look at schedules, but the soonest he could arrange a briefing as preparation for a full oversight hearing would be June. He said "I'm going to have to leave my position with the staff in early 2012 to announce that I'm running. So we don't have a big window for this briefing."

Two months later, Suzanne arrived at the camp in Sicily where she had been attacked. It had been renamed The Teresa Shelter, and it was in much better condition than it had been when she visited. But Suzanne's intelligence team said that it was still being plagued by traffickers who came and went as they pleased. Suzanne had selected it both because it was a center for trafficking activities and because of what had happened to her after she visited it the last time in 2008.

It had taken three years, but all the planning that Suzanne and Felicia had done had paid off. Felicia was no longer part of the action team, but she stayed in close touch with Suzanne from Florence and followed the team's moves closely.

Suzanne had sent her advance team into the camp a week before. They had trained the women in the camp, installed the equipment they would need, and worked out logistics for their defense of the camp. They had also passed the word through an informant about when they would be back. They expected the traffickers' enforcement and recruitment units to show up soon after Suzanne arrived.

They were not disappointed. Shortly after breakfast, the alert from the camp's exterior perimeter team came in. Two truckloads of traffickers were entering the camp through the main gate.

The head of Suzanne's unit was a woman named Marissah Brynner. She was a statuesque, 6-foot tall Latina veteran of a Spanish paramilitary unit with the face of an angel who had served on the coalition forces in Iraq. She moved smoothly through the positioning of her unit on rooftops and concealed among the women in the camp. Then she took up her position next to Suzanne, who stood with a sidearm in a holster in the middle of the square at the center of the camp.

As the trucks pulled up and stopped a few feet from the two women, Marissah signaled to a uniformed woman standing among the camp residents. The woman held up two hands, and then two fingers. There were twelve men with the trucks

The head of the traffickers, whom Suzanne identified from her briefing as a Serb named Miloslav, stepped out of the lead truck, saying in reasonably good English. "A welcoming committee. How wonderful. But you have weapons," he said, pointing to Suzanne's automatic and Marissah's rifle. "What an unfriendly greeting."

Then he looked around. "And I see other women with strange uniforms on. What have you done with the friendly guards that we used to deal with?" He looked at the buildings, and then noticed something. "And there are many new cameras on the tops of the buildings. What is that about? Are we on TV?"

Marissah spoke, saying "Yes, you are."

As she spoke, the women from the camp, all clad in loose, flowing garments, began moving toward the trucks, slowly surrounding the men. Seeing this, Miloslay shouted, "Back away. Do not take another step."

The women stopped moving. A few in the front ranks reached down and began smoothing the folds of their over-garments.

Miloslav was getting angry at the lack of response. "Why are you videoing this?"

Marissah said in an even tone. "So that we can identify your remains."

Furious, he swung his AK-47 up and aimed it at the nearest camera.

But the shot that rang out was not from his weapon, but from a rooftop sniper, and it took off the entire front of his head. As the shot came, thirty of the women nearest the trucks swung open their garments and took out their weapons, training them on the surprised traffickers. At the same time, a loudspeaker boomed out. "Drop your weapons, Drop them now!"

The message was repeated in Arabic, Italian, and again in English. And the traffickers rapidly complied, seeing immediately that in addition to the women surrounding them with leveled weapons, ten women in uniform stood up from the rooftops where they had been concealed, aiming sniper rifles at them.

Suzanne walked up to the nearest trafficker and said, "We are going to lock all of your comrades up in the compound here. You—we will release. You are going to go back and tell your bosses that they are never to come into this camp again. This camp is now under the protection of the RTP Brigade."

Sullen, the trafficker said, "Who is that? Who should I tell them you are? Who pays you?"

"Why, you do. We take your money and give it to these women. They hired us to protect them from scum like you and the rest of these vermin. We are the RTP Brigade. That means Responsibility to Protect. That is our job. Now *go!*"

He jumped into the truck and drove back to the gate and out of it. In the meantime, the uniformed women had been handcuffing the rest of the unit. They started marching them to a low building on the edge of the camp that served as a detention area.

"Is the tracker on the truck?" Marissah asked one of her lieutenants.

"Yes, Major."

"Follow them on the unit and make sure the drone doesn't lose him. He is probably going back to the docks, but track him."

In the after-action report session, three of the camp residents who had been elected by the rest of the women were excitedly telling what they had done. One of them, named Halina, said "All our lives we hide our beauty under these garments. Today we hid our other weapons. It felt so wonderful."

She looked over at the building where the children had been kept, safely out of the line of fire. A few children were watching them from the door, huddled together, talking softly to each other and pointing to their mothers. One of the older girls was pointing at the women who were still standing on the roof with their rifles. Halina smiled. "They saw us, what we did. They saw us protecting them. They will never forget that. They have never seen anything like that before."

But another of the residents looked worried. "Will they come back?"

Suzanne said "Yes, they probably will. That is why we had the drill last week with the helicopters. We won't let them get inside the gates. We'll have our teams watching for them and we'll be ready with much more firepower than they expect. Then they will not come back again."

Halina said, "I have not felt safe since I got here with my children a year ago. Now, for the first time I feel safe. And to think that some of us—some of the women who are in this camp—made some of it happen. I have never been prouder."

Suzanne turned to Marissah and asked "Are all your units on alert?"

She said "Yes. And the helicopters are on standby also."

Suzanne said, "Your teams were excellent."

Marissah smiled and said, "Yes, they were. It all went as planned. The first battle sometimes does. It's the next ones that will test us."

"You'll be ready."

The skirmish was the product of all of Suzanne's plans since the day she and Felicia had begun thinking about how to protect women in the camps and children who were being trafficked. It had taken most of the last three years to prepare for this day. Roberto's initial startup funding was by now only the core of a much larger fund-raising effort that had gone worldwide as soon as Suzanne had called together ten anti-trafficking groups and proposed the five-step program she had outlined to Stan in Washington.

Three of the anti-trafficking groups had refused to participate, and two others set up separate units that would work only on the RTP effort, severed from the agencies' normal operations. But the others had enthusiastically supported Suzanne's carefully staged campaign, moving from a review of the effectiveness of an international inventory of anti-trafficking activities to requests for additional funding from both governments and private donors. Only when those were under way was the paramilitary effort set up.

There were three fronts to the protection efforts. The first was the 'beta unit," as Roberto insisted on calling it, which had led the Camp Teresa action. The second consisted of three private contract groups that were prepared to replicate the Teresa action in three other camps within the next two weeks. The third was the central unit that Suzanne directed, which was responsible for overall coordination, fund-raising, and liaison with the governments in the countries where the camps were located and where trafficking operations were most intense.

The planning team had invited bids for security services through a shadowy network that Suzanne had discovered with Roberto's help. They hired two platoons of women who had worked in the security field, and then something unexpected happened. Women who had heard about the RTP units had begun to volunteer—mostly women who had served in civil action groups in the Middle East. A common denominator among many of the women was that they had been sexually assaulted by their own comrades and officers.

In three months of recruiting during 2011, a total of 120 women signed up for the RTP units and hundreds more had made contact and asked for information. Since some had volunteered and others were part of contractor teams, Suzanne worked out an equal pay scale for all of them, including room and board and their travel to the locations where they would be assigned.

Negotiations were initially difficult with national governments where Suzanne's planning team intended to assign the protective units. Governments at first refused to admit that there was a security or trafficking problem in their country. So Suzanne had to present formal briefings that documented the problems, drawing upon research by the NGOs as well as the background materials she and Felicia had compiled. The sub-text to the negotiations was always that the information about lack of security and trafficking would be made public in ways that could affect the US three-tier rankings of a country's trafficking performance, as well as UN reports on trafficking. After these reviews were presented, only Russia refused to admit that any of its citizens or private firms were involved in trafficking.

Since none of the anti-trafficking groups had a comprehensive overview of all of the programs, the inventory Felicia had organized proved crucial to deciding where to build on existing NGOs' efforts and where new operations were needed.

Four days later, the camp in Sicily was approached again, by traffickers, this time with a force of five trucks. But before they could get within a half mile of the camp, Suzanne and Marissah Ravenna had deployed their backup units, who were assigned to three helicopters that Suzanne had contracted from one of the European security firms. Armed with air-to-ground missiles and 50-caliber cannons, the helicopters needed only to fire a few rounds, destroying one of the trucks, before the entire group wheeled around and drove away.

Within a week, operations modeled on the one in Camp Teresa were carried out in Kenya, Turkey, Cambodia, and Guatemala. Except for the one in Guatemala, all were successful. In Guatemala, the traffickers resisted, and seven of the traffickers were killed. Two of the women in the protective unit were wounded, one severely.

At one of these camps, more than one thousand inexpensive cellphones with cameras were distributed, as a means of equipping the women with means of taping any attacks or threats. New celltowers were built that could rapidly transmit reports of unauthorized entry to the camps to nearby security staff. Videocameras were installed in bulletproof housings through the camps, with settings that ensured they were downloaded hourly in secure cloud-based storage. In addition, some women in the camps volunteered to wear jewelry with hidden cameras, to test whether this would reduce the camp residents' fears of retribution if they were caught taping.

The month-long testing of these added security devices reduced trafficking visits by 90% in the first camp in which they were tested, and the methods were quickly expanded to seven other camps and shelters. Briefings for local police and national military staff were provided, as a near-certain means of getting word to the traffickers who had penetrated these agencies. Security protection was also offered to judges and other court personnel, in an attempt to increase prosecutions and convictions.

By that time Suzanne was ready to return to talk with Stan about the briefing he had been able to schedule in June.

The presentations were intended to focus only on the problems with trafficking and the harm done to children, with a summary at the end by Suzanne. She was prepared to lay out the two basic options: either support anti-trafficking operations at scale or be prepared for paramilitary operations by contractors to protect women living in refugee camps and areas where trafficking was concentrated.

Fortunately or unfortunately—Suzanne could never decide which it was—a reporter for the *Wall Street Journal* who covered women's affairs came across a wire service story on the operation in Guatemala. One of the wounded contract staff had given a lengthy interview in the hospital that mentioned RTP and Suzanne's coalition. At that point, all media hell broke loose and Suzanne had twenty requests for interviews within 24 hours. She knew she would get a blistering call from Stan.

She did. He said, almost shouting at her, "I told you I couldn't make this work if you came in with blood on your hands. You're shooting up refugee camps all over the world. How am I supposed to explain this as part of child protection?"

"Just explain that this is what will happen if governments don't do a better job of providing security themselves. We will immediately shut our operations down in every country where security improves. But we are not going to let women and children get trafficked out of camps where they went to be safe."

The briefing came off in June, despite the media furor over the "vigilante groups," as the RTP teams were inevitably labeled by some reporters and broadcasters. Testimony was given by UNICEF, Treasury, State, and Justice senior staff, several NGOs, and leaders of some of the foundations in the US and Europe who had been funding initiatives aimed at trafficking and sexual violence. Most of the testimony reviewed ongoing programs, despite Stan's repeated questioning about the future efforts and whether programs under way could be scaled up.

When congressional staff asked about the agencies' reactions to the RTP efforts, few of the groups represented went beyond expressing concern about danger to women and children in camps if armed groups intended to operate in the camps. When Stan asked about trafficking operations in the camps, the agencies said they had no information on that.

Suzanne's closing statement to the congressional subcommittee meeting Stan had arranged was carefully controlled, delivered in a level tone that avoided any incendiary content.

She began by factually describing what they had done to recruit and staff the RTP operations with proven military and civil leadership. She explained how they had in each case first asked the host governments to provide adequate security in those locations where the camp operators had said on the record that their security was inadequate to keep the traffickers out. When that failed, they asked the traffickers to cease entering the camps, documenting their requests. She reviewed the data on trafficking in the camps and shelters, making clear that the data were in all cases compiled by neutral agencies and not her own partners.

"The question we are trying to raise is where we should draw the line at those human rights that we will try to protect with mere rhetoric and isolated projects—and those we will defend with technological, police, and, when necessary, armed security forces and military power? Why should we defend the weakest among us with the weakest of methods—mere words and paper promises?

"Stalin is said to have asked, when told the Vatican disapproved of his crushing Eastern Europe's Catholics, 'how many legions has the Pope?' Our question is how many legions do the defenders of children have—and how many will they need to stop the enslavement and abuse of innocent children? If responsibility to protect does not include protecting these children, then what are those words really worth?"

Then she said, speaking very deliberately, "We will close down our operations tomorrow if the requirements for greater security in these camps are being met by host governments and the UN agencies. Those requirements include four things: major expansion of security in the camps, expanded use of financial investigations of the money laundering done by traffickers, confiscation of traffickers' resources to be re-allocated to women and children affected by trafficking, and listing in Tier 3 all countries that do not immediately prosecute traffickers as criminals with sentences proportionate to their crimes.

"I want to add that women in these camps and in the countries most affected by trafficking have given us an amazing response to the RTP efforts. We have had to turn away volunteers who want to join our teams. Women want to be safe and to make sure their children are safe. Given the tools, they will do it themselves.

"We have also received substantial contributions from individual donors and from some of the organizations in this field, who have told us that our efforts are the first time they have seen anyone taking anti-trafficking seriously enough to provide genuine safety for women and their children."

She paused and looked at the staff and the few members of Congress attending the briefing. She continued. "I know there have been some statements of concern about our use of private contractors to protect women and children. Those of you familiar with the recent conflicts in the Middle East, as well as our arrangements for embassy security all over the world, will know that hundreds of millions of dollars have gone to contractors who are responsible for protection of US installations and personnel."

She smiled, thinly. "And those of you with a historical bent may recall that in the 16th and 17th centuries, governments signed contracts with privateers—pirates, to use the less polite term—to raid other countries' ships and bases. That practice was outlawed in the 19th century, but its modern version in private security contracts continues today. Let me be clear again: *there is no need for any contractors if the US government accepts responsibility to protect children in countries where we have ongoing assistance programs.*

"We do not believe that violence is an answer to the violence that has been aimed at thousands of women and children. But if no further efforts are being made to protect these women and prosecute their attackers—we will step in and do what we can to make them safe. That is how we understand the UN responsibility to protect doctrine. It is also how we discern our moral responsibility."

She paused and then added, "A few years ago I met in Italy with some very close friends," smiling at Stan, "who care about these issues. We talked about what could be done, and I valued the advice they gave me. After our meetings, I went to Venice to try to clear my head with the natural beauty of one of the world's most remarkable cities. I found myself at the Guggenheim museum. There's a marble bench there with an inscription by the artist Jenny Holzer. The inscription said '*Go where people sleep and see if they are safe.*'

She stopped and looked at the audience. "That is an unforgettable sentiment if you care about those who have been threatened because they are women or because they are innocent children. 'See if they are safe.' That is our challenge—and yours.

"One final quote, if I may. Martin Luther King once said "It may be true that the law cannot change the heart, but it can restrain the heartless. It may be true that the law cannot make a man love me, but it can keep him from lynching me, and I think that is pretty important." She paused and said, "That's why we need laws, to make the talk about protection real for these children and their mothers."

The moderator, an ally of Stan's announced that there was time for only two or three questions before a quorum call. The first question was a planned softball about the training of the RTP troops.

Suzanne said "All of the women in our Brigade have had full basic and advanced training in infantry or special operations. Half of them have served in combat, and one-fourth have served in repeat deployments. More than a third have decorations earned in combat."

The second question was more hostile. A junior staffer asked "If this mission were critical, why should private contractors provide these services instead of regular troops?"

Stan was delighted at the question, because he knew it would give Suzanne a chance to make a critical point about contractors. And she did just that.

She said, "Our position is that this mission is critical, just as protection of US embassies is critical. A multi-million dollar contract is currently in force with a large private American firm to provide those embassy protection services under the Defense Department's oversight. We believe our forces are at least as well-trained and armed as those private contractors, some of which have recently been prosecuted for war crimes."

She smiled and added, "We would welcome the assignment of regular troops to this duty."

The last question was about the need for the RTP Brigade and how soon forces would be withdrawn.

"As I said in my presentation, we will stand down immediately when the US provides troops or funding to international regular forces to protect women and children in jeopardy. That is how we interpret the responsibility to protect doctrine."

Stan was glad the questioner was unfamiliar with the checkered history of US reservations about that doctrine. The meeting concluded, and Stan winked at Suzanne as she slowly began making her way out of the hearing room with press crowding around her.

Stan called Suzanne two days after the briefing when she got back to London. He said, "I don't know what's going to happen, but you really shook them up. Your message was right on target, Suzanne. And a lot of people who were on the fence heard what you said. I'm going to go at this as hard as I can. The only way people can prove that your solution is wrong is to come up with a serious one of their own. They're debating it now at the White House, State, and all over the place. We'll see what happens—but you did a hell of a job. The spotlight is as bright as it's ever been."

"Thanks for setting it up, Stan. Keep us posted."

Then Suzanne began to expand her coalition's ideas about what was possible. She convinced her partners that they should convene a conference on technology and child protection. After the first publicity on what had happened in the camps once the RTP units were deployed, she had been contacted by other NGOs and private forms who wanted to meet with her to discuss tools they had developed which they thought would be helpful in the RTP efforts. Most of the contacts came from women who were CEOs or major investors in these firms.

Suzanne decided she would invite all of them—and others, from a list Roberto had one of his staff consultants compile—to a three-day conference. The conference was scheduled in London, and she invited Stan to send a representative of his committee.

The meeting was a total success, not only because of the broad range of firms that showed up, but also because she had allowed media from major technological outlets to attend, as a means of publicizing how serious the protection efforts were becoming. Presentations were made by more than two dozen firms, and a display area was set up where vendors could meet with prospective NGO and governmental purchasers.

The products presented included videocams that went well beyond those already installed in some of the camps, some of which were enclosed in bulletproof cases and could upload their pictures to central communications installations monitored by security personnel. Another firm demonstrated inexpensive cellphones with cameras that instantaneously uploaded their files so that destroying the phones did not lose the pictures. Robots that could guard the perimeter of a camp or shelter were also displayed. The presenter brought the house down when she said that if the RTP sponsors wished, "we'll put a skirt on the robots."

A booth showed how easily DNA could be collected from traffickers and others who had been arrested, as a means of tracking repeat offenders in a global data base that would document who was involved in trafficking worldwide. Another showed how a situation room could be set up in a facility where women and children were housed, with alerts when the facility's security was breached. Several kinds of non-lethal weapons were also demonstrated.

A fascinating presentation described the downside of some of the methods, including means by which drones could be highjacked and sent back to attack their controllers. An incident occurred in Iran in 2011 in which control of an American drone was taken over by Iranian forces. A panelist in this presentation warned that drones were being developed all over the world, by more than twenty countries and several international criminal organizations.

A member of the audience reported, without confirmation, a two-day "drone war" over the Texas-Mexico border in which, he claimed, drones from DEA and the cartels competed for airspace and actually shot down the other sides' equipment. The "war" ended, this informant said, when the US controllers succeeded in reversing the directions of the cartels' drones so that they were re-aimed at the cartels' launching sites.

The sessions resulted in even more publicity for the RTP initiatives, increasing pressure on Congress and the UN as they debated the next steps on child protection and the responsibility to protect doctrine. The representatives from nations that still denied that traffickers were working in their countries were overwhelmed by women from organizations in both sending and receiving nations who testified how widespread the dangers to women and children were, and pinpointed specific locations that had been confirmed and mapped by the RTP Brigade's drones.

But there was a backlash, as both Suzanne and Stan had expected. Some clever editor at Fox News had invented the phrase "virgin vigilantes," and it stuck. None of the opponents to the RTP initiative accepted the analogy to private contractors used by the Defense Department, and the full forces of media misogyny were unleashed. Stan knew he was going to have problems.

But at that point, his election was beckoning, and he put aside Suzanne's agenda to make sure he was in a position to do something about it as a Congressman, not a lowly minority staffer.

He called Suzanne, and said that he would do what he could to keep the RTP agenda visible as he disengaged from his staff work to gear up for his campaign. Suzanne was fine with that, since the media attention she had gotten had made fund-raising, recruiting, and launching new sites her highest priorities.

Early 2013

After his election, Stan had carefully prepared proposals for the next authorization bill that would be coming out of the House Foreign Affairs Committee, which he had been assigned to as a new member. He waited a few months for the new Congress to settle in, and then sent his proposals over to the Chairman of the Committee, and waited for his call. It came the next day.

Stan walked into the chairman's office, ready to do some hard negotiating.

The chairman began. "Wright, you and I have always gotten along pretty well while you were minority staff. You don't play to the crazies in your party too much, and I appreciate that. You've respected the duties of the chairman, and that's as it should be." He frowned. "But this draft legislative language you sent over is just out of bounds."

"How so, Mr. Chairman?"

"There's two problems. First, you've got nearly a billion dollars of foreign aid in the middle of this bill. For all this child protection stuff you've been working on. That's not going to go anywhere. I'm not going to clog up the works with a bunch of foreign aid boondoggles the nutballs will go after and sink my whole bill. You want a couple of line items for projects—fine. But no billion-dollar foreign aid package is going to sit in the middle of that bill blinking like a red light and screw it up."

Stan knew that making the case on the merits would go nowhere. It was about the whole package, and he had gambled that he could get his pieces through the committee.

He also knew that a few projects would never be enough to catch the eye of the major liberal donors he needed to attract to build up a campaign fund for re-election—and beyond. Starting early, spreading funds around to other candidates who agreed with his ideas on his agenda would get that ball rolling early. And early money usually beat the alternative.

Roberto was the only one he had shared this strategy with, because he was the only one of their group who was deep enough into finances to understand it.

"What's the other problem, sir?" Stan asked, knowing the answer.

The Chairman chuckled and said. "This is the really weird one. I know you had that briefing a while back by that…that woman who came in and told us all about her army. You've tucked away some language that would ask Defense to put some funding into reconnaissance satellites and drones to help her spot traffickers. I'm fine with doing that through our troops, Wright. But giving that stuff to some virgin vigilantes? What is this—Blackwater for girls?!"

"They're not vigilantes, sir, and they're sure not virgins."

"I'm not in the habit of letting people laugh my bills off the floor, Wright. Take it out. You want to put in some more projects for kids. Fine. But get that women's army out of my bill. Or your projects go too."

Then he added, "Don't forget where you're from, Congressman."

Stan knew that had a deliberate double meaning—it was about South Carolina, and it was about race. And he wasn't going to respond to either.

"All right, sir. I appreciate you letting me know in advance. I'll send over a shortlist of projects, and we can talk further."

"Thanks, Wright. Appreciate your seeing my problems."

As he walked back to his office, Stan knew he was stuck with an offer of a few more projects—the very targets he had gone after in the past as inadequate.

He dreaded telling the Lopez group, but he asked his admin to get them on the line. When he picked up, he briefed them on what had happened, and then fell silent.

Roberto said, "Let me tell you how I see it. Stan, you're stuck between two motives, seems to me. You want to be a Senator—"

"That's way premature," Stan protested.

"Come on, we've known you for fifteen years. You weren't meant to be one of 435, man. Get real."

"Some day, maybe. OK, go on."

"And you want to move the needle for the 400 million."

"Yes. We all do."

"And you want to do it through politics. We all get that. But if you push this now, you may fall off the train. And that doesn't do the kids any good at all."

Suzanne interrupted. "I know I'm supposed to keep quiet, but just let me say one thing. Stan has a chance to make a difference for those kids now. Not ten years from now. *Now.*"

Roberto said, "Suzanne, he doesn't have the votes to make it happen. He needs the chairman, and the chairman has told him the door is closed. We can keep trying to get private funding—you've been doing great."

She snapped back, "It isn't about the money, it's getting the bloody US Congress to act for once for kids. The only nation on earth that hasn't endorsed the UN Convention for Children, funding far below the per capita funding of every developed nation…"

"We know, Suzanne. We took the class too."

She was quiet, and then said, "All right. Let me just leave you with an update. Maybe give you some more context. We worked last month with two of the women's agencies in Afghanistan. They are unbelievably brave and smart. They work with almost no contact with US or coalition agencies, because some of their projects are in Taliban-controlled areas. We offered them protection and they immediately rejected it, explaining to us that woman in military units would make the Taliban go berserk. So we asked them what else we could do that would be helpful, and they said that if we could get contributions that could be channeled through Muslin organizations, it would be very useful to them in getting supplies for their schools. They have hundreds of girls in schools, many in private homes so they don't embarrass the Taliban by opening public schools."

She added, "Those women are just as brave as our troops. Maybe more so, because their only ammunition is books. And their courage."

Roberto called Stan back, saying he wanted to discuss something privately.

"Stan, let me suggest something. We know some people out here who work on reputation clean-up. Someone in entertainment who has been slimed by the blogs, they go in and clean it up. But sometimes they also dig into the slimers' lives, and that backs them off. I think you guys call it opposition research. We could do that on deep sourcing that would never touch you."

Stan said "No. You live by that sword, you die by it."

"You're clean. What's the problem?"

"Doesn't matter, Berto. They make it up. Then you spend all your time denying it."

Stan's final move was to arrange a meeting with the ranking Democrat on the committee, an African-American woman from Los Angeles, Diana King. She had been in Congress for twenty years, representing a safe district in LA, and she had been a strong supporter of Stan's agenda since he first came onto the staff.

Stan explained to the Congresswoman what the Chairman had said. She laughed when she quoted him. "He actually called them virgin vigilantes? He used that stupid label from Fox Never-News?"

"Yeah."

"Well, let me give you some advice worth what you're paying for it. You can keep that language in, and fight for it, and lose. You'll get some good ink from the liberal papers and e-news, and MSNBC will say nice things about you. And then when you get ready to make your move for the Senate seat, they'll find some nice white boy to primary you and throw a ton of quiet money at you, and probably cook up a scandal or two that never happened. And you'll be out of here. And that would be a damned shame."

"So behave and shut up."

"Yes. You'll get some good projects out of it, and you may embarrass the next administration into doing something right if we get the White House again, and maybe they'll help Suzanne and her troops a bit. But if you go against the Chairman it'll be the last line items of yours you'll ever see in one of his bills."

He knew she was right, but he wanted to get her feedback. Now that he had it, he knew what he had to do.

Felicia 2013

Through some of Lopez' contacts on other campuses, the five classmates had developed a network of East Coast college campuses that they visited when they were in the US and when Stan and Jeremy could get free to go with them. Roberto would fly out, and they would deliver seminar sessions at classes like the Lopez class. Several of her colleagues had begun teaching courses on child protection, and the five were frequent invitees to those classes.

At one of these meetings, they were speaking to a small group of about fifteen students. After the class, two of the young women came up to her. One was a good deal taller than the other, but Felicia noted a resemblance and an unspoken connection of some kind between the two. The taller one identified herself as Serena and the shorter one said her name was Lorraine.

Serena spoke, "We're sisters. And we may want to do this work, the kind of work you all do, but in our own way. Maybe with our writing, maybe with art therapy like what you do, maybe with sports or in some other ways." Her face had a quizzical look.

Then her sister spoke. "But how did each of you decide how to do this work? How did you know the best way to get it done?"

They spoke hesitantly, but Felicia could tell that they weren't going to be satisfied with a few well-intentioned words of encouragement.

She told them, "We just built on what we were good at—what we were passionate about. You need to wait to see what is so exciting to you that you can't wait to get up in the morning to go do it. That's what you should be doing."

Lorraine said, "It really isn't 9 to 5 work, is it?"

Felicia smiled at said, "No, it really isn't."

Then Serena said, "But you all seem so happy to be doing it—even though it was sort of depressing to hear about how badly some of the kids are treated."

As they continued to talk, Felicia was intrigued by them. The shorter one spoke rapidly, with great intensity, using her hands and her animated face. The taller one was quieter, speaking softly, sometimes finishing her sister's sentences. They both had marvelous smiles, Felicia saw, and then, as she kept talking with them, she saw that somewhere in their lives they had learned to listen, unlike many of their generation who were better at sending than receiving.

And as she told the others about the exchange that night as they debriefed over dinner, Felicia said, "Maybe one of our real legacies is managing to inspire some kids like those two I was talking to."

Roberto 2010-2015

After Italy, Roberto felt even more dissatisfied with his range of social contacts. He was so refreshed and energized by his contacts with his peers that the contrast with his everyday life was almost painful once he got back to LA. Helping Stan with his campaign was exciting, and it made him wonder if there were political connections that would help him with his work—and his life. He knew that some of the software barons of California had ventured into active roles in politics and entertainment—which, in California, was redundant.

So in late 2012 after Stan's election, Roberto joined a group of Hollywood-based entertainment funders who operated as a loose coalition with full-time staff who scouted out candidates and causes for political investors.

At one of the fund-raising parties he attended at a downtown hotel, he was talking with a partner from his former firm when he noticed a tall woman across the room who looked familiar. Then he noticed that she seemed to have also noticed him, and was headed in his direction.

She came up, put out her hand and said, "Hello, Roberto. You may not remember me. We met when I was still at Cal Tech. I'm Cassie Gramercy."

Despite her stunning good looks, the memory of his disastrous pre-date with her came back to him, and he began looking around for an escape route. She reached out, smiling, and lightly touched his arm. "I just want to say I was a complete jerk when we met and I apologize. I don't think I'm quite the same person. I've had a fairly eventful life since we met. I got married, divorced, had a daughter, and went to work for the social media operation in Dreamworks."

She paused. "And if you'd like to wander away and never speak to me again, I'd understand. Although I hope you won't."

Remembering her forwardness, Roberto was torn between wanting to drop the conversation and hear more about her. She had packed a lot of information into her few sentences, and he was intrigued. She had also moved from B+ pretty to top-rank lovely over the past ten years, and was doing justice to a sheath dress made of some kind of clinging material that was succeeding in its function. Her long blonde hair resonated with his archetype, and that decided him.

"No, everyone gets one atrociously inappropriate moment, and I've had dozens. Tell me more about your work."

They talked for nearly an hour, moving from the ballroom where the fundraiser was being held to the patio outside. She filled him in on her work. She both monitored and wrote for the social media, tracking political trends for a coalition of software and entertainment firms. Her specialty had become conflicts between privacy protection and the relentless data mining that search firms could now do, digging through their users' wants and needs. She described it as "front-line reconnaissance, listening for the footsteps of government as it pokes into our efforts to poke into government."

She was far more vivid in her language than most tech-oriented people he had met, and he was fascinated by her. He told her about the broad outlines of his work, referring to his consulting and not mentioning the anti-trafficking side of it. He touched briefly on what she already knew, which was that he had sold some software and was reasonably wealthy, though not on the top financial floor of the software world. He briefly mentioned the Lopez group and his closeness to the other members of the group.

Then he said, "You said you have a daughter."

"Yes. She's three. My mother lives next door—we're in Pasadena—and she loves watching her. My daughter seems mostly interested in princesses at this point—not sure she'll end up in software."

Then she asked him, "Are you seeing anyone?"

Seeing his reaction, she quickly said "My friends all say I have the social graces of a water buffalo. I don't do small talk very well. It seems to go with the techie background."

"I'm not much on small talk myself. No."

She said, "No, you're not a small talker, or no, you're not seeing anyone?"

"No to both. When can we have dinner?"

"Tonight?"

Roberto pretended to be thinking and then said, smiling. "Tonight's good. I'll have to cancel four or five critical engagements, but that's not a problem."

By this time the electricity and chemistry between them could have fueled several tall buildings, and they quickly said goodbye to the hosts and left.

They never made it to dinner, and spent most of the rest of their lives together.

But Roberto also had plenty to keep him focused on his work. The more he learned about what each of the others in the Lopez group was doing, the more he felt that his own calling was supporting their efforts with his money. His stake in his old firm was doing very well, and his own consulting work was also lucrative.

But he wanted to do more. He followed Jeremy's work closely with regular phone calls and e-mails, and was soon able to identify which religious agencies were doing the most effective work. Jeremy, with a fairly good idea about Roberto's extracurricular activities, had asked that only legitimate funding be used for his activities, and Roberto was glad to comply.

He knew that both Stan's campaigns and his need to funnel contributions to sympathetic allies were going to take additional funding. He donated to Felicia's choirs and her music training programs. And he was fascinated by the discussions he had with Suzanne about her plans for the RTP project, and promised her all the seed funding she would need to launch her efforts to broaden her funding base among human rights and women's organizations.

And so, after careful calculations of the projected returns from his legitimate financial interests, he began a series of further "taps" on trafficking organizations, both those he had hit after the attack on Suzanne and those aligned with the Mexican and South American drug cartels. He had developed good offline relations with two of his former colleagues in the Treasury Department's FinCEN, who were delighted to have an unofficial tester of some of their more exotic methods of tracking banking co-conspirators tied to the cartels.

Starting in 2013 he increased his diversions substantially. He had worked with hacker groups who were pushing the state of the art in cut-outs that would conceal his taps. An unexpected asset in his work turned out to be Cassie's experience with the new field of celebrity privacy. In the aftermath of several e-mail hackings that resulted in widely distributed internet copies of several movie legends' nude photos, the market for privacy software for messaging had expanded rapidly. Cassie worked with several key members of the small elite in the communications and entertainment world who could pay well for such protection. And some of these techniques helped Roberto conceal his own connections.

Cassie had at first been nervous when she learned about Roberto's non-legal activities. But as she learned more about what he was using the money for and how important the Lopez group was to him, she agreed that what seemed a small risk was worth it. She made him promise that he would stop the practice if he ever got the slightest indication that he had been compromised.

Suzanne received a message from Roberto asking her to call him when she had a chance. She finished briefing Marissah and her other staff, and then called him.

"Berto—how you doing?"

"I'm good. I have a serious romantic interest and it feels great. How about you?"

"We're busy. Lots happening, mostly good. And I'm delighted you finally found someone—after all those years of just looking. So what do you need?"

"I need a favor, Suzanne."

She laughed. "You have lots of favors in the RTP bank these days, Berto. Anything."

"I want to go on a mission with your team. Somewhere I can see what you are doing up close." He sounded frustrated. "I'm sitting here playing with shadow accounts in shadow banks in the shadow internet. I want to see something real. I want to see what we're making happen that's good for kids."

Suzanne let herself sound surprised, which she was. "You want to go out with our troops?"

"Yes. I need to get closer than sitting in an office moving other people's money around."

"Your moving that money around has made many good things happen already, Berto."

"I know. But I need to see it up close. Can you make that happen?"

Suzanne was thinking. She had never sent any males out with her troops—it was part of their ethos that they were an all-female operation. But Roberto had standing that no other man had, and she knew she had to respond to him, both as their financer and as a friend.

"I can't do that with our troops, Berto. But I'm planning to join a raid that IJM is doing next month in Luzon. Do you want to go with me?"

"That's perfect. I don't want you to break any precedents with your own teams. But that would give me a much better sense of what's happening that's about kids instead of just money moving around in the dark."

They arranged the details, and she hung up.

A month later, they met in Manila and began the journey to Legazpi. They had joined the team from IJM that had worked in the Philippines for nearly a decade, setting up links to the national police, conducting raids on brothels that used teenagers and even younger girls in their business, and sending the girls to shelters and therapeutic programs where they could live safe and return, when possible, to their families. The IJM staff, a man and a woman, explained that some of the families had in effect sold their daughters into the prostitution rings, and for those girls, permanent recovery homes were arranged far enough away from their families to prevent their parents or relatives from contacting them.

The IJM team met with the police team and Suzanne and Roberto got in the third vehicle in a convoy that drove for an hour to get to a small village outside Legazpi City. As they emerged from the SUVs, they heard the commander of the police unit order five of his team to cover the back door of the brothel.

"They always try to run out the back," he told Roberto and Suzanne with a smile. "And we are always there waiting for them."

The building was a nondescript storefront advertising massages and drinks. The commander said to Suzanne and Roberto that they should stay outside until they were told it was safe to enter. But Roberto noticed a large window, in which a young girl had been sitting until she saw the SUVs pull up. He and Suzanne moved onto the short front porch and watched through the window.

On a signal from the commander, eight men and two women burst into the front door. The girls started screaming but the women officers quickly yelled at them to sit down in a corner of the gaudily decorated front room, and they instantly complied. The other officers were handcuffing the customers and the two men and two women who were apparently the owners or operators of the brothel.

"At least they brought women along on the raid," Suzanne said in a low voice to Roberto. "Imagine those girls being scared to death and having no women to talk to about what has happened to them." She whispered, "This is a good team, but they have no reason to trust most of the police units."

The IJM staff were busy videotaping the operation, careful not to focus their camera on the girls' faces. Then the woman from the team moved over to the girls and began explaining to them, as translated by the male member of the team, that they would be taken to a shelter to live until they could decide what they wanted to do next. She kept repeating a phrase over and over, which the other IJM staffer translated as "She's telling them they're safe now. They're safe and they can leave here and never come back"

A fourth vehicle, a van, had arrived during the operation, and the girls were all herded into it. They had been allowed to go back to their rooms and get anything they wanted to take with them.

Suzanne blinked away rare tears as she saw them emerge and move into the van with blankets and a few pillows. Two of the smallest girls clutched what looked like handmade dolls.

As they drove back to Legazpi, Roberto asked "How many of them will go home?"

She answered, "Some of them will, But others were sold by their families, or by relatives their parents had left the kids with because they were working hundreds of miles away in clothing factories. Those kids can't go back. They'll grow up in shelters, and the shelters will be as good as we can make them—and as safe as we can defend. The schools will be far better than what they would have gotten at home."

"I'd like to help with that."

"You'd be welcome to. I'll have one of our regional staff get in touch with you to arrange it. And maybe you could come visit it sometime. You could see the after-action part of what we do that isn't violent." She smiled. "And you could tell Stan about it, to calm him down a bit about our tactics."

"Will do."

Back home, Roberto had turned up some fascinating research being done in the Defense Advanced Research Projects Agency on identifying and prosecuting criminal networks involved in sex and labor trafficking. Researchers at Arizona State University had developed a search engine that developed infographics linking trafficking ads, phone calls, the location of the person who posted the ad, and the locations where the ads were posted. The search tool, called Memex, was being used by law enforcement agencies around the country to locate patterns of money laundering used by trafficking organizations.

As Roberto compiled information about the use of the tool and its effectiveness in aiding sex-trafficking prosecutors, he realized that the tool could be enhanced with certain capabilities that would move beyond DARPA's authorized uses to more invasive tactics that would make it even more effective—and possibly more illegal as it trespassed on privacy.

He decided to tell two people about it—Stan and Suzanne. He arranged an encrypted phone line, and found a time when the three of them could talk.

He began by saying "I wanted to talk with the two of you because I think I've come across something you should both know about. Let me ask first if you're OK making this a totally off-the-record conversation.

For now I don't want this to be traced back to me, even though some of this is already public."

They both quickly agreed, and he went on. "DARPA has developed a tool called Memex that is being used by law enforcement agencies in New York, Arizona, and other locations to locate and prosecute traffickers." He explained the search tool in enough detail for them to understand how it worked and how it had been used.

Roberto said, "Stan, even though we've both agreed that the feds have not been doing enough to deal with trafficking as a priority, this is one area where they've done some great work. DARPA apparently got into this because they traced some funds going from sex trafficking to the cartels and other illegal activities. I've seen similar patterns in some of the…uh…'research' that I've been doing aimed at groups that work along the border."

Suzanne said, "That explains a phone call we got a few weeks ago. A woman at Arizona State had read about our work and wanted to talk about some software that she thought might be helpful to us. We're scheduled to meet with her next week. That must be what she wanted to talk about. But I'm really glad you called, Roberto, because now I'm ready for the meeting. I've got some volunteers who are nearly as sharp as you are with software, and I was going to bring them to the meeting. Thanks, pal."

Stan said, in an excited tone, "Suzanne, have you ever heard of the SBIR program? It's the small business innovation research program, and it provides funding to small businesses that have a product that could be produced with eventual profits. Some of the money is set aside for minority and women-owned businesses. You could work with a university—or a nonprofit group that has a for-profit subsidiary—and get up-front funding to develop this so that it could be used in your work. I'd be glad to write a letter in support of your application."

He laughed, "It means you can never give me any money again as a campaign contribution, but we'll let Roberto make up the difference."

Roberto said, "Unless Suzanne has won the lottery recently, that shouldn't be a problem."

Suzanne said, "I'm going to regret not having a legitimate outlet for my great wealth, but sacrifices must be made."

Stan laughed again. "We'll get by, somehow." Then he became serious. "Roberto, send me the stuff that has already gone public about this, so I can call the DARPA people and ask for a briefing and not have to bring you into it. I'll tell them I read this background info and wanted to learn more about it."

He was quiet for a minute. "What if we asked Justice to come to the meeting and then suggested that this could beef up their asset confiscation efforts? If they can trace these guys and their funding streams, we could generate some more funding for the anti-trafficking efforts inside the government, maybe in a way that would help your efforts, Suzanne. We'll have to be careful, but I think we can manage that."

Suzanne said, "You guys are great. I know we don't all agree on our different tactics, but this sounds like an area where the three of us can get something going that would make a real difference. Lopez would be proud of us."

Roberto said, "One more thing. The next war is going to be fought mostly on the internet, Stan. These are little skirmishes, testing offense and defense."

He smiled, and then said "I'll bet you could get a ton of funding from research shops in firms whose names you'd recognize immediately—because what we're trying to do in shutting down traffickers is what they need to try to do to shut down logistics for an enemy's army of hackers. We're trying to slow them down before they turn out the lights and start a thousand fires remotely all over this country."

"Well, that's a cheery thought. Seriously, let's get together the next time you're East and talk about this."

"Will do."

Re-connecting with Cassie had begun to shift Roberto's priorities. As committed as he was to helping his friends with their activities, he found himself wanting to spend time with Cassie. Native Californians both, they began organizing weekends around trips to their favorite places in the state, from the wine country in northern California, the Eastern Sierra, the Southern beaches and desert areas, and San Diego. Roberto bought a small RV, and they took it out into the desert and the nearby mountains, as well as the beach parks where RV hookups were available.

Cassie immediately fit into Roberto's family, since his sisters and mother were delighted that he had finally met someone who wasn't completely part of his business world or "hopelessly weird," as Roberto's most candid sister put it, based on prior experience.

And Cassie's daughter Lizzie soon became one of Roberto's favorite projects. Cassie's ex-husband had taken a job in Portugal, so he was not a major factor in his daughter's life. Roberto took her to the preschool she attended in Pasadena, and picked her up when Cassie's work on the west side of LA made that difficult. Her mother was always available, but Roberto liked doing the pick-up, and Lizzie, who called him "Berto," always had a story to tell him about what had happened at school that day.

Roberto soon developed a ritual with Lizzie, based on his own family's dinner table experiences as he was growing up. Once she got in the car for the afternoon pickup, he waited until she got settled and then he invariably asked her three questions: "What did you learn today, who were you kind to, and what did you see or hear that was beautiful?" Her answers were creative, highly variable, and sometimes hilarious—as when her answer to the third question was "Well, it *wasn't* Sammy Decker!"

Cassie and Lizzie were the missing pieces in Roberto's life. From the moment in 2012 that he started talking with her at the party, Roberto and Cassie were happy. He was already preparing for the 2015 gathering, which was going to be held in Washington for Stan's convenience.

After he had begun to spend time with Lizzie, something broke free inside Roberto and he began making notes about his time with her. At first he was just trying to find good software and websites that she could enjoy, that would help her with her reading and teach her a few basic computer skills. But as he made notes, he found he was writing as much about how much he enjoyed his time with Lizzie as he was about the software. Surprisingly, he found writing in words nearly as enjoyable as writing in code—with a much wider audience.

And then he began writing more deliberately, about Lizzie, and then about the lack of good video games that had educational and positive social content. He ended up with an article that he published on his website, which was picked up by one of the software magazines and then published on several blogs.

He soon came across the gender gaps in video games, and the vicious attacks on women who wrote or blogged about the problem. He talked with Suzanne and Felicia, who encouraged him to go further and put him in touch with some of the women who worked in this field. A few were suspicious of his motives, but others were glad to work with him, and equally delighted when he offered to pay them for their time.

It did not escape him that this new arena might help throw people off his trail in the dark Internet, and he felt better about the time he was devoting to these new pursuits. Cassie was also happy that he had headed down this new path, and encouraged him to follow it. She knew it was a much safer line of business than his deep hacking, and she loved seeing his deep affection for Lizzie.

After they had been married for nearly a year, Cassie came to Roberto's office late one afternoon. Surprised to see her, he said, careful to add a smile, "What, you're checking up on me?"

She laughed and said, "No, but it is a business call. You've been very careful to keep me from knowing the details of your work, but I know you are supporting Suzanne's work with the RTP units she's been forming. You saw the story last week in the *Times* about her efforts. She's been trying to get some publicity to see if it will help her fund-raising."

She paused. "Well, it has. I've had five calls this week from women in the entertainment industry—and no, I can't yet tell you who they are. It's my turn to be mysterious because they swore me to secrecy. But here's the thing. Two of them asked what kind of PR I could get if they contributed to Suzanne's projects. And the other three insisted that they be able to make the contributions in secret, because they didn't want word to get out that they had done something so radical."

She sat back in her chair and said "Weird, huh?"

Roberto said, "Not so much. Some people like to be hailed as big givers to women's causes and some like to be anonymous or are scared of what might happen."

Cassie asked, "So what do you recommend?"

He quickly answered "Take all of the money on whatever terms they want. Suzanne needs the help, and I'm glad to have somebody besides me funneling money to her. Do you think it's going to be significant or just token amounts so they can say they're players?"

"One said she wanted to give a lot, and it's someone who could easily go over five million. The others, I don't know."

"Five million goes pretty fast when you're equipping an army that has to be able to move quickly to all the hot spots where RTP is now working. If you can, push them all for more."

"Yes, master strategist. And I won't ask how much you're involved in it." Then she changed her light tone, and said, very seriously. "But you promised me you'd be careful. Are you?"

"Yes." And he left it at that.

Sinaloa 2013

Finally Ruiz had decided he had to inform his top command of the taps on their banking. He had worked carefully, tracking back the taps, which had ceased, then started up again, then stopped. But he could never break the codes that had concealed who had done the taps. He arranged an appointment in the underground bunker where El Jefe spent most of his time.

The briefing was as painful as he expected. The big boss had screamed at him, "Either you find this thief or I will assume it is you or one of your flunkies. You have a week."

Ruiz knew he would not be able to crack the codes being used against their accounts and the Zetas' and whoever else the mystery hacker had invaded. He knew the Zetas had just captured a DEA informant and was working him over. He called Gutierrez and begged him to have them try to get the names of anyone who had ever worked in Treasury who might have the skills to get into their banking transmissions.

Eight days later, the Zetas got the list of names. It was too late for Ruiz, however. On the seventh day of the ultimatum, he had been shot at his desk.

Late 2013

The group learned later some of what had happened from an internal FBI investigation, which Stan had demanded. One of the cartels had captured a DEA agent who had been liaison with FinCEN, and under torture, he had mentioned Roberto's name among several former Treasury employees who had the skills to tap financial transactions. They had watched Roberto for several weeks. Without fully penetrating his systems, they detected his contacts with several banks they often used. They began monitoring the banks' transactions, and picked up the trails of small, frequent withdrawals they couldn't explain.

Finally in early 2014, they sent an emissary to meet with Roberto. The emissary never asked Roberto if he had made the taps, but he introduced himself as being from "international business interests" in Mexico. Roberto could decode the message easily. The emissary went on to praise Roberto's software skills and then talked at length with Roberto about Cassie, Lizzie, his sisters, their children, and where they lived and went to school. Roberto said little, but knew he was at risk. He immediately stopped all tapping operations.

But it was too late. He was summoned to a meeting in Mexico City, and the veiled threats to his family made it an unavoidable trip. When he said goodbye to Cassie, he told her that he would probably be able to bribe his way out of the problem, if there was a problem.

His body was found in a garbage dump in Vera Cruz a week later.

The FBI investigation revealed that the cartels had been able to arrange a rare joint operation, realizing that they had all been hit by Roberto's taps. At the end, the FBI agents were told by an informant, the cartel captors told Roberto that he would be freed if he paid back all that he had taken. Roberto, according to the informant, told them that the money had been spent, but that he would promise not to take any more. He also told them that the money went to help children and that he was glad he had taken it.

Whether his statement of pride was a last straw or not was unclear, but Cassie—and the Lopez group when they heard it—had their sorrow lifted slightly by knowing that he had been proud to the end of what he'd done.

His funeral in Glendale was private and for family only. The Lopez group agreed to celebrate his life when they met a year later in 2015.

Stan 2014

After Roberto was killed, Stan began a single-minded pursuit of answers to his questions about what was happening on the prosecution and confiscation front. The tension between protecting women and children and prosecuting their abusers had always been part of the work the Lopez group had done, with Suzanne on the leading edge of both forms of protection and prevention. Stan remembered what Roberto had once said about the weak efforts at asset confiscation by the federal agencies—as opposed to his own form of it. He wondered whether any more serious efforts were under way. So he asked two of the Republican members of the committee, who had shown that they understood the need for tougher policies aimed at the traffickers and the cartels, to co-convene an informal meeting with the federal agencies

It was not a happy event. Stan and the Republican members quickly cut through the agency staffs' abstract presentations of "progress being made" and "new efforts under way" to demand answers to their questions. After a painful hour of questions and few answers, Stan summed it up.

"We've got a few basic questions, and I don't think we're hearing any answers yet. Why can't you tell us how much you've confiscated and where's the dashboard on the annual totals—and if there isn't one, why not? Why are most of your resources going to monitoring the sanctions on Iran and not the efforts aimed at the traffickers and cartels? How many agencies in the federal government are involved in monitoring the cartels and the traffickers, and how well do you think they're coordinating their efforts? And how do you measure progress against trafficking in this country—is it getting better, or not?"

The agency representative from Treasury then made a bad mistake. He said "Congressman, we're aware of your relationship with Roberto Garcia, and we regret very much his…"

Stan cut him off. "This is not about Roberto Garcia. It's about thousands of women and girls who have been trafficked into and within this country, and what our government is doing about that. So let's keep focused on the target here."

But as hard as he and his Republican colleagues pressed, the answers were not there. The agency officials noted the legislation on trafficking issues that had recently passed the Congress. Stan quickly praised it but pointed out that it mostly focused on trafficking among the small group of children in the child welfare system rather than the much larger numbers of children who never came to the attention of that system, along with the even larger group of children trafficked in other countries. The agency officials cited a 360 percent increase in convictions for the fiscal years 2001-2007 as compared to the previous 7-year period, to which Stan responded by asking what the data showed since 2007. They then cited the average of 24 forced labor cases annually, to which Stan's response was to ask what the total of estimated cases was. There was no response.

One of the Republicans noted that the Justice Department website had no materials more recent than 2010. The 2012 report on the Department of State website reported an international total of 7705 prosecutions—and 4746 convictions. The officials also noted that 166 nations had ratified the United Nations Protocol to Prevent, Suppress, and Punish Trafficking in Persons, which is known as the Palermo Protocol.

Stan let the officials run through these items, and then asked his final question. "Are we making progress in any measurable way? Or is the problem getting worse?"

The ranking official was an Assistant Secretary of State, who looked uncomfortable at the question. "As you know, Congressman, it is very difficult to get good measures on these issues. We view the growing international and US-based efforts as real progress. But I can't tell you that it is not getting worse. The use of the internet for moving people and money has increased the harm done by trafficking in many places."

And then Stan asked his follow-up. "So what can we say to those who are arguing that if women and children are not more secure, they must do what they can with armed security forces to protect women and punish their abusers wherever they can?"

"I can't answer that, Congressman." Then he took a deep breath and said, "But personally, I understand why they would feel that way.

And I hope they succeed in their goals of increasing safety for women and children."

Stan was surprised, and thanked the official at length. He may have jeopardized his career by going beyond the US position on Suzanne's efforts—but he had said it, and that mattered.

Although he had not said it in a public setting yet.

PART SEVEN

The 2015 Gathering

T he 2015 gathering was held in Washington, during the August recess. The seasonal heat and humidity only added to the somber aura of the event, which was held at a hotel south of the Capitol on the Potomac.

They gathered in an executive conference room, drinking hotel coffee and glancing at their cellphones as a way of delaying their mournful updates. They debated the why of Roberto's death over too many beers and too many tears. Stan thought Roberto had pushed out beyond the boundaries he had set earlier because he was supremely confident of his own ability to outhack the cartel's wizards. Felicia disagreed, saying he did it to protect his family, once he knew they had been threatened. But Jeremy said "Maybe it was neither one. Maybe he just knew he was doing the right things, trying to help kids in the ways he knew best." And Suzanne was silent, knowing that in some ways the others held her partly responsible for Roberto's crossing too many lines to try to help her and the RTP effort.

When Cassie Gramercy walked in, the tears flowed yet again, as she greeted them all and thanked them for what they had meant in Roberto's life. She said she couldn't stay, but she had wanted to stop by and tell them all how much she appreciated all they had done for Roberto.

She said "You inspired him with all that you are doing for kids. He told me that everything he did was to try to live up to the goals you had all set for yourselves as a group."

After she had left, Felicia said, "I couldn't bear to tell her what I was thinking—which was that all he did for us was part of the pressure that led him to take terrible risks at the end. I feel awful about that. I never would have wanted his money if I had known the risks he was taking."

And then, through her tears, she began softly singing. *"But the tigers come at night, and they steal your dreams away..."* And then she couldn't go on.

Stan explained what he had heard from the DEA and other agencies that he had talked with about Roberto. "One of the cartel guys got picked up in a raid a few weeks after they found his body, and he was the source for some of what DEA figured out. They took Roberto down to one of their hideouts and told him he had to give back all the money he had taken. He told them it had all been spent and there was no way they could get it back. So they killed him.

"He did a very Roberto thing at the end, though. He had somehow programmed a drone to follow him. After they killed him, one of his tech guys tracked the killers back to their headquarters. The Mexican police—the special unit the President had set up last year—had been chasing these guys for a long time, and when they got the message from Roberto's guy, they surrounded the place. But before they could go in, a bomb or drone strike or *something* hit the buildings the cartel guys were in. Killed nine of them outright and tore the hell out of the place. The Mexicans went in and cleaned up the rest."

"Good," said Suzanne and Felicia at the same time. Jeremy just lowered his head and whispered a few words.

Stan went on. "I don't know if it was the Mexicans, or the DEA, or some private outfit that Roberto had hired. But whoever it was had some very serious ordnance."

After they had talked some more about Roberto, Stan said, "There's something else I have to tell all of you. He got in touch with me several months ago. Looking back on it, I can tell now that he was getting very worried. He told me to tell all of you that if something happened to him, he had done something he wanted us to know about. I tried to laugh him out of it, but it didn't work."

"What was it?" Suzanne asked.

"He wanted you all to know that he had set up a trust—using the trickiest cutouts he ever designed so no one would know it was his money. He made the four of us the only trustees."

Then he laughed, sadly. "There's more. He said that no money could be spent from the trust unless three of the four of us agreed. Cassie has a separate trust, so this is just for us."

Felicia looked involuntarily at Suzanne, and then looked away.

Jeremy said, "Guess he wanted us to debate for a while."

Stan said, "I guess so."

Felicia asked, "How much is in the trust?"

Stan said, "At that point, he told me, it was a little more than fifty million. Plus all of his stock options and other investment returns flow into it—about five million a year more."

Jeremy said, "Wow."

Suzanne said, "Thanks for telling us, but I don't think we should do anything about it now. It's too soon. We need to think about what he'd want. I'm not up for a debate right now."

Stan went on. "He also left something else. He told me he wanted me to get in touch with the unit in Treasury that he had worked with, in case he wasn't able to continue the work. He was guarded about it, but he said the cartels had never cracked his code to get into their banking. I talked with the FBI and they affirmed that they never would have caught up with him if they hadn't tortured the DEA guy who gave them a bunch of names. So the code was good. He gave me a thumb drive and said Treasury would be able to figure out what he had done from what was on the file.

"So I took it over to the Treasury people and they looked over the file and came back to me. They were amazed that one guy working pretty much alone had pulled it off. They said they could use it to increase their surveillance. We've been pushing them pretty hard in closed hearings for not going after the trafficking rings that are working with the cartels dealing with drugs and women—and sometimes children.

"I told them to be very careful—that a friend of mine had been killed for that information. After a few weeks they came back and gave me some information I can't really talk about. But Roberto left some serious tools that Treasury is now using, more than they ever have."

"So it's another part of his amazing legacy. Maybe the cartels didn't win, after all."

Suzanne said, "Maybe he got some more revenge for what happened to his cousin, too."

"I hope so," said Stan.

"Felicia said, "Uh, we have a bit of an announcement too. I hope it's some happier news. We were married in Rome two months ago." She had to stop to acknowledge the applause and cheering. "And it seems I'm pregnant. Jeremy and I know we're having a son. We've discussed it, and we've picked a good name for him…" and then she started crying and couldn't go on.

Jeremy finished it for her. "He will be named Roberto."

For the rest of the day, they sat around on the hotel patio and looked at the river, making very small talk and remembering good times with Roberto. They drank more than they should, and Stan got more phone calls and smoked more cigars than he should have, but all in all they got through their version of mourning as well as could be expected. And the good news about Felicia and Jeremy helped to carry them toward the next phase of their lives, while grieving about Roberto.

The next day, they met in one of the conference rooms, and went through their updates. By now, they understood each other's work in enough depth that there was much more questioning and answering back and forth among them, rather than dry recitals of what they had been doing.

The biggest question mark was what was going to happen between Stan and Suzanne, with her request for congressional action on the RTP agenda. They both waited until Felicia and Jeremy had finished their updates to begin.

Stan, speaking slowly, said "I don't remember which of us first talked about the five paths, but it was—and still is—a good way of telling our story. And now there are four paths. We've each tried to do what we could along our own path, in our own ways. Two of us…" his voice caught and he paused to gain control again, "two of us cared so much about the mission that they went out to the edge of the laws that protect children, and then decided to go beyond, because the laws just weren't working. And that cost Roberto his life, and it cost us our friend."

He turned to Suzanne and said, "Suzanne, I speak for all of us. You must never hesitate to ask us for help, because what you are doing remains dangerous. In some ways, what you've chosen, which we all admire you for tremendously, is more dangerous than what Roberto was doing. He worked in the cyber-shadows, but you are out there with your troops where everyone can see you. And some of the same people that came after him want you stopped, too."

He stopped, trying to get control of his emotions. "Suzanne, we do not have to agree with everything you do to want to protect you in every way we can." And Jeremy and Felicia quickly said "Amen."

And she simply said "Thank you."

Then she added "I appreciate you raising it. We've gone over security for me and the senior leaders very carefully since we heard about Roberto. This is the longest I've been in any one place in a month, and I imagine you've noticed the private security around us when I move around. We're not taking any foolish chances."

She stopped, and now, in a rare moment for Suzanne, she seemed to be trying to get control of her emotions. Then she said, "This is the only family I've ever had. And now that it's smaller, it's all the more important that we stay in touch. I promise I'll be careful."

Then she said, "I don't know what you can get Congress and the agencies to decide to do, Stan. I know you've been trying—down your own path." She smiled. "The one down the center. I respect that. But Roberto helped us see what is coming. Either we are going to combine a serious interpretation of the responsibility to protect and the financial weapons he used with a real attempt at protecting kids and women at scale—or we are going to have to go to Bonhoeffer's answer—to decide that the evil is so bad we will need to try to kill it. I hope we make the right choices."

Suzanne shook her head. "They tried something new at a camp in Lebanon last week. They sent a squad of women in, some with suicide vests, some who tried to talk to the women in camp disguised as refugees. But our detection gear caught the suicide team, who then blew themselves up outside the perimeter we had established. And all but two of the women who were working for the traffickers inside the camp revealed themselves to us and surrendered. They said they had never seen women commanding women with weapons before, and they wanted to be part of that instead of working for the traffickers. The two that left and went back to the traffickers had children who were being held hostage.

"It is such an ugly business. I try to get some kind of break from it, but all I have been able to do is sneak away to a beach somewhere and then I just sit and end up planning the next campaign." She looked away, and then tried to smile. "I know this is the right work, and I know I am good at it. Without Roberto, we could never have come this far."

And then Gabriela Lopez joined them. They had invited her a year before, but hadn't known until a few days before whether she was going to be able to make it. When Jeremy called to make sure she had heard about Roberto, she said that she didn't travel as much as she once had. Now in her early 70's, she was working on Cuban issues again, waiting anxiously for the thaw that had begun to allow progress on contacts between the two governments after so many years.

She came in using a cane, but had the same strong face and stern manner they remembered. But it melted as she came in and sat down and began trying to tell them through her tears how sad she knew they must be at Roberto's death.

"He was an extraordinary young man. So brave, and single-minded. I heard he was married a few years ago. Is that true?"

They caught her up on Cassie and Lizzie and told her what they knew about his killing. She shook her head, saying "I tried to warn him. But he was so confident in his ability. And he wanted so much to help all of you—as I'm sure he did."

"Yes, he did," said Stan.

She smiled then. "And you, Congressman. And you, Suzanne, whom I have been reading about in all the papers and online. And the two of you, Jeremy and Felicia, finally together, doing such important work. What a group! You know, I have taught dozens of classes. But I do not believe I have ever had such a remarkable group. Once in a long while, a group of young people comes along and you know they are special. I worked *hard* for all of you—you pushed me as much as I pushed you."

She looked at all of them, and said "Now tell me the essence of what you have all been doing, because I know you have done so much, and helped each other do it. I am so proud of all of you."

They briefly summarized some of what they had been doing, and she asked her usual excellent, probing questions. She pushed Stan on what he was able to get through the committee, how he was working with the Republicans now that they were dominant in the House, and what his priorities were. She asked Jeremy about his connections with the Catholics, and the other churches, and how well they all worked together.

When Felicia told her she was using music in her work, she clapped her hands and said, "I knew it! I could hear you sometimes humming music under your breath as you walked into class. Oh, that is so good for you—and the women must love it."

And then she looked intensely at Suzanne, and said "Are you being careful? Really careful?"

"Yes, I think I am. I am surrounded by a group of very strong, caring women—women who remind me of you, *senora*."

"Thank you. And please, I am Gabriela now. And I want to invite all of you to have your next gathering—which I hear you do every five years—in a very special place. Can you guess where?"

Felicia was first. "Havana?"

"Exactly. What a good time we will have. And if they lock me up, I will count on the Congressman to negotiate my release."

They laughed, and then talked more, remembering as they did what she had given them, marveling at her ability to help them reflect on what they had done—and what remained.

Lopez said, "I want to ask a favor of you four. A good friend of mine is a reporter who has done a lot of work in Mexico and around the world. He's an older guy, but he's still very sharp. He read about Suzanne's work and knows who Stan is and called me a while ago to ask if I knew all of you—he'd read that you'd graduated from Western. He'd like to interview you. Would you see him? I think he wants to talk about Roberto as well."

Stan asked "What's his name?"

"Sam Leonard. He won a Pulitzer for broadcasts he did a while back about that woman, Maria Chavez, who came up from Mexico to California with all those people."

Stan said, "I've read some of his stuff. He's very good. Sure, we could talk to him. OK with the rest of you?"

They all agreed.

As they "reported in" to Lopez, they gradually began to hear a new tone in their accounts of what they had been doing. They had always listened to each other, more than most of their generation. That was part of what made them a group. Millennial self-declarations were not their style.

But with Lopez this time, they were also listening to how each of their chosen paths differed from the others. They knew enough about each other by this time to know how they were different—and what they had come to share after fifteen years of encounters with the same goals.

Stan told of his committee work on the children's issues, but the subtext they could now hear was the balancing act he was always performing, finding what was possible and weighing it against the ideal. Suzanne, in the greatest contrast with Stan, was the most absolute in her accounting for her work. To the others, she seemed to be answering an unasked question: *what difference does it really make?* Her standard was the hardest to meet, since she demanded absolute safety for her charges, while knowing that the attacks would eventually come, inevitable battles and skirmishes somewhere along the broad fronts she and her allies patrolled.

Jeremy and Felicia had found their niches, both fulfilled in what they were doing, but both pressing to expand their scope. They had found each other as well, and the others could hear the comfort they brought each other. They heard Jeremy, balanced as always, sure-footed in his moves, and Felicia, still the first to ask the blunt question, but with a smile now, and far less impatient with answers she didn't like.

And Roberto was there too, not only in memories, but in what each of them knew about how he had contributed to their own work. They had known but not fully understood the deep menace beneath his efforts to skim more and more from the traffickers and the cartels. They knew he had gotten closer and closer to the line where his efforts could be detected, traced back, and then ended. And they knew he had done some of it for them, as well as for the children they were helping.

And as they felt the loss, they continued to worry about Suzanne, acutely aware now that protecting children was sometimes very dangerous work for those who took it most seriously.

Felicia took Roberto's death the hardest, Jeremy felt. When they returned to New York, she kept going over and over it. She had been unable to speak about it after the gathering and on the plane, but when they got back to their apartment, her feelings overflowed.

"Does this mean we lost? The bastards kill him and we lost?"

Jeremy quietly replied, "No, it means he went too close to the edge and lost control. It was his high, Felicia. It was what made him know he was alive. He did it to help all of us, but it also did it because he was very good at it. It was his gift, and he lost control of it in the end."

"But I feel like we pushed him. We kept taking and taking and he was always there for us."

"Love, he would have done it if we had never met him. It was what he gloried in. You've seen him at the gatherings, working on his laptop in the corner, hands flying over those keys. It was his life."

"And it killed him."

"No, those evil bastards killed him. But they did it because they caught him taking their money to try to do good with it. Look at all the good Suzanne has done with RTP. Look at what Stan has been able to do—for the first time, a member of Congress who totally gets it. Look at the girls and women you've given voices to. Roberto didn't do that—but he was behind it, helping to fuel it, where he wanted to be."

But she could not be consoled. He was gone, and her grief was for the loss of the idea that they—all five of them—would keep doing the work as long as they could, until they were old, spread across the world, but all five together, as they had been at the first. But Roberto died young, and she felt his loss deep in her heart.

A month later, when she returned to Florence with Jeremy, her choir leaders came to her once they realized that she was not yet able to go back to working with them on this visit. The choirmaster, a woman of 30 from Romania who had worked in brothels in Italy, hesitantly said,

"Felicia, we know how sad you are. And we learned some songs about remembering those we lost. Can we sing them for you?"

And they sang her the only Requiem that could have helped, Brahms' gloriously consoling *German Requiem*. And when the soprano sang "*Ihr habt nun Traurigkeit, Ihr will euch trosten*—You now have sadness, but I will comfort you,"—Jeremy and Felicia clung to each other and felt their sorrow begin to lift.

The call from the reporter had come two days after Lopez had mentioned him, while they were still in Washington. He was willing to come to Washington to meet with them if they could give him some time. Because Lopez had asked them, they agreed to fit him in as they prepared to leave Washington.

They had made plans to meet Leonard in Stan's office, to make it easier for his schedule. As Leonard came into the adjoining hearing room that Stan's staff had arranged, they saw an older man, with nearly all white hair, a white moustache, and a tape recorder.

"Thanks for your time." He reached up and adjusted his hearing aids. "Let me get these things in or I'll make notes that won't make any sense. That's why I bring this thing along, too," waving at the recorder.

Leonard began, "Gabriela has told me a lot about you. It's pretty remarkable that you all went into more or less the same area of work after taking a class together, and that you've stayed together and continued to meet regularly. And now two of you are married. Why do you think all that happened?"

Jeremy spoke first. "A lot of it was Professor Lopez. She challenged us in a way few of our teachers ever did. And she got to something that was already inside each of us before we ever got to Western, but she showed us a way to make it real instead of just a lofty idea stuck in our heads."

Felicia said with a smile, "We used to argue among ourselves whether she had infected us with an obsession or inspired us with a vision. For me, it ended up being some of both."

Stan said, "I always knew I wanted to get into politics, and I had a cousin I really admired who worked in children's advocacy. Lopez helped us see what was possible—and what was necessary. But we also drew a lot of it from each other. We've taken very different paths sometimes," glancing at Suzanne, "but we've stayed in touch. I think we've all learned from each other—and from Roberto."

"You must really miss him. He helped all of you, I understand."

"Yes, he did. He had made a lot of money in software and was very generous with us over the years."

Leonard had covered politics in Mexico long enough to know that behind Roberto's death was a deeper story. But his instinct for the investigative details had calmed over the years, and he knew that Roberto's friends were still grieving. So he put that angle of the story aside.

He asked Jeremy, "Gabriela said in some ways you have come the furthest from your days at Western. She said you were fairly fundamentalist when you came into the class, and then began to shift your views after you went to seminary."

Jeremy nodded. "It has been a long journey for me, from the fundies to Niebuhr and Jim Wallis. But that is the journey I had to take. And yet, at its best, I never left the foundation of evangelical attention to the second part of the commandments—the 'do unto others' parts, the 'least of these' parts of the gospels. Those are still bedrock for me. If you take that seriously, you get to a kids agenda right away."

He smiled, and added, looking at Felicia, "And if I ever have doubts, I have some pretty good backup."

She laughed and said, "Damn right." Then, looking at Leonard, she said, "I had to get past some hangups of my own, which these guys all helped me with. I was resisting what music has meant to me, until my grandmother reminded me what these guys had been saying for a long time, that music is another kind of healing—and sometimes even a defense. Stan is our voice in Congress, and I finally figured out a way to get women to raise their own voices through music."

Leonard looked at Suzanne. "You've chosen what is perhaps the most unusual path, Suzanne. What did you get from Gabriela, and what did you get from the rest of your friends?"

Suzanne said, "She first introduced us to the idea of the responsibility to protect children as a logical extension of the UN doctrine that was adopted in 2005. And some of us took it to the next logical extension, which is that if governments won't do that, citizens have to do it. In our case, that meant women had to do it."

She paused, looking at the three, and then said, "Each of the four of them, including Berto, helped me choose the path I'm still on. Jeremy taught me that evil could be confronted, Felicia cared for me when I was in despair, and Stan has given me a forum at some risk to himself. And Berto, as you said, helped us financially and in other ways as well."

Leonard said, "I've read your testimony to the briefing the Congressman arranged for you. It's very powerful. But I know you're aware that your tactics have created major controversy about using violence to combat violence."

Suzanne said, in a level voice, "We are self-defense forces to protect women and children. We don't initiate violence—ever. We sometimes have to respond to it because there are predators out there and because governments have failed to do their job to keep women and children safe. We take the responsibility to protect doctrine seriously. Our tactics are based on what we call the Bonhoeffer rule—named after the theologian who joined a conspiracy to kill Hitler."

Jeremy said, "We might have all ended up in this field one way or another. But without Lopez, we wouldn't have the same sense of urgency and the same focus on what she always called the '400 million problem'—the number of children harmed each year. She never let us shrink what we tried to do down to a few projects. She made us see it whole."

Stan smiled and added "Which sometimes makes us a royal pain in the ass to the well-meaning people working on those projects."

He went on, his voice saddened as he remembered Roberto again. "You can run projects, and that is what most people do. Or you can try to take on the whole system that hurts kids, and hurt it back—hurt it enough that it will stop going after kids. That's what Roberto did, and that's what Suzanne is trying to do. But it can be very dangerous to do that, because somebody is making money from selling kids' bodies, from those little kids making bricks and sewing clothes all day long. And the bastards making the money get pissed off when you get in their way. And then, sometimes, they come after you. So doing projects is safer. Seeing the whole thing can be dangerous."

Leonard said, "The hardest—and maybe the most unfair question I can think of asking you—is why aren't there more people who think the way you do? If Lopez infected you, how much have you been able to try to infect others?"

Stan nodded. "Tough question, as you said. Seeing it whole, as Jeremy just described it, is not always a welcome perspective. The world of international services, like the world of domestic politics, is about programs and projects, and rarely about policy that takes a wider view. Congress does projects, people like to donate to projects, and the media—forgive me—understand projects much better than they do policy and the wider view. So projects often win out in the contest for limited attention span, in Congress, in public opinion, in philanthropy, and in the media. The 400 million number has stuck in our brains for 15 years because Lopez made us see it. She took us to the projects that were working on those issues, but she also showed us the full sweep of those issues in global terms."

Jeremy said, "We try to pass on the ideas she gave us in that class, through our work, our presentations, and our example. We try to make clear the difference, as Stan has said, between projects and moving the needle. There are much better measures of progress now, both in UNICEF's work and in the federal agencies that work on this agenda. But Stan's right. It's much easier to get across the ideas behind projects than what Gabriela taught us about keeping our eyes on the whole prize. And Suzanne continues to remind us, as that bench in Venice says that she quoted in her testimony, that we need to go where people are sleeping and see if they are safe. The one thing Lopez never told us, I guess—or that we didn't hear—was that to keep kids safe somebody was going to have to do things that aren't very safe."

Suzanne added, "The women I work with are all veterans of other wars, either personal or global. They all know the stakes are high. It hasn't been difficult to recruit them to that part of Gabriela's mission."

Leonard asked her, "Suzanne, you've been working in what amounts to a war zone for ten years now. What are you doing to deal with the trauma?"

She looked at him, and smiled, sadly. "It's true, I guess. I've been dealing with trauma for a long time. I've learned some things about how to do that, but it's hard. I won't pretend that it's not. I take vacations. I talk to these guys and my other closest friends about it—I try not to keep it closed off. But what helps the most is when I see one of the kids in the camps that we've rescued, or whose mom we've protected, and the kid is playing with other kids. We get them soccer balls, and dolls, and stuff like that. And sometimes they just play, as if they were growing up in a normal place instead of a bloody camp. And so I play with them, for a while."

She stopped talking, and shook her head. "That helps, sometimes."

Leonard said, "A final question. You're all relatively young, in your mid-30's. You've achieved vastly more than most people your age. Where do you see yourselves in 20 years or so?"

Three of them involuntarily looked at Stan, who threw up his hands and said, "Don't look at me. I have a great job, but it will take all I can do to keep it afloat through the rough waters of South Carolina politics." Then he paused, and said, "I'd like to think we'll have finally gotten the US to endorse the UN Convention on Children. Along with some other landmark legislation we've been working on."

Jeremy said, "I'd like to be running the agency we created, Matthew 19:14, and I hope it's a major player in religious work on this agenda. A serious benchmark for that would be an annual report on spending and measures of progress issued jointly by all religious organizations that work on the child protection agenda. Doing something together for a change instead of lots of smaller slices."

Felicia said, "I'll have children off in college and beyond, and I expect to be writing music of my own instead of just teaching people to sing. And I want to be in Italy at least half of the year."

Suzanne smiled, but sadly, and said "I'd like to be retired, because my work with the Brigade will no longer be needed. That failing, I'll be training my successor to keep children and their mothers safe. And trying, as Roberto did, to use the latest and best technology to do that."

Leonard summed up by saying, "I greatly appreciate your extending your visit to talk with me. I hope I can do justice in what I write to what you have done and to what Gabriela and Roberto did. Thank you."

On to the Futures

In 2030, Stan became a Senator. Over time, with the help of allies from both parties and donors who responded to the agenda, he was able to get the Senate to pass a portion of the package he was unable to get through the House on his first try. The group in Congress supporting the children's protection agenda expanded and formed a caucus, which Stan chaired. He and Dolly had two sons, neither of whom played football, but both were starting pitchers on their baseball teams. Dolly's law practice was successful, with a concentration on veterans' issues.

Jeremy's new agency gained in funding and visibility, and he was in New York most of the time when he was not traveling. Felicia took a year to gradually end her ties with her choirs in Florence and Rome, but found women's programs in New York and Boston that were using music therapy for trafficking victims and women in recovery from their addictions, and became a senior advisor to both programs. She wrote a book about music therapy for women who had been abused, and it became a favorite text in training programs all over the US and in Europe. She visited Italy annually to run music therapy workshops in Florence. She talked with Stan about what she had done, and he agreed to work to expand funding in the Veterans Administration budget for music therapy, building on a small program that had begun a few years before.

And she and her youngest brother reconciled, after his career as a high school music teacher and hers had converged. He became an excellent uncle to Roberto Boxton, who attended a charter school that specialized in international affairs, and to his two sisters Clare and Teresa, as well.

Suzanne continued her work of services, protection, and advocacy for the RTP program, because no government or NGO had yet stepped up to a comprehensive program that met the standards her coalition had demanded. She continued to raise significant amounts of money, and women signed up for her missions in more than fifty locations around the world. At least two attempts on her life were foiled by her own security forces working with national governments who realized that her death would be a hugely disruptive event. Her efforts were partly funded by the market success of the technological innovations her RTP programs had tested and found effective. The trust Roberto had left also continued to fund her core budget.

And over the years, Suzanne had informally "adopted" four children from some of the countries where she had worked. She had acquired a household staff that provided both security and personal support, and all pitched in to help with the children. She had several episodic liaisons with men and women she met along the way in her travels, but never with any intent to make them lasting.

And Lizzie enrolled at Western, with Cassie's full approval, and majored in Diplomacy and World Affairs, in a new sub-concentration on women and children's issues which her step-father had endowed. Stan and Jeremy came to Los Angeles one summer, while Stan was conducting hearings on trafficking from Latin America. They took Lizzie to a revival showing of *The Magnificent Seven*, which she thoroughly disliked, but was too polite to say so.

The group phased their gatherings down to decennial events, enjoying them fully as much as ever but finding their schedules had become too complicated to meet more often. In 2020 they did meet in Havana, as Lopez had hoped, and she joined them again. In 2030 they met in December, after Stan's election, in San Diego. They stayed at the Del Coronado Hotel, which a California billionaire had bought back from the Chinese firm that owned it, enjoying the ever-warming California winter, and remembering their graduation from Western thirty years before. None of them felt old yet, but all of them felt older. They hoped they were wiser, but they all remained committed to what they still called "the Lopez agenda," each in their own way.

And each of them, in their families, tried to make the work-family balance work, and the nine children they shared grew to understand why the work mattered—and why they mattered—and what they would one day need to choose in their own lives about what their parents sought in the world.

And out in the world, the measures of harm to children grew more precise, showing some progress, and some continuing losses. As the world's population grew, the number of children grew as well, but demographic changes in many parts of the world brought larger increases in older people who were living longer, with their own demands for services and income. In most places, unlike children, the older ones voted. So the work of advocating for children continued to be an uphill climb, on which the four remaining friends continued, all on their own paths, but taking time from the quest to walk and talk together as the years unfolded.

The End

AFTERWORD

The role of the writer is to ask questions, not to answer them. Anton Chekov

I've moved a few events around for fictional purposes, but the background events in this novel are all as reported in the media and official documents. The details about trafficking are drawn from news stories and the 2014 UN report on Trafficking by the UN Office on Drugs and Crime and an earlier 2011 report on illegal financial transaction by the same office. The US Army report on female engagement teams came out in 2014, not in 2011, though women were in combat and security roles before then. Private contractors were used in Iraq from the earliest days of US in-country involvement that began in 2003, and the costs of current private security contracts are from federal budget documents. The reference to a child affected by drug smugglers is cited as appearing in the *New York Times* on October 6—but it was October 6, 2014 rather than in 2000. The data on US refugee intake is from the year 2013, as cited in a blog by Carol Giacomo in the *New York Times* on December 8, 2014. The description of the refugee camps on the US border is drawn from Will Hylton's article, "American Nightmare," in the *New York Times Magazine* of February 8, 2015. The details of the Memex system of tracking traffickers are from a *Wall Street Journal* article of February 12, 2015, by Elizabeth Dwoskin.

The description of the work of the Center on Excellence on Children in Adversity is drawn from that agency's website and personal interviews with its staff. Juan Zarate's book, *Treasury's War*, on the US Treasury Department's role in monitoring illicit financial transactions was very helpful. So were Kathryn Joyce's book, *The Child Catchers: Rescue, Trafficking, and the New Gospel of Adoption*, Alexis Aronowitz's book *Human Trafficking*, Diana Russell's work on femicide, Jo Piazza's delightful *If Nuns Ruled the World*, Eric Schmidt and Jared Cohen's *The New Digital Age*, the collection edited by Alison Brysk and Austin Choi-Fitzpatrick, *From Human Trafficking to Human Rights*, and two extraordinarily important books on corruption and the rule of law, Sarah Chayes' *Thieves of State*, and Gary Haugen and Victor Boutros' *The Locust Effect*. A conversation and e-mail exchanges with Professor Laura Hebert of Occidental College also provided important context.

I am indebted to staff at UNICEF in Florence and New York for explaining their work to me, and for their many excellent publications. La Strada is a real organization but does not at present operate in Italy. The other organizations mentioned where the characters worked are fictional. Except, of course, the US Congress, which is only occasionally fictional.

In order to get Stan elected, I somewhat gerrymandered the gerrymandered South Carolina congressional districts. The redistricting in 2011 did not, unfortunately, move toward greater fairness.

This novel about children at risk around the world is intended as a companion to a non-fiction book which I wrote with support from Children and Family Futures where I have my day job. That book, *The Future of the Fifth Child: An Overview of Global Child Protection Programs and Policy*, was published in March 2016.

As with the nonfiction counterpart to this novel, I continue to owe a great deal to my classmates at a college quite like "Western"— Occidental. Carolyn 'Toc' Dunlap and Scott Robinson have been mentors of a sort in helping me at least begin to understand other cultures and problems in the vast, non-American parts of the world. Alan Brown and Selia Wang helped me begin to glimpse the importance of China in these issues and in the 21st century. And I also thank my colleagues at Children and Family Futures who inspire with their work and their lives, especially Russ Bermejo who led me to the work of International Justice Mission. Bob Gardner and Melissa Lujan gave this book great early reads, and Nancy Young and Larisa Owen provided their now-customary and invaluable role of running interference for me in time-carving. Annette Garcia of the CFF staff helped greatly with production and travel. A session of writing at Wellspring House in Massachusetts was very productive.

None of these sources or individuals is responsible for the conclusions I draw in the novel or the ideas voiced by my five characters.

In certain respects, a work of fiction by a WORAWM—Well-off Rapidly Aging White Male—may lack standing in this arena of children, gender, and global poverty. Yet it turns out it takes all types to protect children, and geezers have their place, too. Many of the above-mentioned mentors and mentees alike have helped me try to understand the forces underlying this novel, and I thank all of them for their patience.

Gabriela Lopez is a fictional mentor. But there are academics like her, and others in public, nonprofit, and corporate roles who have a chance to change attitudes among the young about the future of their world. If parents don't take on the task of helping their children see the harm done by violence and slavery, teachers must do it. They must be clear-headed about how viciously those who prosper from that slavery and abuse will defend their "freedom," in their roles as Isaiah Berlin's metaphorical wolves, who are sometimes free to devour the sheep. And those teachers must set forth a clear vision of how much better the lives of children could be if the fences against the wolves were stronger, as Suzanne and Stan and the others sought to make them, and as all of us should as well. To switch animals and metaphors, as Felicia and the song from *Les Miserables* put it, the tigers do come at night, and we should be on the watch for them, for they can steal children's lives away.

Sid Gardner
Mission Viejo/June Lake, California
Wellspring House, Massachusetts
May, 2016

Printed in the United States
By Bookmasters